Praise for *New York Times* bestselling author Lori Foster

"Best friends find hunky men and everlasting love in Foster's latest charmer.... Her no-fail formula is sure to please her fans."
—*Publishers Weekly* on *Don't Tempt Me*

"Foster brings her signature blend of heat and sweet to her addictive third Ultimate martial arts contemporary."
—*Publishers Weekly* on *Tough Love* (starred review)

"Emotionally spellbinding and wicked hot."
—*New York Times* bestselling author Lora Leigh on *No Limits*

"Storytelling at its best! Lori Foster should be on everyone's auto-buy list."
—#1 *New York Times* bestselling author Sherrilyn Kenyon on *No Limits*

"Foster's writing satisfies all appetites with plenty of searing sexual tension and page-turning action in this steamy, edgy, and surprisingly tender novel."
—*Publishers Weekly* on *Getting Rowdy*

"Foster hits every note (or power chord) of the true alpha male hero."
—*Publishers Weekly* on *Bare It All*

"A sexy, believable roller coaster of action and romance."
—*Kirkus Reviews* on *Run the Risk*

"Steamy, edgy, and taut."
—*Library Journal* on *When You Dare*

LORI FOSTER

HARD JUSTICE

HQN™

HQN™

ISBN-13: 978-0-373-79932-9

Recycling programs
for this product may
not exist in your area.

Hard Justice

Dear Reader,

I'm so excited to introduce the second book in my Body Armor series, featuring hot alpha males whose überprotective instincts are put to good use in their role as elite bodyguards.

Justice Wallington, the newest member of the Body Armor agency, is still getting used to his job in personal security, but he knows his background as an MMA heavyweight contender will help any client feel safe. What he doesn't expect is the attraction he feels to Fallon Wade, the sheltered heiress he's been hired to shadow. Distraction is the last thing he needs as he works to determine whether the danger to Fallon is real or a figment of her overprotective family's imagination—but the closer he gets to discovering the truth, the more he finds himself wanting to keep her in his life for good, no matter the cost.

I hope you enjoy Justice and Fallon's romance. And of course, you're always welcome to reach out to me. I'm active on most social media forums, including Facebook, Twitter, Pinterest and Goodreads, and my email address is listed on my website at www.lorifoster.com.

Happy reading!

Lori Foster

CHAPTER ONE

WHEN THE DOORBELL RANG, Fallon Wade's heart jumped into a beat so furious, it stole her breath. *He was here.* She wasn't ready, would never be ready, but she hadn't been given a choice.

Opening her bedroom door very quietly, she tiptoed to the staircase landing and peeked over.

Her father and mother stood before the man, in her line of vision. But it didn't matter. He towered over them and it'd take a giant to block him. Holy smokes. He had to be at least six-five.

Muscles bulged everywhere. Like...seriously. *Everywhere.* Shoulders, biceps, chest, neck; he stood in a casual pose, if a brick wall could ever be casual.

Dark hair stuck up in a messy faux hawk. An untrimmed goatee mixed with beard shadow covered a hard, square jaw. And his nose...well, his nose looked as if it had been broken. At least once.

Or maybe multiple times.

Oddly none of that detracted from his extremely rugged good looks, but rather added a dangerous, sexy edge. He certainly looked more than capable of providing protection.

While her father, no doubt a little shell-shocked, prattled on about what was and wasn't acceptable for his "precious daughter," the man shifted his weight, crossed his arms and, with polite impatience, listened.

Until he glanced up at her.

It was a passing glance at first, as if he'd felt her scrutiny and was only mildly curious. But then those dark sinner's eyes shot back and locked onto her.

Fallon couldn't have been more flustered if he'd reached out and touched her.

Her father, realizing he'd lost his audience, jerked around to see her, too, and then her mother, as well.

Busted.

With all eyes on her, Fallon cleared her very dry throat and squeaked, "I'll be down in a minute." Escaping back into her room with alacrity, she closed the door and collapsed against it.

Hand to her thundering heart, she thought, *potent*.

Definitely macho.

And big. Oh, so big.

Not at all what she'd been expecting.

Okay, maybe having a protection detail wouldn't be so bad after all. She had prepared to meet the usual Men in Black clone with the requisite suit, dark glasses and grim expression.

Instead, he wore sneakers, faded jeans and a graphic T-shirt with an open flannel for added warmth. If she hadn't heard her father lecturing, she would have assumed him to be someone else.

Maybe a landscaper.

Or, given his cross demeanor, something more nefarious—like a burglar.

It took Fallon a few seconds more to get her feet moving, then she darted to the closet with new excitement. Shoot, even having a bodyguard would be an adventure when the bodyguard looked like him.

She stepped into her flat-heeled shoes, found a cardigan to pull on over her top and chose a scarf to drape around her neck. She didn't particularly like the outfit, but no way would she make *him* wait while she went through her wardrobe.

After one last fluff of her brown hair and a quick swipe of gloss over her lips, Fallon squared her shoulders, filled her lungs with a fortifying breath for courage and ventured forth.

The second she stepped out, she heard his deep voice and paused to listen.

"No need to worry. I'll cover her."

Her father choked, turned it into a cough, and said with authority, "She is not to be alone. Not for a single second."

"Promise I'll stick real close."

Alarmed, her father corrected, "But not too close."

"Just close enough, then."

"No one is to get too cozy with her either."

"No cozy shenanigans," he said. "Got it."

"She's naive and doesn't understand that thugs—" here her father paused for effect, his narrowed gaze on the man "—might try to use her to get to her wealth."

"Yeah? That's happened before?"

"Well…no." Her father harrumphed in that familiar way that showed his annoyance. "But it's a very real concern."

"Anyone know her itinerary?" the man asked.

"Even *we* don't know it," her mother explained.

"That's good then. Not like anyone can plan to use her if they don't know where she'll be." The bodyguard sounded accepting of all the rules. "Don't sweat it."

Fallon strangled on a breath. Dear God, he'd just told her mother not to "sweat it." In her memory, no one had ever spoken to the refined Mrs. Rothschild Wade in such a way.

It was, Fallon decided, somewhat hilarious.

"I realize it all seems extreme," her father said. "But Fallon is delicate."

No, I'm not, Fallon wanted to shout. She'd never been *delicate*, or naive. It was her parents who couldn't deal, who couldn't move on. Their worry had all but crippled her—and she'd helped. In trying not to add to their burden, she'd made things worse. For their sake as well as her own, she had to make some changes.

With a note of humor, the big guy replied, "Promise I won't break her."

Fallon snickered, but her mother just stared, so her father rushed to reassure her. And Fallon just wanted to get out the door with her hunky new bodyguard before her parents had a complete meltdown.

Tonight was a meet and greet, and hopefully the path to fun and cutting loose and finally being free. *Safely.* If all went well, if the bodyguard suited her, she'd get to be on her own, living her life without the shackles of the past. Limited freedom, yes. There were some things that, for her, would never change.

She'd had a very sharp reminder of that lately.

However, she could change the scenery. She could change the outlook and her attitude. And she would.

When she reached the landing at the top of the curving staircase, she saw that he stood there at the bottom.

Waiting.

Again his gaze trapped her. He had a way of staring that consumed a person. Beside him her father looked small, even though Clayton Wade stood nearly six feet tall and looked very distinguished with his silver-tipped hair and impeccable manner.

Holding the handrail and attempting a smile, Fallon started down.

"You will remember your place," her father said to the man.

Oh, dear God. Mortified, Fallon wailed, *"Dad."*

"My place?" the man asked.

"As an *avuncular* escort who will, at all costs, ensure her safety."

Fallon wanted to disappear. Did her father honestly think that massive hunk of macho man would be attracted to her?

He looked merely confused, not insulted, so she rushed to move beyond her father's awkward reprimand.

"You're my protection detail?"

"Afraid so."

What did that mean? Did he regret the assignment already—or was he expecting her to regret *him*? She waited, but he said nothing else, just tracked her every step as she descended.

Her father broke the silence. "Justice Wallington, meet my daughter, Fallon Wade. Fallon, Mr. Wallington is the security I've hired from the very respected Body Armor Agency."

As she got closer, she said, "Mr. Wallington," in formal acknowledgment.

"Justice will do, Ms. Wade." His gaze skipped quickly down her body, then forcefully back to her face. He looked to be concentrating.

Did he just check me out? Fallon wasn't at all sure, but it felt like it and her voice went squeaky again. "All right. Then you must call me Fallon."

He tugged at a thickened ear. "Works for me. I'm not much for ceremony."

That prompted her father to start lecturing again. "She is not to be out of your sight."

"I'll keep an eye on her."

"If anything happens to her, we will hold you and the agency responsible."

"Nothing will."

Her father scowled. "Ms. Silver swears you're capable."

"That I am." Though Justice spoke to her father, he didn't look away from Fallon, and she shivered at the deepness of the voice that stroked over her skin like a warm caress.

"She also said you were a professional fighter," her father continued.

"Was once," Justice agreed. "I fought with the SBC, but I don't compete anymore."

"SBC?" her father asked.

"Supreme Battle Challenge. Best known fight organization there is."

Ah, a fighter. Fallon gave him another quick glance. She supposed that explained the damaged ear, crook in his nose and the outrageous hairstyle. "Not a boxer," she guessed.

"Mixed martial arts, so kicking, grappling, submissions, but yeah, I'm a pretty good boxer, too." He jokingly threw a few shadow punches, then, with a glance at her dad, quickly sobered. "Not to brag or anything."

With a critical eye, her father said, "Admittedly, you're not what I expected."

"You were looking for Rocky Balboa? The one in the later movies, not the first? He did get slick in the last few, huh? That's not me, though. Never will be."

Such an outpouring left her father stymied for a moment. "Well, my wife and Ms. Silver did suggest that you'd be able to blend in."

Fallon remained on the last step—and still Justice towered over her. She smiled up at him. "That was my stipulation. That you be able to blend, I mean. I didn't want a bodyguard to be super conspicuous. But seeing you now, I can't imagine you blending in too easily."

He crooked a brow. "Why not?"

"You're rather large to blend."

"Depends on where we go, right?" He took her elbow and very unnecessarily helped her down the last step. "Bar, club, steakhouse—no one will pay much attention to me. In this house?" He looked around as if a little put off by the grandeur. "Or a fancy party?" He rasped a big hand over his beard stubble. "I can shave, spiff up a little and force myself into a suit, but that still might not do the trick."

Fallon couldn't help but laugh; she found this body-guard completely delightful. "Well, we're lucky that there aren't any parties scheduled."

"Fallon," her mother said, her expression curious and expectant. "Are you absolutely certain—"

"Yes and yes," Fallon replied with enthusiasm, hoping to stem their concerns. Spinning around, she embraced her mother in a tight hug. "I'm *very* certain, Mother." Next, she embraced her father. "Please don't worry, Dad. It's absolutely fine. I promise you."

"What time will you be home?"

She smiled as she rolled her eyes. "I don't know, Dad. I'm twenty-four, so I might just stay out all night."

Appalled, her father again looked at the man. Her mother lifted her brows.

Wincing inwardly, Fallon glanced back and said, "That is, unless you have a—"

"I'm yours for the night. Keep me as late as you want."

Everything he said sounded somehow more personal, even intimate. Or maybe that was just her male-deprived brain doing some wishful thinking.

Her smile quavered, but this was too important to turn chicken now. "Perfect. Then if you're ready?"

The corner of his mouth quirked up. "Was born ready." He swept a hand toward the door in a ridiculously gallant gesture. "Ladies first."

Charmed, Fallon hitched her purse strap over her shoulder and started out. Normally she'd wear a coat, too, but late May in Ohio was unseasonably mild this year, even with the frequent rain.

And tonight she wanted to be different. Free.

Eventually, she wanted to be a woman, whole.

AFTER A QUICK glance at Mr. Wade, who remained stiff and horrified by the sight of him, and Mrs. Wade, who looked like she was waiting for him to perform tricks, Justice went out and pulled the door closed behind him. Whew. Glad to have some fresh air, he inhaled deeply and rolled his neck to relieve the vibrating tension.

The freaking mansion had intimidated him. Who the hell needed a house that big? A few times there, he'd thought for sure his voice would echo back at him.

The obvious wealth had intimidated him, too. The ornate staircase alone probably cost more than what he got paid in a year. The rock on Mrs. Wade's finger had all but blinded him. He'd been half-afraid to move for fear he'd bump into some pricey shit and break it.

As if all that weren't enough, Fallon Wade's father had tried—unsuccessfully—to cow him. The man had a cold stare that probably made lackeys buckle. But behind that act, Justice had seen the real concern.

The man loved his daughter, spoiled as she might be.

Thinking of her…little Fallon was quite the surprise. He'd expected a princess, a snooty brat used to snapping her fingers and having her every wish granted. Instead, he'd looked up that sprawling staircase and found a curious mouse peeking through the rails… Then he'd caught her wicked grin and bursting enthusiasm and knew that looks were deceiving.

He watched now as Fallon Wade practically danced down the wide tiled steps to the circular drive where he'd parked. The printed scarf draping her neck blew out to the sides from an increasing wind.

Brown hair, parted on the side with wispy bangs over her forehead, skimmed just below her shoulders, bouncing with her every step. That hair looked silky enough to be liquid.

When he'd first seen her, he'd noticed the smooth, flushed cheeks, a small straight nose and rounded chin... Really nice mouth, too.

But it was her eyes that got him.

For an otherwise unremarkable face, her eyes were amazing, dark like a doe's, framed by long, thick lashes and gently arched brows.

The innocence and curiosity in her face was enough for a second look, but the body...

She wore a plain pink crewneck top tucked into a long black skirt, a darker pink cardigan sweater and that fancy scarf.

For a petite girl with slim legs and arms and a narrow waist, she still had curves. Hard to tell much about those curves in that particular outfit, but he had a feeling she'd be pretty sweet all over.

Following her down the steps to the SUV, Justice noticed she had some nice padding around back. There'd be no hiding that heart-shaped ass.

As she headed for his ride with a happy, brisk walk, her black skirt hugged her hips but swished around her knees.

Her face looked young, her body looked ripe and she behaved like a puppy just let off the leash.

Her parents treated her like she was ten instead of

twenty-four. *Overprotective much?* Hell, it had smothered *him* to see the way they tried to harness her.

Somehow, Justice thought, he had to get a handle on the situation. He'd expected this to be an easy assignment, but so far, nothing added up.

In an effort to understand, Justice drew out his phone and pulled up the internet.

He was aware of Fallon Wade watching him before she asked, "Do you need privacy for your call?"

So even now she wouldn't complain about his lack of deference? He should be focusing solely on her, but first... "I'm just looking up a word."

She tipped her head. "What word?"

"Avuncular."

The wind carried her laugh until it surrounded him. Smiling, Justice asked, "You think that's funny?"

Mirth danced in her dark eyes. "And a little embarrassing."

"Because I don't know the word?" It finally popped up on the screen.

"No, of course not." She looked wrecked by his conclusion. "I was in no way judging you."

That only made his smile widen. He didn't come off as the most professional person and he knew it. "Then why?"

She faced him from a good distance away. "Because my father felt the silly warning was necessary."

Avuncular: of or pertaining to an uncle, especially in kindness and manner. "Ah." Now he got it. "So your dad was warning me against making any moves?"

"It wasn't personal. Dad feels compelled to make

similar warnings to everyone, even though it's never been an issue." She wrinkled her nose. "I'd hardly need to hire you if I had a string of big, strong guys taking me out, right?"

"Oh, I dunno." By the minute, she somehow got sexier. Justice didn't understand it, but maybe it was that quirky smile or those subtle curves she tried to downplay. She definitely didn't seem spoiled, and in fact was downright modest. "I think if you wanted it, you'd have plenty of guys hoping for a shot."

Her brows went up. "A shot?"

Justice gave her a long, heated look. "You know my meaning."

Her dark eyes widened. "Oh." Surprise, then embarrassment, had her ducking her face.

Damn it, why the hell was he flirting with her? "Sorry. I shouldn't have…" He shook his head. "Ignore me."

Appearing both amused and confused by his attitude, she started to speak, and instead lifted her arms out to her sides and turned her face up to the sky. "It's a beautiful night, isn't it?"

Dark clouds rolled over one another and humidity hung thick in the air. He liked storms.

They made him horny.

Though this time, he wasn't sure if it was the storm or the girl. "Sure." Lengthening his stride, more than ready to get the show on the road, Justice opened the door to the backseat of the SUV. "You want to tell me where we're going?"

"You mentioned a bar." She bit her lip. A nice full lip,

he couldn't help but notice. "Is there one you'd recommend?"

Justice couldn't figure her out. Was she a practiced flirt? Too naive to know how she affected him? For sure, she made him forget himself. He kept focusing on her mouth—plump lips and that shiny gloss... She waited for an answer, but he'd forgotten the topic. "One what?"

"A bar?" She grinned, putting dimples into those pink cheeks. "I've never been before."

Justice took a step back. Naive then, and damn it, since when was that a turn-on? "You've never been to a bar?"

"No." She leaned closer in a conspiratorial way, her face turned up to his, her tone teasing. "Is it fun?"

Could be, depending on her idea of fun. But if she'd never been before, why pick now, tonight, with *him* of all people?

Suspicion got the better of him. "What are you hoping to do at this bar?"

"Drink a little." Her nose wrinkled again. "That'd be a first, too."

Justice folded his arms over his chest. "You've never had a drink?"

"Wine a few times at galas, but that was long ago." Though she still smiled, shadows suddenly saddened her expression.

Justice had the awful urge to comfort her. He resisted with stoic effort. "How can it have been long ago when you're so young?"

"Twenty-four isn't that young, and if you want me to be specific, I'll say that I haven't had wine since the night I turned nineteen. Besides, it isn't wine I want to try." The impish grin returned. "I want a beer."

"Beer?" She made beer sound scandalous. Every girl he knew occasionally had a beer, even if she didn't particularly like it.

"Yes."

Justice rubbed the back of his neck. "Okay, well, you can do that at every bar everywhere."

She laughed. "Let's see. I'd also like to dance. Maybe chat with new people. And I want to have fun."

How the hell did she figure to do any of that when her daddy didn't want anyone within spitting distance of her? A raindrop fell, then a few more…and Justice knew the skies would open up soon. He took her arm and tried to urge her into the backseat of the SUV.

She resisted. "I'll ride up front."

Taken by surprise, he did his parrot act and repeated, "Up front?" Clients never rode up front. Definitely not young female clients.

She stared at him with those big soul-sucking eyes. "Unless that's a problem for you."

The only problem, so far, was his reaction to her. But hell, as the client, she got to call the shots, so… "Suit yourself." He switched direction, closing the back door and opening the front.

The raindrops began pelting the ground in earnest, so she hurriedly seated herself.

Jogging around the hood, Justice narrowly avoided the sudden deluge. He checked that Fallon had on her seat belt, then, instead of driving, he returned to her earlier question. "There are a bunch of bars in the area. I don't know much about them, though."

"Really? I thought most guys…that is…" Her cheeks pinked. "You don't drink?"

"Sure. But usually I head back to Warfield to Rowdy's when I want to drink and relax with friends."

"Rowdy's?"

"A bar that's gotten popular with fighters."

"Fighters who are your friends?" she asked with interest.

He eyed her warily. "Yeah."

"I'd love to go there sometime."

A hint? Was she another groupie hoping to hook up with a fighter? God knew they came from all age ranges, backgrounds and interests. "It's a no-go for tonight." Hopefully Ms. Fancy-pants wouldn't insist. "I'd need to ensure first that things aren't too chaotic before I take you there. The bar has some rambunctious parties."

She sighed. "Yes, I suppose tonight we should stick closer to home."

"As to that, I should have been told your plans in advance so I could scope out any place you wanted to go."

Brows coming together, she said, "I've never heard that rule."

She sounded a bit stiff, and Justice bit back his smile. "Yeah, well, now you know."

The frown intensified. "Going forward, I'll plan accordingly."

"Good." Rain made the windows opaque and insulated them from everything outside the car. He could practically hear his own heartbeat, could definitely hear her soft breathing. The sense of intimacy made him uneasy. "So what are we doing now?"

"I'll settle for a more local bar. Anyway, it's probably a good idea that we don't travel too far, just in case."

"In case *what*?"

"In case we don't suit." She gave him a quick, firm glance. "If all goes well tonight, well then, there's a lot more I'd like to schedule."

He'd already been told that when he took the assignment, but still he repeated, "More?"

She ducked her face and pressed her hands over her skirt, smoothing an imaginary crease. "More...like every night? Did no one tell you this could be a month-long detail?"

"Yeah, I knew it." Why was she being so shy now? "I was told we'd be getting acquainted, but I thought most of that would be at your house with your mom and dad."

She laughed. "Nooo."

Yeah, it'd probably be impossible with those two hawks overhead. "So here's how it usually works. You tell me where you want to go, I find the best route to get there, then scope out the place in advance to ensure I know the different exits, if it's secure, stuff like that."

She flapped a hand. "That's not necessary. Honest. I mean, I suppose that makes sense for most people who need protection. But overall, my parents just wanted to ensure I could explore safely. There will be plenty of other people at the bar, right? Lots of people who visit daily?"

"Sure." Long as he didn't take her to a dive, it shouldn't be a problem.

"Why don't you pick one, and we'll give it a shot?" She grinned. "What could go wrong?"

Justice didn't bother answering. If the alarm bells going off in his head were any indication, he figured they'd both find out soon enough.

FALLON REJECTED JUSTICE'S first two choices. One was too swanky for the way she'd dressed, and the other looked more like a club. She wanted a regular, everyday bar with everyday people and, finally, on his third try, she agreed with his choice.

A multitude of fluorescent signs filled the big front window of The Broken Pony. People loitered outside, some openly making out, others smoking, groups talking. The parking lot across the street nearly overflowed.

Because it was still pouring, Fallon said, "Drop me off at the door, please." The thought of walking in there alone made her breathless with nerves, but otherwise she'd be soaked, so—

"No can do," Justice said. "I promised to stick like glue, remember?" He swung the SUV into the lot, drove up one row then down another until he found an empty space a good distance from the bar.

"I'll get wet."

He paused in the process of turning off the car, blew out a long breath, then said evenly, "I've got an umbrella."

He reached around to the backseat, coming very close to her as he did so.

And oh, God, he smelled good. Not like aftershave,

just like…man. Fallon tried to take a deep breath without being too obvious.

He gave her a look as he settled back, now with a black umbrella. "You okay?"

She nodded fast. "Yes."

Without looking convinced, he said, "Stay put. I'll come around."

After pocketing the keys, he opened the door, popped up the umbrella and circled the hood to her side of the car.

By necessity, she had to step out very near him to stay shielded under the umbrella. He didn't bother trying to protect himself from the storm.

"Come under with me," she insisted.

He hesitated.

"Please, Justice? I'll feel terrible otherwise."

Reluctantly, he moved up against her back, his arm around her as he tilted the umbrella to block the worst of the rain blowing toward them. "C'mon."

With every step, their bodies touched. She could smell him again, a rich masculine musk, and better than that, she felt his incredible heat.

Why, even if the bar turned out to be a bust, this alone was a wonderful new experience.

He kept her sheltered from the storm until they'd stepped into the bar, then he turned her so her back was against a wall and he stood in front. While closing the umbrella, he visually scoured the room.

Teasing, Fallon asked, "Safe to proceed?"

"Don't be a smart-ass." His grin took the sting from the comment. "How about those seats at the bar?"

The men to the left of the empty stools looked like a

rough motorcycle club, and the men to the right could have been a college fraternity group. She *loved* the differences. "Yes, please."

"It's crowded, so stay close." He pulled her around in front of him and left one big, warm hand on her shoulder, guiding her as they maneuvered through the crowds. Soon as they reached the bar, he mean mugged the men on either side of them until they turned away.

"So what's it to be?" He helped her onto the high round stool. "Still want a beer?"

She could smell the alcohol in the air. In the background, loud music played. Belatedly, Fallon realized that she probably should have eaten something before now, but earlier she'd been too nervous. "Yes, please."

"You sure? 'Cuz you don't look sure."

Trying for more confidence, she said, "Beer."

"All right, then." He ordered one.

"You aren't going to drink with me?"

"I'm on duty."

"Working for me, yes? So I insist." She leaned close to ensure he'd hear her, then whispered, "I'll feel less awkward."

His gaze went from her eyes to her mouth, then away. "Hey, if you insist, who am I to argue?" He asked for another beer.

The man to her right glanced at her again, then turned for a closer look. Fallon didn't smile. She must have been too surprised by the attention.

The young man glanced at Justice next—then quailed. When she looked at Justice, she saw only an innocent expression, one brow raised. But she wasn't buying it, especially since the man turned back to his friends, spoke low, and together they vacated their seats.

"Hey," Fallon complained. "I was going to talk to him."

Justice snorted. "It wasn't talk he wanted."

"How do you know?"

"The way he looked you over? Besides, he was already crocked. You don't want to deal with that."

From the other side of her, a guy said, "I ain't crocked."

Justice narrowed his eyes. Fallon quickly turned to see the biker grinning at her. She had the fast impression of frazzled brown hair in a long ponytail, a ridiculous handlebar mustache, broad shoulders under a black T-shirt and leather vest.

Fallon said, "Hello."

"'Lo yourself, honey." He ignored Justice and asked, "What's up?"

Lifting her glass, Fallon said, "I'm having a beer."

His grin widened. "I'm guessing this ain't your usual place, is it?"

"Am I that transparent?"

"Little bit." Swinging around to face her, he said, "So besides riling the big guy, what's the plan?"

"Oh, I'm not trying to rile him." But one glimpse at Justice showed he was more than a little fired up. "Justice," she said. "Anything wrong?"

"Not yet." His eyes narrowed on the man. "And it's going to stay that way, isn't it?"

"What's happenin' here?" the biker asked. "You two a thing?"

"No," Fallon denied. "We're—"

"I'm watching out for her." Justice, too, smiled, but it wasn't a nice sight. More like a warning.

She sighed. "Justice is—"

"Look," Justice said, standing and taking her arm. "A booth opened up."

She barely had time to snatch up her beer before he led her away. Two other men got to the seats at the same time, but Justice stared them down until they detoured away without a fuss.

"Really," Fallon said, a little irate. "Was that necessary? I'm here because I want to visit with people."

"Not those people," he said, and he downed his beer in one long impressive swallow.

Digging in, Fallon insisted, "Any people I choose," and she, too, tipped up her beer.

Then almost gagged.

She swallowed the big gulp rather than spit it back into the glass, then stuck her tongue out. "Gak. That's *awful*."

Justice looked at her, then grinned. "Did that quench your thirst?"

Her face still scrunched, Fallon hunted through her purse for a mint. Unfortunately she didn't have any.

Justice pushed the glass toward her. "Take another sip. It'll help."

"I'll vomit."

He chuckled. "Nah, you won't. Trust me."

She did want to learn, so she held her nose and sipped. It wasn't quite as bad since she'd taken such a small taste.

Wearing a lopsided smile, Justice asked, "Better?"

She shook her head, continued to hold her nose, and

drank again. This time, Justice put a finger at the bottom of the glass and held it there, encouraging her to keep drinking.

When she'd finished it, she burped, covered her mouth and blushed.

He laughed. "There you go." He held up two fingers, and a minute later a very pretty waitress carried over two more beers.

Fallon eyed them with disgust, until it dawned on her that Justice had just given the woman money. "I need to pay for the drinks."

"Don't sweat it."

She snickered. "You said the same thing to my mom."

"Did I?" He settled back and watched her.

"No one, ever, has said anything like that to her. It cracked me up."

His expression warmed. "You already feelin' that beer?"

"No." She did feel sleepy though. Holding her nose once more, she again drank, but this time she sat back so Justice couldn't reach her drink. "At least it's cold, huh?"

For such a big guy, he looked awfully gentle as he smiled at her. "So what's the plan? Can you enjoy yourself without hitting on a thug?"

"Thug?" she asked. "Who?"

"Either one of those yahoos at the bar. That first kid was looking for trouble, and the other guy lives trouble."

"So neither one was safe?"

Idly turning the beer, he surveyed her, then shook

his head. "Looking like you do, not sure anyone in here is safe. At least, not to daddy's standards."

Making air quotes with her fingers, Fallon mimicked his voice and said, "Daddy's standards." She started laughing and couldn't stop. "That's so funny."

"You think so?"

When she nodded, her vision swam, so she held her head. "Yes. Dad really is outrageous."

"How come? I mean, what's he so worried about?"

She clammed up, unwilling to give too much away. "We've only lived here a short while—" *like a year* "—and he's unfamiliar with the area."

Justice pushed her drink toward her again.

She dutifully sipped before looking around. "People are dancing. I want to dance."

Wary, Justice straightened and surveyed the gyrating bodies on the floor. "I don't know…"

But she'd already stood. She took one last drink of her nasty beer, then started for the floor.

Justice caught her hand.

Wow, another revelation. For such a big man he had a very gentle hold.

He released her. "Stay where I can see you."

With a sharp salute, she said, "Yes, sir."

She loved to dance but rarely had the opportunity, and never in a place like this. Here, in the boisterous crowd, no one would pay any attention to her.

That is, no one except Justice, because he never took his gaze off her.

CHAPTER TWO

SHE'D DRUNK ONLY two and a half beers, but Justice had a feeling that was two beers too many for little Fallon Wade.

"Dance with me," she'd asked early on.

"I don't dance," he'd lied the first time.

Half an hour later, she'd asked again. "Dance with me."

"Not in my job description." He'd felt like a prick after saying it, but hoped it'd keep her from asking.

It didn't.

"No one else is dancing with me," she complained.

A few guys had tried to sidle up to her.

Justice had stared hard enough to send them all packing. In MMA, he'd learned the value of a really confident, mean, nearly tactile stare. There were times he'd won a fight before it ever started, just with his stare-down.

"Don't worry about it," he said. "Just enjoy yourself."

"I feel foolish."

"You shouldn't." A woman like Fallon stood out from the others, but in a good way. "Trust me, lots of guys are looking."

"Really?" She glanced around. "You're just saying that to make me feel better."

"Gospel truth." He crossed his heart.

Laughing, she rejoined the dancers.

Admittedly, Fallon looked a little lonely. All around her, people brushed against once another but never came within two feet of her.

Several times, the urge to join her burned in his blood.

He couldn't help thinking of her moving against him, the scent of her skin and how soft she'd feel. Twice he'd even gotten to his feet. But he held back.

The things he imagined with her were already taboo enough; he wouldn't cross the line in deed, as well.

So instead he kept his vigil—and tortured himself with carnal fantasies inspired by the rhythmic roll of her hips and the sway of her torso.

Repeatedly, Fallon returned to the booth to sip on her beer. Halfway through the third, she pronounced her words too precisely, a deep flush stained her cheeks, and her dark eyes had that glassy look. Hoping to discourage her, Justice scooted the remainder of the drink to the other side of the table.

It was nearing midnight when some random dude, no doubt guided by liquid courage, caught her in his sights.

Justice read the intent in his gaze, but Fallon, still dancing, remained oblivious.

When the guy elbowed one of his buddies, then pointed her out, his friends started egging him on.

Justice couldn't really blame the guy for trying.

The prim clothes and overprotective upbringing

hadn't stifled Fallon's sensuality. Nope, that came out loud and clear in the way she moved.

The guy had almost reached her when Justice stepped into his path. "Don't," he growled into the idiot's startled face, and the guy literally fled the bar.

Fallon wanted to dance, so by God, she'd get to dance—without getting hassled.

At one o'clock, the crowd finally thinned. Justice took her purse from the seat, grabbed the umbrella and walked out to the dance floor to tell her it was time to go.

She tried to tempt him into dancing.

It wasn't easy, but he held firm. "We need to get going."

She fashioned a very sexy pout. "Why?"

"It's late, the storm let up and you're drunk."

She gave it some thought, then nodded. "I think you might be right."

"So you know you're plastered?"

"No, I meant that the rain has stopped." She grinned at him. "I think I've learned to like beer."

She still held her nose every time she drank, so no, she definitely didn't like it. "If you say so."

"Thank you for your patience."

"It's what I'm paid for." He handed her purse to her, waited while she got the strap up and over her shoulder, which took her three tries, then led her out into the dark night.

Not a single star showed. So much humidity hung in the air that halos formed around each streetlamp. There were a lot less people outside now, and they were more subdued than the earlier crowd, talking low in small groups.

The drone of rain dripping from every surface lent a light music to the night.

Though they no longer shared an umbrella, Fallon stayed very close to him, so he felt it when she shivered.

He was so warm, particularly because of her nearness, that he hadn't even thought about her getting chilled. He glanced down at her and realized she'd gotten dewy with all her dancing in the heated bar. In comparison, the temps outside were cool.

He paused to slip off his flannel shirt then carefully draped it around her shoulders. "Better?"

Surprise had her blinking before she gave him a beautiful smile. "Yes, thank you." Then with concern, she asked, "You're not cold?"

Not even close. Hell, seeing the pleasure on her face sent his temp up a few more notches. "I'm fine."

She looked up at him, maybe gauging his sincerity, then put her palm against his left biceps. "You're actually warm," she whispered with awe.

Yeah, much more of that and he'd combust.

To get her moving and distract his misplaced lust, Justice put his arm around her and steered her forward.

They'd almost reached the car when three bodies slipped out of the shadows. Big, muscular—definitely not slouches. Well, hell.

"Got a cigarette?" the one in front asked.

"Don't smoke." Justice took a step in front of Fallon, planning to protect her as they proceeded, but the other two blocked him. With his patience strained, he loosened his stance. "You don't want to do this."

Ignoring that warning, the lead man said, "I'll take her purse."

"No," Justice replied evenly, "you won't. And if you try, you're gonna get hurt...bad."

The man to his right drew a knife. Justice heard Fallon's gasp, and it infuriated him. She stayed behind him, not even peeking around. Odds were stuff like this never happened in her world—because she didn't go to bars, didn't drink...didn't dance, visit friends or apparently have fun.

Pissed that her night out might end in violence, he growled, "Put that away before I stick it in your fucking ear."

Cowering behind him, Fallon's trembling increased.

The most brazen one laughed. "You're scaring her, dude. Just hand it over and we can all get on our way."

Fuck it. "You're right." He pivoted to the side, as if to face Fallon, but as she started to give him her purse, he kicked out fast, catching the bastard in the face with his heel. The crunch of cartilage satisfied Justice. Even in his sneakers, his kick had likely done more than break the guy's nose, given the way he dropped.

The knife wielder slashed out. With far faster reflexes, Justice ducked back and at the same time grabbed his wrist. With little effort, he broke it, then took the knife from his limp hand.

Remembering Justice's threat, the second attacker turned and, with his damaged arm held close, ran away as fast as he could.

The third man, now more than a little incredulous, eyed his buddy on the ground, then his fleeing friend.

"What do you think?" Justice said. "Make up your mind before I take the decision away from you."

Lifting his hands in submission, the man slowly stepped away until he disappeared back into the shadows.

"Oh, my God," Fallon whispered.

What he'd like to do, Justice realized, was walk away from the mess. But he was on official business with Body Armor, so he had to call it in.

Rule of the agency: don't dick with the law unless given prior permission. For sure Sahara would want him to follow the rules tonight, with a client like Fallon.

When he turned to her, he saw Fallon's eyes were enormous and her lips parted.

"You okay?" he asked.

She closed her mouth and gulped. "You pulverized them."

She sounded so surprised, a smile tried to steal away Justice's black mood. "Not even close, but it's hard to do when the pricks run off."

"You *terrified* them." She looked at where the first guy still sprawled on the ground, out for the count. "I've never seen anyone move that fast."

"Because you haven't watched professional MMA." In comparison to the best fighters, he was fucking slow.

"So impressive. Like…pow!" A little on the tipsy side, she tried to mimic his kick, and almost fell to her nicely rounded butt.

"Easy," Justice said, catching her under the arms and hauling her upright. Knowing he needed to get her in the car before anything else happened, he said, "Come on," and led the way.

As they passed the downed man, she gawked and asked, "Is he dead?"

"Don't be so bloodthirsty. He's just knocked out." At least, Justice hoped that was true. He got Fallon seated, tucked the flannel around her, then hit the automatic lock. "Don't open this for anyone but me."

As he started to close the door, she said, "Wait! What are you doing?"

"Calling the cops. I'll be right here, but I have to let them know."

"Are you sure?" She fretted with the strap of her purse. "I mean, Dad will have a conniption. If you thought he was overprotective before, this will seal my fate."

"You're twenty-four," Justice pointed out. "You're a grown woman and can do as you please." Or was she worried about losing daddy's money? She hadn't seemed that mercenary, but truth be told, he still didn't know shit about her, except that she looked hot as hell dancing and couldn't hold her beer.

"It's not that easy." She looked away. "But they…well, they've been through a lot and I'm all they have left."

The sincerity in her tone did him in. Justice glanced back at the guy he'd kicked. The fool was finally coming to. He staggered to his feet, likely with a broken jaw, but given how quickly he sneaked off, he'd live. The area was quiet; no one else was paying any attention.

Shit, he hated making decisions like this. Sometimes the "right thing to do" wasn't so clear-cut.

"Please, Justice?"

Now, how was he supposed to refuse her when she looked up at him like that?

Decision made, Justice nodded. "All right, fine. Get your seat belt on." Once they were on the road, they'd have a nice long talk about expectations. He'd explain his responsibilities and how he had to fulfill them not only for her father, as the client, but for the agency that employed him.

He drove for five minutes, getting his thoughts in order, deciding what he'd say and tamping down the adrenaline rush from kicking a little ass. He missed competing. Not that the stupid punks had offered any real challenge. Street thugs never did. Whenever possible, Justice avoided them.

But competition…even when he'd lost, he'd loved the sport. 'Course, winning was so much sweeter.

Rather than dwell on opportunities lost, he cleared his throat and glanced at Fallon, his lecture mentally prepared.

She was fast asleep. Deep, even breaths lifted her breasts. Her lips were slightly parted, her hands limp at her sides, her head lolling back against the seat.

Justice should have been disgruntled with her.

Instead, he spent the rest of the drive to her house with a stupid smile on his face.

"WAKE UP, SLEEPYHEAD."

From far away, Fallon heard the words. Too tired to care, she snuggled into her seat and sighed.

"Fallon, c'mon, girl. Up and at 'em."

That gruff voice teased her senses. She pulled the blanket up higher and frowned, trying to refuse.

Rough fingers stroked her cheek, and she heard, "Damn, you are so soft."

Well, that was nice. In fact, this might be the nicest dream she'd ever had.

A second later, a hard hand shook her shoulder. "Knock off the sappy smile and *wake up.* Lights are coming on inside and I expect your dad to charge out here any minute."

Her dad? Fallon lifted her lashes—and found Justice staring into her face. She blinked to bring him into focus.

"Hello," he said with a lopsided grin. "You with me, Fallon?"

"Oh." She sat up, felt her head swim and closed her eyes again. "Yes. Sorry."

She heard his car door open and close again, then hers opened. "Let's go." He unhooked her seat belt for her and practically lifted her out.

More drunk than she'd realized, Fallon fell against him, and the security lights flashed on around them.

Justice groaned. "Now we're in for it."

"What in the world do you think you're doing?"

Shielding her eyes from the lights, Fallon straightened away from Justice, but kept a hand on his arm for necessary support. "Dad?"

Wrapped in his housecoat and wearing slippers, her father did indeed charge. The clothes, or lack thereof, and disheveled hair didn't diminish his stately presence.

With haughty disgruntlement, he looked her over, then turned to glare at Justice with concentrated disapproval.

"You should know," Justice said fast, "I was all kinds of avuncular. But she drank a little too much and—"

Fallon gasped. "You big tattletale! I wasn't going to tell him I drank!"

With a roll of his eyes, Justice said, "It's not something you could have hidden from him when you can't even stand up straight."

"I can stand." She attempted to and teetered to the left. Both Justice and her father reached out. She caught her balance, lifted her chin in triumph…and slowly tipped over.

Justice got to her first, holding her steady. "Just hush now and let me explain."

Feeling very accusatory, Fallon demanded, "Are you going to tell him about the fight, too?"

This time Justice groaned. "Wasn't planning on it."

"Fight?" her father rasped, his face going ashen. He grabbed her shoulders, turned her this way and that to check her over. "Dear God, are you all right?"

"No one was hurt," Justice rushed to explain. "Fallon's fine."

Her father took that in, let out a shaky breath, then drilled them both with his patented stare. "There was a fight?"

"Skirmish," Justice soothed. "Nothing serious."

Well, since her father knew anyway… "He was *amazing*," Fallon gushed. Justice had impressed her and she was dying to share. "He kicked one guy in the face and put him down."

"One guy?" More apoplectic by the second, her father barked, "There was more than one?"

Justice squeezed her when she started to explain, then he took over. "Three knuckleheads wanted to take her purse, that's all. It wasn't a big deal."

A flush of anger replaced the pale disbelief. Through clenched teeth, her dad said, "I don't know where you took her, but you quite obviously used poor judgment."

When Justice started to speak, Fallon fell into him. "I need to sit down."

"Let's take you in, then your father and I can talk." He put an arm around her and led her forward.

She took one step and tripped over her own feet. The concrete drive rushed up at her face.

Before she made impact, Justice scooped her up into his arms. "Make a note, Fallon. You are *not* a beer drinker." He walked past her silently outraged dad.

Her mother, often more reasonable, stood at the door. "Fallon, what in the world have you done?"

"Two beers," Fallon explained. "I swear."

"Close to the truth," Justice said, stepping inside when her mother held the door open. "Add another half a beer to be exact."

Fallon looked at the long stairs, then at Justice. "I don't suppose you could carry me on up?" Her legs felt ridiculously wobbly, and besides, she liked being in his arms. He didn't look the least bit strained.

"No," her dad snapped. "He most definitely cannot. In fact, you will unhand her this instant."

"Clayton," her mother chastised. Then to Justice, "Put her right here."

He strode across the foyer to the small settee her mother had indicated and carefully lowered her to the seat.

Behind them, her father seethed. "You're fired. Leave and do not return."

Going stiff in the neck, Justice said, "She had a terrific time tonight. You know she's not done, and she's already familiar with me and—"

"*Fired!* Now get out."

"Dad!" No, no, no, Fallon thought. It couldn't end like this. "You can't blame him for—"

"If he doesn't leave this instant, I'll call the police and have him removed."

Justice stiffened. "Fine."

As he turned to go, Fallon panicked. "Justice?"

He paused only a second, sent her a look of frustrated regret, then kept on going…right out of her life.

"Shh," her mother told her before she could make a single sound of protest. "Pick your battles, honey, and time them well. Now is definitely not the time."

"But—"

"Come along. I'll help you upstairs."

The night had been so nice. How could she go from happy to devastated in a matter of minutes?

"You need to sleep it off," her mother whispered, "then we'll talk in the morning, I promise."

Behind them, her father glared. Never before had she seen him enraged like this. Certainly she'd never seen him enraged at her.

"Clayton will be fine," her mom assured her. "He's

struggling with his own demons, and like you, he needs a little time. Morning will be soon enough to sort it all out."

God, she hoped so. Halfway up the stairs, Fallon said, "I had a nice time."

"I'm glad."

"Even though no one would dance with me."

Smiling, her mother said, "Perhaps Mr. Wallington wouldn't allow it?"

"Maybe," Fallon said. "He has this crazy death stare, way worse than dad's, and it terrified everyone. I don't think Justice knew that I noticed, but I did."

"Of course you did."

Thinking about the way Justice had watched her, Fallon admitted, "He was wonderful, Mom."

"Was he, now?" Supporting her, her mother kept her walking, up and up that never-ending staircase.

Tonight the stairs seemed a particular challenge. Fallon knew she'd never before overimbibed because this out-of-control feeling was entirely new. She couldn't get her limbs to coordinate, and worse, she felt like bawling.

Once in her room, her mother got out her nightgown and folded down her covers.

Feeling far too clumsy, Fallon finally got her clothes changed and didn't protest when her mother put them away. More than anything, she wanted to drop into bed. However, old habits died hard, so she first went into her bathroom to halfheartedly brush her teeth and wash her face.

When she stepped out, she found her mother sitting

on the side of the bed. Knowing that probably meant a talk, Fallon groaned, but dutifully got into bed.

"How do you feel?"

"Exhausted." And melancholy and excited and...too many emotions for her to differentiate. The night had been fun, but at times scary. Peaceful and exhilarating. And until she'd blundered, she'd felt so incredibly free.

She should never have given up on life, limited as it might be. Now that she'd had a small taste, she wanted more. God, she *craved* more. With new conviction, she decided that if she couldn't have it all, she'd at least take what she could get.

Her mother smiled, then said carefully, "Mr. Wallington is an interesting character."

He fascinated her. "Yes." Interesting, funny, strong, an unbelievable fighter, unique and so protective and gentle without smothering her as her parents often did.

After tucking the covers up around her, her mother smiled. "You know, I met with Ms. Silver and went over all the profiles before selecting Mr. Wallington as your guard."

That was news to Fallon. "You did?" She knew her mother and Ms. Silver had met via their social circles, but she'd assumed her father had made all the arrangements for the protection.

"Yes. Your father was put off by his appearance, but I specifically choose him because, well, I assumed you'd find him unattractive?"

With her mother watching her so closely, Fallon tried not to show any reaction, but inside, she scoffed.

The truth was that she found Justice almost too attractive to bear. But her mother waited for a reply, so Fallon said, "He's okay."

"Yes." Her mother smiled. "Anyway, whether you'd find him handsome or not, I decided his casual manner and dress would make him less obvious as a bodyguard."

Working up what she hoped would be a convincing smile, Fallon said, "I'm glad you did." In the end, it didn't matter how sinfully gorgeous Justice might be: she understood her own limitations.

"I want you to be happy, Fallon."

Fallon sighed. Her mother had her hair loose, no makeup on her face, and still Fallon thought she looked very pretty. She also looked to be fishing.

"I am happy."

"Oh, honey." Her smile went sad. "You know you don't ever need to lie to me."

"I wouldn't." Yes, she could be happier, but she understood her lot. She had parents who loved her, financial security, a custom-made job that she enjoyed and all the comforts she wanted. "Just because I'm…"

"Expanding your horizons?"

Fallon nodded. That was a good way to put it. "It doesn't mean I'm unhappy." She hoped she could clear out the cobwebs sufficiently to reassure her mom.

Teasing, her mother mused aloud, "Now that I've met him in person, I'll admit that Mr. Wallington has a certain rugged appeal."

Rather than admit anything else inflammatory, Fallon pressed her lips together and shrugged.

"And, my Lord, the man is enormous, all of it brute

strength. I imagine any young lady would find him striking on a very basic level."

Pretty much on any level, but Fallon said only, "Yes, so?"

"So he's your guard. It's not only your father he has to answer to, but also his employer. You're a beautiful woman, Fallon, but understand that Mr. Wallington could be completely discredited if he crossed the line while on the job."

"Mom." Heat rushed into her face. "It wasn't like that."

"I'm all for you dating again," her mother continued. "If Marcus doesn't suit—"

"Marcus most definitely does not." She'd see Marcus again, of course. They moved in the same social circle. But she'd never again be alone with him—and she'd never again trust him.

"If you want to talk about it—"

"No." Her mother didn't know the soul-crushing rejection Marcus had delivered, and Fallon hoped to keep it that way. Her way of dealing? Get out there and live without expectations. "I'm fine. Please don't worry."

"I'm a mother. I'm allowed to worry and I imagine I'll be doing so the rest of my life." She softened that with a hug. "Now, about Mr. Wallington."

Fallon would never again delude herself. A strong, confident man like Justice Wallington wouldn't give a woman like her a second look, except as an assignment.

And as a mere assignment, he'd never know her secrets.

"I have no illusions there."

"That's not at all what I'm saying," her mother corrected. "Mr. Wallington would be lucky to have you, and since he seems like a smart man, he probably realizes it. But Fallon, getting drunk and allowing the man to carry you in will only make it more difficult for him to resist you."

Fallon almost laughed. Her mother would be forever biased, no matter what. Justice had resisted her easily enough. "I know. It won't happen again. I promise."

Expression curious, her mother asked, "You think he'll suit as your protection?"

"Yes. He was really terrific, sticking close like Dad asked, but not once getting too familiar." Okay, that was stretching the truth just a tiny bit. She'd had guards before; none of them had been as familiar as Justice.

In fact, none of them had been anything at all like him.

Because of the circumstances, she assumed, as well as his manner, Justice was totally unique. He was far more rough-hewn than any other man she knew, and it showed in his speech, his expressions, his big gorgeous body and his naturally protective nature.

Her mother gave her a knowing look. "I would say carrying you in like an old-fashioned knight went a wee bit beyond familiar."

"That," Fallon assured her, "was entirely my fault." She twisted her mouth to the side. "Apparently two beers are far more potent than a single glass of wine." If she hadn't been so tipsy, she'd never have let him do that, most especially not in front of her father.

"It's late," her mother said with a laugh. "Get some sleep and in the morning you can tell me everything."

"Okay." She turned to her side and burrowed into her pillow. Tomorrow she'd work it out with her dad. She had to. She wasn't ready to let go of her new personal guard so soon. "Mom?"

"Hmm?"

Fallon closed her eyes. "I love you. You know that, right?"

"Yes," her mother said, "we know."

CHAPTER THREE

Justice called Leese Phelps on his drive home. He knew he shouldn't; it was the middle of the night and his buddy would be sleeping, but damn it, he needed to unload. Since Leese was the one who'd gotten him involved with Body Armor, was in fact the one who'd mostly trained him, he seemed the likely person to pester now.

Proving he'd checked the caller ID, Leese answered with, "Everything okay, Justice?"

"Yeah. Sorry for waking you."

"Cat and I went to bed late after a movie. We've only been asleep for a few hours."

Cat, short for Catalina, was Leese's new fiancée and a real peach. "Give her my apologies."

"It's fine. What's up?"

"I got fired."

There was a pause, then Leese asked, "She didn't like you?"

He honestly didn't know what Fallon thought or, once she got sober, if she'd mind that he was canned. "Was her dad who cut me loose." Justice's thoughts churned, interrupted only by the hiss of the tires over wet pavement. There were few people out this late on such a stormy night. "And maybe," Justice admitted, "he had good reason."

As he drove, Justice shared everything that had happened, including the skirmish in the parking lot that he hadn't reported.

When he finished, he waited for Leese to tell him the various ways he'd fucked up the assignment.

Instead, Leese said, "Sounds like it was out of your control."

It took Justice a second to soak that in. "You think?"

"Reporting an attempting mugging is routine, but if the client insists otherwise… I'd have done the same as you. Every so often, things go sideways and you just have to roll with it."

Justice grinned. He knew his friend had gone off script more than a few times where Catalina was concerned. She'd been a pretty damned challenging assignment.

"I have to be at the office tomorrow," Leese said. "Why don't you come on in and we'll talk with Sahara."

"You think Mr. Wade will ask Sahara to assign someone new?" Justice hated the idea of any other guy being Fallon's bodyguard, but still he asked Leese, "Maybe you?"

"Nah," Leese said. "I'm already on detail at the convention center for the outdoor show. Besides, if her dad was that pissed, odds are he'll not only switch guards, but agencies."

Justice winced. Sahara wouldn't be too happy about that. She prided herself on keeping clients happy. "I guess you're right." Having the whole agency lose out was even worse. Body Armor offered the best protection around. If Fallon's dad switched, Fallon would have to settle for second best.

"You should get a new assignment right away," Leese said. "Meet me tomorrow at nine and we'll work it out with Sahara. Another job will help you put this one behind you."

"Yeah, all right." Justice said his farewells and disconnected the call. Hopefully the new assignment would be something easier, maybe a dignitary dodging death threats. That, Justice thought, he could handle.

Hell, *anything* would easier than a nearly impossible to resist, far too innocent, curious and sexy girl... who looked at him with awe. So why did he already miss her?

FALLON WOKE EARLY with a sinking sensation in her stomach.

Not from the alcohol.

Awareness of how badly she'd blundered had her pulling the covers over her head. Good God, she'd gotten smashed and played the fool. When she thought of how carefree she'd been on the dance floor, her face heated.

When she remembered how many times she'd tried to coerce Justice into joining her, each time without success, humiliation made her groan.

He, at least, had behaved with decorum. What must he think of her now? Likely nothing good.

She'd compromised him. Rather than cower, she had to set things right.

The second Fallon left the bed, she realized she'd put her nightgown on backward. Grumbling to herself, she showered and dressed in record time, then entered the breakfast room, anxious to make amends.

Her father was already at the table, his tablet open in front of him as he read the morning news, a cup of hot tea at his elbow. Her mother, dressed in a pretty spring dress and her hair now up, nibbled on toast while typing in email replies for her insanely busy social calendar.

When Fallon cleared her throat, her mother looked up.

Her father did not.

"Fallon? Good morning, sweetheart. How are you feeling?"

Awkward. And anxious. Hopeful to the point of desperation. Fallon said only, "I'm fine, Mom. Thanks." She helped herself to tea, cautiously watching her father.

"No residual effects?"

"No. Except that I'm hungry."

Her mom laughed, but her father continued to ignore her.

Fallon let out a sigh. "Dad."

"Good morning," he said, his gaze still on the tablet.

"Dad," she complained as she took a seat beside him.

Frustration visible, he finally looked up. And waited.

Put on the spot, Fallon cleared her throat again. "I'm sorry about last night."

He nodded, and went back to reading.

"Really?" Fallon narrowed her eyes. "That's all you have to say?" She waited for his reciprocal apology.

After a deep breath, he pressed a button on the tablet to shut it down and gave her his undivided attention. "There's no reason to apologize, Fallon, and no reason to discuss it. Your mother and I talked and we both understand that you haven't had much opportunity to spread your wings. Last night was an aberration, better forgotten." He smiled. "We'll put it behind us as a lesson learned."

Incredulous and insulted, Fallon sucked in a breath. "I don't believe you."

"It's true." He reached out and patted her hand. "I officially dismissed Mr. Wallington first thing this morning. You don't need to worry."

Fury gathered as Fallon stared at her father. "Now I know you're joking."

Her mother interjected, "Unfortunately, Fallon, you know your father rarely jokes."

She flattened her hands on the tabletop. "You already called the agency?"

"And spoke with Ms. Silver herself. She, too, sends her apologies and offered a full refund."

Fallon shoved back her seat. "Call her back!"

"I'll do no such thing." Throwing down his napkin, her father pushed back his chair and he, too, stood.

Her mother quickly circled the table and positioned herself between them. "I know Sahara Silver quite well. Lovely lady. Very shrewd. I'm sure she'll give the situation time to cool down before actually acting—"

"I told her my decision was final." Her father's expression pinched. "I also told her that her man had gotten you drunk to the point that he had to carry you in, and that he'd engaged in violence in your presence."

Fallon saw red. "The bar was *my* idea. I picked the place. I chose to drink. And Justice did exactly as you asked—he kept every other person a mile away." Hoping for a smidge of understanding, Fallon snapped, "I even had to dance alone! Isn't that what you wanted?"

Her father ignored most of what she'd said to focus on one thing. "Justice?" he repeated with a scowl. "Now you're on a first-name basis with the man?"

"Clayton," her mother reprimanded. "Of course they're on a first-name basis. This is a more casual assignment—"

"An assignment the two of you insisted on!" Fallon said, more than ready to fight her own battles. "I didn't need a bodyguard to be a normal person."

"Fallon..." Her father reached for her, but she stepped back.

"The fight wasn't his fault either. He was the perfect protection. I didn't even see what happened, it was over with so quickly. I only know that no one got near me because *he* didn't let them."

Not budging an inch, her father said, "What's done is done."

Giving up, Fallon realized that she wouldn't be able to reason with him. Whenever challenged, the inimitable Mr. Wade dug in. "Fine," Fallon said. "You don't want to hire him, then don't. I'll take care of it myself."

"Oh, dear," her mother whispered. "Fallon, honey, he's quite expensive."

"I have more than enough of my own money." Breathing harder, Fallon said, "I'm twenty-four and it's time I lived my own life."

"I forbid it!"

Her eyes flared at her father's vehemence. "Why? Because then you won't have control?"

Silence fell around them. After several tense seconds, her father removed his reading glasses and rubbed at his forehead. "I've never yelled at you before. Not in anger."

Fallon saw his remorse. "I've never yelled at you either."

Using that as an opening, her mother said, "This is important to her, Clayton. Surely you see that."

Once again, the silence stretched out...until Fallon couldn't take it anymore.

"Dad, I understand how you feel. I really do." But she'd let that understanding isolate her to the point that her parents thought she needed a bodyguard just to go out. "The thing is, I'm doing this with or without your blessing." She clasped his hand. "I'd prefer it with."

Defeated, he nodded, and even managed a dim smile. "And I'd prefer to be the one who hires him."

Fallon almost groaned. Somehow, some way, she needed to gain her independence. "Dad—"

"I'll go call the agency now."

DISGRUNTLED AFTER A sleepless night filled with regret, Justice slouched in a seat in his boss's office at the posh Body Armor Agency. He'd only been on the job for four months. First he'd worked part of a case with Leese—a case that ended with Leese getting engaged. Then he'd had a longer stint with a movie star cast in an MMA movie roll. The duties of that job had been twofold: protect the client from rabid fans during the local shoots and teach him how to portray a fighter during the action scenes.

The first part was a piece of cake compared to the second. The dude, talented at acting but not so much at throwing punches, had a hell of a time catching on. He'd been too arrogant to really learn, determined to think he could overcome the physical aspect of the role—the right stance, the proper moves—with added drama. Justice dreaded seeing the movie, since he knew the actor was going to end up looking like a fool.

Or maybe, he hoped, selective editing and a more athletic stand-in could make it all work. The upside of that job had been the groupies who, when shot down by the star, were more than happy to spend time with a bodyguard. He grinned, remembering how in awe they'd been of his résumé. Not many fighters turned to protection, but for him, so far, it fit.

That is, until Fallon Wade.

His boss's number-one man, Enoch, delivered a tray of much needed coffee and Sahara's favorite pastries.

Less tired and therefore more upright, Leese sat across from Justice. Apparently the late-night call hadn't kept him up. Since getting engaged, Leese looked satisfied more often than not.

Leese accepted coffee but, forever the fitness buff, passed on the sweets. Leese might have left the fight world, but he'd yet to abandon the training.

Sahara Silver, best boss ever, propped her very shapely rear on the edge of her massive desk and, looking orgasmic, bit into a jelly-filled doughnut. She'd dressed as classy as ever in a silky blouse, skinny skirt and crazy-high heels.

He liked Sahara a lot and respected her even more. She was a shark in business, a high-maintenance woman and a loyal friend. After licking her lips and washing down the sugar with a big drink of her coffee, Sahara turned to him, grinned and said, "Buck up, buttercup."

"I got fired," Justice grouched back. "Don't expect me to be happy about it."

"True, you did." She swung one foot. "But I'm guessing *someone* had a fit, because just as I was headed in to this little meeting, Mr. Wade called to say he'd had a change of heart. You are to report to their home at six this evening."

Very slowly, Justice straightened. "You're shi—" he quickly censored himself and corrected "—kidding me?"

Sahara feigned an absurd look of innocence. "Would I do that?"

"You think the daughter forced it?" Leese asked.

"Why else? When Mr. Wade called—at the crack of dawn, by the way—he was most adamant that Justice was through. I do believe he wanted me to hang him by his toenails…or some other more vulnerable body part." She bobbed her eyebrows while giving a pointed look at his crotch. "The man was entirely enraged and I only soothed him by telling him I'd give Justice a strict reprimand."

Justice scowled.

"Consider yourself severely reprimanded, by the way." Sahara made him wait while she took another bite of her doughnut. "Funny thing, though, when Mr. Wade called back, he was subdued to the point of being sullen. He snarled that he'd reconsidered and the contract should stand."

Justice didn't know what to think. Had Fallon had a hissy? That'd fit the princess role, but she hadn't seemed like the hissy type to him.

Still, it wasn't like he knew her well. Shortly after meeting, she'd gotten drunk and people could be very different then.

"None of this makes sense," Justice said. "I'm not even sure why she needs protection."

While sipping coffee, Sahara shrugged. "Her father is wealthy. Threats come out of nowhere."

"But it's more than that," Justice insisted. "They treat her like she's a kid." He glanced at Leese. "She wanted to go to a bar and drink beer. Said she'd never done either one before. What twenty-four-year-old lady's never done that?" And now that he thought of it, it made him wonder what else she hadn't done.

Not a good direction for his thoughts to take.

"That's where you took her?" Leese asked.

"Yeah." He couldn't help but half grin. "She got hammered right off the bat. It would have been funny if her dad wasn't breathing fire down my neck."

Leese gave him a long look. "Had she eaten?"

"I dunno."

The long look became disbelieving. "You didn't find out?" Leese sat forward, his elbows on his knees. "You took a twenty-four-year-old sheltered client on a drinking spree without asking questions first?"

Going on the defensive, Justice said, "'Course I asked questions. She just didn't give a lot of answers."

"Tell me you at least did your research beforehand."

"I told you last night, she didn't give me a chance. She laid out the agenda after I got there, not before."

Leese shook his head. "But you researched her, right?"

Starting to feel uncomfortable, Justice shifted. He knew Leese was big on digging up every bit of info he could, in every way he could. "What was there to research? It was a straightforward job. Just watch over her for a while."

Leese and Sahara shared a look of disappointment.

"What?" he demanded. "There wasn't any specific threat ever mentioned."

"You do your research, regardless." Leese stood. "You know that."

"Sure. But this time, it didn't seem necessary. I mean, I'm like a glorified babysitter or something." Except that now…yeah, now he wished he knew more about her.

"Let's go." Leese returned his coffee cup to the tray. "We'll do it now."

"We will?" Justice quickly gulped down his coffee and went to follow his friend. After all, Leese had fallen much more comfortably into this new gig. For him, it had been an easy transition.

For Justice, he still felt like he had a lot to learn… obviously.

"Yes," Sahara said. "Go, shoo. Do your jobs. Leave the rest of the pastries for me. And Justice? Let me know how it goes."

BY THE TIME Justice pulled through the gate to the Wade home, he felt like he had a better handle on things.

He now knew that Fallon had graduated at the top of her class, so she was obviously smart.

She didn't keep a Facebook page or Twitter account, so she wasn't much for social media—or she was super private. He'd bet on the latter.

The lack of an online persona made it tougher to get a handle on her personal preferences. Leese had thought they'd find out about her friends, past dates, the places she enjoyed hanging…but when they found nothing, they both decided it was her father's wealth that made it difficult to do the usual. Anyone could be tracked online, but as protective as her folks were, they wouldn't like making it easy.

Fallon was young for her job as a decorator for her father's hotel chain. She handled only the local hotels, though. Justice didn't know if that was out of an aversion to traveling or just convenience.

Since most rich people spent a bunch of their time jetting around, Leese had dug a little more, but even he couldn't find a single instance of Fallon leaving the city in years.

Curious, but what Justice found most interesting was an incident from five years ago when Fallon's sister, older by two years, had tragically died in a fire. That alone might be enough to prompt the parents to hover over her.

Losing a kid…he couldn't imagine anything worse than that. But yeah, it could make anyone more protective.

There weren't many details to go by. The parents were super private and had refused all interviews. All Leese could find was a report of the fire, started by accident, saying that the sister had died. Apparently the Wades had enough money and influence to keep their personal business out of the news.

To prepare for the assignment, Justice had left Leese to finish up his cursory research while he checked out all the local establishments that Fallon might want to visit. That had taken most of the afternoon. After figuring he had a handle on things, Justice had eaten his dinner and headed out.

Now that the storms had blown over, the spring day felt too warm and muggy. He'd dressed in a T-shirt and jeans with his usual gym shoes. This time of early evening, the sun settled like a blaze on the horizon, making sunglasses necessary as he drove along the landscaped private drive to the house.

First thing Justice noticed was a black Mercedes parked out front. Slick ride. Curious, he parked behind it, got out and started for the front door. Right before he reached the steps, the door opened and a suited *GQ*-looking guy got ushered out.

Tall, trim, blond—and obviously of the same moneyed ilk as Fallon's family.

Effectively backing him out the door, Fallon said, "Really, Marcus, I've been clear. I'm sorry, but it's over."

Huh. A boyfriend? Maybe *past* boyfriend, given Fallon's frown. Justice held back, watching and waiting.

Marcus took her hands. "Don't say that, Fallon. You can't mean it."

"I do." She tugged, but good ole Marcus didn't let her go.

That irked Justice big-time. He was about to intercede when Mr. Wade stepped out, and for once he looked pissed at someone other than Justice. "Go, Marcus. Don't make this more uncomfortable for her than it has to be."

"Please, sir, I need just a minute to speak with her."

"She doesn't want to talk to you," Mr. Wade insisted.

"Dad," Fallon complained. "I can handle this."

"I screwed up," Marcus rushed to say to her father, ignoring Fallon's objection. "I know that and I'm sorry. It just…took me by surprise."

"Marcus!" Face going red, Fallon glanced at her father, who didn't budge. "You don't have to explain. Seriously." She tugged again, but blondie didn't let go. "I understand. But surely you see—"

"It won't happen again. I swear."

"What," her father asked with growling menace, "won't happen again?"

"*Dad,*" Fallon pleaded more urgently. Then to Marcus, "Don't do this. *Please.*"

Justice decided he'd had enough. Interrupting whatever Marcus would have said, he announced himself. "Hey, Fallon. You about ready?"

Finally noticing him, her face lit up, then pinched in irritation as she forcefully yanked her hands from Marcus. "Yes, of course. I'll need only a minute."

"Sure." As he strode up the steps, Justice pushed

the glasses to the top of his head, letting them catch in the messy fauxhawk that he knew needed a good trim.

She looked nervously to her pushy swain. "Marcus…"

"I'm not leaving," Marcus insisted.

Yeah, Justice decided, he was. "Did I get here just in time to be useful?" His muscles clenched. He felt like cracking his knuckles—or the boyfriend's head.

"No! That is, everything's fine." Fallon floundered, then pulled back her shoulders and glared at Marcus.

"Fallon," the guy pleaded.

"Goodbye." After giving her dad a warning frown, Fallon sent a fast smile to Justice, then hurried inside.

Pinning his gaze to Marcus, Justice approached with as much menace as he could muster.

Marcus quickly stepped aside, caught himself and, instead of leaving, he struck an arrogant stance. "Who are you?"

"None of your business." Satisfied with Marcus's flustered reaction, Justice turned to her father with a cordial nod. "Mr. Wade."

"Mr. Wallington." He blocked the door. "I'd like a word please."

"All right." Justice had figured on getting an earful.

Mr. Wade turned to Marcus again. "Don't come back here uninvited or you'll find yourself out of a job."

Justice whistled low. Far as dismissals went, that was a brutal one.

Face going red, Marcus nodded. "As you wish." Trying to muster some dignity, he needlessly straightened his suit coat. "But I *will* speak with her again." He cast a cautious look at Justice, turned and left.

Both men watched, arms crossed, until Marcus had driven out of view.

Seeing a neutral opening, Justice asked, "Is he a threat?"

"Marcus? No, of course not." Mr. Wade closed the door behind him, giving them privacy outside. "You know that I fired you."

"Not something I would've missed." The man had shouted it at him in a rage.

"I hired you back only because Fallon insisted."

What was he supposed to say about that? No way would he thank him, so instead he settled on a simple, "Okay." He didn't want things to be more awkward than necessary, but hell if he'd grovel.

"I wouldn't have," Mr. Wade stated, "but she threatened to hire you herself. With her own money."

Fallon had enough of her own? Justice wasn't sure. Nothing in the research revealed her finances, and it didn't feel like an appropriate question to ask. Feeling his way, he said, "I gather you don't want her to do that?"

"No, I don't." Showing his frustration, Mr. Wade ran a hand through his hair, disrupting the meticulous style. "But Fallon is independent."

Justice almost choked on that. He banked the skepticism when Mr. Wade glared at him.

"You don't understand," Mr. Wade continued. "I would love to indulge her, but other than agreeing to live at home, she rarely lets me. Even for holidays—her birthday, Christmas—she complains if we give her too many gifts. She buys casual department store clothes, drives an economy car—"

"So far," Justice said, "I don't see a problem." He kind of liked the idea that Fallon was so low-key. Made it easier for him to relate to her.

"I was remiss in explaining things to you." Locking his hands behind his back, Mr. Wade paced. "Fallon received a sizable trust fund from my parents. If she chose to, she could live a very comfortable, independent life off that. However, she almost never touches the money. For the most part, she makes do with her limited salary."

"So it's because of this big inheritance that you wanted her protected?"

"Not entirely, no." Mr. Wade looked off down the drive, visibly gathering his thoughts.

Justice waited for him to explain the threat.

Instead, he said, "I didn't want Fallon to finally spend the money...only to spite me."

Damn, how big of a spat had they had? Justice found himself in the awkward position of feeling bad for Mr. Wade. "Yeah, okay, I get that." He cleared his throat, searching for words to smooth things over. "Look, I don't want to be a bone of contention between father and daughter. If there are strict rules here, just let me know and I'll do my best. But if I can speak up?"

A touch of desperation held her father stiff. "By all means."

"Well..." Justice rubbed the back of his neck, completely out of his comfort zone. Hell, as a fighter, he'd hooked up with plenty of girls and never, not once, had he been forced through a heart-to-heart with a father. "Fallon's not a kid, right? The things she gets excited over, like drinking a beer? That's stuff she should've done years ago. Seems to me she's just spreading her wings a little, playing catch-up with other people her age. Why not let her? So she got a little drunk. You were mid-twenties once, right?"

After a moment, the slightest of smiles tweaked Mr. Wade's mouth. "Yes."

Somehow Justice couldn't see the staid man before him ever cutting loose, but whatever. "No harm was done. And that fight she mentioned wasn't much of a fight at all."

"She said the two of you were accosted by three men."

Bearing his own frustration, Justice propped his hands on his hips. "Yeah, but they were just bozos. I handled it, and I'll handle anything else that comes up." He threw caution to the wind and clapped a hand to the man's shoulder. "Let her cut loose in the way she wants—with me keeping her safe. You'll worry, sure. I get that dads do that."

Brows lifted, Mr. Wade looked first at the hand on his shoulder, then at Justice directly. "Your own father. Does he worry?"

"He passed when I was young. But my mom? That woman could worry paint off the wall." He grinned, gave the smaller man two strong shoulder slaps that left him staggering, then dropped his hand. "Thing is, Mom trusts me. I'm thinking you need to trust Fallon some, too."

"I do."

"Then how about trusting me? I come with good credentials." Not wanting to miss the opportunity, Justice moved on to more important matters. "So about this Marcus character…"

That soured the man's mood even more. "They used to date."

Yeah, he'd figured that much on his own. "Didn't work out?"

After only a second or two of hesitation, Mr. Wade confided in him. "Marcus hurt her. I'm not sure how but they ended their relationship and she hasn't dated since."

Justice went rigid. "What do you mean, he hurt her?"

"Her feelings. He said or did something." In a low voice, Mr. Wade murmured, "Bastard."

Well, what do you know? He and Mr. Wade were finding common ground after all. "Did she date much before that?"

"Not since high school."

Which meant she hadn't dated in college? Why the hell not? "So when did she and Marcus meet?" To keep from sounding too personally interested, Justice said, "It helps if I know what's what, in case he shows up again."

"If he does, it won't go well for him. I meant it when I said I'd fire him."

"What did he do for you?"

Mr. Wade waved a hand. "Management position, created for him—which means he'd be easy to replace."

Hmm. "You think Fallon would be okay with that? I

mean, I got the impression she wanted to handle it herself, not with your influence."

His shoulders dropped. "True." After a huff, he added, "And Rebecca is fond of him."

Fallon's mom? "So maybe you need to be just a little more subtle in how you scare him off."

Mr. Wade scrutinized him. "You?"

Why not? After all, his job was to protect her. "I can easily handle it, and since you're paying me…" Justice left that open-ended, and then waited.

"Keep him away from her," Mr. Wade instructed, "and I just might consider you valuable after all."

"I'll see to it." With pleasure. *What had the prick done to turn her against him?* Hands in his pockets, Justice asked, "You wanna give me any details?"

Mr. Wade grumbled to himself a moment, something about a wasted promotion, then explained, "They were together for about four months and she seemed so happy. Fallon is private, so I don't know what Marcus did to screw it up, but it ended about six weeks ago."

Stalling the million and one questions Justice had, Fallon opened the door—and drew up short when she saw the two men in close conversation.

Suspicion lifted her brows, then animosity lowered them. In a chilling tone of warning, Fallon asked, "Dad?"

CHAPTER FOUR

JUSTICE SAID, "UM..."

Hell, he felt like he'd just gotten caught with his hand in the cookie jar. In truth, Fallon had probably saved him because he'd been close to asking questions that had nothing to do with the job, and had everything to do with the odd protectiveness he felt toward Fallon as a woman.

It went beyond work ethic and nudged into... territorial.

Assignment, assignment, assignment. He'd remind himself as many times as necessary.

Being much smoother, Mr. Wade pasted on a tempered smile. "We were just passing the time until you finished getting ready, honey."

Fallon wasn't buying it. Her doubt showed in the way she looked at Justice out of the corner of her eye.

He grinned at her.

That seemed to confuse her. "I would have been ready if Marcus hadn't dropped in. I'm sorry for making you wait."

"Does he do that often?" *Shut up, Justice.*

"Um, no." She looked between him and her father. "But it did put me just a little behind."

"Not a problem," Justice promised. "I'm on your schedule, remember."

"And it gave us a chance to chat and get better acquainted." Mr. Wade pulled his daughter into an embrace, hugging her close. He looked at Justice over her head while he said, "Have fun, and be safe."

Next he offered his hand to Justice.

Huh. Maybe they really had smoothed over the rough waters. "Right. Better acquainted." Justice accepted the olive branch.

"I'm trusting you to take care of her." After that quiet acceptance, Mr. Wade went in.

Fallon scowled up at Justice. "What was that all about?"

Today she wore slim ankle-length jeans with flat shoes and a loose, blue striped sweater. She looked incredibly cute. "Just talking man to man." Rather than go into detail, Justice gestured for her to precede him to the car. "Where to tonight?"

"I checked out local attractions and found that there's a street fair nearby. It's open for a few more hours."

Justice tripped over his own feet. Damn it, he'd checked everything he could think of, but he hadn't even known about the fair. "Where?"

"It's downtown. Lots of crowds expected."

He grabbed for the door handle right before she could.

Once again, she sat up front.

Like déjà vu, he got behind the wheel but didn't pull away. "Will you need me tomorrow, too?"

She tipped her head. "Is that a problem?"

"Nope. But I'm thinking we save the fair till then."

"Why?"

"I don't know anything about it."

"It's a fair," she said. "There will be vendors, things to buy, food to try."

Justice figured it was past time they made some ground rules. "You need to understand, it's my job to make you secure. I gotta know what's happening a little beforehand, otherwise it's impossible. And when it's impossible, your dad gets pissed and I could end up canned again."

Not giving in, Fallon asked, "What could happen at a fair?"

No idea, but he knew better than to take chances. "Anything, I guess." He tugged at his ear. "See, what I do is figure out how to proceed in case anything does go wrong. Like, I need to know the quickest way out, the best route to take, the neighborhoods we'll go through—"

"You're taking this all too seriously."

"Yeah, says the girl who got shit-faced, had to be carried in, got me fired—"

"Stop!" Barely suppressing a laugh, she pressed her palms to her reddened cheeks. "That's not who I usually am."

Justice noticed how cute she looked with a blush. "Too bad, because that girl was fun."

She blinked at him. "Really?"

Too late to call back the words, Justice said, "I mean—"

"You don't think I was...pathetic?" So much heat now colored her cheeks, she looked scalded.

Bracing a forearm on the steering wheel, Justice

turned to face her. The vulnerability in her dark eyes nearly broke his heart. Softly, he asked, "Why would you think that?"

She looked away, hesitated, then changed the subject. "Maybe we could do the art museum then. There's a special exhibit—"

He cut her off. "Same problem. I'd need to check it out first."

Disappointed, she clutched her hands in her lap. "So then what are we going to do? I'm not anxious to visit another bar."

That surprised him. "I thought you had fun." But maybe her daddy had put the kibosh on drinking.

"I did," she admitted. "But then I woke up this morning and remembered that no one had danced with me. Not that I expected guys to rush over or anything, but... not a single one?"

The smile tugged at his mouth. "You know why, right?"

Her shoulders sagged. "I assume—"

Justice took her hand. It was small in his, delicate. Hell, her dad was right—she was fragile.

Taboo, dude. Knock that shit off.

He retreated, but explained, "Guys tried, honey. More than a few. My job was to keep them away, so that's what I did."

Comprehension came slowly. "You're serious?"

Justice nodded. "Any guy who looked too long, or tried to cozy up, got my best 'back the ef off' stare. You were busy dancing—" *and turning me on in the process* "—so I guess you didn't notice."

She dropped back in her seat. "You actually warned men away?"

"With a mean stare, yeah." In his defense, Justice said, "They weren't your usual refined aristocrats, you know."

A slow simmering anger straightened her shoulders, tightened that soft mouth and narrowed her amazing eyes. "I didn't want to dance with an aristocrat. That's why I went to a local *bar*."

She said it like she spoke to an idiot. Amused by the show of temper, Justice grinned. "Tell you what, if you have enough free time tonight, how about I take you to Rowdy's? I'm already familiar with it and I'm betting the guys I know will be around. If you want to dance with them, no sweat."

She looked tempted, and still riled. "I don't want you coercing anyone to do you a favor. I'm not a charity case."

"Far from it." Hell, he'd probably still have to read the riot act to any man—friend or not—who got too close. "So what do you say?" To help convince her, he added, "You can try another beer, but this time just one."

She stewed a minute more before finally nodding. "Well…all right. But, Justice, you have to trust me to do my own fending off, okay?"

Now that he had a destination, he started the car and pulled away. "That's a no-go. It's my job to—"

"You are only to protect me if things get out of hand!"

Yeah, she had a point. But with a woman like Fallon, that could happen in the blink of an eye.

THEY WEREN'T ON the road long when Justice cleared his throat. Over the next twenty minutes he did it several more times, repeatedly glancing her way, and Fallon assumed he was uneasy about her scolding.

Because he wore his mirrored sunglasses, she couldn't see his eyes. Not that she needed to. The tension in his big body, in his broad shoulders and the set of his jaw, told her he was on edge.

She remained a little irked at his high-handed attitude, but clearly that mood wasn't conducive to a nice evening so she decided to break the ice. With a slight huff, she faced him. "Something on your mind, Justice?"

A long exhale left his posture more relaxed. "Whew." He flashed her a relieved grin. "That silent treatment was getting to me."

Fallon hid her smile. For such a big, bulky guy, he'd really let one little disagreement bother him. "Then why don't we chat?"

As if he'd been waiting for that invitation, Justice said, "Good idea. Who's Marcus?"

Well, shoot. She'd walked right into that one. "Nobody important." Not anymore.

"Nah, don't give me that. He's somebody, or at least he was. You cut ties on him?"

"Yes." Or more like Marcus had cut ties—with his reaction.

He frowned. "Hung up on him still?"

Emphatic, she said, *"Noooo."*

"No?" he clarified.

"Not even a little." Marcus had bruised her pride, wounded her spirit and dashed her hopes, but she knew she'd never really loved him. "He was…convenient." She wrinkled her nose. "That sounds terrible, doesn't it? Very mercenary. The thing is, he works for my dad and my parents liked him. He was familiar with the family." And all her secrets. "It seemed easy to fall into a pattern with him." Easy, and oh, so stupid.

"Well, for what it's worth," Justice said, "I don't like him."

He sounded so sincere, she couldn't help but point out the obvious. "You don't even know him."

"Sure I do. See, fighters learn how to size people up real quick. You get in the cage with a guy and you have to know if he's quiet because he's afraid, or because he's that confident. Does he talk smack to counter insecurities, or because he knows he can back it up? I can read body language and Marcus is a putz."

Fallon laughed. "Sorry to disappoint you, but he really isn't. He's successful and engaging and people love him."

"Not me." Justice squeezed the steering wheel. "Not you."

Good point. "We're the exceptions, then."

"Nope. Your dad wasn't too keen on him either, let me tell you." Justice glanced in the rearview mirror, frowned, and then took an exit. "So what happened? What'd he do?"

She couldn't believe his audacity. "That's private, Justice."

He chewed his upper lip, rolled one shoulder, and said with complete seriousness, "I have to know these things. I mean, what if he shows up and tries to start trouble?"

Fallon laughed. "He won't. In all ways, Marcus is proper."

"Asshole wasn't all that proper today. Proper is letting a lady go when she asks."

"Justice!" It took all her control not to laugh. He did have a way of saying things.

Jaw working, Justice grumbled, "I wanted to cream him."

It was ridiculous, but his vehemence warmed Fallon's heart. She touched his rigid shoulder and said, "I'd prefer that you didn't."

"Okay, so help me out here—what's his crime? If I know, then maybe, *maybe*, I won't feel the need to stomp on him."

For the first time since the breakup, Fallon felt like talking about it. Oh, she wouldn't give him every detail. She'd learned her lesson on sharing too much. But given Justice's defense, and the fact he didn't know all her secrets, he might be the perfect person to listen.

"I'm on the edge of my seat here," he said. "Imagining all kinds of crazy stuff."

Belatedly, she withdrew her hand, but her palm continued to tingle. She curled her fingers into a fist, holding on to the sensation.

Justice's shoulder was boulder hard and so warm that she couldn't help but think about touching him again, wrong as she knew it would be.

"Honestly, it wasn't all that much." The hazy setting sun glared through the windshield, giving her a good excuse to hide behind her own sunglasses. *Now where to begin?* "Marcus and I started out as just friends. I... haven't done much dating."

What an understatement.

Not wanting him to ask about that, she quickly continued. "There are some occasions where you'd really like a date. Weddings, company parties, things like that," she explained. "I knew Marcus through the company, he was nice, others admired him..."

"And you bought into that shit?"

She bit back a smile. "My dad was really pleased when Marcus asked me to a company gathering."

"So what? Your dad didn't have to date him."

That time the laugh broke free. "For some reason you're biased."

"I told you, I'm a good judge of character."

Curiosity got the best of her. "So what do you think of me?"

Becoming uneasy again, Justice said, "Finish your story first."

Fallon thought about it, then decided he was right. Better to get it over with. "We did the whole friend thing for a while until finally, maybe a month later, Marcus wanted more than that, but my parents have been really overprotective."

"Noticed."

Of course he had. Not like he could have missed that. "I didn't have much experience with guys, and Marcus was...patient."

Interest sharpening, Justice growled, "You're talking about sex?"

She wished she could be as plainspoken as him. But his question alone made her face hot. Lifting a hand in a lame gesture, she said, "Stuff that comes before that."

"What stuff?"

Fallon shifted. "You know what I'm saying."

He chewed his lip again. "Okay, so we're talking foreplay, right? Making out, groping a little, testing the water so to speak."

"Yes, exactly." And all that had gone well enough as long as she left on her clothes. "We seemed to suit... until it came time for the deed."

He snorted a laugh. "The *deed*?" he mimicked. With a teasing glance, he asked, "We're still talking sex, right?"

"Yes," she growled, her eyes narrowed as Justice made her feel foolish.

"Let me tell you, if Marcus screwed that up, then good riddance."

Yes, he'd definitely screwed it up. The same strangling humiliation swamped her. "We found we didn't suit and that there could be no future between us. Not in any intimate way."

"Holy shit," Justice breathed. "He *did* screw it up. Jesus, what a putz."

"It wasn't like that."

He snorted another laugh. "If you say so. But now I just feel sorry for him." This time Justice reached out and patted her knee. "The idiot will be regretting that the rest of his life."

It blew her away that Justice seemed to consider

her such a prize. "Why would he regret it? Because he works for my father? I don't think Dad would—"

"Yeah, your dad definitely would. But what I meant was that he'd lost out with you." Justice got back on the expressway before saying, "You know you're a catch, right?"

He didn't know her well enough to make that judgment, but she enjoyed hearing it anyway. "You think so?"

"Know so. I mean, what's not to like, right?"

She half turned to face him. "So tell me, what do you consider my sterling qualities?"

He glanced in the rearview mirror again. "Would that be crossing a line? I mean, I don't look forward to your dad unloading on me again."

"I won't tell if you don't."

He grinned wide enough to put dimples in his whiskery cheeks. "Alrighty, then. For one thing, you're cute as hell. Big bedroom eyes, soft sexy mouth, and you have such a sweet little body."

Fallon ducked her head as guilt swamped her. "I don't."

"See, this is why I should pound on Marcus. Did that prick say or do something to make you—"

"No." Caught between wanting to laugh and dying of embarrassment, Fallon said, "And your language is deteriorating by the second."

"Let's blame Marcus," Justice grumbled. "He brings out the worst in me."

Shaking her head, Fallon said, "You're incorrigible."

"Just speaking the truth." He grew more serious.

"You're also really nice. And smart. You have a good sense of humor. You're daring. And... I dunno. You're *genuine*." With a fast shrug, he added, "I didn't expect that. I thought with you being rich and all, you'd maybe be snooty or bitchy, but you're not. You're real down-to-earth."

Never in her life had she been so flattered. "Thank you, Justice." For obvious reasons, compliments to her character were far nicer than commenting on her physical appearance.

He gave a nod, then said, "You also look really great dancing. Too good, maybe."

Having no idea what he meant by that, Fallon said again, "Thank you. I haven't had much practice dancing either, but I enjoy it."

"I could tell that you did," he murmured. "Hell, every guy there could tell." Then he asked, "Marcus never took you dancing?"

"A few times. Not often." She didn't want to detail everything she hadn't done, so she switched gears. "While we're discussing Marcus, I should probably explain that none of this was his fault."

Justice snorted. "I saw him, remember? He was all butt-hurt and bossy, probably because he knew he'd screwed up."

Fallon choked. "Butt-hurt?"

He grinned again. "Yeah, you know. All pouty and belligerent."

"I've, ah, never heard the term."

He dismissed that with a shrug. "Take my word for

it—men don't act that way unless they're butt-hurt. Not real men, anyway."

With Justice having been a fighter, his ideas of how real men should behave might differ from many others. "Could I ask you something now?"

"Shoot."

"Why did you give up fighting when you're so obviously good?"

"Ouch." He gave a theatrical wince. "Tough question. See, I'm not that good. Not good enough to win a title and that's what it's all about."

"But you're fast, and strong and—"

He grinned at her. "Keep going."

"Admittedly, I don't know that much about fighting, but I was certainly impressed."

"Because," he repeated, "you don't know that much about fighting. The dudes you'll meet tonight at Rowdy's? Some of them are top-notch. Championship quality. Without sounding too cocky, I am good, but only against untrained idiots. You could throw street thugs at me all day long and I wouldn't break a sweat. But in the cage…" He gave a small shake of his head. "Whole different ballgame."

Fascinated, Fallon thought about the men she'd meet, even while wanting to know more about Justice. "How so?"

He lifted one hand from the wheel and curled it into a tight fist. Muscles bulged all along his forearm, his biceps, shoulder and into his neck. "I have bricks for fists. Real knock-out power. Problem is, trained fighters aren't still long enough to let me hit them. MMA is a mixed fighting style, so it's not just boxing. It's grappling, too."

"Grappling?"

"Sort of a mix between wrestling, submission and strikes. My takedowns are too slow and once I'm on the ground the best fighters have an advantage over me with speed. If I get hold of a guy, or if I can land a punch or kick, I can put him down. That's my strength."

She agreed—he looked very strong.

"But any scenario other than that and I'd get in trouble. The losses I had were all submissions."

"How many losses did you have?"

"Twenty wins, six losses."

"Pfft. And for that you gave up?"

He scowled at her. "There wasn't a path to the belt. The heavyweight title holder is a beast. He beat me twice. If I lost weight and dropped down to light heavyweight, my buddy Cannon was in the way."

"You didn't want to fight a buddy?"

"Hell, I don't mind that. Guys compete with their friends all the time. It's a sport, not a grudge match."

He sounded disgruntled, making her smile. "Sorry, I didn't realize."

"I trained at Cannon's camp. I'd seen him fight plenty of times, but even in training he was slicker than most. I knew I'd only beat him with a lucky punch, and so far, no one's gotten a lucky punch in on him. You'll like him."

"You don't sound resentful."

"Of Cannon?" He snorted. "No, 'course not. He's a great guy. Not just at fighting either. That camp? It's his gym, a way for fighters to learn new techniques from each other, but he also runs classes for the neighborhood kids. Everyone in Warfield idolizes him because that's the type of man he is."

She held silent for a bit, noticing that he again checked the rearview mirror, then the side mirror. Just cautious, or was there a problem? She checked her side mirror but saw nothing amiss, just other cars on the road.

As the light faded from the horizon, streetlamps flickered on. They each removed their sunglasses. The headlights automatically flicked on as Justice took another exit and turned down a busy street.

"Do you miss fighting?"

"Yeah. A lot."

She heard the longing in his tone and it bothered her. "Why switch to being a bodyguard then? I'd think if you enjoyed it and you were good—even if not the best—it'd be worth it to continue."

His hands tightened on the steering wheel. "I'm no good at being second best. Too competitive. My last fight was a good win. I was the underdog. Everyone expected me to get my ass handed to me. Instead, I nailed a quick, clean knockout in under thirty seconds. So I figured I'd go out on a high note, you know?"

"Wow." But because she didn't know, she asked, "That's fast, right?"

He laughed. "Yeah. Usually we go three five-minute rounds. Championship fights are five five-minute rounds." He shifted, popped his neck, then admitted, "Nine times out of ten, he'd have beaten me. But he shot in, I threw a punch and *pow*, he went down for the count."

"I'd say there's luck, and then there's being ready. Clearly you took advantage of an opportunity. You were prepared and you did what you needed to do, when you needed to do it."

Grinning, he patted her knee again. "Yeah, that's how I tell it, too."

"Do you still train?"

"Sure. Once a gym rat, always a gym rat. But now I can eat burgers when I want." He patted his flat abdomen. "And drink an occasional beer."

Absurd for him to pretend he had any fat on his body. From what Fallon could tell, he was muscle layered on muscle. But given it was probably a somewhat new occurrence, she was ridiculously pleased that he'd drunk a beer with *her*.

"On top of being competitive, I like a challenge. Let me tell you, this gig is *real* challenging. Hell, every day I learn something new. Another fighter friend, Leese Phelps, was the first to cut out for personal security. He sort of paved the way." With another cocky grin, Justice added, "I still get to be a badass and have some interesting assignments. As a bonus, I get to carry a gun."

Startled, she asked, "You're carrying a gun?"

He gave her a "duh" look. "You thought I wouldn't?"

"I never thought about it either way." She looked him over, but didn't see—

"Want to see for yourself, huh?" He leaned forward a little, lifted his T-shirt and showed her a black automatic in a holster connected to his belt, situated at the small of his back.

It took her a second to find her voice. Justice had

just flashed a swath of firm skin and muscle, and the waistband of black boxers riding low on his hips. Temperature rising, Fallon asked in a whisper, "Have you ever shot anyone?"

"Not so far, no." As he pulled up to a stoplight, he turned to look at her. "But I would if necessary."

She believed him.

Then he flashed another grin, flexed his arms to make massive muscles pop in his biceps. "But with guns like these, it's usually not necessary."

Fallon felt like fanning her face. Good Lord, he looked fine. Needing another switch, she said, "I'm sorry I'm not a more interesting assignment."

"You fit that 'challenge' part, and that keeps it interesting."

Before she could ask him what he meant, the light changed and he moved his foot off the brake.

"Before you," he said, "I worked with Mark Stricker."

Her jaw loosened. "The movie star?"

"Yeah. Let me tell you—that was interesting. Did you know he's, like, five-two?"

"Really? I thought he was taller."

"Me, too."

"In movies, he looks to be at least six feet tall."

"Yeah, but it's a trick. They put him on a platform when he's next to the taller female actors. Crazy, huh?"

"Fascinating." Curious why he'd been assigned to Stricker, she asked, "Was he in danger?"

"Nah. Mostly I helped him train for a new role as a fighter. But there were also times I had to keep the rabid fans away. I can't talk about it much. The deets on the film are still hush-hush."

"Okay, sorry." When he again checked his mirrors, Fallon huffed a breath. "Is there a problem, Justice?"

"What do you mean?"

"You keep checking behind us like you're expecting trouble."

"It's my job to expect trouble."

She started to relax…

Until he added, "Especially when we're being followed."

CHAPTER FIVE

FALLON LOOKED SO STARTLED, Justice decided to distract her. "Tell me about your job now."

She twisted to stare out the rear window. "Justice—"

"Fair's fair. I answered your questions."

Glaring at him, she asked, "Who's following us?"

"Don't know. I'm willing to bet it's Marcus, though."

For a few seconds, she just stared at him—then laughed. "Don't be ridiculous." But she looked again. "Can you see his car?"

"No."

She relaxed back in her seat. "How do you know we're being followed?"

"I know." He took another look in the mirror before leaving the road and pulling into a restaurant lot.

"This is it?" she asked, sounding disappointed by the updated, casual, mom-and-pop diner.

"No." Justice did a U-turn in the lot to face the road, turned off the headlights and waited.

Fallon appeared to be holding her breath, so without taking his gaze off the road, Justice said, "Relax. You're fine."

In reply, she wrapped her arms around herself.

Justice wanted to comfort her but he'd already

crossed too many lines. If he kept it up, he'd deserve to be canned.

A car drove past. A few trucks. And then he saw the fancy sports car.

Fallon seemed unaware as she stared through the windshield.

Was she afraid of Marcus? If so, that was reason enough for Justice to confront him. For some reason—crazy as it might be—he was itching to pulverize the guy.

After the slick black car sped past, Justice asked, "Does Marcus have a Corvette?"

"What?" Drawn from her thoughts, she shook her head. "No—or at least I don't think so. He's more a BMW or Mercedes type of man."

"I saw the Mercedes. Can he afford two cars? Maybe one for business and one for sport?"

"He could, yes. But, Justice, I'm sure that wasn't him. It's not his style to chase after anyone."

"Maybe." Justice stewed a minute more before deciding it would be best to get to their destination so Fallon could enjoy herself. He drove out of the lot, saying, "We'll be there in about five minutes."

"Rowdy's?"

"Yeah." So that he wouldn't make the same mistake twice, he asked, "You hungry? They have some killer burgers there."

She gave it quick thought and nodded. "Very hungry, in fact. Thanks."

Luckily Rowdy had opened up a separate lot adjacent to the bar because the place stayed packed, especially on a Saturday night. Justice kept Fallon close as he stepped inside the busy bar.

Avery, Rowdy's wife who usually worked as the bartender, bustled from table to table. When she spotted him, she got closer and said, "They're in back at the pool tables."

"Thanks. I'll join them in a bit, but we want to grab some food first."

"There's a booth that just emptied. Follow me."

Justice waited until they'd nabbed the seats before doing introductions. "Avery, this is Fallon. Fallon, Avery is married to the owner."

He let the ladies say their hellos before asking, "How come you're on the floor tonight?"

"One of our waitresses called in sick. Rowdy's working the bar and I'm doing my best to keep up here. Some days," she grumbled, "being popular is a bother."

Fallon smiled at her. "Is there some way we can help?"

Justice froze. If Avery said yes, how the hell would he keep track of her?

Luckily, Avery laughed, told Justice he had a "winner," then asked them if they needed to look at the menu.

Sorry that he couldn't lend her a hand, but relieved that Fallon would remain close, he said, "Loaded burgers, plate of fries and I'll take a chocolate milk shake. Fallon?"

"Works for me. Make it two shakes."

Avery's smile was slow and knowing. "Definitely a keeper. I'll get that out to you shortly."

"No rush," Fallon said.

After Avery left, Justice smiled at Fallon. "That was nice of you. To offer to help, I mean."

"I wouldn't mind." She glanced around the bar with a sort of wistful yearning. "In fact, it might be fun."

Yeah, right. "You ever work as a waitress?"

She twitched her mouth to the side. "Dad would have had a heart attack." With the tip of her finger, she traced the wood grain in the tabletop. "Going through school, I worked for him part-time as an apprentice. Now my job is decorating the local hotels he owns. Decor gets old quick in the industry. We like to keep things as fresh and updated as possible."

"The hotels are fancy, aren't they?"

"Not really. I mean, they're nice, but not super upscale or anything. I stay busy with it, but I got ahead on everything so right now I have a whole month off."

Time she'd built in to play. Curious about her, Justice asked, "You like the job?"

"I do. The different locations each have their own character and I get to reflect that in how I decorate them. I do only those in Ohio, Indiana and Northern Kentucky, though Dad has locations all across the country."

He'd wondered about that. "You don't like to travel?"

She shook her head and then deliberately tried to divert him. "What about you?"

Justice shrugged. "It's okay. I haven't traveled much for pleasure, but fighters go all over, either to compete or to support friends. Brazil, Japan, Canada, South Korea—"

"Wow. I had no idea." She folded her arms on the tabletop. "That's so exciting."

"Not if you're fighting. Let me tell you, the packing

and travel and promo is a hassle. Then you have to adjust to the time zone and sometimes the altitude. It's not like you get much opportunity to be a tourist."

"I can't imagine all that running and prep and then having to perform. But I'm impressed."

Sheepish, Justice shook his head. "Don't be. I won in Japan, but not in South Korea or Brazil. Not that I got creamed or anything," he rushed to assure her. "Got bonus bucks for 'fight of the night' in Brazil. It was a real brawl, but I lost two of the three rounds."

"I would love to see a live fight sometime."

He was about to tell her it'd be too risky when Cannon spoke beside them. "You're in luck. Stack Hannigan is fighting next weekend and it's local. Have Justice bring you."

While Fallon stared up in awe at Cannon, Justice tried to signal him by slashing a finger across his neck.

Cannon ignored him. "Introduce me, Justice."

Armie strolled up next to him. "Yeah, introduce us."

"Jesus, Joseph and Mary," Justice mumbled. Did they think she was a date? "I was going to bring her to the pool room for introductions after we ate."

Showing up with the food, Avery bumped Cannon and Armie out of her way with her hip. She set the plates and drinks off her tray, then asked, "Anything else?"

"It smells perfect," Fallon gushed. "Thank you."

Armie said to Avery, "You sure you don't want me to lend a hand?"

"You're sweet," Avery said, "but Crissy just showed up. We're covered."

As soon as Avery got out of the way, Cannon and

Armie muscled their way in. Cannon made Fallon scoot over and Armie would have sat on Justice's lap if he hadn't moved quick enough.

Deadpan, Justice asked, "Why don't you guys join us?"

They ignored his dry tone.

"Think I will," Armie said, stealing one of his fries. To Fallon he said, "I'm Armie. That's Cannon."

She looked…mesmerized, her eyes wide, watchful. "You're both fighters?"

Armie grinned. "Good guess."

"Oh, no. You both look as muscular as Justice."

Cannon grinned now, too. "And you are?"

She poked out a hand. "Fallon Wade."

While Cannon's hand completely swallowed hers, Armie said, "Nice, Eugene. She's a step up."

With surprise, Fallon turned to Justice. "Eugene?"

Cannon leaned near, saying in a loud stage whisper behind his hand, "That's his real name."

Giving Armie a shove that almost put him out of the booth, Justice growled, "You're both assholes, you know that, right?"

Chuckling, Armie righted himself. "Avery just said I was sweet."

"She has to be nice to you because you're a customer."

"Ah, c'mon, Eugene," Armie replied. "Don't be pissy."

"No one," Justice stressed to Fallon, "calls me that."

Armie raised his hand. "Just us A-holes." He slanted a look at Justice. "I, at least, know how to speak in front of a lady."

That was almost too hilarious, given Armie's rep, which wasn't all that distant yet. "Where are your wives? Rissy and Yvette would keep you in line."

"Rissy, Vanity and Cherry are visiting Yvette at our place," Cannon said. "The wives insisted we show up here for Stack's last weekend before the fight."

Justice explained to Fallon, "These two are new dads. Cannon has twins, a boy and a girl, and Armie has a daughter. Usually you can't pry them away from the babies."

"Look who's talking!" Cannon pointed at Justice. "This one does the whole baby-talk thing. It's hilarious."

"And nauseating," Armie chimed in. Then he shrugged. "But the babies adore him."

Justice grinned. "True enough. I'm one of their favorite people."

"There's only four months between our kids' ages." Cannon smiled with pride. "They'll grow up close."

For the next twenty minutes, Justice and Fallon ate while the men told stories.

Like a spectator at a tennis match, Fallon's head bobbed back and forth as she alternately listened to each man gush affectionately. It still amused Justice that the two of them were so affected by their kids. If one of the babies gurgled, they were on it. Drool didn't faze them and they changed diapers like a couple of champions, which they were.

Other than during training, or occasionally at Rowdy's, if you saw one of the men, you saw a baby.

Justice finally interrupted to say, "You get the feeling they're proud papas?"

Smiling, Fallon nodded. "Very. And I think it's lovely."

"So I'm sweet and lovely," Armie said. "I can't wait to tell Stretch."

"My sister will strangle you for calling her that," Cannon reminded Armie. Then to Fallon, he said, "She's almost as tall as me."

"But a lot prettier," Armie added, his eyebrows bobbing.

Justice noticed that Fallon had eaten at least half of the enormous burger and a good share of fries before she pushed back her plate and patted her mouth with the paper napkin.

"Dessert?" he asked her.

She lifted the shake. "This counts." Leaning in, she asked, "So, do you think we could see your friend's fight next weekend?"

Not a good idea. "I don't know," he hedged. "It's going to be crowded."

One brow lifted, Cannon sat back and watched him.

Armie slanted him a look of curiosity.

"I'll cover my own ticket," she promised. "That is, if tickets are still available."

"Not for any good seats."

Cannon and Armie waited to pounce; Justice knew that and tried to think of a way to deter them from interfering, but he came up blank. Wasn't like he could explain that Fallon was only an assignment—and he was already too close.

Finally, Cannon said, "I have tickets. Brand and Miles, friends you can meet in a minute, would be happy to—"

Justice growled, "If she goes, she goes with me."

Fallon's face went pink and she cleared her throat. "It's all ridiculous, but Justice is my bodyguard."

Groaning, Justice stared up at the ceiling. He could feel the guys eyeballing him, the bastards.

"Why's it ridiculous?" Armie asked.

"Because there's no threat against me. It's just that my parents anticipate a boogeyman around every corner."

"We were followed," Justice reminded her.

Cannon said, "You were?"

"Yeah." And now that he remembered, he realized that might be a good excuse to skip the fight at the arena. But before he could mention it, another voice intruded.

"There you are, you chickenshit bastard."

Fallon turned with a start, Armie grumbled and Cannon briefly closed his eyes as if aggrieved.

But Justice laughed as he extended his hand over the booth. "Look who crawled aboveground." He and Tom exchanged a quick, knuckle-breaking hand grip, then Justice did the introductions. "Fallon, this is Tom Nelson, aka Tomahawk."

Tom gave her a quick once-over. "Tell your boyfriend to quit ducking me."

Armie said, "He beat you, Hawk," shortening the man's nickname. "Soundly, in fact. Bellyaching now is pointless. Move on."

"It was a lucky punch and you know it," Tom countered.

"You got caught," Cannon said in that calm way of his. "That wasn't luck, but good training."

"Says the man who trained him." Without losing his good mood, Tom stared down at Armie. "As to moving on…ain't happening. Not until I get a rematch."

Justice ate another fry. "Told you, man, I retired. I'm out of the fight biz."

"Get back in," Tom insisted. Then just to provoke him, he added, "If you can work up the nerve."

As FALLON WATCHED, the man pointed at Justice, grinned and sauntered away.

"Fucking doofus," Armie growled low.

"So much for knowing how to speak in front of a lady," Justice complained, sparing Fallon a glance.

"It's okay." Fallon noticed that Justice didn't seem nearly as bothered by the intruder as his friends were. "He's the one you beat early in the fight?"

Lifting his milk shake, Justice nodded. "None other."

"Tom doesn't want to accept it," Cannon explained to Fallon. "He tries to hide it with jokes, but he's still smarting over getting tuned."

"He's convinced he'd beat me if we fought again," Justice said by way of justification.

Armie gave a shove to Justice's shoulder, almost making him spit out his shake. "If it ever happened, my money would be on you."

Scowling, Justice drew off the straw, finishing his drink.

"People match up differently," Cannon said to Fallon. "A guy who beats everyone else can meet that one guy who gets him every time. Tomahawk's good, no doubt about it. But against Justice? I agree with Armie. Tom's not slick enough to duck those massive fists of his."

Justice gave a self-deprecating laugh. "Guys, really, she's not a date. You don't have to try to soften her up for me."

"He's so freaking humble, too," Armie said with a roll of his eyes.

"I can't beat Cannon."

"And that's your measuring stick?" Armie looked ready to shove Justice again. "Hell, man, there's a reason Cannon's a champion."

Wow. Fallon looked at the man next to her again. "Champion?"

"Light heavyweight."

"That's amazing." She noticed that Cannon leaned toward quiet confidence. He struck her as serious and kind—odd for a guy as big and honed as him.

Armie, on the other hand, was cocky to the extreme. She smiled at him. "What about you?"

"He's also a champion," Justice answered before Armie could. "You're in the presence of real talent."

"I don't understand." Finding this all very fascinating, Fallon twisted in her seat and propped her back against the wall. "Don't you become champion by beating everyone else? How can there be two?"

"Different weight classes." Cannon was happy to explain. "Armie's a middleweight."

"What are you?" she asked Justice.

"I *was* a heavyweight."

That made sense. All the men were big, but Justice towered over them.

"C'mon," Justice said, rudely shouldering Armie out of the booth. "If you want to learn about fighting, we'll join the others for a few games of pool and you can ask all the questions you want."

That sounded like an amazing idea to her.

An hour later, Fallon decided this was the best night of her entire life.

Fighters, she discovered, were hilarious and very friendly.

After Cannon explained the rules of the game, Justice taught her how to hold the cue stick and how to shoot. That in itself made the night memorable; he'd aligned his big body behind hers, surrounded her as he reached around to help her place her hands, then spoken softly into her ear.

She'd taken the shot awkwardly, almost scraping the felt on the tabletop. But no one teased her. The patient instruction continued until she got the hang of it—and once she did, she started sinking balls.

Who knew she had the knack for judging how one ball would rebound off another?

Armie declared her a natural, then immediately wagered five dollars.

She won.

Smiling with pride, Justice stood back, his shoulders braced on the wall, and encouraged her.

Before this very night, Fallon hadn't known she had a knack for shooting pool. Playful accusations of "pool shark" were called out after she'd won her third game.

Twice Avery came in to collect empties and refill drink orders. Though Fallon did indulge in another beer, she only sipped at it, making it last.

One, she decided, was her limit.

When she took the money she'd won and gave it to Avery for an additional tip, everyone cheered her.

Though she blushed, she loved it.

As soon as she declared she was done shooting pool, Justice's friend Miles whisked her away to dance.

Justice protested, but the rest of the guys heckled him so badly, he finally subsided. While he allowed the dance, he clearly didn't like it. Just as he'd done before, he kept her in his sights every second. The only difference now was that his friends paid no attention to his ruthless stares.

In fact, they seemed to enjoy them.

Grinning at her, Miles asked, "You sure you two don't have anything personal going on? Justice is acting mighty territorial."

Fallon didn't know Justice well enough to judge if that was true. She glanced at him, saw his concentrated expression, and wondered if he resented having to keep tabs on her.

Well, if he did, too bad. This was her time out and she intended to enjoy it.

"It's his job to be alert, that's all."

Miles smiled. "If you say so."

As they danced, more than a few ladies watched them. And why not? With his gentle green eyes, dark brown hair and crooked smiles, Miles was a real charmer, who'd instantly put her at ease. As a light heavyweight fighter, he was also as buff as the rest of them.

"Why do they call you the Legend?"

"My legendary sense of humor," he replied with a wink.

Fallon laughed. "I'm not buying that."

"Well, honey, the truth would make you blush."

Shoot, she blushed just from wondering what it could be!

That made his grin widen. "Come on. Spill. You and Justice have a secret fling going on, right?"

That he would think so flattered her. "I promise, we don't. Justice takes his responsibilities very seriously, that's all."

"Being a bodyguard, you mean?"

"Yes." Feeling Justice's alert intensity, she glanced at him again. "He doesn't yet understand that my parents are extreme about everything that concerns me. That doesn't mean a bodyguard is actually necessary."

Miles was about to question her more when Brand cut in.

Brand was another heavyweight. Not quite as tall as Justice, but just as broad in the shoulders. Though he smiled often, his dark eyes always looked a little distant, as if he held himself back.

"Having fun?" he asked as they moved to a fast song.

"Definitely."

"Did I hear that you'll be joining us at the fight next weekend?"

Because she doubted it, given Justice's hesitation on the idea, she asked, "Us?"

"We'll all be there. Front section, good seats." The music ended and everyone paused to wait for the next song. "The wives should be there, too. Have you met any of them yet?"

They all seemed to assume…something, but Fallon wasn't sure what. "This is my first time here, and it's about an hour and a half from where I live. I'm not sure I'll be around often enough to meet anyone else."

"That's a bit of a drive just to have drinks."

"Justice preferred this bar to those more local."

"Yeah, I just bet he did." Brand laughed. "He figures he has a better handle on the competition here."

Fallon tried to deny that. She understood, even if they didn't, that Justice wasn't worried about competition.

"Armie, Cannon, Stack, Denver and Gage are all married. When one of our own fights, we provide the cheering section."

It sounded amazing to Fallon. "I think Justice had other plans, so—"

Stepping in, Tom said, "If he doesn't agree, let me know and I'll bring you along." Then, as another song started, he said to Brand, "I'm cutting in."

This music was slower and Tom quickly caught her waist.

It startled Fallon. "Oh, um…" She watched as Brand got pulled into a dance with another lady. Drat.

"Something wrong?" Tom asked.

Yes, as a matter of fact, his earlier insults to Justice still annoyed her. Justice might not have minded, but she did. Good manners, however, kept her polite. "No, of course not."

He cuddled her closer.

She strained away.

Pretending not to notice, Tom asked, "So I heard you say you don't live nearby."

"I don't, but I'm glad we made the trip. This is a terrific place."

"Agreed. Rowdy and Avery run a good business." He turned a slow circle, and in the process brought her nearer. "I wasn't here before, but they say it was a real foul dive before Rowdy bought it. He did a big reno, kicked out the drug dealers and put in the pool room."

Drug dealers? Fascinated, Fallon asked, "Seriously?"

"Yeah. It's cool now, though. All the fighters hang out here, along with most of the neighborhood."

"You live in the area?" she asked.

"I'm staying here for a while to train. Fighters go to different camps to learn new techniques." He gave a boyish grin and added, "If I can ever sweet-talk Justice into competing again, I want to be ready so I last more than a heartbeat."

Perhaps she'd been wrong about Tom. "You think he will?"

"Fight again? I hope so." He gave her a brief hug and bent to whisper in her ear, "I'm still stung over that knockout."

She laughed with him. "I take it that was unusual for you?"

"To lose, no. Every fighter takes his knocks. But like that? Yeah, first time I was ever KO'd, and for it to happen so fast, well, let me tell ya, it sucked." He circled again and Fallon found herself plastered to his rock-hard body. "Justice has sledgehammers for fists, and that lucky punch caught me just right."

From directly behind her, Justice said, "Know what? I'm feeling pretty damned lucky again."

Fallon jumped; Tom did not, so apparently he'd seen Justice approach.

Keeping her trapped to his body, Tom smiled. Now that he again had Justice's attention, he reverted back to the insults. "One-trick ponies only go so far."

"Maybe you only saw the one trick because you haven't been paying attention. Besides, with you, one trick was all I needed."

"Ouch," Tom said with a grin. They'd stopped dancing, but he didn't let her go. "So that's what it takes to motivate you, huh? A little cuddle with your lady friend?"

"She's a client."

"You still sticking with that?"

"Hey!" Fallon finally caught on. Shoving her way free with a little more force than necessary, she glared up at Tom. "If you want to goad him into a fight, use someone other than me!"

She turned to march away, but Justice caught her hand and anchored her to his side, ruining her dramatic exit.

"Not just yet, Fallon," Justice said when she tugged against his restraint. "Tom has something he wants to tell you."

Oh, good grief. She didn't want to hear anything else he had to say.

Voice jovial, Tom said, "He's right. I promise I only

wanted to dance, not incite violence. I'm sorry if my teasing made you think otherwise."

So…had she overreacted?

It didn't matter because Justice said, "She's off-limits."

Tom lifted a brow. "Yeah? For what?"

Sounding as if he chewed gravel, Justice growled, "Everything."

"Ah, I didn't realize." Still fighting a smile, Tom looked down at her. "Really, no insult intended, so will you forgive me?"

She felt like a spectacle. "Yes, of course."

Tom clapped Justice on the shoulder. "Call a truce, Justice. You're making her nervous."

Justice said nothing, but he nodded.

"Good. I want a rematch, you know that. But I don't want or need a barroom brawl. You gotta know I'm not after that."

Justice loosened his stance. "Yeah, I do."

"Thanks." Tom saluted them both and departed.

When she and Justice turned and headed toward a table, Cannon and Armie applauded.

After that, the guys razzed Justice endlessly about being a bodyguard. They heralded him for being oh-so-meticulous in his duties, calling him keenly thorough in exploring every possible threat, both real and imagined.

Fallon would have been offended for him again, except that the guys infused enough obvious respect in their tones for her to know it was only good-natured ribbing.

Justice grinned, in fact, when he gave them each a one-finger salute. Minutes later when the questions started, he patiently answered each one. Miles, especially, seemed interested in the different duties required of a bodyguard.

Fallon didn't mind any of it, until the talk turned to Marcus.

"Ex-boyfriend?" Cannon asked. "I've had some experience with those."

Armie raised his hand. "Me, too."

"No," Fallon denied. "He was never really—"

"He was," Justice interrupted. "But not anymore. Now he's just a pita."

"Pita?" Fallon asked.

"Pain in the ass," Justice explained.

Because she couldn't deny that, Fallon turned the topic to kids, and for the next forty minutes or so, the men talked about their babies. It seemed they had enough stories to last the night.

When Cannon got a text, he read it and stood. "The party finally broke up at my house. I'm heading home."

Armie was right behind him. "That means I can go now, too."

Stack, who she'd met earlier, shook his head at both of them, then finished his bottle of water. "Pathetic." He yawned elaborately and claimed his wife, Vanity, would be waiting for him.

Justice brought her to her feet. "You ready to call it a night?"

"I—" Her words got cut off as each of the men drew her around for a hug. She got passed from one big, hard body to the next, with praise on her pool shooting skills, her dancing, how she'd put Tom in his place, how well she handled Justice…on and on with invented qualities. Well, except for the games of pool. She really had done well there.

Lastly, Stack asked, "You'll be there next weekend for the fights? Vanity would enjoy meeting you."

She glanced at Justice in time to see him rolling his eyes.

Guessing that it was a special weekend for him to spend with his close friends, she knew she couldn't interrupt. "It's probably better if I don't—"

"You can all stop twisting my arm," Justice announced right before hauling her back over to his side. "She'll be there."

Fallon would have objected, but Justice hurried her out the door. She glanced back in time to see the others all grinning.

CHAPTER SIX

THE FOLLOWING WEEK passed in a near blur of happiness. As requested, Fallon presented Justice with an itinerary of the places she wanted to go. Because she'd listed a lot, she didn't expect to get to everything. She'd assumed Justice would pick and choose and let her know what was easiest.

Instead, he covered everything on her wish list, which meant they spent all day, every day, together.

Usually, he'd show up late morning to early afternoon after spending a few hours scoping out their immediate destination. Given the time of day, they'd head to lunch first thing. Justice arranged it so she got to visit nearly every area restaurant, from the mom-and-pop diners to the fast-food chains to the trendy spots. Fallon got him to try a few new things, and she learned the places he liked best.

They spent an entire day at the street fair and even got a caricature drawing of them together. Because the artist drew Justice so comically big, and her eyes so enormous, Fallon couldn't stop laughing over it.

Other days were spent at the art museum, a flower show, a butterfly show at the conservatory, a Star Trek exhibit and an outdoor sculpture display at a park. Justice enjoyed the Star Trek exhibit best, and she most enjoyed the flower show. But all of it was terrific.

Tomorrow would be his friend's fight and she was excited, so when Justice showed up late morning, she had a dozen questions ready for him.

When she opened the door and saw him, though, she forgot much of what she'd planned to ask. "You look tired."

Around a wide yawn, he said, "I'm fine."

"Fine my foot." Had she been running him too much? True, they'd been on the go almost nonstop for days. But he hadn't once complained.

It was only ten, a little earlier than usual, and bright sunshine poured over the steps and surrounding landscape, reflecting off the black SUV Justice drove. A perfect day for the river walk she'd planned, but Fallon was ready to call it quits. Justice, she decided, looked like he needed a nice long nap.

She was about to tell him the change in plans when her mother stepped up behind her and invited him in.

"Join us for a cup of tea."

He quickly removed the dark sunglasses, saying, "No thank you, ma'am. Not a tea drinker."

"Coffee then."

"I brought my own. It's in the car."

Her mother, unfortunately, wasn't taking no for an answer. "Fallon needs to get her sunscreen. Please, come in." Her mother held the door open and waited.

Hooking his glasses on the front of his T-shirt, Justice reluctantly stepped in, and immediately looked ill at ease.

"My husband is gone for the weekend or I'm certain he'd enjoy saying hello, as well."

Justice didn't look convinced. "Off on business?"

"Yes." She indicated a chair, leaving Justice no choice but to sit. "Fallon, honey, would you make some coffee?"

She didn't want to, but the kitchen was close enough to the sitting room that she'd be able to listen in. "All right." She rushed off to do the prep so she could rejoin them while it perked.

From a distance, she heard her mother say, "May I ask you something, Justice?"

"Shoot."

"Is that hairstyle popular among fighters?"

Fallon almost choked.

Justice just laughed. "Not sure I'd say it's popular anywhere, especially right now. I haven't trimmed it in a while. When I was fighting, though, I'd dye it orange."

"Orange? Somewhat like a…rooster?"

"Somewhat," he agreed, his tone teasing. "But there are a lot of words for rooster, ya know?"

Oh, dear Lord. Fallon dumped water into the coffeemaker and rushed back to the room. She got there in time to see her mother laughing.

Justice smiled at her, then ran a hand over his head. "Now that I'm not fighting, I've kinda lost interest. Guess I should either shape it up or shave it off."

"Well," her mother said, "I find it interesting. So please don't bother on my account."

His mouth quirked. "No, ma'am."

Horrified over the subject for several reasons, Fallon

bit her lip. Luckily, he mother didn't seem scandalized, and Justice didn't look offended.

"The coffee will be ready in a minute." She studied Justice's face and saw the tiredness there. "We can reschedule for another day if you'd like to rest."

He clutched his heart and groaned. "Don't unman me in front of your ma. What would she think of me if you're all bushytailed and I'm pooped out when we've been doing the same thing?"

"Her ma," Mrs. Wade quipped, "would think you're hilarious."

For some reason, Fallon's face went hot. Probably from the way he spoke so casually in front of her very formal mother—and how her mother teased back. "We haven't been. You leave earlier each day to inspect the route and venue and…whatever else it is bodyguards do."

Justice gave her a level, very intense look. "I ensure your safety. That's everything I do."

She had no reply for that, but it didn't matter because Justice wasn't done yet anyway.

"And I go where you go. This is your time, so don't worry about me." He stretched. "Besides, I'm tired because of my grandma."

"Your grandma?" she asked.

"That coffee ready yet?"

"Oh, yes." With haste so she wouldn't miss the story, Fallon filled a cup and brought it to him. Creamer and sugar were already on the table. "So," she said as she handed him the cup, "what was that about your grandma?"

"She had to go into the hospital last night." He dropped a spoonful of sugar into the coffee and sipped appreciatively. "I spent the night there with her. My mother came up this morning, so I was able to leave."

Fallon and her mother both stared at him. He'd spent the night with his grandmother at the hospital?

"I hope she's okay," Fallon finally thought to say.

"Yeah, she's a tough old bird. Insists on living alone and for the most part, she gets around okay. But even though her eyesight is bad, she refuses to wear glasses, so it's no surprise that she tripped over the stoop. We thought she might have broken a hip in the fall. Since she gives the docs a really hard time, it's always better if my mom or I are with her to sort of smooth things over." He grinned. "Otherwise she might've gotten herself shoved out the door just for being so ornery."

"You say that with a great deal of affection," her mother noted.

"Yeah. Granny's a keeper." Justice drank more of his coffee, then sat back. Muscles rolled in his shoulders as he relaxed, and yet his abdomen stayed firm and flat beneath the T-shirt. "The doc came in to see her this morning right before my mom got there. She's bruised up real good, but no breaks, thank goodness. She and my mom were arguing when I left." He grinned.

"Arguing?" Fallon asked.

"Yeah, see, Mom says Granny has to come home with her until she's fit again, but Granny said she wasn't a baby and didn't need a sitter. Still, I'd put my money on Mom. She can be stubborn as a goat when the mood strikes her. Not stubborn enough to get Granny to wear her glasses, but otherwise, she usually wins."

"Why won't she wear her glasses?" her mom asked.

Justice shrugged. "Says it makes her look old."

Fascinated by this glimpse into his life, Fallon pulled out a chair. "How old is your grandmother?"

Justice rubbed his jaw. "Let's see. Mom's sixty now, so Granny must be eighty-five or thereabouts. It's hard to believe, with me being such a lug, but they're both itty-bitty things. Mom's maybe five-one, and now that she doesn't stand so straight, Granny's barely five feet."

"Amazing." Fallon's mother sat forward. "So your father is a large man?"

"Was. He died when I was real young. An accident at the factory where he worked. I was only three so I don't remember much about him, but Mom has the house full of photos and between her and Granny, I've heard every story there is about Dad, twice."

Sympathy left a knot in Fallon's chest. "I'm sorry. I didn't realize."

He shrugged. "It's okay."

"So…" Her mother faltered, cleared her throat, and continued with "*Granny* is your father's mother?"

"Nope. But she loved my dad, too, said he really made my mom shine." Justice smiled with some memory. "Dad and Granny liked to play poker. To hear my mom tell it, they had some serious competition going. Knowing my grandma, I can imagine it got loud and rowdy on occasion."

"Your mother never remarried?"

He laughed. "No. She said she started with the best and wasn't taking second pick for anyone. I think she's been content." After finishing off his coffee, he pushed back his chair and looked toward Fallon. "You ready to go?"

Lost to thoughts of Justice as a little boy, she jumped. "Oh, yes. Of course." She quickly gathered up their cups and carried them to the dishwasher.

Her mother protested. "You don't have to fool with that, honey. Lindsey will be in later today."

"I don't mind."

Minutes later, she and Justice got into the SUV. She noticed the shirts in the backseat and was going to ask him about it, but Justice diverted her.

"Who's Lindsey?"

Because she liked the woman a lot, Fallon smiled. "She helps out around the house."

"Helps out how?"

"During the first part of the week she only does light housekeeping, but on Friday she does the bigger stuff, like laundry and changing the sheets on the beds and grocery shopping. That's why I don't like to leave little messes for her to contend with. She's got enough to do today."

"I'm guessing in a house that size, you have other staff?"

"Yes." Fallon tipped her head, watching him drive. "We have a landscaper who takes care of the property. Lindsey's there every day except the weekends, and once a month a cleaning crew comes in to do the heavier work, like washing down all the walls, polishing the floors, things like that." Now that she said it, it sounded extravagant when she'd never really thought of it like that before. "Why do you ask?"

"Seems like there are a lot of people coming and going. I don't like it." His brows pulled together. "Mind giving me some names and their contact info?"

Unbelievable. The man looked exhausted, but he wanted to take on more work? Crazy.

Folding her arms across her chest, Fallon said, "Actually, yes. I mind." She didn't want things to get out of hand. "I promise you, my father is extremely diligent in ensuring all personal employees are vetted. You don't need to worry about it."

"But he's out of town for the weekend."

"That happens a lot, Justice. Dad travels often for business, plus he takes a lot of golfing trips."

She could see that Justice didn't want to let it go.

Sighing, Fallon added, "We have a top-of-the-line security system. You should realize that. I mean, look at how overboard Dad is about me going out anywhere."

They were almost out of the long drive when Marcus turned in.

Justice looked first stunned, then irate. He steered into the middle of the drive, blocking Marcus, and put the car in Park.

Uh-oh. "Do not start anything," Fallon warned.

"Wouldn't." The corners of his mouth lifted in a mean smile. "But he's not coming in. I heard your dad forbid him."

"Dad did *what*?" How come she didn't know about that?

"Told him not to come around uninvited."

She jumped on that. "So maybe my mother invited him."

Doubtful, he glanced at her. "You really think she might've?"

No, she didn't. Huffing, Fallon said, "How should I know?"

"You big faker." He reached out and tweaked her chin. "I'm betting your mom doesn't like him enough to go against your dad's wishes."

Marcus got out of his idling car and slammed the door.

Fallon grabbed Justice's arm. "I mean it, Justice. Don't you dare do anything...physical."

"Afraid I'll smash the little worm?"

"No. You don't strike me as a bully."

"I'm not, so quit worrying about him."

Mostly she was afraid Marcus would humiliate her. But how could she end this peacefully? Both men looked ready to implode.

When Marcus started around to her side of the car, Justice muttered, "Like hell," and threw open his door.

Fallon hurriedly got out of the car, too. "Marcus," she said, her voice too high. "What are you doing here? Do you have an appointment with Mom?"

"What? No." Marcus kept flicking his gaze to Justice. "I came to see you."

"Well, as you can see, I'm on my way out." She tried to sound cheerful instead of panicked.

When Justice stopped beside her, massive arms crossed, posture relaxed as he leaned on the car, Marcus must have decided he wasn't a problem and finally gave her his full attention.

"We need to talk."

She didn't want to talk. "Another time, maybe."

"You keep dodging me."

"'Cuz she doesn't want to talk to you, you dipshit." Justice smiled at him. "Let it sink in, then go away."

Marcus turned on him. "Bodyguards are supposed to be respectful!"

"Not to dipshits," Justice muttered. "I'm plenty respectful to Fallon, which is more than I can say for you."

Marcus all but vibrated in frustration as he tried to focus on her again. "I'm sorry I hurt you. It was thoughtless and if I'd been better prepared—"

No, no, no. "It's fine," she squeaked. "I've already forgotten about it."

"Then—"

"We're done, Marcus. Over. Please, *please* get that through your head."

"I won't accept that." He reached for her—

And Justice moved. "Nope. Touch her and I'll break something. Or to be more specific, something on you. Like…an arm? Maybe just a hand. I dunno, yet."

"You cannot just go around threatening people!"

Unconcerned, Justice said, "Wasn't a threat."

Fallon pointed at Justice. "Get in the car!"

"Will when you do."

She glared at Marcus, saw he wouldn't budge, and turned to Justice again. "I'm going to speak to Marcus over there." She pointed to the side of the road. "You are not to intrude, do you understand me?"

"Long as he doesn't touch you, I can restrain myself." After cracking his knuckles, he lounged back against the side of the car again. "I won't like it, but I'll do as told."

"Like a trained ape," Marcus sneered.

Fallon gave him a shove. "Shut up or I won't talk to you at all. Ever again!"

Petulant, Marcus turned and stomped away to where she'd indicated, near a flowering hedge.

With one last warning look at Justice, who managed to appear amused, Fallon joined her ex.

The second she reached him, Marcus started to speak.

Fallon cut him off with a slash of her hand. "I don't want to hear it," she hissed low. "If you can't understand how I feel, at least respect what I say."

"Not when you keep saying it's over." He swallowed hard and whispered, "I love you, Fallon."

Her temples started to throb. "You don't," she replied gently. Of that much she was quite certain. "If you'd stop pretending to be wounded, you'd realize it." Again he tried to speak and again, she didn't allow it. "Men who love women are not repulsed by them."

"Oh, God, honey, I wasn't," he denied fervently. "It's just… I assumed your family had paid for…"

"There are some things money can't buy."

Frantically, he shook his head. "There are specialists who could—"

"No." Fallon had to make him understand. "Don't you see, Marcus? This is a problem for you, and it's not going away."

Determined, he squared his shoulders. "There are ways around it."

She didn't want to know what he might mean by that. Did he expect her to hide her entire life? No, she wouldn't.

Trying to reason with him, she put a hand on his arm. "I didn't know my father had banned you. If you promise to stop pursuing me, I'll get him to let up on that."

"You ask the impossible."

With her goodwill gone, she snapped, "Fine. Suit yourself. But I'm not discussing this anymore." Heart punching in slow, painful beats, Fallon pivoted on her heel and strode back toward Justice.

Marcus yelled, "Any man would have a problem with those scars!"

Oh, God.

Shoulders lifting, she froze, horrified and panicked. An invisible fist squeezed her heart, making her gasp.

Her gaze shot to Justice's.

Eyes narrowed, arms crossed, he leaned a hip against the car and watched her.

In that moment he reminded her of a coiled panther who only pretended to be at ease.

As Marcus rushed toward her, Justice moved—and reached her in two long steps. Before she could even draw breath, Justice stood behind her and he stopped Marcus's approach with one long, outstretched arm. His hand flattened on Marcus's shoulder.

"Word of advice." Justice sounded cold and furious. "Leave."

Hearing that tone, Marcus finally showed some sense. She could feel Justice at her back, his big body ema-

nating waves of anger. She prayed Marcus would go—
and finally he did, stalking away with a muttered curse.

Fallon was still standing there, too mortified to
move, when Marcus made a U-turn through the me-
ticulously trimmed grass and sped out of the driveway.
The sound of his revving engine gradually faded until
all she could hear were the birds in the trees, the rustling
of leaves and her own heartbeat pounding in her ears.

What would Justice say now? What would he do?
She was oh so aware of him behind her, backing her
up, protecting her from hurts he didn't know and probably wouldn't understand. She felt sick with worry, ap-
prehensive of what would happen next.

Then Justice's big hands settled on her shoulders,
softly massaging. He said nothing. Didn't question her,
didn't force the issue.

He'd heard Marcus, she knew it.

She didn't know what to think.

Time ticked by and he only caressed her. By small
degrees the panic quieted and her heartbeat returned
to normal. She knew she couldn't remain a mute, trembling mess, so she cleared her throat, reached up to pat
his hand and asked as casually as she could muster,
"Are you ready to go?"

"Sure." Yet he didn't move.

Fearing her reprieve might be slipping away, she said
hesitantly, "Justice…"

Suddenly his massive arms came around her, stun-
ning her stupid. He drew her back against his chest and
held her, enfolded in that delicious embrace.

Why was he always so warm? And oh my, how could

she think when his scent of musk and sexy man surrounded her? Savoring it, she sucked in a long, slow breath.

Justice lowered his chin to the top of her head, gently hugging her. Voice pitched low and rough, he muttered, "Your dad would shoot me if he saw me doing this."

She strangled out, "This?"

"Comforting you."

Pride made her protest. "I don't need—"

He squeezed her quiet. "Holding you makes *me* feel better, okay? So just go with it."

She nodded, even managed to settle more comfortably against him. Never had a man so large held her so gently. Actually, she'd never known a man as large as him. His forearms, folded over her breasts, flexed with roped muscle when his thumbs brushed her skin. Fascinated, she lightly touched the soft hair there, then with one fingertip, she traced a line up to his bulging biceps.

He was so big, so hard.

And speaking of hard, against her back she felt—

His mouth touched her temple, and he muttered, "That's about enough of that or I'm gonna get carried away." Hands on her shoulders, he turned her toward him, studied her face and asked with concern, "You okay?"

The abrupt change was like a dash of ice water. *Now* he would ask about Marcus. "I'm fine."

He smiled at her crisp tone. "I don't know what that dumbass was blathering on about. Shh. I promise I won't ask." He tipped up her chin. "But know that you can talk to me, okay?"

He did that amazing "look into her soul" thing and it

left her flustered. His eyes were so dark, so serious and too intense. She nodded fast. "Yes, thank you. Now we should get going." Pulling away, she hurried to the car.

As usual, Justice reached the door before she could and opened it for her. "If he comes back, I want to know."

She wouldn't report to him, but it didn't seem worth arguing over, so she made a noncommittal sound of acknowledgment.

They were on the road a few minutes before she remembered the T-shirts in the backseat. "Taking your laundry somewhere?"

Distracted, he glanced at her, caught her meaning and grinned. "Those are for you. You'll be with the team tomorrow, so you need an official shirt. I brought a few different ones for you to choose from." Pretending to be stern, he added, "Most of the chicks wear them really tight and low. But I don't want to have to beat the guys away with a baseball bat, so the shirts I brought for you are crew necked. Hope that's okay."

Better than okay, it was preferable. "Thank you." She gestured at the shirts. "May I?"

"Sure."

She reached back and pulled four shirts into her lap. Two were black, one gray and one white. Each had a wolf head on the front. She read aloud, "'Howl for the Wolf.'"

"That's Stack. We'll all be rooting for him." He winked at her. "Now you're official."

"Why do they call him the Wolf?"

Justice laughed.

"There's a joke?"

"Nah, see, there're two meanings behind the name and I'm not sure you want to hear them both."

"But I do," she insisted.

He glanced at her two more times before shrugging. "All right then. He got the fight name because of the way he stalks his prey in the cage."

"Ah, like a wolf. I get it."

Justice's grin widened. "It was a good, legit, badass name. But then a bunch of ladies started rumors, and now most say he's called Wolf because of how he makes women howl in the bedroom."

Fallon blinked in surprise—and felt her mouth twitch. "You're serious?"

"Yup. Old Stack used to be a real player. That was before Vanity, though." He tried to put on a straight face as he said, "Now he only makes her howl."

When Fallon snickered, Justice laughed with her.

It felt...nice. Casual and easy. So very different from her relationship with Marcus, which despite their longer association had always felt somehow superficial, too polite and proper. "Now that I know, I'm going to feel silly wearing the shirt."

"Even guys will wear some version of it, so don't give it a thought. I'll be wearing the gray one."

"Okay, then I'll choose the black one." It had short sleeves, but that suited her. "With jeans?"

"Perfect."

For the rest of their drive, Justice detailed what she should expect at the venue. It would be a late night with a lot of raucous men in close quarters and, according to

Justice, women hoping to "hook up" who would probably attend the after party at Rowdy's bar.

It all sounded very exciting, and yes, very fun.

She could hardly wait.

HE HUNG BACK, keeping his distance until they finally parked near the river. So they'd be doing the river walk? That could take all day. Perfect.

Turning the car around, he went back the way they'd come. With them occupied, he'd have time to visit both residences.

He tightened his hands on the wheel and thought about things—then decided exactly what to do.

IT WAS LATE when Justice brought Fallon home.

Today more than any other day, she'd been so damned hard to resist. Maybe because she was so natural, so sweet, and her smiles, man those smiles, they nearly did him in. He loved seeing her happy, relaxed. For much of the day, he'd barely been able to take his eyes off her.

They'd walked for miles and miles, and neither of them had complained. He enjoyed the way Fallon had appreciated each spring flower, cloud formations and various animals they encountered on the trails. She seemed to see everything, in ways he hadn't before.

Not until she showed him.

In one of the more wooded sections of the hike, he'd overturned a fallen log and found her a salamander. She'd admired it from five feet away, making him laugh. When she insisted he carefully replace the creature and the log, his heart had squeezed with a weird sensation of…respect. Yeah, he respected her. A lot. She was rich, but compassionate. Pampered, but vulnerable. Sweet, but also amazingly sexy.

They'd eaten picnic-style along the riverbank; hot dogs and bagged chips and cold colas had never tasted so good. He should have chosen a shadier spot, given her now-pink nose and cheekbones, but she hadn't protested. Some geese swam by, frogs occasionally sang and tiny fish glittered in the shallower water along the shore. Butterflies had been everywhere and the air smelled good, like wildflowers, water and…Fallon.

He taught her how to skip rocks and how to overhand throw. She wasn't very good at either, but they'd done a lot of laughing. Before they left, she'd chosen a smooth rock as a souvenir.

A rock. It still astounded him, and made her even more endearing.

Though the air had cooled now, they were both a little sweaty. Justice couldn't remember the last time he'd taken so much pleasure in a day—hell, a week.

Something about Fallon made it impossible for him to be detached. The way she saw the world and her happy outlook, the simple joy she took in the smallest things, affected him.

And yeah, he liked the way she looked at him. She might not realize it, but she wore her heart on her sleeve. If she'd been anyone else, anyone other than a client, maybe someone just a tad more experienced, he'd have already made a move on her.

Instead, he'd repeated the facts in his head like a litany.

Client, innocent, inexperienced. Those three things made her as taboo as a woman could get.

Didn't stop him from thinking things, but for the most part it did help him to keep those thoughts to himself…and his hands off her.

The glow of the headlights from the SUV bounded around the area as he turned into her private drive—and that's when he saw it. At first glance he thought it was blood.

Everywhere.

Then he realized it was too bright, and the arcing splatter looked as if someone had literally thrown it from a paint can. He stopped the car.

Fallon, who'd looked to be dozing, her eyes closed, her mouth curled in a serene smile, turned to him. "What's the matter?"

Justice hated to ruin her day, but there was no way around it. He couldn't pull into the drive without getting the paint on the tires and further spreading it. He drew a slow breath and nodded at the destruction. "Someone is playing vandal, and I'm betting I know who it is."

CHAPTER SEVEN

WIDE-EYED, FALLON started to open her car door.

Justice stopped her. "No. It could be a trap."

"A trap?" She looked shocked, unable to understand the concept.

Already backing out, Justice said, "We can't drive through, so it stands to reason we'd get out of the car. That could be the whole point."

She scoffed, but didn't argue. Justice drove farther down the road to the start of an upscale community, then pulled over to the side. Leaving the car running, he locked the doors and used hands-free dialing on the SUV's Bluetooth to dial 911.

"Is that necessary?" Fallon quickly asked. "It seems like such a fuss."

"It's necessary." As soon as he finished talking to the police, who promised to meet him shortly back at the house, he dialed the agency. Everyone was gone for the day, but he left a message that Sahara would get first thing in the morning.

Next he insisted on calling her mother.

"She'll be in bed."

"Probably. But won't you feel better once you know she's okay?"

Clearly she hadn't considered any other possibility, but as soon as he mentioned it, she agreed.

Mrs. Wade answered on the third ring, and she did indeed sound half-asleep.

"Mom?" Fallon said in a rush. "Are you okay?"

More alert, her mother said, "Fallon? What's wrong?"

Justice sighed and took over. "Everyone is okay, Mrs. Wade. Did we wake you?"

Bemused to realize she was on speaker, Mrs. Wade cleared her throat. "Yes. I'm sorry. What time is it?"

"It's late. I was just bringing Fallon home, but someone vandalized your entryway. There's red paint everywhere. I'm going to speak to the police, and then I'll walk her up to the door and arrange for someone to come clean it so it doesn't get tracked anywhere else."

There was a startled silence before Mrs. Wade said, "I'll be right there!"

"No," Justice insisted. "Let the cops do their thing first. They need to make sure no one is hanging around, and they might want to take a few pictures or something. I'll let you know when they're done."

"Oh, yes, I guess that makes sense." She paused. "Red paint, you said?"

"That's what it looks like to me." Justice assumed it was supposed to look like blood. But whatever idiot did it had no real clue how spilled blood should look.

Lights flashed behind them as a police car pulled up.

Justice said, "The cops are here. Gotta go. But I'll let you know what's happening as soon as I know."

It was another hour before Justice finally walked Fallon up to her front door. He'd left the car on the street and together they'd edged around the mess. A twenty-four-hour cleanup company would arrive shortly.

He would stay until the job was done, but he wanted to get Fallon inside, and let her mother get back to bed.

Mrs. Wade greeted them the second they got close, then she insisted that Justice come in.

The poor woman looked frazzled, so Justice tried his best to put her mind at ease. "The mess will be gone in no time. The cops agreed it's only paint. Likely just vandals." Not that he believed it. "Fallon says you have a terrific security system, but only on the house and nearby grounds."

"Yes. Clayton had it set up, but I doubt he ever considered a situation like this."

"No reason he should have." Now though, Justice thought, things had changed. "Any chance you can put a security camera at the street entrance in case anything like this ever happens again? In fact, I can take care of it if you want, since I know Mr. Wade is away for the weekend."

She reached out and touched his wrist. "Please, let's move on to first names. We're Rebecca and Clayton."

Reacting to her smile, Justice nodded. "All right, Rebecca. Thanks. Now about that security?"

"You don't think it can wait until Monday when Clayton returns?"

Aware of Fallon quietly watching him, he rubbed the back of his neck. "I'd rather not." Gesturing, he said, "With the paint being red, I think someone might've wanted us to think it was…blood."

"Oh, my God." Eyes wider, Rebecca put a hand to her throat. "But why?"

Justice was taking it as an implied threat, but he saw no reason to spook the two of them further. "No idea." Moving on from that, he asked, "Mind if I have a look at the security?"

"Oh, yes, of course." Dressed in a pretty robe and delicate slippers, Rebecca led him around the first floor to all the security cameras.

He also checked the different locks on the doors and windows. "How about downstairs?"

"It's a finished rec area. Why?"

"Assuming there are doors and windows, I'd like to check it out, too."

She agreed, leading the way to what literally appeared to be a rec center. There was a theater room, bar and kitchen, game room, sauna, workout area and even an indoor pool. Trying not to feel intimidated again, Justice concentrated on the double doors that opened to an opulent outdoor entertaining area, and when he found them to be adequately secure, he checked all the windows.

"What do you think?" Rebecca asked him.

He smiled at her. "I'm reassured. Now about upstairs?"

"You already checked the main floor."

"I meant up from that. Those are bedrooms up there, right? Is there any way for someone to get in?"

She gave it some thought. "There are balconies off the bedrooms…"

"Let's have a look, okay?"

"All right."

It surprised Justice that Fallon's mom was so agreeable to letting him prowl the house. As he followed her up the stairs, he asked, "How many people have been through your house?"

"Up here? No one that I can think of. When we entertain at home, guests generally remain on the main floor."

The first room she led Justice to was her and Clayton's bedroom. It was so formal, he didn't know how the hell they managed to sleep—or get frisky. He sort of hated to even step in the room for fear he'd damage something.

Windows made up one entire wall with a remote to open and close the curtains and to darken the panes. He looked out and saw an amazing view of the grounds, leaving him almost speechless.

The windows were, of course, secure.

A decadent bathroom, sitting room and a closet big enough to live in completed the suite.

Irritated, with no idea why, Justice next viewed two guest bedrooms, an upstairs library and then, with a teasing smile, Rebecca led him into Fallon's room.

"She's still a little messy," Rebecca said. "And she certainly didn't expect anyone to be in here, so pay no mind to that."

Messy? Other than a pair of shoes not quite in the open closet, a cardigan draped over the arm of an oversize, padded rocking chair and a selection of jewelry atop a dresser, the room looked perfect.

Like Fallon.

"When we hired a designer, Fallon insisted on doing her own room." Pride glowed from her eyes. "She has a fresh style."

"Fallon is a decorator, but you hired an outsider?" That seemed curious to him—and insulting to Fallon.

Rebecca quickly turned away, but not before Justice saw a flash of regret, and something more, in her eyes.

"Fallon wasn't feeling well at the time." Proving she didn't want to be questioned on that, Rebecca rushed on. "She made the quilt herself. Isn't it beautiful?"

"Yeah." But Justice only gave a quick glance to the pretty quilt made in shades of blue that seemed to blend from light to dark. He was too busy watching Fallon's mom.

"As you can see, her windows also lock tight. She didn't want a whole wall of windows like her father and I have. But the architectural windows are nice, aren't they? To keep a balance in the outside view of the house, there's a wall of windows in the adjacent study."

Jabbering? Justice figured she really didn't want to focus on Fallon, so instead he dutifully looked over the locks on the two arched windows. Sheer curtains, also in layered shades of blue, would keep out the worst of the sunshine during the day, but wouldn't really provide any privacy at night.

The immense backyard, however, ensured there were no close neighbors to peek inside.

She, too, had a connecting bath, decorated all in cream with a plush rug in front of the claw-foot tub and another in front of the glass-walled shower. When

Justice took a deep breath, he caught the scent of her shampoo and lotion.

Dangerous.

When he finished checking everything, he and Rebecca went back to the front door where a panel held the security code. In the basement he'd seen the panel that contained all the settings.

"The cameras are also accessible from our cell phones and tablets," Rebecca told him. "Our privacy is very important to us."

Speaking of privacy…it suddenly occurred to Justice that Fallon had disappeared. Where was she? He knew she hadn't gone to bed because he'd just been in her room. Was she peeved at him for something? Maybe thinking he was too high-handed in trying to keep her safe?

"Well?" Rebecca asked. "What do you think?"

"Mr. Wade did a great job. Everything is as safe as you can make it without around-the-clock guards. I know the system. It's top-of-the-line and easily customizable. Adding a few more cameras wouldn't be a big deal, or too costly." Not that they'd probably mind the expense. "I'll come by a few hours early tomorrow and take care of it. Tonight, though, make sure you lock up behind me, okay?"

"I will, and thank you for your concern."

He glanced around but still didn't see Fallon, so he asked, "Who else knows about your system? What it covers and doesn't cover?"

"I don't really know." She thought about it. "Fallon, of course."

"None of your employees? The people who work around the house?"

"No. Clayton would never tell them." She pursed her mouth and gave Justice close scrutiny while saying, "I believe Marcus is aware, since he and Fallon were practically engaged."

Whoa. That was news to him! Trying to sound neutral, he asked, "Engaged?"

"Yes. He'd often bring her home from events."

Marcus. Just thinking his name made Justice frown. "When's the last time you saw him?"

Brows lifted, Rebecca said, "Oh, he came by earlier today—not long after you and Fallon had left."

Tension crawled into Justice's shoulders. "Why?"

"He wants to work with me on the reading program for underprivileged kids. Marcus is very generous and gives freely of his time as well as his money."

It took some effort, but Justice managed not to snarl when he said, "I thought your husband disliked him."

She flapped a hand. "Clayton gets touchy when it comes to Fallon. Doesn't matter how old she gets, he still wants to treat her like his little girl." The way she said it told Justice that Rebecca didn't really see that as a flaw. "However, I trust her to make good choices. She and Marcus are no longer together, but Fallon has said there's no reason for us to break ties with him."

Justice wished he had a vote—he'd side with Clayton for sure. "You don't think it's a little coincidental that I ran him off, then he returned and now someone has vandalized your property?"

Her brows went up. "What do you mean, you ran him off?"

Carrying a tray with sandwiches and tea, Fallon chose that exact moment to return. She set the tray on the foyer table with a clatter that deliberately drew their attention.

After a cross glare at Justice, she said to her mother, "Marcus was being pushy. But *I'm* the one who sent him away."

Justice shrugged. She could tell that fairy tale if she wanted, but they both knew Marcus would have continued to press her if he hadn't intervened. "The point is, he was here, hassling you, then snuck in to see your ma after we left—"

"He didn't exactly sneak," Rebecca said.

"And now your driveway is splattered in bloodred paint."

Fallon shoved a plate at him.

He eyed the sandwich made from some small, round, fancy-type bread. Placed artfully beside it were a pickle spear and kettle chips. Until that moment, he hadn't thought about being hungry. "Thanks."

While handing a plate to her mother, Fallon said, "I'm sure Marcus had nothing to do with the paint."

Relieved, Rebecca nodded. "I can't imagine that he would."

"Bodyguards," Fallon added in an incriminating tone, "are apparently prone to melodrama."

Rebecca murmured, "I see," while attempting to hide her smile.

Justice snorted. "It's called doing my job." Then he ate the tiny sandwich in one big bite.

Bemused, Fallon watched him chew and swallow, looked at her own sandwich, and offered him half.

He grinned. "Nah, thanks. Even we melodramatic types know not to take other people's share."

"Fallon usually only eats half anyway," Rebecca offered, while ushering them to the dining room.

Each lady ended up putting half a sandwich on his plate. And true enough, he'd finished every bite while they were still nibbling on theirs. "So what do you say? I can grab what I need and get here in the afternoon. We won't need to leave for the fights until five."

Fallon hesitated with a chip almost to her mouth. "I thought the first fight started at eight."

"Prelims start at eight. Stack will be with the main event starting at ten. But I always get there early when someone from the same camp is fighting. Moral support and all that." It'd be interesting to see how Fallon fared in the loud, testosterone-laden atmosphere. Half hoping she'd decline, but also anxious to introduce her to his world, he asked, "That work for you?"

"Oh, sure. Whatever you want."

So accommodating, he mused, knowing she had no idea of everything he wanted. Not that he should be thinking about that, especially not with her mother watching him as if she, at least, knew exactly where his mind had gone.

The beeping of his cell saved him. He answered the call from the cleaning company, replied that he'd be right out and pushed back his chair.

"I'll stick around until they're done with the mess, but you two can go on to bed." *Yeah, shouldn't be thinking about Fallon curling up in that cozy-looking bed either.* "I'll bring you the invoice for the work tomorrow when I come by to add to the security."

"It's too much," Rebecca protested. "I can see to the—"

"No, ma'am. I'd rather you didn't." Melodramatic or not, at this point Justice chose to trust very few people. "Let me handle it, okay?"

She subsided. "If you wish. But, Justice?"

He lifted a brow.

"Thank you."

"Thank me by locking up behind me. And try not to let Marcus in until I've cleared him."

Rolling her eyes, Fallon abandoned her plate and stood to join him.

"He's persistent," her mother said, smiling at Justice as if she didn't mind.

"Seems so."

Folding his arms, Justice held his ground. "Promise me."

"Fine by me," Fallon grumbled. "I don't particularly want to see him anyway."

He'd noticed. *What scar could she possibly have?*

From what Justice could tell, she was physically perfect. Curved in all the right places, sleek in others. For sure her boobs were real; they didn't appear large, but the way they bounced when she walked nearly made him nuts.

Marcus was an idiot. *Did she have an appendectomy scar?*

He snorted again, gaining added attention from both women. Going for some cover, he said, "Your mom is working with the man." A fact Justice hated. "You're bound to see him."

"Going forward," Rebecca promised, "Marcus and I will hold our meetings elsewhere."

Better than nothing. Justice nodded. "Just be careful around him."

She treated him to an indulgent smile. "Yes, Justice."

Fallon grabbed his arm and practically dragged him from the room. Of course, he allowed the dragging. She looked extra cute when she got all riled up.

As soon as they were out of earshot, he asked, "Was your ma patronizing me?"

Releasing him at the door, she faced him with hands on her hips. "Yes, with good reason."

Justice frowned. He'd kind of liked having her hands on him. "How's that?"

"Oh, no, you don't. You're not going to divert me. I have something important I want to explain to you."

Her grave tone put his chin in the air with wary defiance. "What?"

She glanced back toward where they'd left her mother, then lowered her voice. "I'm trying to break away from insanely overprotective people."

"Your parents?" he asked, wanting to make sure.

She threw up her hands. "Yes, my parents. They love me—"

"But they smother you. Yeah, I get that."

"Then *get* that you're doing the same thing!"

"Shhh," he cautioned. "Your ma will hear and you'll hurt her feelings." Justice knew instinctively that Fallon wouldn't want to do that.

She drew a breath, then managed a thin smile. "This is important to me, Justice. For once I want to be free, not treated like an infant."

One of these days he'd understand her...maybe after he figured out why her folks were so watchful—and why she'd allowed it. "Trust me, honey, I know you're not a child."

The way her eyes flared, Justice knew he definitely shouldn't have said that.

Annoyed with himself, he started to explain. "I mean—"

"Thank you." Her expression softened. "I appreciate the sentiment and I'm glad that *someone* realizes I can take care of myself."

He hadn't said that, but he was glad she'd let him off the hook, so he muttered, "No problem."

"How about instead of worrying about me, you head home to get some much-needed rest?"

Rest? At least this time she hadn't insulted him in front of her mother. "Do I look frail to you?"

"No."

"Weak?"

"Of course not."

"Then why would you think I need to *rest*?"

She barely muffled a laugh. "You say it like a slur. Everyone needs to rest sometimes. You've had several busy days and—"

Thinking she needed to understand just how energetic he felt, he took a step closer—but caught himself before he did anything stupid. Like touch her. Or kiss her.

God, he wanted to kiss her.

Instead, he waffled. He'd never been this uncertain with a woman, but damn it, Fallon wasn't just a woman.

She was a client.

He needed to remember that.

Eyes big and dark, Fallon stared up at him, unsure of herself, her gaze searching his. "Justice?" she whispered, sounding a little breathless and completely on board for whatever he might want to do in that moment.

"Shit."

She blinked, the fog of interest clearing. "What?"

"Just...shit." He laughed at himself and ran both hands over his face. "I gotta roll. Lock this door behind me, and don't let anyone else in. I'll see you tomorrow."

He didn't wait to learn if she had anything else to say. Instead, he strode down the drive, which now felt a mile long, though he knew it wasn't. And with every step he felt her gaze on his back. He'd confused her.

But hell, she couldn't be more confused than him.

It took nearly two hours to clean up the paint. Luckily, it was a cheap, water-based paint and they were able to get it completely removed from the concrete drive. The lawn, however, looked like hell. The crew promised the paint wouldn't actually kill anything and that after mowing two more times, it wouldn't even be noticeable.

With the spring rains, even the grass should look good as new very soon.

By the time Justice got to the small house he'd recently purchased, he really was dragging. Thanks to Fallon feeding him, he needed only a quick shower and then he could fall into bed.

Soon as his headlights hit the front of the house, he realized he'd had a visitor.

Some asshole had stomped on all the new flowers he'd planted in the beds around the front porch.

Son of a bitch. The Wades weren't the only ones to be vandalized. Could that mean someone didn't like his connection to them? Probably, and as far as Justice was concerned, Marcus was his number-one suspect.

SITTING IN THE Body Armor Agency, ensconced in his boss's office with the requisite coffee and treats, Justice updated Leese and Sahara. Knowing they'd be curious, he'd even taken photos with his cell phone to better show the damage done to the houses.

They both frowned over the red paint and sympathized with him over his squished flowers.

"Sucks," Leese said. "But it still surprises me that you'd plant all those flowers."

"My granny and mom bought them for me. I didn't have much choice. They're both going to be pissed when they see the mess."

Sahara looked at him over her coffee cup, and when she finished her drink, she suggested, "Replant. Don't tell them."

"Maybe." The idea had merit, though he knew how disappointed his mom always got whenever he'd told her even the smallest lie. Still, she'd start in worrying if he didn't.

Absolutely *no one* could worry like his mom. She'd cornered the market. If Fallon wanted to see melodrama, he should introduce the two of them— No. *What the hell was he thinking?*

All kinds of crazy connotations went along with a girl meeting a guy's mom. He definitely couldn't go there.

"What?" Leese asked. "Did you think of something else?"

"No." Nothing that he could share with anyone.

Leese said, "I think more research is in order. There's probably a connection somewhere that we're missing."

"Fallon and her family swear there isn't any real threat. They just want her protected against anything that might come up."

"So maybe they don't know. Maybe they're over-looking something."

Sahara saluted Leese with her coffee. "You know, you're proving to be the best at research, often even better than my PI. You have an innate knack for know-ing what trails to follow. If you have any free time, maybe you could lend Justice a hand. Just log in your hours for me."

Leese glanced at Justice. "I don't want to step on your toes. If you'd rather do some digging yourself—"

"Not offended," Justice promised. "I'm not nearly as good at it as you are, and I know it, so I welcome the help."

Leese smiled in anticipation. "Then consider it done."

"I'm glad that's settled." Sahara moved to sit behind her desk, dismissing them with a shooing motion of her hand. "Keep me updated," she said absently, already logging into her PC.

In silence, Justice and Leese walked out together and boarded the elevator. As soon as the doors closed, Leese asked, "You okay?"

Surprised by the question, Justice growled, "Yeah, 'course." But he stewed.

Leese snorted. "Give it up. You've got something on your mind. I can tell."

Should he tell? He'd found Leese to be a good confidant, but still, some shit should be kept private.

Folding his arms and resting back in the elevator, Leese waited.

Well, hell. Justice scowled. "Thing is, it's going to sound ridiculous." As melodramatic as Fallon had accused.

"Probably not as much as you're thinking."

Scrubbing a hand over his face, Justice tried to think of where to start, and finally just said it. "I don't feel like me anymore. Hell, I don't even know what I'm doing. It's like, for so long I was a fighter. End of story, ya know? I woke up and knew what I'd be doing that day. What I wanted to happen and how I'd work on it."

Leese nodded. "There's more of a routine to fighting. Training, travel, competition. Whether it goes good or bad, you know what to expect. With this job, not so much."

"Right," Justice agreed, jumping on his understanding of the situation. "I'm doing this shit and I like it. A lot. But the guy I used to know isn't there anymore. The things that come naturally to me, I can't do. The stuff

I *can* do…well, it feels way too fucking natural. Like I was born to do it." Frustration crawled over him; he knew most of it centered around Fallon.

They stepped out of the elevator but didn't head for the front doors.

"I get it," Leese assured him.

"Do you?" Because Justice wasn't entirely sure he did, so how could Leese?

"I've gone through a few transformations myself." With a self-deprecating smile, Leese said, "I used to be a dick."

Justice tried to deny that. "You were just—"

"We both know it's true. Then I got involved in Cannon's camp and I finally felt focused. I gave my all to following what I thought I wanted—fighting."

"That *is* what you wanted," Justice countered. Hell, Leese had more heart than a lot of champions.

"No. Once I accepted reality, that I'd never be the best, I starting thinking about other options, and the stuff I enjoyed more."

"That's how you ended up at Body Armor?"

"Yeah." Leese looked as uncomfortable with the conversation as Justice. "And good thing, because now I know this is what I was always meant to do. It feels like the right fit, you know? Far more so than fighting ever did. It's more natural for me."

"See," Justice said, "that's sort of how I feel. Except there are conflicts, too."

Leese slowly smiled. "The girl? That's the conflict we're talking about, right?"

Would it be disloyal to Fallon to say so?

"I've been there, too," Leese reminded him. "I'm definitely not one to judge."

True. Leese was going to marry the girl he'd been conflicted over, so he'd been farther down the road than Justice planned to travel. After remembering that, he didn't need much prodding. He spilled his guts, telling Leese about Marcus, his mention of a scar and Fallon's reaction. "What do you make of that?"

Brows together, Leese gave it quick thought, then shared his advice. "I think I need to dig a little deeper into her background."

"I thought you already did that."

"I did a surface search looking for the obvious stuff, but now I might have more direction." He clapped Justice on the shoulder. "In the meantime, stay sharp—and make damned sure she's on board before you push for anything beyond a business relationship."

Justice put his hands on his hips. "S'that what you did with Catalina?"

Grinning, Leese said, "Catalina didn't give me much choice in the matter. I tried to resist, but she was pretty damned insistent."

After a shared laugh, they parted ways, with Leese heading to the shooting range in the basement and Justice heading for his car. He had a lot to accomplish before he went to the Wade house.

Unlike Catalina, he knew Fallon would never push for a relationship. She was too shy, too sheltered. That meant he had to concentrate on keeping it professional, no matter how difficult that might be.

CHAPTER EIGHT

FALLON WAS SO EXCITED, she couldn't contain her smiles. The parking lot would be jam-packed, Justice explained, so he parked in a pay lot a block from the venue. On their way in, they passed crowds of people ready for the fights, many of them wearing the same type of shirt as the one Justice had given to her, but with different fighters featured on the front.

Groups of young men hung together, already tipsy. Women, dressed to impress, flirted as they went by.

A couple of guys recognized Justice and asked for a photo with him. Even after he explained that he didn't compete anymore, they were still impressed and adoring, so he gave in, all while keeping Fallon close at hand.

He got them into the venue through a side door, away from the long line of people awaiting entry. They went down a hallway filled with men in shorts and T-shirts, some pacing, some hurrying along, others carrying supplies.

When passage got difficult, Justice took her hand, presumably so he wouldn't lose track of her. Whatever the reason, she felt a ridiculous thrill from his touch. His hand was easily twice the size of hers, strong and warm. Her heart started thumping hard, and when he glanced back at her with a cocky smile, she realized she was squeezing him.

They ducked through a closed door. She was surprised to find Cannon, Armie and Denver inside.

"You made it," Cannon said to her, coming forward for a greeting.

"It's so exciting," she whispered, then stalled when Cannon drew her in for a hug. Armie got her next, then passed her along to Denver.

If she lived to be a hundred, she'd never get used to how these big, ripped specimens were so demonstrative—and so gentle. It was enough to leave a woman with permanent heart palpitations.

Knowing she blushed, Fallon didn't object when Justice pulled her back to his side.

She stayed quiet as he asked the group, "How's Stack doing?"

"He's ready," Cannon said with confidence. "I'll be rejoining him in a few minutes." Then to Fallon he said, "There's food if you're hungry." He indicated a table filled with a variety of things to eat and drinks in a cooler. "Or if you're interested, Justice can show you around, introduce you to some people."

"Whatever Justice wants to do is fine by me."

All the men grinned at her while Justice rubbed the back of his neck. She realized what she'd said, twisted her mouth and added, "Within reason."

That made them laugh.

Armie nodded at her chest. "Nice shirt."

She looked down at it with a smile. "Justice gave it to me." She'd worn the oversize black fighter tee over a long-sleeved white shirt. Justice wore his gray shirt alone.

And my, how he filled it out. She had to admit, it looked much better on him than it looked on her.

Armie said, "When the ladies wear it, they tie it on the side." He smiled. "Mind if I show you?"

"Oh…um…" She glanced at Justice.

He rolled his eyes. "Do it," he said to Armie, "but make damned sure you're behaving."

"Stretch would have my hide if I didn't."

Stretch, she recalled, was Cannon's little sister and Armie's wife.

Armie stepped up to her, turned her to the side, then took the hem of the shirt and knotted it at her hip. It didn't affect the wolf design on front, but did make it fit her better and look more stylish.

He turned her toward a mirror and asked, "What do you think?"

Apparently Armie had many talents. "I like it. Thank you."

"You're going to get warm with that undershirt," Denver predicted. "It gets downright steamy about half-way through the night."

"Oh, well…" She couldn't lose the layer, so she merely shrugged and tried to act like it didn't matter. "It'll be fine, I'm sure."

Justice watched her until the door opened and more people stepped in. Clearly these were other fighters in the group and since she was the only woman, she started to feel like an intruder.

It got more awkward when one of the men asked if

she was "with" Justice and he explained they weren't dating.

The man immediately tried to cozy up to her.

Justice immediately protested—and that had his friends all laughing.

Armie pulled him aside for a private conversation, and while Justice was otherwise occupied, two more men smoothly stepped in with questions about her availability. Fallon was both flattered and flustered. She'd never before garnered so much attention.

Even as she made excuses about why she shouldn't give out her phone number, she smiled until her cheeks hurt.

Minutes later, Justice rejoined her and that got rid of the interested men real quick.

It might have had something to do with Justice's sudden cross mood. He glared at everyone, including Armie, who kept snickering.

With the growled excuse that he'd show her around, Justice flipped off Armie, gave a halfhearted wave to the others and urged her from the room.

"What's going on?" Fallon asked.

"Nothing."

It was far too crowded to debate while walking in the hallway, so Fallon simply stopped. When Justice turned to her, she said, "*Something*, and I want to know what."

He stepped close, backing her to the wall and using his body to block her from passersby. He braced one thick arm on the wall above her head and leaned in. "Fine. You want to know what's got me irked?"

She'd never seen him in a mood like this. And, good

Lord, he surrounded her! With every breath, she inhaled his hot scent, leaving her stomach filled with butter-flies. No longer quite so certain, she whispered, "Yes?"

He angled closer still until his face was near hers and she could see her own reflection in his dark eyes. Then he said nothing.

His gaze dipped to her mouth.

Her heart went into her throat and her toes curled inside her shoes. "Justice?"

He drew a slow breath and his eyes met hers again. The impact was enough to weaken her knees.

Suddenly his mouth tilted. "Don't faint on me."

She shook her head, unwilling to make any promises.

"Guys are hittin' on you."

"They are?" Is that what bothered him?

"Yeah, and don't give me that innocent act." He tweaked her chin. "You liked it. But, honey, this isn't the place for it. Half the dudes here will be toasted by the end of the night, and half the ladies will be willing regardless. So Armie made a suggestion."

Was it the suggestion, then, that had him riled? Feel-ing very daring, she prodded him. "Let's hear it."

Justice took his time, tucking back her hair, then stroking her cheek with his thumb. "Tonight, if anyone asks, you're with me."

Going breathless, she repeated, "With you?"

"Yeah. That's the safest way for us to play it." He drifted the backs of his knuckles down her throat, then lightly cupped her shoulder. "So we'll be doing some of this tonight."

"This...what?"

"Touching. Teasing. Me making it clear to every yahoo out there that you're mine."

She had absolutely nothing to say to that. Little jittery explosions were going off in her body, making it hard to breathe, hard to think, but not to feel. Nope, she could feel just fine and the way he'd touched her…

"Okay?"

Well, shoot. He expected conversation. She managed a nod.

When Justice grinned, crinkles showed in the corners of his dark sinner's eyes. "You are so sweet." He looked her over, then playfully asked, "You sure you won't faint?"

No. "Pretty sure."

His grin widened. "You sound all raspy." He dipped his head, then said softly into her ear, "Don't get nervous. I won't be pushing the boundaries. We just need to convince everyone else."

Right. In order to protect her heart—and her pride— she seriously needed to remember that, for Justice, this was no more than a job. All the sudden flirting and intimacy was a game played to make the job easier. It would be beyond foolish for her to keep reacting to him so emotionally.

What she needed to do, she decided, was take advantage of the awesome opportunity now afforded her. How many big, buff, badass and sexy men would want to be this close to her? She could enjoy every second of it while keeping it in perspective by reminding herself that it wasn't real.

Play it cool, she told herself, but definitely go ahead and play.

"Fallon?"

Justice's low, gruff voice and the way his warm breath teased her ear wasn't helping her to get control.

He stayed very near to her, and his scruffy jaw brushed hers.

"Hmm?"

"You ready?"

For what? She didn't actually ask, because she knew whatever it was, yes, she was more than ready. Anxious even. She'd wanted some new experiences; now it appeared she'd get her money's worth.

In a lust-induced stupor, she nodded. Satisfied, he pressed his warm mouth to her temple in a brief kiss that made her breath catch.

"For anyone watching," he explained, then he levered back and slung his arm around her shoulders, keeping her close as he headed back down the wide hall.

Luckily they had a few minutes before she was expected to speak to anyone. The crowds got thicker, giving her time to get her wits together as they wended in and out of human congestion. Eventually they ended up near the "cage." Justice showed her where their seats would be, right behind the announcers. An entire section was roped off for the group.

Many people—fighters and their wives, past and present champions, a few celebrities who'd shown up to watch, referees and announcers—all greeted Justice like a friend. The scope of his social circle amazed her.

He introduced her each time and allowed people

to make the assumption they were a couple. One man grinned and gave him a fist bump with the murmured praise, "Nice."

After the man walked away, Justice whispered, "He means you," and gave her an affectionate squeeze.

Fallon bit her lip, but the implied flattery still made her grin.

Once the fight started, many of the women sat together but Justice didn't like that arrangement. He kept her at his side and she ended up sandwiched between him and Denver.

Since they were both gigantic men, she felt extra tiny and completely insulated from some of the jostling as people surged to their feet again and again to cheer or shout instructions. Fallon didn't think the men fighting heard all the yelling. If they did, they didn't acknowledge it. She figured the spectators just liked to give suggestions regardless.

Armie sat back with the ladies, including his wife. Fallon learned that Cannon's wife had stayed home with the babies. Apparently she and Armie's wife took turns on that.

Because Justice was so engrossed in the fight, Fallon asked Denver about Cannon. He explained that as an assistant coach, Cannon was in back with Stack, and when it came time for the fight, he'd be cage-side.

Trying to understand, she asked, "So Cannon not only runs a gym and fights, but he coaches, too?"

Denver started to lean close to reply and she suddenly found herself hauled up to Justice's side. He took over the explanations. "Cannon started the gym but everyone pitches in to help out there. And depending on who's fighting, different fighters step up as assistant coaches. They leave the real training to a dedicated, full-time coach, though." When the prelims ended, Justice went into more depth about the process, and the other guys chimed in, giving her a lot of insight.

The women, too, had much to say, and their perspectives, she found, were vastly different from the men.

Overall, she gathered that the fighters were something of a family. They stuck together, supported each other and accepted imperfections.

Even though he no longer competed, Justice was clearly still part of the family, and Fallon loved that for him. Her own family had always been small and after losing her sister—

"Son of a bitch."

Justice's muttered complaint drew her from her wayward thoughts. She glanced up—and found Marcus staring at her from across the aisle, several rows away. He, too, had good seats, but in a different section.

"That's Marcus," she said in surprise.

"Yeah, and I'll bet my ass the little weasel isn't an MMA fan."

Justice sounded accusatory and more than furious.

"Maybe not," she rushed to say. "But it appears he's here with clients. Notice the other men around him? They're probably fans and Marcus is wooing them for business."

When he started their way, Justice said, "Let me handle this," with evil relish. He started out of the row.

"No." Fallon caught the back of his waistband, which

was the only thing she could reach, and inadvertently got pulled from her seat. She almost tripped over a seat, but three pair of male hands caught her.

Mortified, she thanked everyone, then in a very low voice hissed to Justice, "Don't you dare embarrass me by causing a scene. I mean it."

Expression fierce, Denver said, "I wouldn't."

Already the others were staring at them, wondering what had happened. Fallon pasted on a smile before ushering Justice along. When they reached the aisle, she requested, "Give a minute."

He laughed like she was nuts. "Hell, no."

"Justice," she growled.

He cupped his hand around the nape of her neck, stalling her complaints. "With or without your boyfriend, I wouldn't let you out of my sight here. But I'll let you take the lead. How's that?"

Not good enough; however, debating it in front of everyone would only cause more conflict. So instead she said, "He's *not* my boyfriend," then looked at Marcus and pointed to the hall behind them.

He nodded and headed in that direction.

Giving Justice a stern frown, she said, "I'm trusting you to behave."

"Yes, ma'am." Keeping his hand on her nape, he walked with her to the very congested main hall.

WATCHING THEM TOGETHER, he realized their relationship was more than client and bodyguard. Were they a couple? It sure appeared so.

Being classy, rich and pampered, Fallon Wade

couldn't be Justice's usual type. Maybe the differences made her more appealing, perhaps even special to him.

If so, that'd make things easier. Justice was a real hard-ass who didn't feel the need to prove anything to anyone.

Women, however, had a knack for weakening even the strongest of men.

He'd definitely work this to his advantage.

Every locked door could be opened, as long as you had a key. He smiled, thinking he'd just acquired the key he needed.

"GOOD HEAVENS, IT'S PACKED."

Justice pulled her closer, moving her in front of him and using his arms to shield her from being jostled. "Everyone is heading to get a drink before the main fights start."

"Is it always this busy?"

"Yeah." He steered her into a slight alcove near the fire exit. As they waited for Marcus, he figured he might as well set her straight. "This is your show—"

"Thank you."

"As long as he doesn't insult you."

She rounded on him with a lot of attitude. "If he insults me—"

"He'll get flattened."

"I'll handle it." Her eyes narrowed. "We've discussed this, Justice."

"Yeah." Justice had a hard time thinking straight. Out of necessity, he'd followed Armie's suggestion and kept her as close as he would a bed partner. But that just naturally led to him thinking more about her actually being one.

"And?" she asked, sounding a little breathless.

"I dunno." The longer he stared down at her, the less angry she seemed. He touched her cheek and found it every bit as soft and warm as he remembered.

She shifted, cleared her throat, licked her lips. "Justice?"

God he loved her eyes, so big and deep with emotion. And her mouth—all pink and wet... Without meaning to, he leaned a little closer, more than ready for a taste.

"What are you doing here?"

At Marcus's brusque question, Fallon jumped as if someone had goosed her. She whipped around, snapping, "Damn it!"

Marcus scowled.

"Fallon, Fallon," Justice playfully chided. "I had no idea you had such a potty mouth."

Her elbow connected with his gut.

Taken by surprise, he grunted, "Oof," then caught her arm. "Violent, too."

She forced a smile for Marcus. "I'm here to watch the fights of course."

Very deliberately, Marcus kept his gaze on Fallon. Even with Justice giving him a death stare, the bastard avoided his gaze.

Shoving his hands in his pockets, Marcus nodded. "I didn't know you were a fan."

"And you are?"

"Not really. But I have some potential donors for the

literacy fund-raiser with me. When a friend had tickets he couldn't use, I bought them from him."

Justice propped a shoulder against the wall and suffered through the cordial conversation. He detested hearing Fallon talk so sweetly to her ex, and he especially hated that the ex was being reasonable for once.

He liked Marcus better as an asshole he could revile.

"So they enjoy the sport?" Fallon asked.

"I really don't know," Marcus said. "But they're competitive brothers and enjoy any kind of wager there is."

Fallon frowned. "They're betting on the fights?"

"They bet on everything, and they especially favor friendly wagers over sports of any kind." He made a face. "They've left it to me to keep a tally of the bets, since I'm not joining in the competition."

"I take it they have deep pockets?" Fallon teased.

"Yes, very deep. But they don't just gamble with money. I've seen them put up cars, houses and, a few times, women. Whoever loses always pays up."

Fallon stiffened. "Exactly how do you pay up with a woman?"

Marcus smiled slightly. "No one is being forced, I'm sure. When you're as well off as those two are, women are always available and willing to oblige."

She narrowed her eyes. "It's still wrong."

He shrugged. "I'm not disagreeing."

To switch the topic a bit, Justice spoke up. "You said they're businessmen?"

Face tightening, Marcus looked away. "They have a willingness to contribute."

Something in his tone and manner sharpened Justice's interest even more. "So *not* businessmen?"

"Of course they have businesses."

"And those are?"

Instead of answering, Marcus ignored him and asked Fallon, "Are you enjoying yourself?"

"Yes. It's so exciting. I'd never realized."

His expression warmed. "You wouldn't even watch boxing with me."

"In comparison, boxing seems boring."

"Boring?" he teased. "Maybe you need to give it another try."

Justice sawed his teeth together.

"From what I remember of boxing," Fallon said, "it's just punching. This is punching and kicking, elbows and knees, grappling and—"

Indulgent, Marcus smiled. "You've become an expert?"

"Far from it. But I am learning a lot from Justice's friends. In fact, one of his friends is the main fight of the night."

"Main event? Really?" There was no real surprise in Marcus's eyes when he looked at Justice again. "So you know Stack Hannigan?"

"Know him and gave Fallon the shirt."

Using both thumbs, Fallon pointed to her chest to show off the wolf logo.

Justice took her hand and lowered it. The last thing he wanted her to do was draw Marcus's attention to her boobs.

Unfortunately, he was too late.

With his gaze where it shouldn't be, Marcus swallowed. "Nice."

Resisting the urge to clock him, Justice said, "Damn, man, you must be one of Stack's more rabid fans the way you're drooling."

As if only then realizing where he'd been looking, Marcus snapped to. He coughed and tried to hurry along with a question. "I take it you'll be rooting for him?"

Pretending to miss the male conflict, Fallon nodded. "Yes. And Justice promises me that he'll win."

"Fact," Justice said.

"I'll pass along that inside info, then," Marcus promised. "The brothers will appreciate it." He glanced at Justice, glanced over his shoulder, then said to Fallon, "Do you think we could—"

Gleefully, Justice said, "Nope."

Since he held her arm, Fallon couldn't elbow him again. Instead, she tried to yank free of his hold. But Justice didn't let go, even when she tried to shake him off.

Naturally Marcus couldn't help but notice.

Eyes going flinty, the ex took a step forward. "Now wait just—"

To keep Marcus from interceding, Fallon did an immediate about-face. "Mother told me you'll be working with her on the literacy charity. That's very generous of you."

Divided, Marcus waffled between showing his anger and grabbing her olive branch.

Knowing which one he'd prefer, Justice waited.

Marcus finally settled on the branch. "Yes. It's a

great cause." Voice softer, he said, "And I was hoping I'd get to see you."

Ha! Justice had guessed all along that Marcus had ulterior motives.

Staying firm, Fallon shook her head. "That's not going to happen."

"But—"

"Mother has agreed that she'll only meet with you away from our home."

Marcus turned his hate-filled glare on Justice. "I suppose that's what *he* wants?"

Justice gave an evil smile.

"It's what *I* want," Fallon hurried to say.

Done with the dramatics, Justice drew her into his side and draped his arm over her shoulders to keep her anchored there. "The fights will be starting soon. We should get back to our seats."

Luckily Fallon agreed, and for once, Marcus didn't kick up a fuss. He glanced over his shoulder again, nodded to Fallon and said, "I'll see you soon."

Something made Justice uneasy.

Maybe it was the wary way Marcus kept looking around, how he went the opposite direction from which he'd come. Skin prickling, Justice, too, did a quick survey of the area—and found one of Marcus's betting buddies standing a few yards away, arms crossed, watching them with too much interest.

In an instinctive move to meet a threat head-on, Justice stepped forward. Almost at the same time, Fallon turned into his path, probably to blast him—which, okay, he maybe deserved.

They collided.

Justice caught her upper arms to keep her from stumbling. She automatically braced her hands against his chest. They both went still.

Maybe it was Marcus hitting on her, or maybe it was all the other dudes trying to get her attention. Whatever the reason, he felt all territorial and determined to stake a claim.

Resisting a woman wasn't easy. Hell, it wasn't even natural. Resisting Fallon…now that was almost impossible, but he hung on by a thread.

Torturous, especially when she turned her face up to his.

The awareness in her eyes damn near knocked him over the edge.

Everything around him faded away as sexual tension sank in. Fallon's gaze dipped to his mouth, she licked her lips and, choosing to see that as an invitation, Justice gave in.

He cupped a hand to the back of her neck, drew her up and covered her mouth with his own. He couldn't say exactly what got into him, and he sure as hell couldn't justify it, but in that moment, he felt explosive with need.

Should'a made it a light kiss.

Should'a kept it quick.

But damn, her mouth was soft and damp, and with a shuddering breath she parted her lips.

He lost his head a little, especially when she melted against him and her small hands clutched at his chest.

Again on instinct, he turned them so that her back

was against the wall, her front shielded by his body, ensuring no one could see her.

It was insane. Definitely wrong. But he had to taste her.

His tongue slipped over her lips, dipped inside to touch her teeth, then her tongue. She teased back with her own.

On a groan, he nudged her mouth open, deepening the kiss with a bold stroke of his tongue. Her mouth was warm and sweet, and he couldn't get enough.

Her soft sound of surprise gave him a second of sanity. *What the hell was he doing?*

He decided he had to stop, and tried to by lifting his head. He expected Fallon to say something, maybe even push him away. Instead, her breathing labored, she kept her eyes closed—her swollen mouth looked so pink, so wet…

This time he kissed her without any reserve at all. He couldn't get enough of her as he held her nape in one hand, and with the other, coasted down her narrow back to her hip.

In a sign of acceptance, her arms slid up and around his neck.

He pressed against her—

"Jesus, Justice, what are you doing?"

Harsh reality crashed into him. Oh, fuck.

Justice glanced over his shoulder and saw Leese scowling, Armie grinning. *Busted.* After clearing his throat, he asked, "When'd you get here?"

"Just now," Leese said, disapproval in his tone and expression.

Armie cocked a brow. "Really getting into the act,

huh? It's convincing. No one will doubt that you're into each other."

"Yeah, um…" What to do? Fallon had tucked her face against his chest, clearly hiding, and damn, he could feel her hot breath even through his T-shirt. He also felt her trembling.

It took him a second to wrap his brain around the fact that he'd now be stopped cold, when seconds before he'd been smoldering.

The idea of watching Stack compete no longer seemed so important, but no way could he do what he really wanted, which involved finding someplace private and scoring big with sweet little Fallon Wade.

"Would you like a minute?" Armie asked with absurd formality. "Not to finish, you know. I mean, you're right here in the open. But maybe to make your apologies to the lady? To set up plans for later?"

"Fuck off, Armie."

That got his friend laughing. Clutching his hands together, Armie said, "Young love. So beautiful. So… lusty."

Leese shoved Armie, then scowled again at Justice. "Wrap it up," he suggested, his tone terse. With yet another shove, he prodded Armie along to give them privacy.

Feeling damned ridiculous, Justice turned back to Fallon.

She continued to hide against him, and now her shoulders shook.

Oh, shit. If he'd made her cry, he'd kick his own ass. "Fallon?" He tried to lift her chin.

She resisted by tucking tighter to him.

He didn't know what to do. He stroked her silky hair, then her back. He pressed a kiss to her temple—and got himself all hot and bothered again.

Frowning at his own lack of control, Justice whispered, "You okay, honey?"

Her hands fisted in his shirt, and she made this strangled sound that alarmed him.

"Fallon?"

He heard it again, not quite a sob, but maybe—

She looked up at him and Justice saw that her big doe eyes were bright with laughter, her cheeks hot, and she couldn't quit snickering.

Hilarity?

He quirked a smile of relief. "Tickled your funny bone, huh?"

Choking on her humor, she hugged him again.

God, she looked incredibly beautiful to him. "Get it together, woman. We're in public."

Around a chuckle, she admitted, "Right—*now* I remember!"

Meaning she'd forgotten, too? "You're not the one who had to face Leese and Armie."

She did more snickering before she could face him again. "Oh, God, that was *so* embarrassing."

But rather than blast him, she laughed? Nice. Justice liked that reaction. He tangled a hand in her hair, saying, "Trust me, Armie's done worse."

That only put her into a fit of giggles—until Justice murmured, "You taste good, Fallon."

With a sharp inhale, she stared at him and bit her lip.

Renewed need clenched his guts. As much to himself as her, he said, "We have to get back to our seats."

"Right." She looked away, smoothing her hair and shirt. "I guess that kiss was to help convince people we're together?"

Sure, and I got hard for the same reason.

No, he couldn't say that; it'd only make things worse.

But because he didn't have a good answer, and he didn't want to outright lie to her, he kissed her again instead.

This time he managed to keep it light and quick.

"Sorry I embarrassed you." With an arm around her, he steered her out of the alcove and along the wide hall to their aisle entrance. "Don't ask me to apologize, though."

"Okay."

Justice frowned. She shouldn't have been so damned agreeable. "Not for the kiss, I mean."

"I knew what you meant."

Damn it. "It was wrong to maul you like that, especially here and now, but—"

"Justice, I'm not complaining."

No, she wasn't.

He didn't know what to think about that.

Talking became impossible as they squeezed through the crowds returning to their seats. He noticed Marcus and his cronies were again seated, now with drinks in their hands.

Feeling more surly than ever, Justice looked at each of them. The same man who'd been eyeballing him earlier looked up to meet his gaze. The guy smiled, then lifted his drink in a mock toast.

Justice continued to stare at him—until Fallon tugged on his hand to get him seated. There was a lot of ribbing from the guys as they waited for the next fight. Justice ignored them until he saw Fallon blushing.

Then he tried to mean-mug them all—without much success.

"Aw, he's sensitive," Denver said in a loud stage whisper.

Armie grinned. "And damned indiscreet."

"Rude as hell, too," Leese added, "because he hasn't introduced me yet."

Fallon turned with a smile and took care of the introduction herself. For a few minutes she and Leese talked about the bodyguard business. Justice thought about Marcus and wondered how he could get the names of the men with him.

When Tom came up to him, he almost groaned with frustration, especially when Tom took the seat beside him.

"Good night of fights, so far."

"Yeah," Justice agreed, not exactly in a chatty mood.

Tom elbowed him. "Makes you want to get back in it, doesn't it?"

"No."

"Bullshit. It's in your blood, Justice."

Used to be. But now? He had so many other things on his mind that he—

Tom thwacked him hard on the shoulder. "Give me the word and I'll talk to the powers that be. They already promised they'd set us up quick. And you know fans would love it."

Justice tried ignoring him.

"Your little lady would love to see you compete."

Sitting back in his seat, Justice said, "Ain't happening. Let it go."

"Can't, man. You're part of the plan and you know it."

"Get a new plan."

Tom grinned widely, but the annoyance was there in his eyes. "Fallon, honey, wouldn't you like to see Justice in the cage?"

Being drawn into the discussion caused her to falter, but not for long. "Justice can make his own decisions."

"But you'd like to see it, right? Or maybe you don't, considering how badly he'll lose."

She took the bait, saying, "Maybe I'll just watch the fight where he already knocked you out."

"I have it recorded," Armie said. "You're welcome to it."

"That was a fluke," Tom scoffed. "If Justice was really so damned cocksure, he'd have already given me a rematch."

Armie laughed. "If you want to stick with that fluke story, a rematch is a bad idea."

"You chicken?" Tom leaned around Justice to see Fallon. "Normally I wouldn't believe that of him, but since he's dodging me…"

Justice took Fallon's hand to stifle her denial. "Believe what you want, but I'm still done."

Finally Tom's smile slipped. "Damn it, man. I can't accept that."

Justice looked him in the eyes. "That's your problem then."

Fallon glanced anxiously from one man to the other. Justice gave her hand a squeeze to let her know he wasn't bothered. But, yeah, that was a lie. Tom got to him—not enough to make him backtrack, though.

Just enough to make him want to throw a punch.

Then he saw the guys with Marcus watching with interest. No way could they hear anything being said, not from that distance, but body language alone probably showed a conflict, and it had caught their interest.

Tom said, "I'll give you half my pay." Then with quiet force, "Take the fucking fight."

Fed up, Justice half turned to face him. "Your ego wants to fight, but here's a news flash for you—I don't give a shit about your ego, so leave me the hell alone."

Tom looked surprised for just a moment, then his face split with a grin. "I'm wearin' you down, buddy, I can tell. No, don't start gnashing your teeth. I'll let it go—for now."

Luckily the music started as fighters made their entrance with deafening fanfare. This was the start of the main card with a lot of fan favorites competing.

Fallon held his hand and listened intently to the introductions. Leese, he noticed, kept a sharp watch everywhere else.

Did he feel the same thing Justice did? It must have been catching, because by the end of the fight, Armie and Denver were also more alert.

Something was happening, Justice only wished he knew *what*.

CHAPTER NINE

THE EXCITEMENT WAS CONTAGIOUS, and although Fallon didn't know any of the athletes, out of loyalty she cheered for whomever Justice preferred.

The competitions proved more thrilling than she'd ever imagined possible. Bloody, yes. Brutal, no question. But she noted a mesmerizing fluidity to the defense and offense of each fighter. It didn't take her long to understand the styles and to recognize when a fighter wanted to stay on his feet versus preferring a ground game.

She was glad they had the "good seats," given how many people milled around going for more beer. She found it very distracting even though they weren't passing in front of her.

Denver leaned toward her ear to ensure she'd hear him. "Too many people are here without any real interest in the fights. But you seem to be enjoying them."

"Oh, yes, definitely." Secretly, she kept imagining Justice competing and, each time, a secret thrill unfurled inside her. Then again, the brush of his arm against hers, the way he smiled, also affected her.

She watched as he shouted suggestions and enacted them from his seat. He'd twist, tighten and duck as if he, himself, were in the fight.

Studying his profile, she asked, "Do you miss it?"

He glanced down at her. "What?"

"Competing. I know you said you didn't, but—"

"Sometimes," he admitted with a crooked grin. "But I have no intention of going back, so don't tell Tom or he'll be even more relentless."

Fallon didn't know Tom well, but she assumed, from what she'd seen so far, he'd be relentless anyway. If he ever did get Justice back in the cage, she'd put her faith in Justice every time. His modesty didn't matter. There was an amazing quiet confidence about him that she found incredibly appealing.

And good heavens, he knew how to kiss.

Just thinking about it now made her lips tingle and left her a little breathless.

She was so lost in daydreams, she almost missed a submission. When everyone surged to their feet, she shook off the sensual haze and jumped up, too.

Oh, it was awful!

She might have screamed…but then the referee called the fight and she watched as the poor guy who'd just gotten his arm cranked bounded to his feet with a low curse—before slapping his opponent on the shoulder.

Justice slipped his arm around her waist. Amused, he said, "You're on the squeamish side."

She made a face. "I thought his arm would break."

Tom leaned around Justice to say, "It happens on occasion."

Dear God. She blanched. "You're joking."

"Nope."

"I'm glad that didn't happen tonight."

"One more fight to go," Justice said. "But Stack's pretty good at avoiding submissions."

Tom stood. "I'm running out for a drink. Either of you want anything?"

Justice shook his head and Fallon said, "Thank you, but I'm fine."

With a nod, he left.

A few minutes later Armie returned and leaned forward, his arms braced on the back of her and Justice's seats. "So Tom knows your…friend?"

Fallon half turned. "My friend? Who?"

Armie tipped his head toward where Marcus had been sitting, but now the seats were empty.

Justice scowled. "What are you talking about?"

"Tom's out there with the three of them, chatting like they're old pals."

"The hell you say!" Justice surged to his feet before Fallon could stop him.

He'd only taken two steps when the intro music started for Stack's fight, making him hesitate. And then Marcus and his friends reentered—but not with Tom.

"Justice," she said, hooking her fingers over the back pocket of his jeans, which was the only part of him she could reach. "Why do you care?"

As he slowly turned to face her, the chilling anger left his eyes, replaced by something else. Something far from chilly.

His gaze shifted to her hand on his butt pocket, then to her face with a raised brow.

Armie started snickering. "Dude, you are in a bad way."

He'd had to shout to be heard over the music, and that got the attention of the other guys, who all started in with outrageous comments about their buddy being molested.

When she started to retreat, Justice laced his fingers with hers and stared toward Marcus and the others. He ignored his friends' provoking comments.

Finally Tom rejoined them, empty-handed, she noticed.

Justice didn't remark on it, but he was still scowling when he claimed his seat again.

Leese leaned past her to ask him, "What are you thinking?"

"That something's going on."

Fallon looked back and forth between the men. "What are you talking about?"

New music blared, and then Stack and his entourage, led by Cannon, entered the arena through a side door and all conversation died as the men raucously shouted for their fighter.

Clearly, Stack was a fan favorite. Most people were on their feet, some holding signs, many snapping pictures. Fallon forgot all about Tom and Marcus and whatever clandestine message had passed between Leese and Justice.

For this fight, anxiety riddled her. Everyone was so certain Stack would win, she kept wondering what would happen if he didn't. And of course, the other fighter had plenty of fans, too. How disappointed would they be?

She thought of Tom; clearly, he hadn't yet gotten over his loss.

With every punch or kick thrown, each takedown and submission attempt, she got more tense until she thought she might break. For once Justice was too caught up in the fight to notice how she fretted.

The torture lasted until the middle of the third round. Both fighters were battered. Stack had a severe black eye and the other guy had a cut on his forehead. Sweat covered their muscles, which had seemed to pump up with each punch thrown. Though Stack continued to breathe evenly, the other guy was getting gassed and it showed.

Earning his fight name, Stack prowled relentlessly forward, and when his opponent stepped back, Stack shot in. They ended in a tangle on the floor.

Beside her, Justice went nuts. The shouting from all the men nearly deafened her. She continually shifted her position to see around all the now-standing people and when she finally had a clear view again, she saw that Stack had a full mount. He landed four punches in a row, and the body beneath him went slack.

The ref called the knockout.

Pandemonium ensued while several of the fighters seated near her surged forward to the cage. Fallon could tell that Justice wanted to join them, but instead he swung her up in his arms and hugged her while laughing.

He held her as if she weighed nothing, and being in his arms made her nerve endings all go on alert.

As he set her back on her feet, she noticed that Armie

had also stayed behind with the wives, who hugged each other, alternately laughing and crying.

They were such protective, considerate men, and she sighed in distraction.

Until Justice cupped the side of her face and pressed his mouth to hers.

It was no more than a celebratory smooch, there and gone too quickly for her to kiss him back, but her blasted knees almost buckled.

While congratulations and back slaps got passed around their triumphant group, Fallon subtly fanned her face. Justice talked with others, and her mind wandered—to kisses and handholding, protectiveness and affection.

The truth settled into her heart and she knew…she cared far too much for him.

For so long she'd tried to keep her private life just that—private. In doing so, she felt like Justice only knew bits and pieces of her. Nothing of depth.

Nothing *real*.

Now with new awareness, she decided he had a right to know why she'd never dated. He needed to understand her issues, awful as they would be to share. Whether he considered the touching and kissing tonight as part of an act, for her it was real.

How would he react once he knew all of her?

Denver returned to their row of seats to collect his wife, who threw herself into his arms. While cuddling her close, he said to Justice, "After party at the club."

Justice was already shaking his head. "Not this time."

Denver glanced at her, then nodded. "Got it. Well, if you're interested, we're all going to Cannon's place tomorrow to hang out."

"Celebrating Stack's win?"

Denver shrugged. "The plans were already made, but sure."

Laughing, Justice told her, "Anyone can get caught, so if he'd lost we'd get together to grumble."

"That's about it," Denver agreed.

Justice put his arm around her. "What do you think? Did you have any plans for Sunday?"

Thrilled that he would include her, she quickly shook her head. "I'm free."

After giving her a one-arm hug, he told Denver, "Then count us in."

With plans made, everyone began exiting in a crush far worse than when they'd entered. Because some of the guys and their wives went a different direction to join up with Stack, she and Justice were among strangers. He kept her in front of him, occasionally raising a forearm to keep anyone from bumping into her.

They'd finally made it to the main hall that led to an escalator when something happened. People began cursing and the sounds of a scuffle were heard. She tried to go on tiptoe to better see, but Justice immediately tucked her behind him, saying, "Hold on to me."

She flattened a hand to the middle of his back.

Muscles flexed under her palm; the man was so hard all over.

Then a guy behind her shoved past in excitement, saying, "Fight!" as if he relished the idea.

A woman pushed in front of her, separating her from Justice while pressing close to his back.

Someone else wedged past her, then more people— and more. In a matter of seconds, she couldn't even see Justice. Uncertainty gripped her as she got jostled left and right.

Thinking it might be a good idea to get out of the main flow of bodies, she edged to the side, hoping to stand against the wall until Justice came back for her.

She almost made it, too, until someone shouldered her hard and she lost her footing. Her purse got jerked off her shoulder. She stumbled.

Without even realizing she was near the stairs, she went down them, nearly taking a few other startled people with her. Her hip hit the rail, her shin cracked against a step.

At a short landing where the stairs took a turn before continuing down, she finally crashed into a corner wall, her body in a disheveled heap. Somewhere along the way, she must have clunked her head because stars danced in her vision. In a daze, she struggled to get her bearings.

"Hey now." Tom crouched down in front of her. "You okay, honey?"

His big body blocked others from crowding her. "Justice…"

"I'm sure he's coming." He put a hand to her shoulder when she started to stand. "How about you hold on just a sec? Catch your breath and let me see if anything's hurt?"

Honestly, everything hurt, especially her pride. People who'd given up on the escalator continued to gawk at her as they passed down the stairs.

She brushed her hair back and winced. Looking at her wrist, she saw the bruise starting.

Tom took her hand and gently turned it. "Did you brace yourself as you fell?"

"I don't know. It happened so fast."

She heard an enraged shout and a second later Justice shoved Tom aside. "Fallon? Ah, shit." He touched her face. "Baby, what happened?"

Feeling like an utter fool, Fallon reached for him.

He drew her up and against him.

"I fell," she said with a hot blush. She wished there weren't so many people around to witness her embarrassment.

Scowling darkly, Justice asked, "Down the steps?" He looked back at them.

"Yes. Don't ask me how. It just…happened."

He slowly tipped up her face. "Banged yourself up, too."

He didn't know the half of it. Her hip ached, her shin throbbed, but at least the twirling stars were gone.

Tom stepped close again. "Got her purse."

Fallon gave up her stranglehold on Justice, limped as she put her weight on her leg, and attempted a smile. "Thank you, Tom." She took her purse from him. "Stuff went everywhere—"

"So did you." Like Justice, Tom appeared furious. "I think I got most of it."

Justice kissed her temple, then said to Tom, "Sorry if I—"

"No worries." Tom bent to look at her. "You seemed a little loopy when I first got to you. You sure you're okay?"

"Yes. Just humiliated."

Tom said, "Want me to lead the way?"

Nodding, Justice kept her close as they continued slowly down the stairs, following the flow of people out a side door into a near empty lot.

"We're parked around front," Justice said with a frown. "Can you walk okay?"

"Of course." The brisk air helped to revive her and after a few more steps, the pain in her hip eased. To get the attention off her, she asked, "Was there a fight?"

His expression carved in stone, Justice said, "No. Just two idiots arguing." He continued to watch her closely, proving her ploy hadn't worked.

"Does that happen often?"

Tom answered her. "I've seen a few crowd disputes but they're usually over before they really get any steam."

"You've got a bruise on your cheek."

"I do?" Surprised by Justice's growl, Fallon touched her face.

He caught her hand and moved it down. "Don't prod it. We need to get some ice."

"Want me to go back in and grab an ice pack?" Tom offered.

Fallon answered before Justice could. "That's not necessary. I really am fine."

Neither man agreed.

Even after they reached the parking lot, they both looked far too grim.

Why was Tom still hanging around? "Are you parked close to us?" Fallon asked.

He shook his head. "Got a second?" he asked Justice. "I mean, maybe after you get her seated?"

Justice's expression tightened even more, and he nodded. He treated Fallon like breakable glass as she got into the car, then he closed the door and walked a small distance away to where Tom waited.

Knowing they deliberately excluded her irked Fallon. She wanted to protest, but even more than that, she wanted to take inventory of her injuries.

She found a large purpling bruise on her shin and a peek in the visor mirror showed a nasty swelling on her cheekbone. Checking her hip would have to wait until she had privacy. She wasn't about to pull down her pants with people so close to the car.

She glanced up and found Justice watching her intently as he listened to whatever Tom said. By the second his expression darkened until he looked quietly enraged.

The two men finished their conversation, briefly shook hands, and Justice started her way.

Ho, boy. Fallon didn't know what had made him so angry, but she assumed she was about to find out.

SOMEONE HAD PUSHED HER.

Justice still couldn't wrap his mind around it. Why would anyone want to hurt Fallon? And how the hell did Tom know what Fallon didn't?

He'd already demanded she tell him what had happened, but she repeatedly insisted that she'd lost her balance in the crush. No one, she promised him, had pushed her.

He wanted to believe that—only Tom had been adamant. He claimed he saw it, Fallon struggling to reach the wall but two men had deliberately corralled her nearer and nearer to the steps, then shouldered her hard.

Picturing it put Justice in a murderous rage.

He'd fucked up, letting her out of his sight, and that pissed him off, too. They were almost to her house when he growled in accusation, "You were supposed to be holding on to me."

She stiffened with indignation. "I was until people got in front of me. How could you have not noticed that I was gone?"

"I felt a hand on my back and I thought it was yours."

She snapped back, "Great to know I'm indistinguishable from the crowd."

Justice drew a slow breath, reaching for calm. "You're distinguishable, believe me."

"Oh, really?"

With that sarcastic tone, she sounded as pissed as him. "Yeah."

"So when exactly did you realize I wasn't with you?"

He cleared his throat. "When the chick cupped me from behind."

Fallon went rigid and in a deadly whisper, asked, "She did what?"

Shrugging, Justice explained, "Reached down between my legs and grabbed a handful. I about jumped a foot." He glanced at her. "Knew right then it wasn't you."

Agitation narrowed her eyes. "Of all the—"

"She only copped a quick feel. Then I saw you were gone…" His own anger edged back in. "You could have been killed," he muttered.

"That's ridiculous. Bruised, yes. Dead? Doubtful."

Justice pulled to the side of the road less than a mile from her home.

"What are you doing?"

"I want to talk to you." *And touch you.* "I want this resolved before I let you go tonight."

"Justice." She softened her tone. "I promise, I'm fine."

Taking her hand in his, he kissed her sore wrist. "I should have protected you better."

A little breathless, she whispered, "It wasn't your fault."

He didn't remind her that she'd just been blaming him for not noticing sooner how they'd gotten separated. "Whether Tom is right or not, I want you to be careful."

"I'm always careful."

No, she wasn't. Her exuberance kept her wide-eyed with absorption, but not caution. At times it seemed to Justice as if she rushed to soak up as many new experiences as she could, as quickly as possible, as if she thought the opportunity would only last so long.

In doing so, she also gave him a new perspective. He began to notice things he'd long taken for granted.

Thanks to Fallon, he had a new outlook on life. Accepting the necessary changes he'd made came easier than expected. Hell, he was starting to feel as if he'd only just discovered what he'd always meant to be.

Featherlight, he brushed his fingertips over her bruised cheek. "I'm sorry." It pained him to see her hurt. He wanted to hold her close, and he wanted to rage.

If it had been deliberate, he'd damn well find out.

She leaned into his palm.

That simple show of trust did crazy things to him. "Fallon…"

"Hmm?"

Using care, he tunneled his fingers into her silky hair, then nudged her closer. Trying again, he said, "Fallon."

She stared at him with those big, dark eyes, making him hard with need. "Yes?"

"God, you tempt me." There, let her deal with that.

Her eyes widened in surprise, then grew heavy lidded in understanding. She looked at his mouth—and did the unthinkable.

She leaned toward him in silent consent.

"Damn," he whispered, already dragging her closer and pressing his mouth to hers. He started slow and easy, but when she made a small, hungry sound, his good intentions snapped. He tilted his head, nudged her lips open, and tasted her with his tongue.

So sweet.

Justice told himself to pull back, but Fallon settled her hand on his shoulder, lightly dug her fingers into his muscles, and it set him off.

Crazy how such a simple touch from her affected him.

The kiss was a little wild in ways he hadn't known were possible. He knew good old chemistry, but this was something else.

From a *kiss*.

Because of Fallon.

He was supposed to be protecting her, not pawing her in the front seat of a car.

But before he could think better of it, his hand was on her breast, lightly cuddling. God almighty, she felt good. Even through the layers she wore, her stiffened nipple grazed his palm and that, too, fired his blood.

Her gasp of surprise turned into a throaty moan, proving she enjoyed the touch as much as he did.

While teasing his thumb over one thrusting nipple, Justice pulled back and put his forehead to hers. Their heavy breaths mingled.

"We need to stop," he murmured low, trying to convince himself as much as her. Despite that, he continued to play with her, loving how she trembled, how she clutched at him. Her breasts were sensitive and he knew if he ever got the chance to have her, he'd enjoy spending an extra amount of time there.

He was just about to get it together and retreat when she touched her lips to his again.

Approval had never felt so hot.

The damned center console was in his way, but still he managed to kiss her firmly enough to press her head back against her seat. Needing to feel her skin, he reached for the hem of her shirt.

Getting under the oversize SBC fighter T-shirt was

easy, but she wore another shirt under that, tucked in. Continually kissing her and feeling like a bumbling high school boy again, Justice inched it away.

Fallon never once protested, but then, she seemed so involved in dueling with his tongue, so lost to sensation, Justice wasn't sure she even noticed.

When he finally stroked his palm over the soft, naked flesh of her waist—yup, she noticed that.

She jerked back with a yelp, frantically righting her shirts and retreating as far away from him as she could.

Justice was left holding air.

Breathing hard, he watched her, concerned, wary. "Guess I stepped over the line?" He wanted to kick his own ass. *Of course that was over the line.* Hell, he wasn't supposed to be kissing her, much less fondling her.

"I didn't realize... I can't..." She folded her arms around her middle and stared at him. "I can't."

Trying to figure out how to proceed, he nodded. "Okay." He had a raging boner and adjusted his jeans.

She watched his every move as if expecting him to pounce on her.

"I understand." He sat back, giving her as much space as he could. "Sorry. I didn't mean to rush you."

She said nothing.

Damn it, he couldn't take it and reached out to gently brush her cheek. "Honey, it really is okay. My bad. I shouldn't have let things get so far."

As if pained, she closed her eyes. "No, I'm the one who should apologize. I've overreacted. It's just..."

She looked so pained, he asked softly, "Just what?"

"I... I meant to talk to you. To explain."

He waited, but again she went silent. "You want to tell me something?"

"No. Not tonight." She dropped back in her seat, her posture far too defeated. Then just as quickly she sat forward and faced him. "Tomorrow. Could we talk tomorrow?"

Whatever it was, Justice didn't know if he wanted to hear it. "Sure. We're going to Cannon's, right?"

Immediately she shook her head. "No, it needs to be before that. Maybe over breakfast?"

Did she plan to fire him then? He probably deserved no less. Not that it'd matter. Whether working for her or not, he'd continue to protect her—and pursue her. At this point, he couldn't seem to help himself. "I had planned to do some gardening."

She blinked. "Gardening?"

"Yeah. The same time someone tossed paint on your driveway, my flowers got trampled."

"Flowers?"

Did she have to sound so disbelieving? "You know those colorful things you plant around the bushes?" He lifted his chin. "My mom and granny got them for me as a housewarming gift, so I used them in the landscaping. If Mom finds out they got destroyed, it'll upset her. So I'm going to replace them before she has a chance to visit." Defensively, he added, "I don't want her upset."

Very slowly the shock left Fallon's face and her brows

pinched down. "What do you mean they got trampled?" And in a higher pitch, she added, "On *purpose*?"

"Looked like."

Getting riled, she demanded, "Why didn't you tell me?"

Confused by that reaction, Justice shrugged. "You had enough on your mind."

"Enough on…"

Sighing, he draped an arm over the steering wheel and looked her over. "You keep repeating my words. Did a little groping cause that, or was it the kissing?"

She drew back. "Neither!"

"Settle down," he soothed, relieved that she was no longer so withdrawn. He'd take her irritation over shock any day. "I just wondered."

"You had no right not to tell me! If your flowers were sabotaged, there's a good chance the two incidents are related."

Was there any doubt? "I assume so." Which meant there was definitely a threat, whether she wanted to see it or not.

As if she'd read his thoughts, Fallon huffed. "You keep thinking someone is harassing me, but did it occur to you that *you* could be the one being harassed?"

Justice snorted. "No." But now that she said it… He considered it only a second or two before saying, "I'm not worried about me. I can handle myself."

"Apparently you can't handle your flowers."

Boy, she really was in a snit. To smooth things over, he said, "Sorry I didn't tell you. You're right. The more you know, the more cautious you'll be." Hopefully, anyway.

The annoyance faded under grudging acceptance. "Thank you."

To seal the deal, he added, "If I get done in time, I can come by early and we can talk then."

He watched as she chewed her bottom lip.

"Or," she offered, "I could help you plant tomorrow?"

She looked very uncertain, as if she expected him to refuse. Shoot, he'd love the company. Problem was, a woman like Fallon shouldn't be digging in the dirt, especially not with her bodyguard. "I have about three dozen flowers to get in the ground and it's going to be warm tomorrow."

"I won't wilt."

He thought about it for only a second. He could best protect her by keeping her close—and yeah, that excuse worked as well as any, and was definitely more acceptable than just wanting her company. "If you're sure you don't mind, then I can pick you up in the morning."

Amazingly, her face lit up. "What time should I expect you?"

Damn it, he badly wanted to kiss her again. He had enough sense to resist, but it wasn't easy.

After they made their plans, he drove the rest of the way to her house and walked her up to the door. With his hands in pockets to keep from touching her, he said, "Put some ice on those bruises, okay?"

"All right." And still she stared up at him.

"Good night, Fallon."

Her gaze went to his mouth. "Good night." In a flash, she went on tiptoe to kiss him. Just a warm touch of her mouth to his before she darted into the house and shut the door.

His hands were still in his pockets, but a smile split his face.

Amazing how something so wrong could feel so right.

GODDAMN IT, HE needed this win.

Rising frustration burned in his guts. Things weren't working out as quickly as he needed them to and his patience wore dangerously thin.

He was a man of action, a man who made things happen, but all he could do now was stay vigilant until he found the leverage he needed.

Why wouldn't Justice get on board?

Why did he have to be so goddamned stubborn?

By pure luck, he'd gotten ahead of them today. He'd waited in a driveway, headlights off, and he'd planned a clever accident for when Justice's car got close.

When they'd pulled over to the side of the road, he'd gotten diverted. From the bright moonlight, he'd watched them making out.

Interesting.

Apparently, the girl's spill down the stairs had sparked Justice's possessive instincts after all.

When they'd finally driven on, he'd made the split-second decision not to interfere. He'd hold on to his plans for the accident and use it another, more propitious night. The stakes grew higher with time, and that was in his favor.

Now that he knew he could use the girl as motivation, he didn't want to rush and risk a misstep.

He needed to plan carefully.

Finally, everything was falling into place.

CHAPTER TEN

FALLON KNELT IN the soft grass, gardening gloves on her hands, surrounded by pots of daffodils and pansies.

She loved Justice's home.

It was a moderately sized ranch with three bedrooms, two bathrooms, a one-car garage and a front porch that ran the length of the house.

"I painted everything after I moved in," he explained while opening a bag of fertilizer. "Used to be this dull army green."

"I love the yellow with white trim. And the black roof and shutters are classic. The front door is really beautiful, too. Is that also new?"

"Yeah. Used to be just a plain door, but I put in the sidelights and transom."

"It looks amazing."

Crouched next to her, Justice sat back on his heels. "The whole house is about the size of your garage."

"Size doesn't matter."

He snorted. "Depends on who you ask."

Catching on to his thoughts, she ducked her face. "You know what I mean."

"I do." He studied her. "The amazing part is that I think you really believe it."

"Of course I do." Carrying on a normal conversation wasn't easy. Today Justice wore athletic shorts and sneakers. When he'd picked her up, she'd admired his white T-shirt, but as soon as they reached his house he'd peeled it off and she admired his bare chest so much more.

The sight of him was enough to make her breathless. Add in the stirring aroma of his skin, amplified by the bright morning sunshine, and it was a wonder she could string together two words.

When she saw his mouth curl into a smile, she realized she'd been staring and quickly cleared her throat. "Besides, if you recall, that's my parents' house, not mine." She placed a cluster of daffodils into the prepared hole and gently pressed the rich soil around it.

Justice, too, got back to work and without looking at her, he said, "It's the type of house you're used to."

Is that what he thought? That she expected a mansion throughout her life? Softly, she shared a confession. "I've stayed there because it meant so much to Mom and Dad. But when I imagine moving out—and I will, eventually—it isn't into a mansion."

"What do you imagine?" he asked.

She glanced up at his home. She really did love it and the neighborhood seemed nice. The houses weren't too close together, but children would have friends to play with and that was a bonus.

But to be honest… "I've always thought about living someplace remote. Where I could step outside and there wouldn't be anyone around to see me. I could come and go without being…noticed."

He thought about that, nodded, and asked, "Why?"

With one plant done, she scooted down to work on another. The silence stretched out, but Justice didn't press her.

He'd always been patient. Too patient.

Fallon really wished he'd prod her. Now, in the light of day, she dreaded the talk and needed the encouragement.

"I'm just private." *Liar.* Being private was very different from hiding.

"Did your mom see your bruises?"

Glad for the temporary reprieve, Fallon shook her head. "She was asleep when I got home, and I was asleep when she left this morning. She peeked into my room long enough to tell me she wouldn't be home until supper. My father will be home by then, too." Using the back of her hand, she brushed perspiration from her brow. "Just as well that I tell them both together. They tend to flip out whenever I get injured."

"You've been injured before?"

A perfect opening, but her courage fled. Putting all her concentration on carefully removing another flower from a plastic pot without damaging the roots, she said, "If I skin my toe, they carry on."

He nodded. "Want me to stay with you when you explain?"

That was the nicest offer she'd ever gotten. Justice was her bodyguard, but he was also the most down-to-earth person she'd ever known. He'd kissed her. Repeatedly. And now he offered to face her disgruntled parents with her.

Her reticence melted away and she whispered, "Remember that talk I wanted to have?"

His head jerked up and he stared at her. "Yes."

She hadn't been prepared for that reaction. He'd seemed so relaxed about it, almost disinterested. But at the first mention he bit.

Because she couldn't maintain eye contact, Fallon went back to planting. It'd be easier if she wasn't looking at him when she bared her soul. "I had a sister who died in a fire."

Very gently, he said, "I knew that."

"You did?"

He nodded. "There weren't many details to be found. I'm guessing your folks kept as much of it out of the news as they could."

Fallon let a humorless laugh escape before she could stop it. *Dig*, she told herself. *Plant. Focus on something other than his sympathy.*

She moved on to a pansy. "It was five years ago. We were—"

"We?"

He'd jumped on that clarification pretty quickly. But then, she'd already noticed how he stayed so attuned to her.

A lump formed in her throat. "I was there." Because she concentrated so closely on the plant, she didn't realize Justice had stood and was now behind her, not until he caught her upper arms and pulled her to her feet.

He didn't force her to face him, but he did caress her, his big hands warm on her shoulders. "Go on."

Resisting the urge to lean back against him, she drew

a breath and whispered her explanation. "It was five years ago. I was nineteen and Cindy was twenty-one. She was always a little…freer than me. Where I was shy, she was the life of the party."

"Were you close?"

"Very." Her smile hurt her heart and her voice cracked. "She wasn't only my older sister. She was also my best friend and my hero." It took several gulping breaths before she could admit the truth. "It's my fault she's dead."

Justice stilled, his hot hands firm on her shoulders, before pulling her closer. In a low, soothing voice, he asked, "Will you tell me what happened?"

Giving herself time to regain her control, Fallon nodded. It felt odd to stand out in the open, in Justice's small yard with other houses nearby and neighbors passing by, while talking about such a life-changing moment.

But she did it anyway—because he deserved to know.

"My parents had bought some new lakefront property. It came with a small fishing cabin. They planned to build a nice vacation home and figured the contractors could use the cabin until that was done, then they'd have it torn down. But since it was there, Cindy decided she and I should have a girls' weekend away."

"Just the two of you?"

"Yes." A bee buzzed near Fallon's face and she waved it away. The sun was so bright, almost blinding, giving her a good excuse to close her eyes. "We'd packed a bunch of junk food and our bathing suits and planned to just catch up. She'd been abroad and I'd missed her, so it sounded like a wonderful plan. Dad didn't like the idea much but we convinced him. And Mom always thought we were safe together."

Justice wrapped his arms around her, hugging her back to his chest, his chin on top of her head. "What happened?"

"Cindy brought a few joints and I was…shocked."

He hesitated. "It's not uncommon for someone her age—"

"I know. But Rebecca Rothschild Wade's daughters did not smoke pot." Another smile took Fallon by surprise. "That's what Mom said whenever we did something she disapproved of. I once got a D on a paper because I hadn't studied, and she gave me this look, then said, 'The daughter of Rebecca Rothschild Wade always does her best—and, Fallon, this is not your best.'"

Justice nuzzled her temple. "I like your mom."

"Me, too."

"So you girls were cutting loose a little, having fun, and something went wrong?"

"I didn't cut loose," she protested, twisting to see him. "I've never in my life smoked pot."

He smoothed back her bangs. "Such a good girl."

"No," she whispered. "I wasn't." A deep breath helped her to continue. "Cindy was teasing me, trying to egg me into trying it, calling me chicken and Goody Two-shoes. I decided to get even, so I went to the front window and pretended our parents had showed up. I acted all panicked, like we were caught."

Justice kept her close. "But they weren't there?"

"No. We were still very much alone on a deserted country road in an isolated area on a lake."

Worry darkened his expression. "Shit."

"Yeah." An understatement. "Cindy panicked, which cracked me up because she was twenty-one and usually did whatever she wanted. But like me, she didn't want to upset Mom. So she tried to throw everything in the trash."

Justice guessed, "Only the ash was still hot and the trash caught on fire?"

"It spread so fast." Fallon hated to relive it all. She saw again the flames licking out from beneath the cabinet, the way Cindy tried to drag out the can but ended up tipping it over. "Everything was so old and brittle, it seemed one moment I was laughing at her, and then suddenly the fire went everywhere. To the cabinets and walls." Her throat closed up. "On Cindy."

Justice crushed her close. "God, babe, I'm so sorry."

She fisted her hands against him. "I tried to help her, but I couldn't get the flames out and then she wasn't moving. I couldn't breathe. I couldn't breathe!"

Justice rocked her, his hold tight. "Shh. I'm so sorry. It's okay now."

"I got hurt. Cindy died and I got hurt."

He froze.

"I left her, Justice." Tears ran down her face and she choked with shame and remembered pain. "I left her."

"You escaped," he insisted.

If she'd kept her head, they both might have lived. But instead, she'd left her poor sister behind in a shack engulfed in flames.

Justice gave her a small shake. *"You survived."*

True, she had. And she didn't know if she could ever forgive herself. "I got as far as the porch before the over-hang caved in on me." Memories flowed over her and she absently rubbed her shoulder. "I got pinned for a minute by burning wood."

Horrified, Justice stared down at her. In a tortured rasp, he asked, "Burned?"

She pushed back from him, one step and then two. Making herself look him in the eyes, she nodded. "My shoulder and part of my chest."

Breathing harshly, he listened, his gaze never leaving hers.

"In the car...when you touched me..." There was so much emotion in his face, but she didn't know how to read it. "I didn't want to take you by surprise."

Very slowly, he inhaled, then reached out a hand to her.

Uncertain, wary, she accepted, twining her fingers with his.

He tugged her in close, pressed his mouth to her forehead, her bruised cheek, then briefly to her mouth. "Will you show me?"

HER HAND, SO SMALL in his, trembled just a little. The look on her face...so much devastation broke Justice's heart. He wished for a way to change the past, to make it easier for her, but she'd so obviously suffered, not only the physical pain but the emotional torture she'd put herself through since then.

His heart beat heavily as he led Fallon into his house.

He didn't take her far, stopping just inside the closed front door. He'd given her a tour earlier, not that there was that much to see. But having her near his bedroom, even for those few minutes, had truly tested his resolve.

He sang a litany in his head: she wants to talk, she wants to talk.

If he'd known what she had to say, he'd have been better prepared. But he never would have guessed...

"Will the rest of the flowers be okay?" She shifted, crossed her arms and uncrossed them. "We should probably get them into the ground. Or at least set them in the shade. If you want, I could—"

By cupping her face and kissing her, Justice ended her nervous questions. It wasn't a hungry kiss, but one that, maybe, showed her how much he cared.

Against her lips, he rasped, "It's killing me, honey."

She tentatively flattened her hands to his bare chest. "What?"

"Thinking about you hurt." Closing his arms around her again, he pressed her head to his shoulder.

"Mother was hurt more." Her fingers, cool against his feverish skin, idly stroked him. "She had to make funeral preparations from the hospital."

When her voice broke, Justice damn near broke, too. He tangled a hand in her hair, squeezing her a bit more, needing the contact, wanting to get her as close to his heart as he could.

"She never left me. Every time I opened my eyes she was there. If she didn't know I'd awakened, I'd catch her crying very, very quietly. But...but as soon as she'd see me, she'd smile and touch me and tell me she...loved me."

Tears stung Justice's eyes and he fucking couldn't bear it. God, what her mother must have gone through. No one should ever have to be that strong. And her dad... Mr. Wade was so controlled, so dignified, but Justice knew the guy had to have broken down. How could he not?

As if she'd read his thoughts, Fallon whispered, "Dad was there a lot, too. He always looked so grim, so heart-sick. But he, too, would smile at me—like somehow everything would be okay."

Her voice had faded until Justice could barely hear her. "I respect your parents a lot."

"They're amazing." She hesitated, drew a breath. "I was in the hospital for three weeks, so I missed the funeral. It was the only time I was there alone."

And it was probably the worst time to be alone. Not that it could have been helped. His heart ached for her and for her parents.

Justice didn't think about it. He just scooped her up and headed to the couch, then sat down with her in his lap.

Fallon didn't complain. She settled against him with a sigh. "I haven't talked about it much. Mom and Dad... it hurts them still. And not many other people know about it."

"When Leese and I did research, we didn't see anything about you being hurt."

She lifted her head to look at him. "Leese?"

"Yeah, remember we bodyguards do some background checking before taking a case." And going forward, Justice would remember how thorough that important step should be. "Leese is better at it than I am, but he didn't see anything about you being hurt. If he had, he would have told me."

"Money can buy a lot of privacy," Fallon said. "Hired guards stood watch outside my room while I was in the hospital so no one could come up to ask me questions without Dad knowing. There was already too much about Cindy...dying."

She had a hard time saying it, Justice noticed, as if the pain from the loss was still fresh.

"People speculated on how Mom and Dad might feel, and reporters constantly tried to get the inside scoop. Because of who he is and his financial influence, Dad had to make a statement, but he didn't mention me. He didn't want me put under the spotlight, too."

"It was a very personal matter," Justice agreed. "No one else had the right to prod any of you."

She nodded, waiting a moment or two, then whispered, "I wanted out of that hospital so badly, but they couldn't do the skin graft for seven days. Burns like mine require wound care first. Because of the damage... from the fire..."

Justice stroked her hair.

"The wounds can worsen for the first few days."

So even after she was safe in a hospital, her injuries didn't improve? As she talked, she seemed calmer about it and he wondered if she'd gotten to share with anyone. Getting things out in the open, his mom always said, was the best way to deal with them.

But if her involvement in the fire was kept secret, and her parents were so obviously grieving, had Fallon been given the chance to talk to *anyone*?

Somehow he didn't think so. "Will you tell me about it?"

"Why?"

"Because it happened to you, and I care."

She watched him, maybe gauging his sincerity, then nodded. "When they took the skin from the donor site, in a lot of ways that was more painful."

"Worse than the burns?"

She nodded. "They take that whole top layer of skin, down to the nerves. The nerves are alive and exposed—"

Jesus. He hugged her again.

Suddenly she skipped ahead, maybe sparing him some of the uglier details. "When I was finally able to go home, I still had a month of care, and I had to wear a compression vest and sleeve for what felt like forever."

"How long?"

She wrinkled her nose and admitted, "More than a year."

He whistled low.

Fallon surprised him with a half smile. "They weren't very comfortable, but they supposedly helped with scarring."

It wasn't the physical scarring that concerned him. "You're okay now?"

Her brows twitched, like maybe she thought he didn't understand. "Yes, I'm fine." Then she stressed, "But I'm *scarred*."

Though Justice didn't give a shit about any stupid scars, clearly Fallon did. "Where?"

She touched her shoulder and partially down her chest toward her breast. "Those are the worst ones." Glancing at him, she smoothed a hand over her thigh, too. "I've got another one here, but not from being burned. It's the donor site, where they took skin from my thigh to graft onto the burns."

His big hand settled over her thigh. "I hate that you had so much pain." Then, before she could say anything, he asked, "Will you show me?" To him, the best way to prove to her that it didn't matter was to get it out in the open. After that, they could move on.

Her gaze clashed with his. She looked horrified by the idea of baring herself to him. Horrified, but also resigned.

Eventually she nodded. "If you really want to see."

Oh, he wanted to see every single inch of her. And since the burn marks were such a problem for her, they'd start there. "I do."

She warned, "I won't drop my pants."

"Spoilsport," he teased, trying to lighten her fatalistic mood.

Her mouth opened, she paused, then closed it. It took her another second to say, "I can open my shirt."

Justice nodded. "Yeah." He had to be a heartless perv because even now, with such a sensitive concern for her, he felt himself stirring. Hell, he couldn't joke with her about dropping pants and opening blouses without getting a little turned on. He wouldn't do a damned thing about it, but it was happening all the same.

She sat up on his lap, half facing him, and her fingers went to the buttons on her shirt.

He held his breath.

Timidly, she opened one button, peeked at him, then opened another. He could see her upper chest now and just a hint of cleavage.

Keeping his hands to himself wasn't easy. He really wanted to help her hurry along. Being passive while a woman on his lap undressed was a new thing for him.

But then, a woman like Fallon was new, too, and he'd never dealt with an issue like hers.

Attempting to relax, he hooked one hand around her waist, leaving the other to rest on her thigh.

Sounding hoarse, he said, "You don't have to be shy with me."

"It's not that," she promised. "It's just…"

Heightened awareness had a stranglehold on him. "What?"

"They're ugly."

"They're just scars," he chided.

"Marcus thought that, too, until he saw them, then—"

"Fallon."

At his gentle rebuke, she lifted her brows.

"Don't compare me to that dick, okay?"

Nodding, she squared her shoulders, opened three more buttons and with a lot of palpable dread, pulled the loosened material down her right shoulder, taking her bra strap down at the same time.

Justice had difficulty getting his gaze off her face. She looked to be in an agony of suspense while she awaited judgment.

Silly woman. Finally he looked down.

He could only see a little of the mark, and as he'd suspected, it looked like what it was—scarring. He wasn't squeamish about it, and to prove it to her, he lightly traced the uppermost raised edges of her skin with a fingertip.

She would have recoiled, but he spread his fingers open on her back and kept her still.

Because he couldn't see much of it, Justice asked, "How big is it?"

Hesitantly, she opened three more buttons.

The puckered, damaged skin spread out in an arc over her shoulder, midway down her bicep on her arm, over to the bottom of her collarbone and feathered into the swelling of her breast. The skin was thicker, a darker pink, little tails reaching out in different directions.

Seeing the evidence of what she'd suffered made Justice swallow hard. Only the fact that she might misconstrue sympathy or concern kept him from reacting in any way.

"Anywhere else?" he asked.

Her confusion obvious, Fallon shook her head. She was so stiff that she looked ready to break. "Well, on my thigh. I told you that." Strain left her voice thready. "It's not as irregular."

He started to say more when he heard a car pull into his drive. He glanced through the window and saw Leese parking.

Before he ran out of time, Justice carefully pulled the material back together and closed the buttons.

"Justice?"

He drew her in for a soft kiss before explaining, "We have company."

She blinked fast. "We do?"

He smiled at her obvious confusion. She'd had herself all prepared for him to react a certain way, but he hadn't and now she didn't know what to say or do. No doubt she wondered what he thought, but she wasn't ready to hear the truth, and he needed time to figure out his next move.

"Leese is here." He lifted her to her feet just as the knock sounded on the front door. Stepping around her, Justice opened it.

"We have to talk," Leese said as he stepped in—then drew up short when he noticed Fallon. He stalled. "Sorry. I didn't realize you had company."

Fallon blurted, "We were planting flowers."

Biting off his grin, Justice nodded. "Yeah, that's exactly what we were doing."

Leese elbowed him. "Don't embarrass her, you ass." He turned to smile at Fallon. "Ms. Wade. How are you?"

"Fallon, please. And I'm well." She flashed a worried, uncertain look at Justice. "I'll just…go work on the flowers while you two talk."

"I'll only be a minute," Justice promised.

Once she'd politely pulled the door closed behind her, Leese slowly turned to stare at him.

"Shut up."

"I didn't say anything."

"But you're going to." Justice walked over to the window and saw Fallon standing there by the flowers, staring down at the grass, unmoving. Something inside him shifted, as if making room for unfamiliar emotions. It wasn't a comfortable feeling—but it wasn't bad either.

"She was in the fire," Leese said.

If he expected a big reaction, he'd be disappointed. "Just found that out for myself."

"She told you?"

"Yeah." Justice headed into the kitchen for a drink. "She has some scars and is really touchy about them."

"From what I read, it was pretty damned awful."

It was, but Justice felt the need to protect her privacy. "What'd you find?"

"One of the companies her father owns did a small report about it, mostly to let other employees know so they could share their condolences. Mr. Wade found out and squashed it, but you know how that goes. Digital trails are never completely erased."

"Her father didn't want her hassled. I don't blame him."

Leese leaned against the kitchen counter while Justice poured tea. "I wanted to talk to you about something else, too."

Determination rushed through Justice. He hated that Fallon had suffered, that she undervalued her physical appeal now, and he really wanted to go stomp on Marcus because he just knew the bastard had further damaged her delicate ego. Even more than that, he wanted to prove to her that the scars, no matter how harsh, in no way detracted from her appeal.

However, he didn't want Leese to know anything about it, so he shrugged and said, "Shoot. I'm all ears."

"I heard she took a fall down the steps last night."

"Yeah." And Justice really felt guilty about it. "I thought she was right behind me but—"

Leese interrupted to say, "Someone called the agency with an accusation."

Justice paused with the tea halfway to his mouth. "The hell you say. Who called?"

"Anonymous."

Very slowly, he set the tea aside. "To accuse me of *what*?"

Leese shook his head as he stepped away from the counter. "The guy who called claims he saw Tom with Fallon."

A smoldering anger softened Justice's tone when he asked, "Doing what?"

"Well…" Leese rubbed the back of his neck. "Supposedly he was giving her a shove—down the stairs."

FALLON TRIED TO hide her hurt as Justice unexpectedly hustled her to the car and drove her home. He'd been in such a rush to get rid of her, he'd barely given her time to wash the dirt from her hands.

When she'd protested that there was one more flower to go in the ground, Leese offered to do it.

But damn it, *she* wanted to plant that flower.

And she wanted to know Justice's thoughts.

He'd looked at her, at the evidence of her burns and what she'd caused to happen five years ago…but he hadn't said a word. Was he repulsed?

No. Justice wasn't like that.

But had his interest turned to pity? That she could believe. Above all else, Justice was protective. He'd seemed as bothered by the retelling of the ordeal as she'd been.

So what had she expected to happen? For him to tell her it didn't matter? To say he would overlook the fact that he was her bodyguard and she was a scarred mess and that they'd…what?

Date?

Humiliation left her sick to her stomach. She was a complete fool to think—

"Thanks for planting the flowers." Reaching across the seat, Justice took her hand.

She badly wanted to hang on to him, to draw on his strength, but instead she squeezed his hand, said, "No problem. I enjoyed it," and pulled away.

He was so lost in thought, he barely seemed to notice. She wasn't used to him being this remote. Even that very first day, he'd been more…personal.

As soon as he pulled up in front of the house, she removed her seat belt. "You don't have to walk me in."

He scowled and put the car in Park. "Yeah, I do." He got out and crossed around to her even though she'd already left the car and was halfway up the steps.

When he reached her, he took her elbow. "Fallon—"

Oh, God no. She couldn't hear this, not yet. Not now. She turned to him and forced a bright smile. "Make sure you water those flowers when you get home. I'd hate for them to all die. Your mom wouldn't be happy."

He quirked a smile. "Can't have her unhappy."

She waited.

Suddenly his cell pinged. He pulled it from his pocket for a quick look, scowled some more and said,

"I gotta run. Thanks again, honey." And with that, he turned and left.

He hadn't mentioned going to his friend's tonight. Did he plan to cancel? Given his rush in leaving, she should probably assume so.

Of course, she could ask… *No.*

It was all she could do to hold it together. If she started asking questions, she'd force him to make excuses.

She couldn't go through that again.

Glad that her parents weren't yet home, Fallon watched Justice drive away before going inside, doggedly climbing the stairs to her bedroom, then sitting down to cry.

CHAPTER ELEVEN

JUSTICE STRODE INTO the rec center, his gaze scanning the interior as he looked for Tom. He didn't notice anyone else or anything else, so he was surprised when suddenly Armie stood in front of him. He almost plowed him over.

Mildly, Armie said, "Justice. What's up?"

"S'Tom here?" He continued to look past Armie—until his friend stepped closer. Backing up a step, Justice barked, "What the hell?"

Still casual, Armie asked, "Can I talk to you a minute?"

"I'm busy."

"Let's talk." He gave Justice a shove toward the front desk, away from the workout gear and padded mats crowded with fighters, both new and veteran.

Frustrated, Justice decided it'd be easier to deal with Armie than ignore him. He found an isolated corner and turned to say, "Make it quick."

Armie nodded. "Want to tell me what's going on?"

"No." Bristling with impatience, he asked, "S'that it?"

Shaking his head, Armie denied him. "Sorry, dude, but the thing is, you look ready to commit murder and

I have a class of kids coming by in an hour. Don't want them to have to wade through blood and guts and shit like that, so take a breath, get a grip, and tell me what's going on."

The hell he would! "None of your business."

"It is if it involves the rec center."

Justice growled. Armie might be smaller than him, but that didn't make him small. He was the best fighter Justice had ever known. Lightning quick reflexes, unending endurance, deceptive strength and a twisted sense of loyalty to his friends.

Which meant he wanted to save Justice from himself.

Sighing, Justice gave up and explained what had transpired.

Armie listened, nodding occasionally, then asked, "Remember what I told you about facing off with a real asshole?"

"Yeah. Keep my cool."

"You are currently not cool, Justice."

Couldn't argue with that. Hell, from his toes to his ears, he was bunched up and ready for violence.

Didn't faze Armie though. "I'm not buying that Tom had anything to do with it, and until you have proof, you shouldn't buy it either. Anything anonymous pisses me off."

"Yeah, that part pissed me off, too."

"Looks to me like every part pissed you off. But my point is that you shouldn't put too much stock into an anonymous accusation."

"I didn't." Or had he? "I was just going to talk to him."

"Fine. Talk to him, hear what he has to say. But it's guaranteed he's going to blow up—same as you or I would over an accusation like that—so *you* have to keep it together to get the facts."

Justice hated to admit it, but Armie made sense.

"Can you really see Tom hurting a woman?"

Not really. But the bastard was awful pushy about a rematch. Justice drew a deep breath, let it out real slow and felt some of the tension seep from his muscles. "Got it. Now get out of my way."

"He's in the locker room." Grinning, Armie clapped him on the shoulder and warned, "Know this, Justice— if any punches get thrown, I'm going to stomp both of you." And with that he returned to instructing some newer fighters.

Justice barked a short laugh. Now that he'd cooled down, he had to admit he appreciated Armie's interference. He didn't want to cause a scene, especially with kids coming in soon. It was a known fact that any dishonorable behavior at the rec center could get a guy kicked to the curb.

When Cannon had started the club, the primary use was for the guys to train. But because of Cannon and Armie, who were longtime best friends, it had soon become an integral part of the community. Now fighters at every level trained there, women took self-defense classes, at-risk kids had an outlet and positive influence, and it all appeared seamless because everyone took turns helping out by teaching, cleaning and training.

Though he was MMA's fastest rising star, Armie was still the one who usually organized everything.

He had more energy than any three people combined and shared a special affinity for the rec center's origins and purpose.

With a new mindset, Justice started off again. He'd talk to Tom, gauge his reaction and then decide what to do.

Steam filled the locker room when he walked in. Fresh from a shower, Tom sat on a bench wearing only jeans while he pulled on shoes and socks. He glanced up, said, "Hey, Justice," and went back to dressing.

Same congenial greeting as always.

Folding his arms over his chest and leaning back against a set of lockers, Justice studied him.

Brows lifted, Tom sat up straighter and asked, "What?"

"You said Fallon was pushed down the steps."

"Elbowed. Some scruffy little dude who disappeared right after."

"You didn't bother to grab the guy?"

"With Fallon tumbling down the steps? I was more concerned with getting to her."

Justice slowly nodded. "You were there, looming over her, when I reached you both."

"I wasn't looming, you ass." Starting to sound irritated, Tom said, "Everyone knows she's with you."

Well, hell. "I'm her bodyguard."

"Yeah, keep spinning that tale if you want, but no one's buying it." Tom eyed him. "Gotta admit, she's different from the usual babes you like."

Since he didn't want to compare Fallon with the very

casual relationships he'd had in the past, Justice bypassed the comment. "So why were you trailing her?"

"I wasn't." Tom sat straighter, his brows knit together. "Okay, so I was hoping to chew your ear a little more, try to talk some sense into you about the rematch. But then I saw Fallon veer off from you. Right after that, she started getting jostled and down she went. Hard as she fell, I didn't know if she'd broken anything or knocked herself out."

That all sounded plausible. "You think the guy elbowed her on purpose?"

"Sure looked like it to me."

"Seems like a hell of a coincidence that you were right there when it happened, but didn't grab the guy who supposedly caused her fall."

Slowly, Tom came to his feet. "If you're accusing me of something, get on with it."

Justice could see the anger starting to spark. Tom had never had great control. As to that, Justice often didn't either, but he was learning. From Leese, from Armie. And good thing, too, because a showdown between two pissed-off heavyweights didn't always end well. "Just asking."

"You know what?" Tom stepped closer, his stance combative. "I *did* watch her once I saw she was alone and looking a little lost. Where the hell were you, Justice?"

He rolled a shoulder. "We got separated. Soon as I realized it, I backtracked to get her."

"Not in time."

Justice couldn't deny that.

Crowding closer still, Tom growled, "You should be thanking me for being there. She might've gotten trampled otherwise."

He was so obviously looking for a fight, Justice had to wonder if Tom would stoop that low just to get his attention, to maybe force a confrontation. Anything was possible, and when it came to Fallon's welfare, he planned to cover all his bases.

Without retreating, Justice relaxed his stance in a deceptive way.

If Tom lunged, he'd flatten him.

"Someone," he said casually, watching Tom's reaction, "called the agency where I work."

"Yeah, who?"

"Whoever it was didn't leave his name."

Bristling with impatience, Tom waited.

"The caller said you were with Fallon."

"You already knew that. I was..." Blank surprise wiped every other emotion off Tom's face, quickly replaced with indignation. "Wait a minute. You accusing me of something?"

Justice stared at him.

Clenching with outrage, Tom said, "If you think I had anything to do with her getting hurt—"

Justice relaxed. Tom suddenly looked apoplectic, and not with guilt but insult. "You didn't push her?"

"No, I didn't fucking push her! *I don't mistreat ladies!*"

"Take it easy."

"You take it easy!"

Justice laughed. Good thing Armie had forced that

little talk on him or they'd be throwing punches right now. And where would that get him? He didn't really suspect Tom, not anymore, but he wouldn't entirely let him off the hook either, not until he found out what was going on.

"Relax," Justice said. "Given the information I have, I had to ask."

"I will not relax!" Tom practically heaved with fury. "How the hell would you feel if I accused you of doing something like that?"

"I'd be pissed." Because Justice knew for a fact he'd never hurt a woman.

Tom threw up his arms in an "exactly" pose. "Going after your lady would be chickenshit."

"Agreed."

"I'm not chickenshit."

Justice shrugged. Eventually Tom would understand that he wouldn't get a qualifying fight in the cage, so maybe he thought to rile Justice by using Fallon. Would he be content with an old-fashioned beat down in private, out of the limelight?

"I'll take you at your word," Justice said.

"Well, hallelujah, you prick."

"But stay away from Fallon."

Justice's attitude only infuriated Tom more.

Not that Justice cared. Because if it wasn't Tom, he'd need to figure out who *did* push her—and why someone wanted Tom blamed.

A FEW HOURS LATER, when her mother checked in on her, Fallon pretended to be napping. She didn't want her

mother to see her swollen eyes. Tears were useless—
she knew that, and she was now ashamed that she'd
given in to them.

She had no intention of sharing her grief with her
mother or father. It would only upset them. She'd
learned years ago how badly they reacted to any show
of sadness.

Keeping her eyes closed, Fallon expected her mother
to turn around and leave—instead, she sat on the side
of the bed and shook her.

"Fallon, wake up!"

The urgency in her mother's tone startled her and
she came up to an elbow before she thought better of
it. "What? What's the matter?"

Her mother got one good look at her and sat back in
horror. "You've been crying!" She looked more closely,
then gasped. "And dear God, you're bruised!"

Rushing to reassure her, Fallon explained, "I fell,
that's all. I'm fine."

Her mother scowled with accusation. "If you're fine,
then why have you been crying?"

No immediate answer came to mind, so Fallon
stalled. "Why did you wake me, Mom? What's wrong?
Has something happened?"

As if only then remembering, her mother stood and
said, "We'll talk about your fall later. Right now you
have to hurry. Justice is downstairs and he's talking to
your father." She added with emphasis, *"Alone."*

A dousing with ice water wouldn't have been as
shocking. "Justice is here?"

"Yes. He wants to see you, as well, but first he said he needed a private word with your father."

No way. Fallon threw back the covers, stood, and then paused. Confusion warred with urgency. "Did he say what he wants?"

Her mother shook her head. "He didn't, but he looks different and very determined, and he was insistent that he had to talk to Clayton first before I came to get you."

Dejection made her chest tight. Justice was here to quit. Sinking back to sit on the side of the bed, Fallon folded her hands and concentrated on not looking lost. "I can't interrupt them."

"Why not?"

She sighed, searched for an out, but finally decided that she'd have to tell the truth. "I showed Justice my scars."

Her mother's eyes widened, then immediately softened. "And?"

"I don't know."

Her mother quickly sat beside her and took her hand. "Tell me everything that happened."

It was beyond embarrassing, but Fallon needed someone to talk to, so she shared it all without admitting that Marcus had seen them first, or his reaction.

"Justice was silent all the way home." Fallon drew a breath. "I think…I think he's probably quitting."

Her mother pushed to her feet. "Go down there and confront him. Tell him you deserve to know what he's doing."

"Mom! I can't do that."

"Oh, yes, you can, young lady!" She tugged Fallon to her feet, quickly smoothed her hair, straightened her now wrinkled clothing and stepped back. "There. Much better."

Fallon knew that was a lie. She looked horrible. "Mom—"

"You will get yourself downstairs this instant, young lady. Rebecca Rothschild Wade's daughter does not cower in her bedroom."

Hearing her mom reprimand her like a schoolgirl, Fallon half smiled. "I'm not a child any longer."

"Exactly. Now let's go."

Before Fallon could think of a way to dissuade her mother, she had the door open and was prodding Fallon into the hall. She was so emotionally distraught, it seemed easier to give in than to fight her mother.

In the end, what difference would it make if she heard from Justice face-to-face, or if her father had to explain things to her?

Halfway down the steps, raised voices caused Fallon and her mother both to pause. *Justice and her father were arguing!*

The men were in the dining room. Through the open archway, Fallon could see Justice's profile—and his appearance further shocked her.

He'd shaved! Gone was the sexy scruff she liked so much; his goatee was now neatly trimmed. And…and his hair was cut short to the same length all over, eliminating his messy fauxhawk!

She blinked twice trying to take it in.

In his usual jeans, but with a black polo shirt that

hugged his massive shoulders, he still looked gorgeous, yet also very, very different.

What did it mean?

And then she heard him say, "Quitting is the only option."

Even though she'd expected it, the truth hit her so hard, she had to slap a hand to her mouth to keep from making a sound.

How had he come to mean so much to her in such a short time? *Why had she so stupidly let that happen?*

"I'm paying you," her father insisted.

Above her hurt, Fallon's pride rebelled. She would not let her father beg for Justice's service.

"This is pointless," Justice replied, just as irate. "Whether you pay me or not, I'm not budging. I'd be looking out for her anyway. It's personal now, not business."

Wait...*what*?

Trying to understand, Fallon gulped in air. How could he be her bodyguard if he quit? She glanced at her mother, and found her smiling. Even more confused now, Fallon turned back to stare at Justice.

"You say that like it's your decision," her father barked. "Fallon has some say in this, too, you know."

"I'll convince her." Justice folded his arms in what she now recognized as an arrogant and determined stance. "And since I'll be dating her, it'd be ludicrous for you to pay me as a bodyguard."

Dating her?

Before she fell down the steps in an ignominious heap, Fallon hurried down the rest of the way. "What's going on? Justice, what are you talking about? Why are the two of you shouting?"

Justice turned fast, saw her face and scowled. "What happened to you?"

Her father pushed rudely past him. "You've been crying."

"Crying?" Justice repeated. Then he glared at her father. "You made her cry?"

"Me?" He glowered right back. "I've only just gotten home!"

Her mother said, "I believe it was you, Justice, who did the damage."

"Mother!" Fallon knew a blush would add nothing to her ravaged appearance. She was such an ugly crier. With the very first tear her nose turned red, her eyes got puffy and blotches marred her cheeks.

"Dear God." Slowly, her father stepped closer, his gaze examining her face. With blood in his eyes, he pivoted to face Justice. "How did she get bruised?"

Fallon couldn't believe the level of accusation in her father's tone. "I fell down some steps, Dad, that's all."

"You *fell*?" he asked, incredulous.

"Yes, and it's absurd for you to act like Justice had anything to do with it."

"It is partially my fault," Justice said, willingly taking blame. "I should have had hold of her—"

Her father gaped at him, maybe because he didn't want Justice holding her.

Before this debacle could get any worse, Fallon redirected a frown at Justice. "We should talk privately."

He shook his head, refusing her, then wagged a finger from her to himself and back again. "Something's going on between us. You know it as well as I do. I'm trying to be upfront with your folks about it."

Furious, her father said to her, "He took advantage of you, made you cry, allowed you to get hurt and now he wants to quit."

Her mother said, "Hush, Clayton. Let them talk."

"He wants to talk about *dating* her!"

"Yes, I know." Unlike her father, her mother sounded pleased.

"He is completely unsuitable—"

"That's enough!" Not about to let her dad interfere, Fallon huffed out a breath. "Justice did not take advantage of me, falling was my own fault and if he wants to quit, well—" It would break her heart, but she didn't want to guilt him into staying.

Justice took a step toward Fallon. "I know it shouldn't have happened, honey. On every level it was wrong. But I'm already more than a bodyguard and we both know it. I'm tired of being hampered by ethics."

"Of all the—"

"Clayton," her mother snapped, her voice shrill, "I told you to hush!"

He clamped his mouth shut and settled on an evil scowl.

Justice and Fallon both ignored her parents.

"I'll talk to my boss tomorrow, tell her how I screwed up and accept the consequences there. But understand, Fallon, regardless of anything else, you're stuck with me."

"Stuck with you?" She had a hard time taking it in.

"Yeah." He came closer still. "Whether Sahara black-balls me out of the industry, or your dad kicks my butt to the curb, even if you don't want to see me on a more personal level, there's no way in hell I'm going to let anything happen to you."

Her mother sighed happily.

"You can't just shadow her," her father barked. "It's absurd."

Justice touched her face, skimming his fingers over her bruise. "Why were you crying?"

No way would she explain it to him now, not with her parents both watching so avidly. "Would you step outside with me?"

He nodded. "After you tell me I can quit our business association and move on to a personal relationship."

Her teeth locked. She did not appreciate the forced confrontation.

"I want you protecting her," her mother said, smoothing over the moment. "Especially with that confusion the other night."

"Confusion?" Her dad jumped on that. "What confusion?"

"I'll explain in a minute," her mom said to soothe him before turning back to Justice. "However, I agree with Clayton. We must continue to pay."

Justice took a hard stance. "I'm not accepting your money."

"You," her father snapped, "signed a contract!" Then he stomped away.

"There, that's settled." Fallon's mother hugged her, and surprised Justice by hugging him, too. "I'm so pleased." She turned and went after her husband, already detailing the issue with the paint, the added camera on the driveway and Justice's concerns.

Justice cursed low, his demeanor rife with frustration. "Your parents are going to be really disappointed when things don't go their way."

Fallon's heart tripped with uncertainty and with… hope. "Meaning?"

"I won't take money to be with you. It wouldn't be right." He stared at her intently, his voice going gruff. "Ah, babe, I can't bear to see you cry."

"I'm not." Not anymore, though she knew she still looked hideous.

His fingers brushed over her cheek. "It hurts that much?"

"I'm not a wimp." Insulted, she attempted to explain. "It wasn't the fall. It's just that I thought…the way you brought me home, and you were so silent, I wasn't sure…" She sighed. How could she find out what was going on if she couldn't even finish a coherent sentence? Everything felt so awkward. She detested making a fool of herself. She detested the idea of not seeing Justice.

She detested being a coward.

As if it were the most natural thing in the world, Justice gathered her into his arms and pressed his warm mouth to hers, lingering for several seconds. His hand cradled the side of her face, his touch so incredibly gentle.

"I don't understand," she finally said, and to get to the point, she stated, "You saw my scars."

"Yeah, I saw them."

His matter-of-fact acknowledgment only bewildered her further. "I have more," she thought to remind him. "On my leg from the donor site and—"

"I know." His hands, so big and hot—*she loved his hands*—stroked up and down her back while his breathing went deeper. Against her lips, he murmured, "I want to see that one, too."

All but smothering in confusion, Fallon stared up at him. "Why?"

"They're a part of you, and every part of you fascinates me." He kissed her again, stroked her bottom lip with his tongue, then lightly tugged on it with his teeth.

"Justice…"

Almost in accusation, he said, "You opened your top and I got hard, babe. I *hate* that you were hurt. I wish I could take the memories from you. But damn, did you really think a scar or two would matter so much?"

Of course she did, because the scars had mattered to everyone else. They obviously repulsed Marcus, despite his current regret and assertions that they didn't. Seeing them still made her parents weepy. And the memories associated with them… She swallowed hard, nodded and said, "Yes."

He gave her a small, sexy smile. "I'm just a man, and anytime a gorgeous woman starts opening her top, I react." Voice even lower, he confessed, "If I hadn't gotten away from you, I'd have done things ass-backward, shaming the agency and myself."

"What do you mean?"

His hands went suggestively to her hips as he looked down her body. "If you'd dropped your pants…" His nostrils flared with a deep breath, then he half laughed as he let it out. "It's a fact I wouldn't be able to keep my hands off you."

So even after seeing the disfiguring marks on her, marks that spread out to one of her breasts, he still wanted her?

"I'm trying to be honorable and upfront," Justice asserted. "That's what you deserve."

Fallon really needed clarification. "You weren't…" How did she ask him? "That is…"

His mouth took hers again, a little hungrier, a little less restrained. When he pulled back, he rasped, "You're killing me here, honey."

She blurted, "You want me to believe the scars didn't bother you at all?"

"They almost leveled me." He closed his arms around her, hugging her in close to his broad chest. "If I could somehow go back in time and take the hurt for you, I swear to God I would." Levering her back again, he gave her a look so serious, so stern, she held her breath. "But in no way did they make me want you any less. Hell, I'm not sure anything could."

Fallon thought of the scars, of what he'd seen and how he'd reacted, and she badly wanted to believe him.

His dark eyes stared into hers. "Tell me you want me, too, and I promise I'll prove it to you."

She nodded in quick confirmation. "I do." As soon as the words left her mouth, heat filled her cheeks. That sounded far too much like an acceptance of marriage. "I mean—"

Smiling, Justice gave her a quick smooch. "Too late

to take it back now." He smoothed a hand over her hair. "We need to get going if we want to make it to Cannon's on time. You about ready?"

Oh, good grief! "We're still going there?"

"You don't want to?"

"I do!" Damn it, she'd said it again. "I just thought—"

"A bunch of nonsense, that's what you thought." His gaze moved over her, but he didn't seem repulsed by the signs of her tears either.

Apparently, nothing bothered him.

"I'd like you to get to know the guys even better, and their wives will be there again. You like everyone, right?"

"Yes. They're all very nice."

"They're the best." Obviously relieved, he brushed a thumb over the corner of her mouth and asked, "You ready to go?"

Fallon loved how he kept touching her, like he couldn't resist. He made her feel pretty, when she knew she currently looked wretched in every way possible. "No, of course I'm not ready."

As if he really didn't see it, Justice asked, "Why not?"

She had to laugh. He was such an elemental male, so accepting, that he lightened her world just by being in it. "I'm a total wreck, Justice, that's why. I have to change my wrinkled clothes and repair my face and..."

"You're beautiful," he whispered.

Those words were so soft and earnest, she could have sworn her heart melted. "Justice—"

"Every part of you, Fallon." Looking and sounding

utterly sincere, he teased her lips with a butterfly kiss. "I'm going to keep saying it until you believe it."

Hand to her mouth, she half cried, half laughed. "You're nuts."

He leaned closer to whisper, "Let's blame prolonged horniness, okay?" With a light swat on her butt, he added, "Now get a move on before your folks come back to grill me again."

"Five minutes," she promised, and ran up the steps, anxious to return to him.

Today, she decided, everything would be different.

MARCUS CHECKED HIS WATCH, then stared at his two companions. He grew impatient waiting for them to negotiate the lofty proposal for their participation. "I have to get going soon." He knew they would reject his first request, but he also assumed they'd give something, even if it was more meager than what he'd asked for. In business, Marcus had always found it beneficial to start high and gradually concede, rather than start out too low.

"Meeting up with your girlfriend?" Kern Arnold, the oldest of the two brothers, asked as he closed the file he'd been perusing. Kern turned to his brother, York. "What's her name again?"

"Fallon," York supplied with a sly grin. "And she's a cutie."

"She is," Kern agreed, resting his arms on the table. "Cute, apparently smart and obviously from a good family. She's a catch, Marcus."

Marcus detested these personal questions, but he wanted the contributions Kern and York would give to the literacy fund-raiser. God knew the men could afford it.

At the MMA fights, they'd wagered twenty grand as if it were nothing, and when Kern lost to his younger brother for the third time in a row, he'd only laughed. Apparently York was on a winning streak, because he'd ribbed Kern mercilessly. Marcus was far from a pauper, but still it boggled his mind to see how easily the two men tossed around money.

With a benign smile, Marcus corrected the assumptions. "Actually, I'm meeting with Ms. Wade."

"Ah, the cutie's mom?" York asked.

"Yes." Marcus nodded to the file. "I'm working with her on the fund-raiser."

"Finding a way to edge back in, huh? Clever," Kern praised. "If the mom approves of you, the daughter will be more inclined."

"Actually," Marcus said, his jaw tensing, "I sincerely wanted to help."

York slapped him on the shoulder and laughed. "What about that big bruiser with her?"

"I told you, he's her bodyguard."

"Uh-huh." York bobbed his brows at his brother. "Looked to me like he was guarding every inch of her body."

"Seemed to be loving his job, too," Kern added with a chuckle.

More irate by the moment, Marcus held silent.

"Who was that other fighter we met? Tomahawk, right?"

Something in the way York asked that, as if he held

a private secret, put Marcus on edge. He replied with a clipped, "Yes."

"Tomahawk wants the bodyguard back in the cage. Just think, if he succeeds that'll leave sweet Fallon yours for the taking." Kern gave him a steely-eyed stare. "You could swoop in and be the little darling's protector."

"He could score big," York added, "especially if she's got real need of protection."

Marcus stared at the brothers while fighting the urge to react. Though he recognized there were subtleties afoot that he didn't entirely understand, he still detested hearing the two men discuss Fallon with so little respect. Never mind that he'd screwed up; he still cared for Fallon—for her whole family—but he also wanted the security that would come from such an alliance. One way or another he'd get her back. When she was his wife, spoiled rich boys like Kern and York wouldn't dare malign her.

He forced a smile. "Fallon and I have a history. It'll work out eventually. Now, about the fund-raiser—"

"Count us in," Kern said, sliding the folder back toward him.

Terrific. More than ready to wrap it up, Marcus segued straight into his sales pitch. "If you're ready to commit an amount—"

"The proposal works fine."

Incredulous, Marcus slowly withdrew while searching their faces. Wondering if this was more bullshit, he asked, "All of it?"

"Sure."

York added, "From each of us."

Stunned, Marcus gathered his thoughts. He couldn't keep staring like an idiot. "I see." But to be sure, he opened the file and turned the final figure toward the two men. "You understand—"

Kern gently closed it again and smiled. "We understand perfectly, and we're on board."

Marcus had no idea what to say. He'd have been happy with half as much from one of them, not the full amount from both. "I…" *Shut up and be grateful*, he warned himself. "Thank you. This is wonderful."

York shrugged. "It's a tax write-off."

"Well, whatever your motives for such generosity, I'm very grateful." They were right that getting on Mrs. Rothschild Wade's good side would aid his cause to win back Fallon. Since both ladies cared deeply about the less fortunate, this would be an amazing start.

As if he'd read Marcus's thoughts, Kern smiled. "Let me know when and where you'd like us to present the checks."

Easy, Marcus thought. Maybe *too* easy. Yes, the brothers threw around money, but usually with a wager attached. However, he wouldn't question his good fortune too much.

He didn't want them to renege.

After quickly discussing the arrangements and gaining their signed commitments, Marcus left the bar.

The brothers were spoiled, but he smiled because for once their money would go to very worthy causes—the fund-raiser…and his own.

CHAPTER TWELVE

JUSTICE LEANED AGAINST a deck post, a beer in hand, and watched while Leese, Catalina, Stack and Vanity chatted with Fallon. It warmed him, seeing his friends become hers.

She deserved more friends. Good friends—like his.

"Did you notice she's as far from the bonfire as she can get?" Armie sounded both curious and puzzled.

Yeah, he had noticed. Fallon had subtly nudged her lawn chair backward—farther and farther—until she was a good ten feet behind everyone else. Without questioning her, the others had gradually relocated, too.

They kept her surrounded and distracted and, in their own unique ways, protected—though they might not realize it.

Miles watched her intently. "Whenever the fire pops, so does she." Even as he said it, wood crackled and Fallon jumped.

But she didn't leave and the pride swelling inside Justice amplified every complicated feeling he had for her until he damn near shook with his need. He'd have to get her alone, and soon. He wanted her—more than he could ever recall wanting anyone or anything.

Armie and Miles stood with Justice, talking quietly

while they took turns grilling hamburgers—and noticing Fallon.

They were each still looking at her when Justice explained, "She doesn't advertise it, but she was burned once."

Miles jerked around to stare at him, a frown in place. "Bad?"

Justice couldn't think about what she'd suffered without a resurgence of rage, empathy and an overwhelming desire to shelter her.

"Bad," he quietly confirmed. "Physically and emotionally." So others wouldn't overhear, he explained in a low voice what Fallon had gone through. "When I saw the setup for the party, I told her we didn't have to stay, but she wanted to, even insisted on joining the others around the fire."

"She has guts," Armie remarked with admiration. "I like her."

Miles nodded. "Me, too."

Justice didn't mind admitting it. "I more than like her."

Brows raised, Miles asked, "Is that allowed?"

"Because I'm her bodyguard? Probably not." Justice scrubbed a hand over his face. "For sure, Sahara is going to have a fit."

Armie grinned. "She doesn't know yet?"

"I told Fallon's parents today. They finally accepted it—I think." In fact, Rebecca had seemed to be on his side. Not that he needed their agreement or support, because he'd have gone after Fallon either way. "Tomorrow, first thing, I'll tell Sahara. I figured I should do it face-to-face."

"First Leese and now you," Miles laughingly complained. "I was thinking of checking out the whole bodyguard gig, too, but the boss lady isn't going to like her track record with fighters."

Justice assumed Miles was joking—hell, he still had a long fight career ahead of him. Sure, he'd taken some serious hits in his last fight, but he'd still won.

With concern shadowing his features, Armie stared toward the group around the fire. "It doesn't feel right, letting her do this. Look at her face. She's almost panicked."

True, and her panic put a vise around Justice's heart. More than anything he wanted to go to her, scoop her up and take her away from the source of her torment.

But he also wanted more than that.

"She needs to talk about it. She hasn't had much opportunity to do that. Even when she told me, I could tell it was new for her. For so long now she's kept everything bottled up and I think it's past time she let it out."

"It was a secret?" Miles asked.

"Of sorts," Justice admitted. "Her folks get upset if she mentions it." Before either man could get too riled about that, he added, "They're off-the-charts protective now after losing their other daughter and seeing Fallon so hurt. I'm not sure any of them have really recovered."

"It'd be tough," Armie admitted.

"Her dad was trying to shield Fallon when he kept all mention of her out of the news. He was dealing with his older daughter's funeral and with Fallon in the hospital

and his wife's grief...he wanted to spare Fallon from reporters, and in doing that, only a few people even knew
she'd been hurt. She couldn't talk about it with anyone
even if she'd wanted to."

"Jesus," Armie whispered. "Her poor folks."

"Yeah."

"Good intentions," Miles noted. "I can't even imagine what they were suffering."

"Pure hell." Justice stepped away from his friends
and loaded up two hamburgers. "Don't say anything to
her yet, but if she gives you an opening—"

"We'll be all ears," Armie promised.

"Make sure you don't show her any pity. She'd hate
that."

"Have you told the others?" Miles asked.

"No, but feel free. Just be discreet. I want her to feel
accepted, not like the center of gossip." Justice headed
off with a plate of food for both of them, drinks in his
other hand, and on his way he announced to the collec-
tive group, "Food's ready."

That got the desired effect. Everyone headed for the
grill, giving Justice a few moments alone with Fallon.

She'd just stood up when he reached her and, hands
full, he bent down and settled his mouth over hers with
new possessiveness. Knowing others might witness the
kiss didn't bother Justice.

He wanted everyone to know about this new facet
of their relationship.

As a couple, Fallon would have all the acceptance,
backup and loyalty that he had from his friends. She
deserved that, and more.

At first she was stiff with surprise, but she quickly melted against him, her hands sliding up his chest and around his neck.

Feeling her small, warm body pressed to his, Justice almost dropped the food, then he caught himself and lifted away. "Hi."

Still leaning against him, her eyes heavy, she smiled. "Hi."

"I missed you." He kissed her again, briefly this time, and then handed her the drinks.

She looked at them a moment before catching up. From the light of the bonfire, Justice watched the blush tinge her cheeks. She took the beers from him.

"If you don't mind sitting here, I'll join you."

"It's fine."

No, it wasn't. Now that he'd reminded her of the fire, the wariness came back into her gaze. "We don't have to stay."

"I want to." She sat down in her lawn chair and took the plate from him so he could pull a chair closer to her. "Could I ask you something, Justice?"

He settled himself beside her. "You can ask me anything."

She surprised him by reaching over and stroking a hand over his smoothly shaven jaw. "Why did you change so much?"

"Change?"

Her smile was gentle and curious. "The haircut, the close shave, the shirt?"

"Well now, honey, I wasn't just wooing you, was I?"

He picked up a loaded burger. "Had to win over your folks, too."

"So you did it for them?"

"For you." He took a big bite while watching her, encouraging her to do the same.

She nibbled—and waited for an explanation.

After he'd swallowed, Justice opened a beer for each of them. "Just one for me—I'll be driving, and only one for you 'cuz now I know you can't hold your liquor." He leaned closer to whisper, "And I want you clearheaded for later."

Immediately diverted, she whispered, "Later?"

"When I plan to kiss you head to toes."

She flushed…with interest. Swallowing, she looked around to ensure no one had overheard, then jumped back to her original question which, honestly, Justice had hoped to avoid.

"So you changed everything—"

"Not everything. Not how much I want you. Not who I am." He scratched his chin. "I just figured it might be easier for your folks to swallow the idea of you and me together if they knew I wasn't totally irredeemable. I mean, a shave and haircut isn't much, but it shows compromise, right?"

"I don't want you to change at all."

He smiled, inside and out. "No?"

"Everything about you is appealing. The scruff you wore before, and the way you're shaved now. The messy fauxhawk and the shorter hair. Whatever you wear—" she slanted him a look "—or don't wear, I already like you." She took a shaky breath, her attention on her burger. "I just thought you should know that."

The smile spread into a satisfied grin. Damn, but she pleased him. "So if I don't shave every day, or my hair gets shaggy again, you won't mind?"

There was a load of emotion in her eyes when she looked up at him. She started to say something—

And others joined them.

Justice assumed Miles and Armie had filled them in on Fallon's background, but it didn't show. They didn't treat her any differently. But he noticed that a few of the women mentioned their own backgrounds, the difficulties they'd faced—and how they'd gotten beyond them.

Armie, too, talked about his dad, a subject that had once been very taboo but seemed to come easier to him these days now that he was a father, too. All in all, they created an atmosphere of camaraderie that felt both safe and accepting.

Fallon listened to each person with genuine concern and caring. She didn't shy away from their confessions, but she also didn't get too nosy with her questions.

Justice wasn't disappointed that Fallon hadn't yet chimed in; she needed time, he understood that.

But tonight, he felt, was a good start.

Tomahawk showed up an hour or so later, along with a few of the newer fighters. Everyone who joined them brought along beer or snacks and soon everyone was mellow from food, drink and friendship.

A million stars hung in the dark sky. A gentle breeze teased the air. All around them crickets sang.

And Justice was so horny, he could barely breathe.

It was nearing midnight when he decided he couldn't wait any longer.

The bonfire had died down and no one seemed interested in keeping it blazing. Some people had already left with the designated drivers, and the remaining couples were cuddled up together, talking quietly. Occasionally a soft laugh filled the air.

Justice lifted Fallon into his lap and nuzzled her neck with damp kisses. "You ready to go?"

The question, along with the intimate familiarity, left her muddled. "I… That is…"

Deliberately, he'd put his mouth near her burn scars. He needed her to know that he found every inch of her sexy.

Cupping a hand to her cheek, he encouraged, "Say yes."

She let out a shaky breath and nodded. "Yes."

Justice had to grin. Her reply had sounded like an answer to a lot more than what he'd asked. "I have a few things to say, but it'll wait until we're alone in the car."

Their goodbyes to the others took them a few minutes more. As usual, all the guys had to hug her, most of the ladies, too. This time, though, Fallon seemed more at ease with it.

Soon as that was done, she eased close to his side again. He put an arm around her shoulders and together they walked to the side yard.

It was as soon as they rounded the house to the front that Justice saw the dark Corvette parked on the street.

The same car that had tailed them days before.

After taking quick inventory of the other vehicles

and assigning each to the people he knew, he jerked around to stare at the backyard—and realized Tom had arrived last. So was it his car?

Was it Tom who'd been following them? Was he possibly the one who'd…

But why? What was his end game?

Justice remembered that Tom was with Fallon when she fell—or was *pushed*—and his fury expanded.

"Justice?" Fallon peered up at him, her skin pale in the wash of moonlight, her eyes huge and luminous. "Is something wrong?"

The moment she spoke, he realized that he'd tightened his hold on her. Immediately, he let up, saying, "Everything's fine." He needed to corral his rioting thoughts and temper his automatic anger until he could talk with Tom.

It wouldn't be tonight. In fact, he thought, maybe he shouldn't say anything at all. He'd keep Fallon safe, so he knew no harm would come to her. And maybe if he gave Tom enough rope, he'd either hang himself, or prove his innocence.

Justice decided he liked that plan. Tomorrow, after he fessed up to Sahara, he'd discuss this new twist with Leese. Maybe Armie and Cannon, too, since they'd be around Tom more often.

"Come on." He walked with Fallon across the dew-wet grass to the curb where he'd parked. Keeping watch up and down the street, he unlocked the door and waited while she got settled inside, then went around to the driver's side.

Justice waited until he'd pulled away from the curb

and driven two blocks before speaking. "I don't want you to be nervous."

She folded her arms around herself and, after glancing at him, looked out the windshield. "I'm not."

"Fibber," he teased. His heart pounded, he was already half-hard, but he didn't want her to be uncertain with him. "You know I want you, Fallon. So damned much. But that doesn't obligate you in any way. If you'd rather take this slow, I understand. It's your show, and if you want some time to think about things—"

"Things?"

Thinking about it stirred him. "Hot, sweaty, naked sex. With me."

When she drew in a sharp breath and blinked fast, Justice realized he shouldn't have been so blunt.

He smiled crookedly. "Sorry, honey, but no one's ever accused me of being smooth. You already know I want you. But I want you to want me, too. And until you do—"

"I do!" Then she frowned. And laughed. "Why do I keep saying that?" She didn't give him time to answer. "I want you just as much."

Justice blew out a relieved breath. "Best news I've heard in a really long time."

"It's just…" She waffled, cleared her throat. "The thing is, I've never… I mean, I almost did with Marcus, but then—"

"Yeah, let's don't go there, okay? If I hear the history of you and Marcus, I might get the urge to stomp on him a little, and I'd rather talk about you wanting me." He considered what she'd said. Curiosity and need sharpened to an acute ache softened only by tenderness. "You're telling me you're a virgin?"

She rushed into defensive explanation. "I was young, and then I got burned, and—"

"And you'll have to trust me that any guy would have been thrilled to get you horizontal."

She bit her lip and fell silent.

Sooner or later, Justice knew he'd get her to believe him. For now, though, she needed to know he understood. "But yeah, I get it. You've been reserved for a while." He shifted, wishing he could ease the restriction in his jeans because now he had a full-blown boner. "I get to be your first?" To himself he thought, *your only.* "Gotta say, that's pretty freaking awesome."

With a jittery laugh, she pressed her hands to her cheeks. After a moment or two, she asked around a relieved grin, "You really think so?"

Almost too turned-on to talk, Justice rolled one shoulder. "I mean, if you weren't, I'd be okay with that, too. God knows I'm as far from a virgin as a guy can get."

A scowl overshadowed her grin.

That made him chuckle. "I'm thirty years old, honey. I hope you weren't expecting a monk."

She put up her chin. "I'm not dumb. Of course I expected you to…have experience."

Done with that topic before he ruined her agreeable mood, Justice said, "So what do you think? My house?"

"Okay."

That squeaky voice got to him and he glanced at her. "In case you're wondering, I'm not going to rush you right to bed." No, he'd do a lot of kissing and touching first.

"Okay."

Still squeaky. He almost grinned, but instead shifted the subject to give her a different focus. "How weird will it be for your folks if you don't come home tonight?"

That stumped her. "I don't know. I've never done that."

Amazing. He knew she was twenty-four, almost twenty-five, but her life had been on hold for so long. Softly, Justice suggested, "You wanna call them and let them know?"

Watching him, she asked just as quietly, "Will I be spending the night?"

Hell, yeah. "I'd like for you to."

"You're sure?"

Justice gave it some thought. He hadn't made a habit of sleepovers. Whenever he did spend the whole night with a woman, it was out of convenience, and never with a woman like Fallon. More often than not, he leaned toward female fans who just wanted a notch on their bedpost. Like him, they wanted a little fun, a little relief and nothing more.

For so long, his focus had been on training. But not anymore. Now he could look at other things, like the future.

"Yup, I'm sure. Even if you aren't ready for everything I want—" *and he wanted a lot* "—I'd still enjoy keeping you close."

"You want me to sleep with you even if we don't..."

When she trailed off, Justice nodded. "Even if we don't have sex. What do you think?"

Reaching out, she lightly touched his shoulder. Her voice was as gentle as her touch. "I think I want everything, and yes, I'd love to stay over." She withdrew her hand and pulled her phone from her purse, then hesitated. "What should I say?"

Hell, he had no idea, not with parents like hers. "When I was nineteen and still living at home, and I knew I'd be out all night, I'd call my mom so she wouldn't worry." He glanced at Fallon. "I already told you she's an award-winning worrier, right? Anyway, I'd just hedge all her warnings by promising upfront that I'd be safe, I'd use protection and I'd be home for breakfast. That was her cue not to wait up for me."

"Would she do that?" Fallon asked with a smile. "Wait up?"

"Nah, but there were a few occasions when I forgot to call. I'd get home in the morning and she'd be passed out on the couch, snoring real loud, then she'd jerk awake with a start and almost fall on the floor. She'd start right in giving me hell and swearing she hadn't slept a wink all night." He laughed remembering it. "No matter how big I got, she claimed she could still give me a whoopin' if I needed it." The laughter faded to a slight smile. "So I tried to remember."

Fallon sighed. "My parents are nothing like your mother. They really might stay up and they'd be thinking every terrible thing you could imagine."

"Yeah, and I guess the same reassurances wouldn't work for them, right?" When she looked puzzled, Justice said, "You'll be safe, I'll use protection and I can have you home in time for breakfast if you want."

Fallon laughed and blushed, and in the process turned him on even more.

"You are so pretty."

She ducked her face, but he could see her mouth curling over the compliment. "Thank you." She touched in a number and put the phone to her ear. After a moment, she said quietly, "Hi, Mom. I'm sorry if I woke you. Yes, everything is fine. I just wanted to let you know that I'll be out the rest of the night." She listened, gave a slight nod. "Yes, I'm still with Justice. He thought I should let you know so you wouldn't worry." She glanced at him, her gaze playful. "Yes, he is very sweet."

Justice felt awkward as hell listening in. It was a first, hearing a girl call her mom to make her excuses. Hell, not since high school had he dated anyone who still lived at home.

Fallon glanced at him. "Okay, yes, I'll tell him. Love you, too. Good night."

"You woke her up?" he asked as he made the turn onto the street where he lived.

"I think so. But she wanted you to know that she appreciated your consideration."

No recriminations? Rebecca was astute, so she had to know how the evening would roll out. She couldn't be happy that Fallon would be with a man like him—that is, unless she preferred him because she knew he'd protect Fallon.

It was something to think about—but later. Right

now, as he reached his driveway, the last thing he wanted to think about was Fallon's parents.

Using a remote, he opened the garage door and drove in.

Fallon was remarkably silent.

Wooing was not his strong suit, Justice knew. Before now, it had never been necessary.

After he turned off the car, he paused with his hands on the steering wheel, his grip tight as he tried to find the right words.

Fallon's seat belt clicked as she released it, and the light flashed on when she opened her door and stepped out.

Well hell. She was moving faster than he was!

Justice quit worrying about rushing her as he hurried from the car.

FALLON DIDN'T WANT to acknowledge her own uncertainty. After all, Justice was definitely different from Marcus. The two men didn't have a single thing in common, so it stood to reason that Justice's reaction to her scars would be different.

But fears weren't rational.

He'd already seen the worst, she reminded herself, and hadn't in any way appeared repulsed. Encouraged by her internal pep talk, she promised herself it would be okay—if she could just get her erratic heartbeat to slow down a little.

The garage opened into a short hall between the dining and living room, leading into the kitchen.

"Want a drink?"

She shook her head. "No."

His boyish smile took her by surprise. "How about a kiss, then?"

"Yes." When he kissed her, she couldn't think enough to worry.

Slowly, right there in the hallway, he pinned her to the wall. With excruciating buildup, he settled his hot mouth to hers in a damp, firm kiss. At first, he indulged a gentle exploration, his lips teasing over hers, his tongue touching her bottom lip, lightly dipping inside.

The way his hard chest pressed to her breasts made her nipples grow tight. Somehow, in some subtle way, he insinuated one thick thigh between hers—then pressed against her. Fallon ached, already wanting, needing, more.

Coasting her hands over his bulging shoulders, she thrilled at his strength and the flex of firm muscles. He crowded in closer until she felt surrounded by him and the press of his big body curled her toes.

His mouth opened hers with ease and his tongue stroked deeper, hotter.

God, he tasted good and smelled even better. She deeply inhaled his wonderful, stirring scent, then arched up against him, asking for more.

With a hungry sound, Justice held her face in both of his hands and ravaged her mouth. His tongue thrust in to play with her own. She couldn't think and didn't want to. Loving how out of control he seemed, Fallon wrapped her arms around his neck and held on.

Long minutes later when he took his mouth to her throat, he whispered, "God, you're hot." He drew her skin in against his teeth, making her inhale sharply at the pleasure.

Justice had it wrong. It was his mouth, his damp tongue and his hard frame that was hot.

Near her ear he breathed, "I want to fuck you, Fallon."

No one had ever spoken to her like that, and hearing it now, in such a gravelly voice, thrilled her.

He grazed the edge of his teeth down the side of her neck to a sensitive spot where it met her shoulder, then gave her a sizzling love bite.

In reaction, her nails bit into his shoulders.

He lifted away to look at her and her knees almost buckled.

Justice had the most beautiful, sinfully compelling eyes, currently filled with raw hunger.

His gaze moved over her face, repeatedly lingering on her mouth until he touched it with gentle fingertips. "I also want to treat you carefully, love you slowly and kiss you everywhere."

Her heart went into double-time.

Locking his gaze with hers, he whispered, "I want to make this so good for you, Fallon."

Holding on to him, trying to catch her breath, Fallon knew what she wanted: for him to not stop. She tried a smile to reassure him, but breathing was tough enough. "Honestly, I'm good with either way."

That heart-melting smile of his made him almost too gorgeous. "Beautiful, sexy and a real sweet-talker. Damn, Fallon, could you be more perfect?"

That sobered her mood. "I'm not perfect," she whispered. "You know that."

"Close enough to level me." Leaning down slowly this time, Justice nibbled along her jaw, her throat, and as he pulled the neckline of her shirt aside, he licked her neck. She felt the rasp of his tongue and his hot breath.

She hadn't realized her neck would be so sensitive. The way he drew on her skin kept her heart slamming in her chest. When his teeth tugged on her earlobe, she groaned softly.

She felt one of his big hands going down her spine all the way to her backside. He cuddled her, made another rough sound and came back to her mouth, but not for long.

Grabbing her hand, he started for his bedroom in a long, hurried stride.

Breathing hard in anticipation, Fallon laughed and rushed to keep up.

CHAPTER THIRTEEN

JUSTICE KNEW HE was about to lose it. Damn it, she deserved better than a wham-bam quickie, but it was all he could do to keep from having her there in the hallway. He wanted her naked, him naked, skin on skin.

He wanted to slide into her, feel her squeezing him tight.

And he wanted it *now*.

The bedroom, he decided. He at least had to make it to the bedroom—even though it felt too damned far away.

He got her into the room, closed the door and very deliberately put a little space between them. He couldn't touch her. Not yet. If he felt her softness, he'd cave again and be all over her.

Even amid the raging lust, he knew getting her clothes off was important. She had to know—had to *see*—that he wouldn't be put off by her burns.

Hell, at the moment, a tornado might not dampen his need.

Had he ever wanted a woman with this much desperate, clawing need? Maybe his first, but he doubted it. He knew what blind lust felt like, but this, with Fallon, was hotter, stronger, deeper.

It almost overwhelmed him.

As if she needed the support, Fallon leaned back against the wall, her chest billowing with her fast, deep breaths. Her heavy lidded eyes watched him closely, her expression sultry.

Justice held her gaze as he peeled off his shirt and tossed it aside. Sitting on the bed, he removed his shoes and socks. His attention never left her.

If she got skittish, he needed to know.

As she stared at his naked chest and shoulders, her lips parted and she breathed faster. She put a hand to her throat, her cheeks flushing. He stood again, and her concentrated gaze dropped down to his abs.

God almighty, he loved the way Fallon looked at him, with so much innocent, curious fascination. He was so hard that he strained his jeans. Knowing what would happen, what he'd do, that he'd soon be over her, sliding into her, made his muscles clench.

When he just stood there, letting her look her fill and trying to regain some control, she encouraged, "Go on."

Justice tried and failed to hold back his grin. "Jeans gotta stay on for now, babe. At least until you catch up." Once his pants were gone, he'd be gone, too.

In every way, Fallon was a priority—even over his own pleasure. He wanted her to enjoy every second of what they'd do.

She stared at his crotch and Justice felt himself twitch. Much more of that and he'd lose the battle.

"Okay." Lifting a hand, she touched the buttons at the top of her blouse.

"No." Anxious to fulfill a private fantasy, he stepped

toward her. "Let me." He'd been dreaming about stripping Fallon bare since the day they'd first met, and by God, he'd savor every second of it.

She went still, a little wary.

"Keep breathing," he instructed, wanting her as into it as he was.

She nodded, and tensed up even more.

Instead of making a beeline for the buttons, which would quickly leave her exposed, Justice held her face in his hands and spent some time plying her soft, damp mouth with heated kisses. Not a chore at all; the lady had an *amazing* mouth, and the taste of her…

Thinking of her taste made him throb. He couldn't wait to lick, suck and nibble on every inch of her fragrant skin, and he would; her breasts, her belly…between her soft, tender thighs.

He held back the groan the visual caused.

Fallon's skin was warm and silky and he wanted to rub himself all over her.

Lazily, as if he wasn't on the verge of exploding, he cupped a hand over her left breast—for the moment, steering clear of her scars. Even through her bra and shirt, he found her stiffened nipple with his thumb and strummed over it, drawing it tighter.

She ended the kiss with a sharp breath.

Intent on devastating her, Justice took her mouth again. With a tilt of his head he deepened the kiss, eating at her soft mouth until she melted against him. Carefully, reining in the lust so he could go slowly, he slipped his hand under the hem of her shirt. He forced himself to go slow, to be content stroking his fingers over her narrow waist, absorbing the warmth of her skin before sliding his palm up her side, feeling her through her bra, teasing his fingertips over the upper swell—and then, with only the barest hesitation, he tucked his palm inside to hold her bare flesh.

She quickly ended the kiss again to stare at him with dark, dazed eyes, hazy with need.

Forcing the sturdy bra cup lower, Justice cuddled her breast in his hand. "You little faker," he murmured, loving the fullness of her, the weight of her heavy breast. "How come your bra hides this?"

"This?" she rasped as her eyes sank shut.

"How large you are." God, she was stacked and he hadn't even realized it. "Don't get me wrong, it's a nice surprise, but you must squish these poor babies down."

"Minimizer bra," she gasped, distracted by how he touched her.

"What woman wants to minimize her rack? You should be showing it off."

She dropped her head back with a strained sound of pleasure. "I didn't want attention…ah, Justice."

Tugging her hands away from his neck, he held them both in one of his and pressed them to the wall above her head. His heart drummed furiously as he found the front closure to her bra and with a practiced flick of his fingers, released it. "Ah, that's better." Putting a tiny bit of space between them, he inched up her shirt until he could see her.

Breathing became a struggle.

Her utilitarian white bra had done a hell of a job restraining her lush breasts, now snugly framed by the cotton cups. *Could a woman be more beautiful?* He didn't think so.

With the shirt tucked up high, her scars remained hidden. Hopefully, that would keep her confidence in place, at least for now.

Holding her wrists over her head, Justice studied her. She had a rockin' body, more so than anyone would guess.

He stroked the backs of his knuckles over her midriff. "You look like this, and no one knows except me." His gaze came up to meet hers. "It's going to make me extra nuts every time I see you in your casual clothes."

She shifted, but didn't pull her hands free. Sultry need darkened her gaze. "You're embarrassing me."

"Nah, I'm turning you on." Lightly, he tugged at one nipple. "But just you wait." He leaned down and, after dampening the nipple with his tongue, drew it into his mouth to suck hungrily.

Her high, vibrating moan felt like a stroke to his dick.

She pulled her hands away from his, but only to press him closer. "Oh, God," she whispered.

He loved how she curled into him, and how she gasped for air.

Moving to her other breast, he gently nuzzled while using his fingers to play with the nipple he'd left wet and tight. He was now close to her scars, but she didn't seem to notice.

"Justice, please..."

Intent on keeping her thoughts scattered, he pressed one thigh between her legs, his hand clasping her bottom and rocking her while he leisurely enjoyed her breasts.

When her breathing turned ragged, broken only by small, desperate moans, Justice gave in to the urge to know more of her. Murmuring to her, he coasted a hand over her smooth belly down to her pelvis, then over the crotch of her pants.

Her fingertips dug into his shoulders.

"Easy now." Holding her, letting her get used to his hand between her thighs, he kissed a path back up her chest, her throat and to her mouth.

This time it was her kissing him with demanding intensity, and when she moved against his palm, sharing her need without words, he knew she was getting closer.

Not quite there, but maybe—

"My legs are shaking," she whispered breathlessly. "I need to sit down."

He scooped her up and took her to the bed, lowering her to her back, and as he straightened, he took her shirt with him, stripping it off over her head in one smooth movement.

She gasped and quickly covered her upper body. Shock widened her eyes, but he wouldn't let her dwell on anything but the need.

"My hands are bigger." Slowly, one by one, Justice caught each wrist and pressed her arms up to either side of her head. "Let me."

She closed her eyes, turned her head away.

Sitting beside her, he brushed the bra cups away and just looked at her. She was such a slender woman, her rib cage narrow, her stomach showing only the slightest, sexy curve. With each fast breath, her lush breasts rose and fell. A pulse beat frantically in her throat. Her nipples were flushed dark, stiff and still damp from his mouth.

Using care, he covered her with his palms, cupping his fingers around each breast.

Firm, full and so damned soft. Her nipples were stiff against his palms. He closed his eyes at the sensation, but only for a moment. He didn't want to miss a thing.

"Justice?"

She sounded as affected as him but also anxious to know his thoughts.

Of course he saw the scars, and he didn't shy away from looking at them. Fallon wasn't a dummy; she'd catch on real quick if he tried to pretend they weren't there. She watched him so closely, he didn't bother hiding anything he thought or felt.

"Say something," she whispered.

"I don't know what to say. I'm struggling to go slow here, babe. But you're everything I imagined and a hell of a lot more." He gave her body quick scrutiny and admitted, "Your boobs are so much bigger than I expected."

Blinking at him in surprise, Fallon's mouth twitched. "My...boobs?"

"Should I have said *breasts*? I should have, right?" He continued to caress her as he spoke. "You're a classy lady and probably don't hear things like—"

Fallon touched his mouth. "I want you to be you, Justice. You don't have to say anything differently. You just took me by surprise."

In a growl, he said, "I want you so bad, I'm starting to sweat."

Relief filled her eyes and her smile widened. "That's so romantic."

"Are you teasing me?" he asked, pleased to see her tension visibly ebbing away.

She nodded. "You're making me nuts, too. I've never felt like this."

"'Cuz no man's ever done this to you before." He had to keep reminding himself of that. She was a virgin, and her one attempt at sex had been botched, thanks to Marcus—the prick.

"Yes, but I promise, you don't have to treat me with kid gloves. I just want to be like every other woman."

Only she wasn't, not to him. "The way you react to me..." He got his attention off her body long enough to look into her beautiful eyes. He saw the same heat and need reflected in her expression that he suffered. Even as he held her breasts, he felt her trembling. "God, Fallon, that's such a turn-on. I'm on a hair trigger here, but this is your first time so I wanna go slow. This is special."

She bit her lip, then asked, "Because I'm a virgin?"

"Because you're you," he said with grave seriousness. "Because you're special."

She pressed a hand to his jaw. "So...not because I'm scarred?"

Frowning, Justice lightly touched the roughened skin on her shoulder, part of her chest and the top of her breast. She resisted, trying to stop him, but he did as he pleased anyway.

Even when she went stiff, he didn't let that sway him.

"They're just marks, honey. Emotionally, they're huge, I know. But physically, they aren't a big deal at all." He glanced at her face, saw her eyes were squeezed shut and asked, "Does it bother you that my ears are thicker?"

Her eyes popped open. "What?"

"From fighting. I have some cauliflower ear goin' on. Not as bad as some I've seen, but I notice it. My right ear is worse than the left. Doesn't mean enough to me to want to do surgery or anything—"

"You're gorgeous!"

A grin tugged at his mouth. No woman had ever angrily shouted that at him before. "My nose has been broken a few times, too. No way could you have missed the kink there. It's crooked as hell."

"Maybe a little, but it just adds to your appeal."

Did her blindness to his flaws mean she, too, cared beyond the sexual attraction? He hoped so, but with Fallon it was tough to tell. She'd lived such a sheltered life, and because he refused to count Marcus, Justice was, in effect, her first adult boyfriend. He was the first to be sexual with her. He was the lucky bastard who happened to show up when she decided to spread her wings.

While he had her talking again, he reached down to open her slacks. "See, that's how it is for me, too. I look at you and you're so hot, so sexy, who cares about a few scars? I sure as hell don't."

"Marcus did."

Scowling, he stripped the pants off her, taking her panties, too. She gasped, but didn't object. Looking her over, Justice fought for control. "Let's don't ever say his name again, okay? Definitely not at times like this." He drew her upright, untangled the bra straps from her arms and tossed it with her pants.

"But—"

He levered her back down on the bed. "He's an idiot not worth your breath." Because he couldn't resist, he briefly trailed his fingers down her body, ending at the neat triangle of dark pubic hair. She kept her legs together, but he didn't let it bother him as he stroked her, then on impulse, he bent to kiss her hip bone.

Her breath hitched and she blurted, "I told you I had a scar on my leg, too—"

He stood and stripped off his jeans.

That got her quiet. And alert.

While he looked at her naked body, she visually explored his. Justice didn't mind. She could look all she wanted.

He sure planned to.

Fallon cleared her throat. "You're…impressive."

"My dick?"

She half laughed, half coughed. "I meant all of you. You're so hard all over."

"Especially my dick."

This time the sound she made was all humor. "Are you trying to amuse me?"

"Trying to get you to relax." Standing close to the bed, he again trailed his fingertips over her body, starting with her breasts, down to her stomach, over a hip bone and to her outer thigh where he touched the other scar, the one where they'd taken skin to treat her burns. A donor site, she'd told him.

This scar was flatter, a neat rectangle with a grid-like pattern to it.

Though she didn't fight him, Justice chose not to linger there. He had the rest of her to play with, too.

He went back to caressing the taut muscles of her thighs. "Ease up, honey."

"I don't want to ease up," she said. "I want to touch you like you're touching me."

"Yeah," he growled, thinking about her small hands on him. "I'd like that, too." *Control*, he reminded himself. "If you relax, I can touch you more."

Reaching for him, she said, "I'll relax more if you kiss me."

"Is that so?" Justice willingly came down beside her, pulling her close against him. She automatically lifted a leg over his, and when he felt the heat of her against him, he damn near lost it. Tangling a hand in her silky hair, he drew her face up to his and kissed her hard, sinking his tongue into her mouth, stealing her small groan.

With his free hand, he touched her everywhere, sweeping over her body, wanting to learn all of her, her every secret. He loved the softness of her skin, disrupted only by the scars.

"Shh," he murmured, when she shied away from his touch. Deliberately, he cupped her breast, letting his long fingers stretch up to the scar. He lifted his head to look into her eyes, saying just as quietly, "No secrets between us, okay?"

After several heartbeats, she cautiously nodded.

"I like touching you, Fallon. I don't want any hang-ups in the way."

She nodded again, then whispered, "Okay."

"You're beautiful and sexy. Believe me?"

Her mouth twitched even as her eyes grew damp. On a choked laugh, she agreed. "Okay."

Damn, she was special. He took her mouth again, voracious in his need, while he cuddled her plump backside, stroked her slender thighs and her downy soft stomach. With each caress, Fallon squirmed against him, into him, her hands on his shoulders holding him tight.

Justice couldn't get enough, fast enough.

Urging her to her back, he bent to one nipple, sucking strongly, insistently, and at the same time worked his fingers between her legs.

This time she was pliant, willingly giving him access, even arching up to him. He took his time exploring her, growing bolder with each touch.

Shifting restlessly, she groaned.

With one finger he stroked over the sleek, swollen folds until they parted, then he pressed in to the second knuckle. She was creamy wet, so damned hot and *tight*.

Her inner muscles clamped down on him, and he felt a surge of lust so strong, he almost came.

After taking a moment to regain his control, he levered up to his elbow and watched her expressions while he slowly worked his finger deeper inside her.

Her thick lashes were lowered, her eyes glazed with sultry need. A rosy flush colored her cheeks.

"Damn," he rasped, before looking down her body.

The sight of his rough hand between her tender, parted thighs gained all his attention.

He added a second finger and her thighs spread wider, her hips lifting into the touch.

Such a natural, carnal reaction; Justice liked that a lot.

He liked having her all stretched out, shivering with pleasure, waiting for him to continue…yeah, as hot as it got.

He brought his thumb up to her clit and watched her slender body tense. He forgot that he was trying to take it easy with her, that he wanted her to feel cherished.

He went blind to everything but having her.

On a path down her heated body, he licked, kissed, taunted with his teeth, until finally he settled himself between her spread thighs. In a voice gravelly with lust, he asked, "You want this, don't you?" He needed to hear her say it.

Taut with expectation, Fallon dropped an arm over her eyes and kept quiet—except for her harsh, unsteady breathing.

Justice lifted her thighs over his shoulders, pressed his face close and inhaled the scent of sweet, aroused woman. Heady stuff. Using just his fingertips, he parted her sex, drew his tongue along the glistening pink flesh, up and over the little stiffened clitoris.

The taste of her here only made him greedier for more.

As he ate at her, Fallon cried out over the sharp sensations.

"Tell me, Fallon," he growled, licking over her again,

pressing his tongue into her heat to gather every drop of her excitement.

She whimpered, *"Yes."*

Keeping her still with one hand flattened on her stomach, he closed his mouth around her, using his tongue to mimic the sex act, then curling it around her clit and tugging rhythmically.

She almost came undone—and he *loved* it. His erection pressed into the mattress; he was so damned hard, throbbing with his need, he knew he'd lose it the minute he got inside her. Before that, he had to guarantee her climax.

He would not leave her with regrets.

When her hips began to move in time to her small gasping breaths, he knew she was close. Again he pressed two long fingers into her, stretching up inside her as far as he could go.

She was drenched, bathing his fingers, her body ripe and ready, trembling on the cusp of release.

Knowing it'd make this first time easier for her, he thrust in and out, twisting his hand each time, stretching her. She coiled tighter and tighter—and suddenly the climax hit her.

Wet heat accompanied her raw cries and the urgent, uncontrolled movements of her body. Pleasure contorted her expression, her release real and honest.

It was the hottest, most exciting thing ever, and it set him off.

The second she began to ease, her legs going lax, Justice stood. He damn near pulled the drawer out of the nightstand in his rush to find a condom. He jerked the packet open with his teeth and looked at Fallon with a burning gaze while he rolled on the protection.

Her thighs were sprawled, her long lashes resting on her cheeks damp with perspiration, her breasts heaving as she continued to gulp deep breaths.

Coming down over her, Justice kissed her parted lips and kneed her thighs wider. "I'm in a bad way here, honey, or I'd give you more time to recoup."

With a visible effort, her slumberous eyes opened. "I don't need time," she breathed. "I just need you."

She knew how to level him.

Justice put a forearm under her, raising her hips and instructed, "Put your legs around me."

Languidly, she did as ordered.

His vision narrowed until he saw only her. "Hold on tight."

"Yes, sir." Smiling, she looped her limp arms around his neck.

He promised, "Next time I'll be easier." He adjusted the head of his erection against her, nudged forward and, without warning, drove his full length into her.

Well, that took care of her smile.

She gasped hard, her fingertips digging into his shoulders.

Growling with the pleasure of it, Justice did his best to hold still when every fiber of his being told him to move. "You're so tight."

She tried to shift and he groaned. Immediately, she went still again.

"It'll be fine in a second." At least he hoped that was

true. He couldn't think of any other virgins he'd had. Not even back in high school.

"I'm...I'm okay."

"I know it." His voice was rough, but he couldn't help it. Caught in an unfamiliar maelstrom of physical need and incredible emotion, he nuzzled her lips. "You sure you know it, too?"

"Yes. Sorry. You just surprised me."

Even now, in a haze of lust, he couldn't resist teasing her. "You thought we'd be doing something else?" Talking was pretty damned tough. The hot, sleek grip of her body squeezing around his cock in little aftershocks left him rigid from head to toes. Her lush breasts cushioned his chest, and her nipples were still drawn tight. Her breath fanned his collarbone, adding to his fever.

It was like very sweet torture, but he was determined not to hurt her.

"Justice?"

"Hmm?"

"Will you kiss me again?"

On a vibrating groan, he took her mouth. Hell, he could lose himself in kissing her. He ruthlessly held himself in check until she finally unclenched. The second she did, he drew back, only to slide in deeply again. She freed her mouth on a soft, high-pitched cry.

"Yeah, that's what I want." This time she gripped him with need instead of discomfort. Keeping his thrusts measured, he concentrated on her reactions, taking much of his pleasure from hers.

When she whispered, *"Harder,"* he gave up on all

restraint and began driving into her, rushing them both toward completion.

Head arching back, slender body bowed, Fallon cried out another release. Her beautiful response triggered his own, and he put his face in her neck, crushing her close until the nearly painful pleasure finally began to fade.

WHILE REGAINING HER BREATH, Fallon idly smoothed her fingers over Justice's shoulders and back, and down the deep groove of his spine to a very tight behind.

Lord help her, the man was rock solid all over.

She didn't need experience to know that a man like Justice was rare. So earthy, so considerate and so incredibly hot. For now, he was hers, and she intended to make the most of it.

Nerve endings all over her body still pulsed with new awareness. His body covering hers was a delicious sensation, his hips holding her legs open, his breath on her throat, his chest hair tickling her breasts.

Unable to contain her happiness, she lightly hugged him.

"Mmm," he grumbled, with a faint, "G'me a minute."

Satisfaction curved her mouth in a secret smile. She'd gladly give him a lifetime if he wanted it.

Odds were he didn't. They hadn't known each other long enough for her to be thinking such things, much less for him to be thinking it.

However, she had here and now, and she wouldn't ruin it by reaching for more. "I'm good." She stroked back up to those broad shoulders, now damp with a light sheen of sweat that amplified his scent.

How could a man smell so incredibly good?

She breathed a little deeper and felt those still-tingly places flutter anew.

She'd never before noticed anything like it. She'd enjoyed the scents of aftershave and expensive cologne, sure. But this fresh, masculine, toe-curling scent, like earth and man and sex, made her want to eat him up. It was unique to Justice and everything female in her reacted to it.

She ran a hand over his short cropped hair. She'd liked his cut before and already missed it, but the new trim didn't detract at all from his sex appeal.

Feeling daring, she trailed her toes up the back of one hairy calf.

Suddenly Justice leaned up to see her.

His gaze was intent, a little curious, a lot triumphant.

She felt ridiculously shy, especially since he was still inside her, not as much now, but she felt him there teasing her sensitized flesh.

Without a word he leaned down and treated her to a warm, lingering kiss.

God, she loved his kisses.

When she thought of what he'd done with that mouth, how crazy he'd made her, the explosion of pleasure, she moaned softly.

Justice stole the sound from her, taking advantage and deepening the kiss with a stroke of his tongue.

Fallon didn't recall doing it, but when he finally let up, she had her legs wrapped around his waist, her arms locked around his neck.

He switched to her throat. "You tasted so fucking good, Fallon."

She hadn't expected him to talk about it! A little flushed, she whispered, "Thank you?"

His laugh teased her skin. "You're welcome." Then he shifted away. "I don't want to crush you." Leaving her body, he moved to his side and pulled her into his embrace.

She could have told him how much she'd enjoyed his weight over her, but this position was nice, too.

He touched her mouth. "You okay?"

"Very." Better than she'd ever been.

"Not sore?"

Though she was just a little, she shook her head. "Thank you for asking me to stay over. We're going to do this again, right?"

His eyes warmed, and his grin came slowly. "That would be my preference."

"Good." Feeling more free than she had in years, Fallon turned to her back and stretched. She was as aware of her scars as ever, but not in a tragic way. Their existence seemed more bearable, less…shameful.

Justice rested a big hand on her stomach, then leaned forward and brushed his mouth over the burn marks on her shoulder. It surprised her, until he casually remarked, "You left me weak. I'll need a few minutes, and maybe I can talk you into showering with me. Hopefully our next time I can keep it together and show you some of my better moves."

Fallon laughed at his hilarious comment and the easy way he treated her scars. She was honestly starting to believe that they didn't bother him, and somehow that made them bother her less, too.

"*Better* moves?" She turned her head to smile at him. "I can't imagine anything better than what you already did."

"Good." Feigning a serious attitude, he said, "Low expectations will make it easier on me." He pressed his hand down, insinuating it between her legs.

Her heart thumped at his easy familiarity with her body.

"Before long," he murmured, "you'll know all my moves. I want you to promise to tell me what you like the most, okay?"

Easy enough to do. Hoping she wouldn't overstep, she whispered, "I like you."

Her concerns disappeared when he said, "That's a fine start."

So not only could she freely show her body, she could also speak her mind? The urge to laugh, maybe even dance, swelled inside her. Justice's acceptance worked toward liberating her from the chains of the past five years.

Her thoughts buzzed about her future, and in rapid order she made several decisions, all thanks to Justice.

"I like you plenty too," he said. "You know that, right?"

Actually, she did. Sure, she was an easy conquest, but Justice wasn't a user. He wasn't the type of man to take advantage of anyone, much less a woman. Knowing her parents wouldn't approve, knowing it went against the agency protocol and could damage his career, he'd still come after her. If he'd only wanted sex, she had no doubt he could have had his choice of women. And if he'd wanted her specifically, well, he could have had her without anyone ever knowing.

His openness, the way he'd approached things, meant he cared. How much, she didn't know. Heck, she didn't even know how much *she* cared.

But she looked forward to finding out.

With a growing frown, Justice muttered, "You're taking a mighty long time to answer me."

"Just thinking—and yes, I know you like me."

His gaze warmed. "Good." Sitting up, he stretched his arms high, making those bulging biceps roll and the muscles in his back flex and pull. He twisted to see her. "Stay put and I'll play the gentleman."

Not understanding, she quirked a brow.

He whistled as he left the bed, returning a moment later with the condom gone and a damp washcloth in hand.

Until he went to bathe her between the legs, she didn't understand his intent. As usual, he didn't let her shy away and once he'd finished, he crawled back into bed and drew her close.

She couldn't remember ever feeling so content.

CHAPTER FOURTEEN

IT WAS LATE MORNING, the sun slowly crawling into the sky and lightening the shadows in the bedroom, when Justice began to stir again. Fallon watched him with fascination. She should have been exhausted, but instead she fairly burst with energy.

They'd had sex three times throughout the night before taking a shower together and finally sleeping.

She rather liked his insatiable appetites because they indulged her own.

An hour or so ago she'd awakened, immediately aware of Justice beside her. His heavy arm had draped her body, one big rough hand opened over her breast.

His fingertips had touched the worst of her scar, but that had had little relevance against the reality of being naked in bed with him, filled with the memory of all they'd done and all they could yet do.

By slow degrees she'd freed herself of his hold and now rested on an elbow, just looking at him.

Even with the beard shadow darkening his jaw, he didn't appear as intimidating, not with his face so utterly relaxed. Visually she traced his well-defined lips and the slight kink in his strong nose.

Grumbling something in his sleep, he shifted and the sheet went lower, barely maintaining his modesty.

Not that he had much.

Justice Wallington was an extremely carnal man, and very unapologetic about it. In fact, last night he'd blamed her, saying she made him that way. Fallon smiled remembering it.

It was one of the nicest compliments she'd ever gotten.

Shifting again, he lowered one hand to his abdomen to scratch.

She breathed deeper. *His abs were stupendous.* "Justice?"

One eye opened, he looked at her, then stretched more deeply and turned toward her. "Come here, you."

Straight-arming him, she laughed. "Hold up."

He pulled her in anyway and his warm lips brushed her temple. "What's up—besides me?" To emphasize that, he nudged his morning erection against her belly.

"Yes, you are," she murmured, smoothing her hand over his crisp chest hair. "Before you take over, you should know that I want to touch you, too."

"Yeah," he growled with that now familiar edgy arousal in his tone.

Tucking her nose into his neck, she breathed deeply while moving her palm over his shoulder and biceps. She could spend a day just touching Justice, and still not get her fill.

"Is all this cuddling going to add up to morning sex?" he asked while dragging her pelvis into closer contact with his. "If so, I should warn you that I have to be at the office in two hours to talk to Sahara, and it's going to take me an hour to get you home and backtrack."

Thinking to save time, she asked, "Would it help if I took a cab home?"

"Hell, no. It'd help if we hurried things along, though."

"Yeah?" Smiling, she brought her hand down past his ribs, those solid abs she'd just been admiring, across his hip...and then to his erection.

Justice went still, but only for a moment. "Now we're talkin'." With a groan, he turned to his back, inviting her to touch all she wanted.

"Talking first is just what I had in mind." Keeping her fingers firmly curled around him, she sat up to ensure she didn't miss anything. Now able to look him over as much as she wanted, she whispered, "You are such a stud."

When he said nothing, she glanced at his face. Smoldering heat burned in his dark eyes, giving her a taste of sexual power.

"You've got my full attention, babe."

Yes, she did. Though he didn't touch her, a man couldn't be more attuned to a woman. Not just now, but from the day she'd first met him.

Before she got carried away, she needed to explain something. "Yesterday, when I was stupidly crying—"

"Nothing stupid about it." More softly, he added, "I'm sorry I hurt you."

"You didn't. It was my own insecurity that did it. I know that. I promise I don't usually weep like a baby.

In fact, I rarely cry." Crying had always felt so self-indulgent.

When his erection flexed in her hand, she decided to finish her talk in haste. After all, he was being incredibly patient with her.

So how did she explain? Since Justice was always so plainspoken, she decided to follow his lead. "The scar on my leg doesn't bother me as much because it's not in such an…intimate place. No one sees it either. I mean, I can easily wear longer shorts and it's hidden."

"You don't need to hide."

She loved that he thought that. "But these—" She shrugged her shoulder forward to indicate the uglier scar. "That's such a female part of me. A sexual part."

"I guess. But you're more than a stacked body, honey. A lot more. Any asshole who doesn't see that isn't worth your time."

Humor curled her mouth. "I thought we weren't going to talk about Marcus."

"No, we're not." Smug, he pointed out, "But you knew exactly who I meant."

"I want to thank you."

"For letting you hold my junk and not complaining that you're *only* holding it?"

Justice was so damned funny, even at the most awkward of times, that she had to laugh. "For that, too, yes. But I meant for reinforcing that the scars aren't what define me."

"Not even close."

"I don't want to be shy anymore."

"You still were? Because damn, honey, you've got a grip on my dick and—"

She halted his jokes by gently squeezing him.

"Go ahead," he rasped, his hands knotting in the sheet. "Be shy or bold or whatever. Long as you keep touching me."

"I plan to." The feel of him, smooth velvet over rigid steel, amazed her. Curious about every inch of him, she briefly cupped his testicles, now drawn tight, then trailed her fingertips up his length before clasping him again. He was thick enough that her fingers didn't quite meet her thumb, but while entering her, she felt only indescribable pleasure.

Fascinated by the drop of fluid beading the tip, she brushed her thumb over it.

As if pained, he briefly closed his eyes, locked his jaw and his body tensed.

"You liked that."

His eyes slowly opened. "Yeah."

"I'm not entirely sure where this is going—and no, I don't mean this," she said, giving his erection a slow pump.

The harsh groan interrupted whatever quip he'd planned to make.

"I mean you and me, in a bed. You said you wanted to date. I'm not so naive that I don't understand *dating* as a euphemism for sex." Lying to him and herself, she said, "I want you to know, if sex is all you want, I can be content with that."

"Goody for you, but I sure as hell can't."

She quickly continued past his denial, needing to get

it all said. "I've been starving for this." She got more comfortable, straddling his thick thighs and coasting a hand down his big, gorgeous body. "So many nights I thought about being with a man, kissing and touching and doing all the things most women do." With a soft laugh, she admitted, "I never envisioned a man like you." With his size, his muscles and his body hair, he was pure male perfection. She'd been too realistic to ever hope for anyone like him. "But I have you now and I want to take advantage of every second we have together."

He caught both her wrists and carefully dragged her down to rest atop him, then folded his long arms around her. "You can get back to torturing me in a minute. There's something I want to say to you first, though, and I can't think clearly with you doing that."

She smiled. "Okay."

Beneath her cheek, his chest billowed on a long, slow breath. "First, hell yeah, I wanted to have sex with you. Still do. And I know I will tomorrow and the day after."

He didn't offer forever, and after knowing him such a short time, that made sense—to her head. Her heart, however, wanted to grab for it all.

Her head reminded her heart that she had to be reasonable.

Pressuring him wouldn't gain her anything, and who knew if they'd even suit for the long haul. Scarred or not, she deserved happiness. For right now, that meant Justice.

She turned her face to kiss his throat. "Okay."

"You know what I noticed about you right off? Your eyes. So big and soft and dark. Those eyes got to me from the start. Then your honesty. The way you react to everything." His fingers tunneled into her hair, close to her scalp. "And this baby-fine hair, all sleek and sexy."

Her hair? She levered up to see his eyes. "Seriously?" Her hair was…plain. She could grow it longer, could wear it more stylish, but she'd spent so much of her life trying to avoid notice as a woman…

"Okay, so maybe I noticed your ass, too." Justice kissed her forehead. "But your hair got my attention, too. So did your skin." His lips brushed her ear. "And the things you say and do." He moved to her throat, and she felt the hot brush of his tongue. "The way you smile." Growling softly, he added, "How good you smell, so good I could just eat you up."

He *had* eaten her up, and her entire body flushed anew with the memory.

When his hands coasted down her body and he began to rock her against his erection, she knew she had to regain control.

She pushed free of his hold to sit on his abs. "So," she began, only to gasp when he cupped her breasts. *Talk about making it hard to think.*

"You want to know what we're doing? We're dating. Exclusively."

Since he waited—while toying with her nipples— she quickly nodded agreement.

"Good."

"We're dating," she repeated, "and taking it one day at a time."

"Sure." He didn't sound enthusiastic about that part, but she took heart that he didn't deny her either.

"I won't pressure you," she promised. "And you won't hold back if there's anything you want to say to me."

"Know what, Fallon?"

"What?"

"You talk too much." He reached for her.

Laughing, she swatted his hands away. "One more thing."

His long groan was too amusing.

"You know how you wanted me to tell you what I like?"

That sharpened his interest. "Yeah? Got specifics for me?"

She shook her head. "The same goes for you." Leaning forward, she kissed his sexy mouth and whispered, "Let me know if I do anything wrong."

He inhaled sharply, especially when she kissed a damp path down his now-tensed body. His fingers tunneled into her hair, and when she reached his groin, he groaned in an agony of suspense.

Fallon loved his taut anticipation, the way he kept himself so still, almost as if he feared deterring her somehow.

"You like this?" she asked, and held him in her hand.

"Yeah." Strained, he added, "Tighter."

She squeezed, and got rewarded with his low growl.

"And this?" She feathered kisses all along his length.

"Yup."

Above her fingers where she held him, she slowly licked, up and over the tip of him. "And how about—"

He gasped for breath. *"Hell, yeah."*

Filling her head with the musky scent of him, Fallon drew him into her mouth, sucking as she took him deeper.

She'd expected a reaction, but got even more than she'd counted on. Justice held her head, his breaths laboring, his muscles shifting. After only a few minutes, he roughly drew her up and under him, taking her mouth hard. She felt him fumbling on the nightstand, then he rolled to his back, donned protection, and a second later, joined their bodies in one hard, smooth thrust.

As he began rocking into her, he growled against her lips, "Hope you're into a quickie, 'cuz I won't last."

She was into *him*, and given the sharp pleasure already coiling tight, it wouldn't be a problem. Putting her legs around him, hugging him close, she breathed, "Ah, God, don't wait," as the climax hit her.

Holding her hips, he moved harder, faster—and ground out his own release.

When he finished, he sank against her, kissed her brow and whispered, "Damn, Fallon, you make me wild."

For a brand-new relationship, she figured that was a pretty good start.

MAKING IT TO the Body Armor Agency with two minutes to spare, Justice strode through the foyer and headed for the elevator. Right before he stepped inside the car, Miles joined him.

"Hey, Justice." Miles did a double-take and asked, "What'd you do to yourself?"

"Nothing." Self-conscious, Justice ran a hand over his clean-shaven jaw. "What are you doing here?"

"Got an appointment with Ms. Silver."

"No shit."

Miles grinned. "No shit."

"Huh." The doors closed and belatedly, Justice remembered to push the button for the right floor. "So, what's up?"

"Don't make a big deal of it, Justice. I'm just checking it out."

Slowly, Justice grinned. "You're joining us, aren't you?"

"I don't know yet."

At first, the idea of Miles getting on board seemed great. Then he rethought it. "You're on a winning streak. Why would you want to leave—"

The doors opened a floor early and Leese stepped in. Like Miles, he showed his surprise at Justice's spiffed-up appearance. "Is this Fallon's doing?"

"It's a shave, all right? No big deal."

"And a haircut. When was the last time I saw you without the shitty hair?"

"Go screw yourself."

Grinning, Leese shifted his gaze to Miles. "What's up?"

"He's joining us," Justice offered.

"I didn't say that," Miles corrected, looking harassed. "Only that I'm checking it out."

Leese frowned. "But you're on a winning streak."

"That's what I told him." Justice was relieved to have their attention diverted. "Now that I think about it, though, he mentioned last night at Cannon's that he was interested. I thought he was joking."

Leese gave him a speculative gaze.

"I've been considering it, that's all." Miles shrugged. "Ms. Silver has a terrific pitch."

"She does," Leese agreed. "And I'd be the first to say it's a good gig. But it's not fighting."

Pinching the air, Justice said, "Maybe just a little fighting."

The elevator dinged as they reached the floor for Sahara's office. Probably to escape the inquisition, Miles quickly stepped out.

Bounding after him, Justice said, "Hey, I have to talk to her first." He had no idea how Sahara might react, if she'd raise hell with him or whether or not he might even be out of a job. The unknown sucked, so he wanted to get it over with.

"I have an appointment," Miles countered. "So get in line."

"I work here, damn it!"

Grinning, Leese followed them. "I think I'll just go along to watch."

Both Miles and Justice scowled at him.

Sahara's door stood open, which, when it came to his classy boss, was as good as an invitation. Justice slid in front of Miles and, after a perfunctory knock on the frame, sauntered in.

Miles crowded in behind him.

Leese leaned in the doorway, arms folded.

Justice did *not* want an audience for what he had to do. "Sahara—"

At the same time, Miles said, "Ms. Silver—"

With one finger raised in the air, Sahara quieted them both.

She sat behind her massive desk listening to her agenda from her personal assistant, Enoch, while making notes on her calendar. As usual, Enoch had already delivered coffee and pastries.

Sahara took her time, changing a few appointments, adding in a few others and organizing the calls she had to make. All in all she did a fine job of ignoring the men, not even looking up at them.

After she'd finished and Enoch headed out for his own office, she glanced up—and her eyes flared. "Justice!"

Grousing, he said, "It's just a shave and a haircut. I was past due, that's all."

"Well, my word." Looking from one of them to the other, Sahara clasped a manicured hand to her heart. "You gentlemen make a nice visual first thing in the morning. It's like an advertisement for testosterone." She fanned her face. "I must think about a billboard with the three of you on it to represent the agency."

"I don't work here," Miles said.

"Yet. But I'll win you over."

With a shake of his head, Leese said, "You're bordering on sexual harassment."

Sahara laughed and left her seat to circle to the front of her desk. Per her usual preference, she hoisted her rump onto the edge and got comfortable. "I'm serious. We could bring in all sorts of new clientele."

"Too expensive," Leese said. "Most people seeing

the billboard wouldn't be able to afford your exorbitant pricing."

She shrugged a delicate shoulder. "You get what you pay for."

Bristling, Justice took a step forward. "Enough nonsense, already. I have to talk to you."

Very slowly, she turned her head and skewered him with her blue-eyed gaze. "Oh, I'm not sure that you do, Justice. You see, Rebecca Rothschild Wade called me bright and early this morning."

Justice tucked in his chin. "It isn't even nine o'clock yet."

"She said she wanted to beat you to any self-castigation."

He had no idea what she meant. With suspicion, he said, "That sounds nasty."

"You know what's nasty? Being awakened at 6:00 a.m. by a client."

Justice wasn't sure what to say about that. He tried, "Sorry?" and knew by Sahara's withering look that it hadn't helped.

Turning back to Miles, she smiled. "I like order, you all know that. So, Justice, take a seat while I talk with your friend."

"What?" He knew Sahara could be unpredictable. A great boss, but he didn't understand this current mood of hers. "Why does he go first?"

Her eyes narrowed. "Because I said so."

Well, hell. He could feel Miles and Leese staring at him and he felt like a kid being sent to the corner. "Fine, no biggie." Refusing to look cowed, he folded his arms and planted his feet. "At least tell me if I'm fired."

A mean smile curled her glossy lips. "Now Justice, do you honestly think I'd let you off that easy?"

"Um…"

"Not a chance."

Huh. Okay, so at least he still had his job. Holding up his hands in a conciliatory gesture, he moved to the sofa and sat down to wait. Already he felt better. If Sahara had to vent, fine. He'd take it. He didn't mind being bitched out. He did like the job, though, and really didn't want to have to start over somewhere else.

For Fallon, he would have. But staying at Body Armor suited him.

After a deep, calming breath, Sahara released him from her stare. "Leese, this involves you, so please come inside."

Now Leese and Miles both looked uneasy, too. Good. Misery loved company. Justice smirked at them when they edged farther inside.

"Please, gentlemen, get comfortable."

"What's up with the gentlemen stuff?" Leese asked.

She rolled her eyes. "I'm wooing Miles so I'm trying to be more solicitous."

Justice grunted. She hadn't been solicitous to him.

"Wooing me?" Miles asked. "I'm just here—"

"He's only *curious*," Leese said, mocking their friend.

Sahara pretended to cast a line toward Miles, then slowly reeled it in. "I've got you hooked and we both know it. Don't fight me too hard, okay? Justice has taken all my patience for the day."

Appearing more uncomfortable by the moment, Miles rolled a shoulder. "Honestly, the way he's over there quaking in his boots, I'm thinking about running the other way."

"I'm not quaking!"

Laughing, Sahara said, "No, he's not. The big lug knows I value his role in the agency."

She did? Justice tried to hide his surprise. Sure, Sahara always made him feel important, and he knew she trusted him. But he also understood how important the agency was to her. She'd inherited it from her brother after his murder and she'd do just about anything to keep it as successful as possible.

That meant keeping the reputation golden.

Him hooking up with a client could cause real damage, so he'd have understood if she'd raged at him.

Under the circumstances, a few killing looks weren't so bad.

For the next twenty minutes, Justice had to sit there while Sahara extolled Body Armor, doing her best to win over Miles. He still didn't understand why Miles would even be interested, but he saw for himself how his friend asked enough questions to cover all the bases.

Sahara elaborated on the necessary requirements, the training regimen, the possible scenarios and the perks of working for the agency.

When she wound down, Leese asked, "Why am I here?"

"I want you to show Miles around the building. Not just the places he's seen while visiting one of you, but everything shut off to the general public, like where he could exercise and practice shooting and—"

"Got it," Leese said.

"If he takes the job, you'll be training him." She cast another dark look at Justice. "This one is going to be busy for a while."

Miles started laughing. "I get the feeling this is like a big family instead of a boss and employees."

"Don't," Justice said. "She can be very boss-like when it suits her."

"Yes," Sahara agreed. "I can." She crossed her legs and studied Miles. "But it's also true that a certain familiarity is necessary given the nature of the job. There could be times when, depending on what the client wants, you work around the clock."

Justice opened his mouth and she snapped, "Hush it!"

He clamped his lips together.

Scowling at him, she added, "Around the clock does not, in the usual course of things, include intimate involvement with the client."

Justice wasn't the only one to flush. Leese did his own fair share of looking chastised, and with good reason. His wife, Catalina, had started out as a client.

"Right," Miles said, clearing his throat. "I get that. But for the sake of clarity, I'm curious what's happening, too, so if you want to deal with Justice, I'm happy to stick around."

"Dick," Justice muttered.

"You may as well," Sahara agreed. Sighing, she shifted to face Justice.

As the silence stretched out, he said, "Well?"

"Rebecca is thrilled with how things are progressing."

Huh. Hadn't seen that one coming. "She is?"

"Very."

For reasons that had nothing to do with the job, Justice smiled. "Well…that's good, then, right?"

"If it's all fine," Leese interjected, "what's the problem?"

"The problem is that if Justice breaks her heart, I'm going to have some seriously irate clients on my hands."

Justice pushed to his feet. "I told them they weren't clients anymore."

Brows up, Sahara immediately understood. "You're that serious about her?"

"I am."

"You haven't known her that long."

Justice waved that away. "Have you met her?"

"Not personally, no."

"Well, they have," he said, nodding at his friends. "There was no way to resist her."

Miles said, "I resisted her just fine."

"Ha! Because you knew I'd flatten you if you didn't."

"I resisted her, too," Leese pointed out.

"You're disgustingly in love with your wife, so it doesn't count. And if you recall, you didn't resist Catalina worth a damn."

Leese smiled. "True."

"Boys," Sahara warned…but then she laughed. "Ah, this is starting to be a trend. At least I know Leese is now off the market, so he can henceforth perform his protection details without intimate involvement."

"Absolutely," Leese said.

"Same here," Justice assured her. "If Fallon hadn't been so…different, I'd have done fine with her, too. Hell, I worked for that movie star with chicks throwing themselves at both of us nonstop and I wasn't once tempted to be inappropriate. But Fallon got to me."

"You were different with her," Miles said, offering up some defense. "We all noticed that right off."

He sighed. "Yeah."

Sahara pointed at Justice. "I won't ask for details—"

"Good." He wouldn't have shared anything private anyway.

"But Rebecca insists that they continue to pay, so they're still clients—and no, don't argue about it. It's not your decision to make." Leaving her desk, she muttered, "I'm running an agency, not a dating service."

"Yes, ma'am."

She shot him a look so mean, he had to bite back a smile.

"Do not screw this up, Justice."

"Won't."

In a silent command for everyone to go, Sahara opened her office door. "Miles, let me know if you have any questions. If you decide to join us, we can meet again and go over any unanswered questions you might have."

"I'll be in touch," he promised.

Leese said, "I have time to give him a tour before I head out."

As Justice passed her, she touched his arm to get him to pause. To Leese, she said, "You're meeting with the lottery winner this morning?"

"Him and his wife. Seems like a real nice guy."

"Good, keep me posted." Pitching her voice low so the others wouldn't hear, she said to Justice, "At this point I'm starting to feel like a pimp but…keep up the good work."

She closed the door on his look of surprise.

Slowly, the grin spread over his face. Working for Body Armor was a hell of a good decision.

And thinking of the job… He jogged to catch up with Leese and Miles. "I'm joining you on your tour so I can talk to you about something."

"Something like Fallon Wade?" Leese asked.

He shook his head. "Something like…Tomahawk Nelson."

CHAPTER FIFTEEN

JUSTICE PARKED IN front of the Wade household and bounded up the steps. Anytime he was away from Fallon, he looked forward to seeing her again.

Every time he had her, he wanted her more.

He'd managed to cool his jets enough to actually help her experience some of the things she'd missed out on. The woman was a true movie junkie and wallowed in any theater experience. Together they could go through an entire tub of popcorn, two colas and a box of candy.

Her favorite flicks were of the action variety, and man, he loved her for it. He could tolerate a sappy movie just barely, and had in the past done so just to appease a date.

With Fallon, it wasn't necessary.

Scary movies spooked her, but that just meant she cuddled closer, especially once he had her in bed. He couldn't get enough of that.

Two weeks had passed, and he'd tried to be considerate with her parents by only keeping her overnight on the weekends. Little by little, she was coming into her own and he couldn't have been happier about it.

The whole bodyguard thing, though…nothing else had happened. They dated, had sex, enjoyed each other, and there wasn't a single risk to be found. So how did he justify charging them when he didn't do anything differently because of the job? He would always protect her when she was with him, and he wanted her with him more.

He figured he'd talk to her dad about it today.

Before he could knock, Rebecca opened the door.

"Good morning, Justice. How are you today?"

"Terrific." He looked past her but didn't see Fallon. "How about you?"

She drew him inside. "I'm well, thank you. But I have a favor to ask."

With the way she looked at him, suspicions sparked. He said only, "Yeah?"

Glancing around, she tugged him toward the dining room. "If Fallon heard me ask you this, she'd overreact."

Yeah...he was getting a really bad vibe about things.

"However, I'm not only certain you'll understand, I'm positive you'll agree."

Having no idea what she wanted, he said, "Yes, ma'am."

"Clayton and I are going out of town together for ten days. We haven't done so in a very long time."

Given the way they hovered over her, he figured they probably hadn't left Fallon alone since she'd been burned. "Someplace special?"

"Clayton has business in New York. I used to always go along and shop, then join him for dinners. But..." She faltered, then looked away.

Justice gently patted her shoulder. "I understand." He really did. Losing one child, having another so badly hurt, it made sense that they hadn't wanted her out of their sight.

"I'll be better able to enjoy myself if Fallon stays with you." Flapping a hand, she said, "Oh, I realize there hasn't been any real danger, but I'm still very anxious about it. The two of you have spent some nights together, so I was hoping, if it wouldn't be an imposition—"

"Totally works for me," he rushed to tell her. Have Fallon all to himself for ten days? Hell, yeah. "Don't give it another thought."

"If Fallon knows I asked you—"

"Yeah, about that." He rubbed the back of his neck. "I don't want to keep secrets from her, so how about I make the suggestion that she stay with me, then later— like after it's a done deal—I can tell her that you explained things to me up front?"

The way Rebecca's eyes softened and her mouth curled, Justice wasn't surprised when she hugged him.

It did startle him when she said, "You're just too, *too* wonderful, Justice. Thank you."

Wonderful? He didn't know how she figured that just because he agreed to keep her daughter close. True, he didn't know much about long-term relationships, definitely didn't have much experience with them, but everyone knew lies, even lies of omission, weren't the way to go.

"Is something wrong, Mom?"

They both turned to Fallon, who watched them closely.

"I was just telling Justice how I plan to join your father on his trip to New York tomorrow."

"Oh." She dusted her hands over trim denim capris that hugged her thighs and ass. "You're leaving early, right?"

"Too early," Rebecca agreed with a laugh. "But Clayton's first meeting is at lunch tomorrow and he wanted me settled in the hotel first." To Justice, she said, "We'll use the suite in our own hotel. Since so many people greet us, it takes a few minutes to actually get to the rooms."

Keeping his attention glued to Fallon, Justice barely heard her mom. It pleased him a lot to see her wearing a top with a more open neckline. The peach colored, V-neck T-shirt was still modest and her scar didn't show, but at least she hadn't bundled her neck in a scarf. Her hair was a little more tousled, her eyes bright and already he wanted her.

"You look nice," he told her in a voice gone deep. But damn, now he knew what she looked like naked, and it wasn't like he'd be forgetting anytime soon.

"Thank you."

He watched as she stepped into casual flip-flops, then tracked her every step as she came to hug her mother.

She said, "I can be home earlier tonight to help you pack."

"I've already gotten it done," Rebecca assured her. "You go and have fun." She flashed a conspiratorial glance at Justice. "Stay out as late as you'd like. In fact, we can make this our goodbye right now."

Justice drew Fallon to his side, then said to Rebecca, "Call if you need anything."

"Thank you, I will. And you have my cell number, as well."

It got more awkward by the second, so Justice urged Fallon from the house. Wasting no time at all, the second they pulled out of the drive, he asked, "Why don't you stay with me while your folks are out of town?" He bobbed his eyebrows. "We can play house."

Her smile twitched. "And how, exactly, do we play that?"

"It could start with us getting naked."

She laughed. "And getting into bed?"

"Or the shower or the couch or, hell, the dining table works for me." Once he thought it, he pictured it, and he started to get hard. "I'd love to see you laid out there on the table, like my own private dessert."

"Justice."

"Well, I would."

After a steadying breath, Fallon nodded. "Okay, I like those ideas, too."

His cock jumped up in joy.

"But first…"

First? He glanced over and saw her withdrawing a list from her purse. *Time to rein it in.*

He cleared his throat. "Got something else you wanted to do?" Fallon had lived such an inhibited life that now he wanted her to see and do and experience everything that interested her. If that meant putting his own wants on hold for a while, he didn't mind at all.

"These are listings for apartments that interested me."

Apartments? Whoa. He squeezed the steering wheel and hoped he misunderstood. "Apartments for who?"

"Me." She laughed. "I've enjoyed myself so much lately, I've decided it's time for the next step."

"Your own place?"

"Exactly."

God, he hated that idea. "Why? I mean, we've been getting out a lot, right? Having fun?"

"So much fun," she whispered. "But at twenty-four I'm old enough that I shouldn't have to explain to my parents anytime I'm out all night."

So it was her nights with him that had put the idea in her head? Well, hell.

True, there hadn't been any recent threats. That didn't mean he was convinced that her fall down the stairs was an accident. Someone *had* tromped his flowers and painted her driveway.

Also, he couldn't forget that anonymous call claiming Tomahawk had pushed her…

Both Miles and Leese were helping to keep an eye on Tom. If he was anywhere around, one of them knew it. Yet they hadn't seen anything suspicious. Other than being a major pain in his ass, Tom hadn't made any untoward moves.

Justice decided he needed to reason with Fallon, and what better way to do that than to point out her close relationship with her parents. "You know, I think Rebecca might be more understanding than you think. She knows you'll be staying with me while she's away, and she didn't mind at all."

Fallon's head snapped up from her perusal of her list. "What do you mean, she *knows*?"

Uh-oh. "She, ah…" How to word it? "She would assume we'll be spending more time together while she's away. You know, because the opportunity is there and everything."

Fallon seemed to accept that but shrugged it off. "I'm not spending two weeks with you."

Wow. Okay, that hurt. He didn't bother hiding his scowl. "Why not?"

"Because I'm not going to intrude on you like that." Before he could set her straight, she added, "And you've known from the jump that I wanted to get out on my own."

But…yeah. He had known. Fallon deserved to be "free"—her word, not his. If living on her own would do that for her, how could he selfishly ask her to move in with him instead?

Was moving in together even the right move? They'd known each other close to a month. Sure, they'd packed a lot of together time in there, being nearly inseparable for most of those days.

He'd loved every second of it—but had she?

Was he being too clingy? Grabbing for more than she wanted to give?

Could be.

After all, when it all boiled down, he was still her bodyguard. Her best interests had to be his priority.

Hating it, Justice nonetheless agreed with her. At a stoplight, he said, "Let me see the list."

She handed it over without argument. The first two places he automatically discounted. They weren't in the best parts of town and they were too damned far away from him.

The third…yeah, the third was *maybe* doable. He

did a quick calculation in his head and figured it was no more than ten minutes from his house.

Aware of Fallon watching him closely, he folded the list to the third address and handed it back to her. "We can check out that one."

"Justice," she said calmly. "I wasn't asking."

"I know." The light changed and he pulled away. "But I'm your protection and my recommendation—" *a better word choice than what he wanted to use* "—is that the first two are in dangerous areas. Your folks would worry endlessly." Hoping that'd seal the deal for her, he glanced her way. "You don't want that, right?"

"No, I don't."

Stalling for time, he said, "You know we can't go today, right? I'll have to scope it out first."

"Now you're just being silly."

As he started to deny that, he got a call on his cell. He glanced at the Bluetooth screen in the car, saw it was his mom and answered with a push of a button.

"Hey, Mom. I've got you on speaker, okay? There's a girl with me—"

"There's a skunk in the shed! A raccoon I could deal with, but not a skunk. Mom's here and she's insisting she can handle it, but, Eugene, you know the woman can barely walk after her accident!"

He winced at the name, avoided eye contact with Fallon, and said, "Is she at least wearing her glasses? Maybe she doesn't know it's a skunk."

"Oh, she knows because I told her. She said I was being a wimp and that she'd handle it."

Justice bit back his grin. "I'll be right over, okay?

Tell Granny I'll wash her in the creek if she gets sprayed by that skunk."

In the background, he and Fallon both heard her yell, "He's going to drop you in the creek, Mom! You know he will, too."

His granny's voice came through loud and clear when she barked, "I'd like to see him try!"

Oh, man.

"I'll be right there, Mom. Sit on her if you have to." He disconnected, wondering what to say.

Fallon snickered.

Taking that as a good sign, he asked, "Mind if we make a detour?"

"Of course not. I'm sort of anxious to meet your family."

He reached for her hand. "The other women in my life, you mean?" Being honest with her, he said, "They're nothing like your folks, but they're great. I think you'll like them."

"They raised you, so I already do."

Nice. Justice knew his mom would go nuts over Fallon. He only hoped she didn't chase her away with her enthusiasm.

ALONE IN THE living room with the two women, Fallon tried not to blush. The way they both stared at her, fixed smiles on their faces, didn't make it easy.

"You have a lovely home." Avoiding their piercing gazes, Fallon glanced around at the cozy home done in a traditional style with upholstered furniture, an enormous television, and plenty of colorful throw pillows.

Homemade curtains covered the windows and a variety of braided rugs covered the hardwood floors. It was clean but a little cluttered; photos of Justice at various ages filled the mantel, the walls and the side tables, with photos of his father beside them.

"Thank you." Iris, his mother, never looked away. "I like the privacy here."

"I would, too. It's beautiful." Large shade trees filled the spacious lot, which was bisected by a long gravel drive that led to the house set a good distance from the main road. Woods on one side and to the back probably caused the problems with skunks and other critters. To the other side was the long creek separating the property from a farmer's field.

As Justice had said, both women were very petite, but that was where the similarities ended.

Iris, his mother, had the same flair for "style" as her son. Her shoulder-length hair had turned to silver, but she'd enhanced it with a wide purple streak off to one side. Bold makeup played up her dark eyes, and close-fitting jeans with a tank top emphasized her trim, toned figure. She didn't look trashy in any way, but she would most definitely turn heads.

His granny was the opposite. She wore her silvery white hair in a long loose braid with little soft wisps framing her tanned, weathered face. She didn't wear a speck of makeup, but wore a loosely fitted, tea-length cotton dress made for comfort, not style. Regardless, Fallon could see that she, too, had maintained her figure.

"How long have you and Eugene been dating?"

"A few weeks." Fallon didn't mention that he'd been—still was—her bodyguard.

"He never mentioned you," Mona grumbled. "I'm going to kick his butt for that."

Both women were a delight, and very openly nosy. "He's been sweet, and I'm afraid I've kept him quite busy."

Dark eyes brightening, Mona said, "Do tell," with a lot of suggestion.

"Mom," Iris chastised, but she did so with a smile.

Realizing how that had sounded, Fallon quickly clarified. "That is, we've done a lot each day—"

Their smiles widened.

Worse and worse. "I mean—"

Mona barked a laugh and slapped her knee. "We've got her blushing, Iris. When was the last time Eugene brought around a girl who even knew how to blush?"

"He never brings around *any* girls," Iris pointed out. "I was never sure if that was because of the girls, or because of us."

"Oh, he's really proud of both of you," Fallon rushed to assure them. "It's easy to see how close you are whenever you've been mentioned."

"He's mentioned us?" Iris asked.

"Well, when he met my father—"

Hand to her throat, Iris said to Mona, "He's met her father!"

Fallon knew she was botching her first meeting but had no clue how to fix it.

Luckily, Justice stepped in then. Even better, he didn't stink of skunk. He took one look at how his granny and mother sat in chairs facing Fallon on the couch, and cocked a brow. "Are you two behaving?"

Mona said, "No. I was trying to get some details, but so far all I know is that you're proud of us."

He grinned, bent to kiss the top of her head and said, "Wonder if I was drunk when I gave that impression."

Iris laughed, not in the least insulted. "Got the skunk taken care of?"

"Yup. It was a young one and didn't give me too much trouble when I relocated him a good distance into the woods. I found where he was getting into the shed, too. A couple of rotted floorboards at the back behind the mower made it easy for him. I nailed down a temporary barrier, but I think the whole floor probably needs to be replaced."

"Should I call someone?" Iris asked.

"Nah. I'll get to it."

Iris's gaze shifted to Fallon. "I don't want to interrupt your romance."

"You won't," he said without a single twinge nor any denials about a romantic relationship. "I can bring Fallon along with me."

Everyone looked at her. Put on the spot, Fallon said, "That's fine by me, but I don't want to intrude—"

"You're not," said three voices at once.

Fascinated by these women who'd known Justice—or rather, Eugene—as a little boy, she grinned. "All right, *Eugene*. Thank you. I'd love to visit more."

Iris popped to her feet. "While you're here, mind if I show you a few other things that need work? You could fix it all on the same day."

"Sure, Mom."

Clearly wanting to get him alone, Iris said, "Fallon, you just relax. I won't keep him long, I promise."

Justice cast Fallon a look, then Mona. "No shenanigans, Granny, or you might end up in the creek yet."

Mona put her nose in the air. "I haven't skinny dipped in forever. Might be refreshing."

Making a horrified face, Justice followed his mother out.

"Now." Mona quickly moved to sit beside Fallon. "Tell me everything before he comes back in."

"Everything?" Fallon asked.

"How you met, how long you've been together, and how serious it is. Hurry. There's no way that boy will leave me alone with you for more than a few minutes."

Seeing no way around it, Fallon shrugged. "Actually, it's a pretty romantic story." She smiled. "Justice started out as my bodyguard."

THE SECOND THEY were alone, Justice took his mother by the shoulders. "Okay, Mom. First, quit calling me Eugene."

Her mouth twitched. "It's your name."

"I know, but you're doing it on purpose to tease me." Most of the time she called him *son* or *sweetie* or some other endearment. "Second, don't go grilling Fallon."

She smacked his shoulder. "I wouldn't have to if you'd told me about her."

"She's special," he said, catching her off guard. "There, now you've been told."

Her eyes widened and her smile turned huge. "Oh,

sweetie, that's awesome!" She threw herself against him and squeezed him tight.

Used to her demonstrative shows of affection, Justice hugged her right off her feet. "Thanks, Mom, but don't go getting ahead of yourself. I haven't known her that long, and just because I'm half in love already—" *what an understatement* "—doesn't mean Fallon is, too."

Iris pushed back to scowl into his face. "Well, of course she is. Look at you, son. You're a catch. Any smart girl can see that."

He laughed. "It's fair to say, you're a little bit biased."

"A good son makes a good husband."

"Mom," he warned. "Now you're definitely getting ahead of yourself!"

Tamping down some of her enthusiasm, she patted his chest. "I'm just saying, she'd be lucky to have you."

Justice figured she might have that wrong. Knowing his mother would see it differently, he paced away to the corner of the deck where a few screws were loose. "She's wealthy."

Iris caught up to him. "What's that?"

"She and her family. They're big bucks." Only that didn't really describe Fallon at all, so he added, "She's really sweet, though, and down-to-earth."

"Seems to be," Iris agreed. "And pretty, too."

"Yeah." Justice worked his jaw, then gave up. "She was hurt once."

"Hurt?"

Leave it to his mother to focus more on that than money. Caring for Fallon as he did now, it pained him to talk about it, so he gave her the quick version of the story.

His mother didn't need the nitty-gritty to understand the emotional damage. "Oh, honey, I'm so sorry. That poor, sweet girl."

"She's touchy about the scars."

His mom leveled a look on him. "You made it clear that they don't matter?"

"Yes, ma'am." Because physically, they didn't. "Little by little, she's starting to believe me. But now she's got this new confidence, and she wants to live a little."

"She can live a little with you."

He smiled. "Yeah, she has." The smile waned. Fallon wanted to move out on her own. He'd rather ask her to move in with him, but he couldn't steal anything from her. She deserved to have everything she wanted.

"What?" his mom asked.

Justice shook his head. There were some things he wasn't yet ready to share. "You're always my biggest cheerleader."

"It's easy to cheer for a winner."

Damn, he loved her. His granny, too. They always had his back, always... *His granny.* "Oh, shit."

"Language," Iris cautioned.

"Sorry." Already striding toward the house, Justice said, "Granny's in there putting Fallon through a cross-examination right now, isn't she?"

"Probably." Jogging to keep up with his long-legged gait, Iris laughed. "Slow down! Your Fallon didn't strike me as the type to let a little curiosity offend her."

"Granny's curiosity is the equivalent of a runaway Mack truck." He burst through the door, but ground to a halt when he found the two ladies sitting close together on the couch, looking through a photo album. Heat burned his face. "Damn it, Granny—"

"Language," his mom and Granny snapped at the same time.

Eyes soft and smile wide, Fallon looked up at him. "You were so stinkin' adorable."

Justice hated to look but couldn't seem to stop himself. He peered over her shoulder and saw the god-awful photo of him as a naked infant...sucking his thumb.

Fallon touched the photo, as if she touched the baby him.

"He was a big newborn," his mom said, crowding onto the couch on Fallon's other side. "And he was always a sweet baby."

Seeing that the women would be occupied for a while—which, okay, kept Fallon from looking at apartments, so ultimately worked in his favor—he grumbled, "I'm going to go over the house and see what other repairs are needed. Might even go get some supplies since I'm already here."

No one replied. They were too busy turning pages in the album.

MARCUS WALKED INTO the office where Kern and York waited on him. Smiling at the brothers, he said, "Sorry I'm late."

"You're not," Kern told him, extending his hand. "We were a few minutes early."

Right there on the tabletop rested the check written out for the full amount.

"How've you been?" York asked. "Things going well with your lady?"

For a moment, Marcus didn't know what he meant. "Who?"

"Ms. Wade. You win her over yet?"

Bristling, Marcus took time to pour himself a drink. It was only three o'clock, but Kern and York already had drinks; no reason he shouldn't join them. After taking a fortifying sip, Marcus pulled out his chair opposite the brothers. "Ms. Wade and I are friends."

"Ms. Wade?" York repeated. "You're that formal with her still?"

He'd been trying, obviously without success, to move away from an intimate topic. "Of course not. As I said, we're friends."

Kern snorted. "Being *friends* is not what you want."

No, it wasn't. However, by all appearances, he had lost his opportunity. Fallon might not believe it, but what he wanted most was for her to be happy.

Damn it all, she appeared to be very happy with the bodyguard.

York hit the tabletop. "What the hell, man? Where are your balls? You've given up, and I would have put odds on you."

Yes, he likely would have. God knew the brothers loved a bet. Well, let them deal with a little reality.

Studiously avoiding looking at the check, Marcus sat back in his seat. "Actually, I haven't seen Fallon in a while. Mrs. Rothschild Wade arranged the fund-raising meetings away from the home." He didn't mention that Mr. Wade had also told him to stay away.

"So?" Kern barked. "Her daughter hasn't been around her house much anyway."

Marcus went still. *How would Kern know that?* A dozen concerns tripped through his brain before he found the composure to hide his surprise and distrust. Trying for a note of mere curiosity, he murmured, "Oh?" as if he wasn't all that interested in the answer.

He even opened the folder to the paperwork that would finalize their donation.

York cast a worried look at Kern, then pasted on a smile. "I told my brother that I'd seen her out and about with the bodyguard. Quite a few times, in fact. It appears he, at least, is on game."

"Meaning?" Marcus stared at the papers as if searching for a necessary notation, when in reality, the text blurred together as the ramifications of anyone spying on Fallon slowly sank in.

"Meaning he's beating you, man." Kern pushed back his chair and stood. "I thought that nice donation would give you a fighting chance, but you haven't even tried to use it to your advantage."

Ah, and since he hadn't produced the results they wanted, Kern now might pull the donation? *Not if I can help it.* Collecting his thoughts, Marcus tapped his fingertips together. "It still could help. Once it's presented, there's no way Fallon won't notice." Because he would tell her—about the donation and about his concern. "I'm flattered that you're both taking such an interest in my personal life, but is there a reason why?" Pretending amusement, he half smiled. "Perhaps a bet as to who wins the girl?"

Kern looked struck, then turned to York. "Hell of an idea."

Great, so he'd just encouraged them. Yet, Marcus knew that wasn't the only bet.

"One at a time," York said with some sly meaning.

Interrupting their debate on the odds, he asked, "Why, specifically, does it matter to either of you?"

They held silent, but not for long. The brothers were too cocky, too arrogant concerning their own wealth and influence, to understand his suspicions. They considered themselves beyond the reach of social boundaries. "The bodyguard keeps dodging Tomahawk."

Marcus gave a short laugh. "I seriously doubt that he dodges anyone. If he doesn't take the fight, it's because he has no interest in it."

Wearing his most charming grin, York added, "Do your part and we'll figure out the rest."

"The rest of what?"

Pushing the check toward Marcus, Kern added, "But do it soon." His smile looked like a threat. "Honest to God, I don't give a shit about literacy." He stormed out, his laughing brother behind him.

That check began to look like a bribe, and finally, Marcus knew what he had to do.

CHAPTER SIXTEEN

INSTEAD OF LOOKING at apartments as she'd intended, Fallon ended up visiting with Justice's mother and grandmother nearly every day.

The women were absolutely delightful, very different from her relatives…and oh-so-similar to Justice, like tinier, female versions of his humor, warmth, caring and integrity.

Never, not once, had Fallon ever doubted the love of her parents. In a million ways, they'd shown her the depth of their feelings for her. Their love was quiet and fierce, an unwavering comfort.

For Justice's family, the love was bold and in your face, hilariously demonstrative and heart-meltingly unashamed.

From the start, they included her in those tight hugs, outrageous jokes and happy welcomes.

During the times that Justice did routine repairs to Iris's property, Fallon learned to make bean soup and braid a rug. She got a tour of Justice's old room, saw his many sporting trophies, heard stories of past girlfriends and watched all the DVDs of his fight career.

In some ways, she felt like an insider with the women, especially when they ganged up to tease Justice.

"Eugene" never seemed to mind, though. In fact, he would smile in an indulgent way, as if pleased to see them growing closer.

On the eighth day after her parents left, Fallon and Justice were finally going to check out the only apartment that was still available. Later they'd take his mother and grandmother out to dinner and she already looked forward to it. She wanted to go by her house first to get a change of clothes, and when they were five minutes away, she got a call.

She pulled out her cell, glanced at the screen and saw it was Marcus.

Justice said, "Ignore it."

He'd been in a sullen mood ever since she'd insisted on seeing the apartment. It wasn't as if she wanted to give up staying with him. Now that he'd involved her in his life and his family, losing either would be like losing a piece of her heart.

But it wouldn't be fair to him. Being her bodyguard had pulled him into her problems, and now she feared he was as overprotective as her parents. She couldn't burden him.

He needed choices. He needed to know that she'd be fine on her own. If their relationship grew after that, then and only then could she entirely trust in his feelings, accepting them for what she wanted them to be rather than what they might be—worry, or worse, sympathy.

"Of course I have to answer," she said, and put the phone to her ear. He needed to understand that Marcus was not a threat. "Hello, Marcus."

"Fallon. I haven't seen you in a while."

She watched Justice's profile. "There's no reason that you would."

Genuine sadness came through his reply. "I'd like to think we're still friends."

He'd humiliated her so badly that, before Justice, seeing Marcus only reinforced her insecurity. Now, however, she felt more than capable of being around him without a single twinge. "Of course we are."

"I'm sorry, Fallon. You don't know how many times I've regretted my reaction—"

Unwilling to rehash what had been a most mortifying situation for them both, she cut him off. "I'm over it, Marcus, I promise." Just as quickly, she asked, "Is there a reason for your call?"

She heard his sigh before he said, "Yes. I need to see you. And no, it's not to rekindle anything. There's something you need to know."

What could Marcus possibly have to tell her? Whatever it was, she didn't care. "Just tell me now."

He suddenly growled, "Is your bodyguard with you?"

She looked again at Justice. "Yes."

"I assumed," he said with resigned annoyance. "Let me speak with him, please."

Fallon didn't like the sound of that at all.

"Why do you want to talk to Justice?"

Brows shooting up, Justice glanced at her.

"It's important. Since he's with you and I'm not, I'm sure he can explain better than me."

Annoyance rising, Fallon scowled. "I'd prefer that you explain."

Justice held out his hand. "Give over, Fallon."

"No." Then to Marcus, she demanded, "Tell me right now or I'll hang up."

"If you do, I'll just have to call the agency where he works and hunt him down that way. And honestly, Fallon, that might take too long. Now please, put him on."

Marcus said nothing else, damn him. She didn't know what to do.

Wiggling his fingers, Justice asked, "Do you trust the putz or not?"

"Fine." Fallon put the phone on speaker and then slapped it into his hand, unwilling to mask her irritation with manners.

"Marcus," Justice said with malicious humor. "How's it shaking?"

"Rather than be harassed, I'll get right to it."

"Yeah, why don't you?"

"We need to get together to talk, and before you turn obnoxious again, you should know, I think it's possible that Fallon is in danger."

Justice glanced at her, frowned, and said, "Yeah, let's meet."

"No," Fallon insisted, wanting to ensure that they both heard her loud and clear. "This concerns me and I want to know what's going on. *Right now*, Marcus."

After a heavy pause, Marcus muttered, "You didn't tell me I was on speaker."

Justice shrugged. "Didn't know you'd have anything worthwhile to say."

"This is difficult to explain, especially over the phone. I'm free now if we can meet."

"*All* of us," Fallon said.

"Of course."

They agreed to meet at her parents' house, in the driveway near the road.

Justice didn't want him any closer than that and Fallon didn't care enough to debate it.

For the rest of the short drive, her thoughts whirled. *What could Marcus possibly know about a threat?*

Justice reached over and squeezed her knee. "You know I won't let anyone hurt you, right?"

Snorting, she said, "No one is trying to. Marcus is up to something. It's ridiculous."

"I thought you trusted him."

Why did Justice have to decide now to defend her ex? "It infuriates me that he would attempt to bypass me to talk to you."

Justice pulled into the driveway, drove all the way up to the house, turned around, then went back to the entrance, now facing the street. "I think he's trying to be considerate."

She gaped at him.

"He could be really concerned about something and doesn't want to alarm you."

"I am a grown woman!"

He grinned. "I know. So we'll talk to him together and find out what's what. Okay? Just don't run him off until I've finished asking questions."

Fallon didn't point out that it was usually Justice who sent Marcus packing. "If this last apartment is gone before we get there—"

Rather than listen to her grumble, Justice got out of

the car and leaned against the front bumper, his arms crossed. That made her grumble even more, especially since she assumed her mention of the apartment was what had him looking cross.

She joined him, her hands on her hips and her good mood deteriorating. How could she get Justice to see her as a completely independent woman with no need of a bodyguard if Marcus planned to introduce some trumped-up danger?

Even now, feeling irked, Fallon couldn't help but notice how impressive Justice looked with his biceps bulging and a light breeze blowing his T-shirt flat against his abs.

"Stop it," she snapped, giving him a light shove.

Startled, he dropped his arms and scowled at her. "Stop what?"

"Posturing," she accused. "Looking all macho and disgruntled. You're doing it on purpose, aren't you? Know what I call that, Justice?"

Cautiously, his frown fierce, he asked, "What?"

"Pouting."

"Pouting!" He straightened to his impressive height to stare down at her. "I do *not* pout." He stepped closer. "Actually, I was contemplating things."

"What things?"

"If Marcus is right and there is a problem, you can't be alone in an apartment."

Fallon threw up her hands. She'd known his thoughts would take that path and it infuriated her. "How come every single time I try to prove that I'm the same as other women, something stupid comes up?"

"For one thing, you're not like other women." He cooled her anger by saying, "You're a damned heiress or something. No idea what kind of money your family has, but any idiot can see that you're loaded. That makes you a target."

He had a slight point. "Justice—"

"And whether you want to accept it or not, someone is up to something." He stepped closer still, until she had to tip her head way back to maintain eye contact. "Remember the red paint? My trampled flowers?"

"I don't have a faulty memory and it wasn't that long ago."

"Well, smart-ass, that's a problem. Sure, we could write it off as vandalism, except that you were *pushed down stairs*."

She tried not to waver under his conviction. Honestly, she didn't want to believe that someone planned to harm her. She'd never hurt anyone—except her sister. "Damn." Now was not the time to get maudlin. "I could have just stumbled."

Justice tipped up her chin. "Stop dodging reality. Let me do what I do, okay?" He bent to brush his mouth over hers. "I couldn't stand it if anything happened to you."

She wanted to say that nothing would, but suddenly she wasn't so sure. Justice's concern was affecting her. *Could I really have an enemy?* The idea chilled her.

They both looked up at the sound of Marcus's Mercedes pulling into the drive. He parked to the side of Justice's car and, without pause, got out to stride toward them.

The breeze, growing stronger, played with his blond hair and blew his tie to the side. He looked trim, stylish and, she could admit, handsome. His toned physique showed the designer suit to best advantage.

It didn't matter. Next to Justice, he seemed completely insubstantial.

Marcus took one look at Fallon and his brows went up while his jaw slackened.

She shifted uneasily under his stare. Yes, little by little she'd changed her look. Today she wore a casual spring dress, yellow with splashes of floral that complemented her figure. Rather than conceal, the fit of the dress showed off her bust. The scooped neckline was high enough to hide her scars, but showed much more skin than usual, even a hint of cleavage. A sash belt was tied at her waist and the full skirt skimmed just above her knees. She'd finished the outfit with strappy sandals and a yellow cardigan.

"Fallon," Marcus murmured, and it sounded like a verbal caress.

Justice put his arm around her shoulders and drew her into his side. "Keep it up," he warned, "and I'm going to flatten you."

Drawn back to reality, Marcus blinked. "You look so different. Nice, I mean. Very nice."

Justice growled.

Ignoring him, Marcus said softly, "I just… You took me by surprise. It's as if you've bloomed."

Flushing, Fallon nodded. "Justice and I have plans, so if you wouldn't mind.?" She loved it when Justice looked at her with so much appreciation. From Marcus, it left her cold.

He looked momentarily wounded, then shifted his gaze to Justice. "I wanted to speak in person. The entire thing is awkward, maybe even far-fetched, but it just doesn't feel right."

"Tell us what it is," Fallon insisted, and she got a squeeze from Justice. Right, he wanted her to let him do the questioning. She leaned into him, which was as much approval as he'd get.

"I think it's best if we keep this between us. You'll understand why—I hope—when I've finished." Marcus looked at each of them, then settled on Fallon. "You remember the men I had with me at the MMA competition?"

She lifted a shoulder. "A little."

"I remember them," Justice said.

"I believe I explained to you then that Kern and York Arnold are very wealthy men and they enjoy spending their money in outrageous ways."

It came back to Fallon in a rush. "You said they even bet with women as the prizes."

"Willing women," Marcus made clear. "But yes, it's as if they try to outdo each other in their extreme gambles." He shoved his hands into his pants pockets, his gaze on the ground. "Frankly, I've seen shocking behavior from both of them."

"They spoke with Tomahawk at the event," Justice said. "He knows them?"

His gaze shooting up to meet Justice's, Marcus frowned. "I don't know. Or rather, I'm not sure how well he knows them." He paced away, turned back. "They gave me an astounding amount for the literacy fund-raiser. Their one check equals the total we had hoped to gather in donations."

Fallon didn't understand. "That's good, isn't it?"

Justice took a step forward, his posture and tone hard. "Not if they're trying to buy him."

Marcus surprised them both by nodding. "My concern exactly."

Tucking her slightly behind him, Justice said, "So what is it they want you to do, and what does it have to do with Fallon?"

Looking past Justice, Marcus locked his gaze with hers. Softly, he said, "They want me to win you back."

"LIKE HELL." JUSTICE WASN'T about to let some wealthy dude in a fancy suit get in his way. Fallon was his and she'd damn well stay his. It didn't matter that Marcus, Kern and York fit better into Fallon's world. It didn't even matter that he, himself, made good money, first as a fighter and now as a bodyguard. Fallon wasn't a woman who cared about material wealth.

She cares about me.

He believed it, and soon she'd admit it—preferably before she plunked down first and last months' rent for an apartment she wouldn't be using.

Having her around his mom and granny had been a stroke of genius. Fallon flourished under their easy acceptance and lack of formality. In no time at all she'd become a cozy part of the family.

The problem was, she'd loosened up enough that

other guys took more notice of her—Marcus included. That wouldn't do. The sooner he got this settled and got her away from her ex, the more he'd like it.

Jealousy was a bitch.

"Just so I'm clear here," Justice said in what he hoped was a mild tone, "you have about thirty seconds to get the point."

"I'm trying, but it's not easy. Most of my concern is just a feeling."

"Gut instinct," Justice said, willing to give him his due. "Never ignore it."

Nodding, he glanced at Fallon, but seemed to find it easier to speak directly to Justice. "The brothers were in my office today and they were more than curious as to whether or not Fallon and I were back together."

Justice's jaw tightened and his eyes narrowed. "I hope you set them straight."

"In fact, I did. I explained that we were only friends now." Lower, he said, "I've never liked to hear them say her name or speak of her."

Fallon asked, "Why would they talk about me?"

"That's just it, I didn't know. They tried to be subtle about it playing it off like male camaraderie or something, but no matter what they said, it felt disrespectful." He drew in a breath. "Believe it or not, Fallon, I care for you. Beyond that, I respect you a great deal and I don't want anyone in any way to slander you."

Muscles tensing, Justice asked through his teeth, "Exactly what did they say?"

"Nothing specific, definitely not any direct insults. It's that they're—" he searched for the words "—irreverent.

Spoiled. Obnoxious. Selfish." He glanced at Fallon. "All things I would never associate with you. It doesn't matter what money they have or how much power that money brings them. They aren't good enough to joke about you as if you're just another woman, a woman they would know or would use in a bet."

Justice didn't like the small understanding nod Fallon gave Marcus. "Why the hell didn't you shut them up?"

"I'm a businessman," he snapped. "I can't go around alienating every person who's a jerk. Because of my position, I'm forced to use diplomacy."

"We understand." Fallon tipped her head. "But I still don't hear a threat."

Hands on his hips, head dropped forward, Marcus muttered, "They know the two of you are dating."

"So?" Justice said. "We haven't made it a secret."

"Justice." Fallon touched his arm, and the quietness in her tone alarmed him. "They don't travel in the same circles. Seeing them at the fights, that was a fluke. Since then, we've been to low-key places, or at your mother's. If these men know we're dating, someone is telling them."

"Or they've been spying on you." Marcus lifted his head. "They know she's been staying with you, that she hasn't been home." Quietly, Marcus repeated everything that had been said.

Gut instinct. Justice felt it now and he wanted to whisk Fallon away from any possible harm. First, though, he had to uncover the source of the danger.

Doing his best to stay clearheaded and keep the rage at bay, he asked, "Any ideas?"

Marcus gave a brief shake of head. "I don't know

anything for sure, but I suspect they have a wager on a fight."

"They want to see a rematch with Tom and me." Grim, Justice cursed low, his hands curling into fists. "I still don't see how Fallon plays into this, or why they'd be keeping tabs on her. Is Tom somehow in on it?"

"I don't know that," Marcus said quickly. "But an idea occurred to me for how we could find out."

Justice stiffened. "No."

"What?" Fallon asked, looking from one of them to the other.

"No," he said again.

"Tell me," Fallon insisted.

Marcus folded his arms over his chest and stared at Justice. "We need to pretend to give them what they want."

MILES SAT AT a booth in Rowdy's bar, slowly nursing a beer. At another table with a few other fighters, Tom brooded. He didn't join in on the jokes and he wasn't drinking as much.

Suspicions sucked. He liked Tom all right, but he trusted Justice more. Leese felt the same. If Justice had reason to doubt Tom, that was good enough for them.

A slim, familiar figure wearing designer jeans and a body-hugging top walked through the front door of the bar. Maxi Nevar's dark blond hair trailed down her back, and her brown eyes searched the crowd.

For him.

Miles waited, deciding if he felt like giving in to

Maxi tonight. He had twice before and both times the sex had been…well, incredible. Mind-blowing, even.

The lady wasn't shy, and she knew what she wanted.

Her gaze met his and she smiled, proving that tonight, *again*, she wanted him.

As she made her way toward him, Miles finished off his beer. He couldn't say what it was about Maxi that made him want to stay detached. Possibly her own detachment. She enjoyed sex with him, but wanted nothing else.

Other men in the bar tracked her progress as she maneuvered her way across the floor. He should just be flattered, but God, he'd suffered from a weird mood lately.

When she finally reached him, she asked, "Alone tonight?" as if it didn't matter all that much, as if, if he had a date, she'd be okay with it and would just mosey on.

"I'm alone," he said. "But sort of working." His gaze skipped over to Tomahawk. Miles watched him smile at something someone said, then turn distracted again.

"Working on getting drunk?" Maxi asked with a laugh as she settled her sexy behind across from him in the booth.

"Only one beer," he said, then resented that he'd explained. He never got drunk, but since they only had a very limited relationship—which was exactly how he wanted it—she didn't need to know his habits.

"Just a cola for me," she said to the waitress who stopped by their booth.

"Another for me," Miles added, handing over the empty bottle.

Maxi tipped her head, causing that dark golden hair to cascade over her breast. "Would you rather be alone tonight?"

Not really. "Just weighing my options."

To his consternation, she laughed. "Another woman has caught your eye? Should I vacate the booth before she gets the wrong impression?"

Sitting back, he stared at her. It wasn't natural, damn it. "What's the lure, Maxi? That I'm a fighter?" Because he might not be for much longer.

"That's a joke, right? The first night I came in here, I noticed you right off. When I hit on you, I had no idea what you did—and I don't care."

"So if I decide to take up waiting tables?"

"I assume you'd still have an occasional night off and I'd see you here, right?"

For a booty call. Frowning, more at himself than her, Miles said, "I don't know."

For only a heartbeat, her dark eyes looked troubled, then she quickly brightened again. "Well, that would be a waste, but I'm sure I'd survive."

No, he hadn't imagined it. He'd seen something, maybe worry? "Actually, I'm thinking about being a bodyguard." *Why the hell did I just tell her that?* He waited, wondering how she'd react.

"To protect someone specific?" She crossed her arms on the tabletop and leaned forward enough that he could see her cleavage.

Maxi had a nice pair on her, full and soft with sensitive mauve nipples. Once, she'd damn near come from him sucking on her. He stirred remembering it.

But then, the second she'd walked in, his temperature had spiked.

Without giving him a chance to answer, she added, "Not being nosy, but if you're involved, then I'll definitely move on."

Knowing she would, Miles shook his head. "I meant as a career choice."

"Sounds exciting—and I go back to my original question. You'd have the occasional night off?"

The server brought their drinks, giving him a moment to think and time to check on Tom. He saw a woman leaning over Tom, whispering in his ear. *Good*, he thought. *Go home with her so I can quit watching you.*

To Miles's surprise, Tom kissed her palm, whispered something back to her and sent her away. The others at his table heckled him, but Tom only shook his head.

What the hell was going on?

A small, warm hand covered his, drawing Miles back from his curiosity. He met Maxi's dark eyes, already heavy with interest. While they looked at each other, she toyed with him, trailing her fingertips down the seam between two of his.

"So," she whispered. "Are you going to be free for a few hours tonight or not?"

A few hours. Nothing more. She wouldn't ask him why he planned to leave fighting, or why he was sulking over his beers. She never pried. Never asked anything personal.

She just enjoyed his body for a few hours, the orgasms he'd give her, and then she'd leave his house and he wouldn't even know if he'd see her again or not.

"Depends," Miles said, watching her. "Your place tonight?"

Her smile never slipped. "No."

"I'm starting to wonder if you're a serial killer. Maybe an escaped convict? Do you have a husband and kids at home?"

Slowly, she sat back, her smile gone. She stared at her drink. She seemed somehow…hurt.

"Maxi—"

"I'm not married. No kids. I don't like cheaters."

Well, that was something at least.

"I've never broken a law in my life. Not even the speed limit."

"A paragon of virtue, huh?"

"Hardly that, but I'm a coward." Her dark gaze met his. "Much too much of a coward to ever be a serial killer."

Pushing her, Miles asked, "What do you do for a living?"

"I'm a personal shopper."

Huh. That fit, given her great style. "One more question."

"I won't be grilled. You're either into it or you're not."

"It" being meaningless sex. *And since when has that been a problem for you?* "Why me?"

Her arched brows twitched. "That's it? That's your question?"

"Yeah."

The smile returned and she leaned forward again. "Let's go to your place, get naked and I'll show you."

Maybe his dissatisfaction was because the guys

were all starting to settle down. Gage, Cannon, Denver, Stack, Armie and Leese. Now even Justice appeared hooked. Like dominoes, once the first one fell, the rest tumbled. But here he was, feeling…fuck it. He felt a little lost, and admitting that, even to himself, burned his ass big-time.

"I told you, I'm working."

She bit her lip and, resigned, sat back again. Miles watched her play with her purse strap, tuck her hair behind her ears, look out at the bar and at the front door where she'd entered.

"What are you thinking, Maxi?" It struck him and he asked, "Your name *is* Maxi, right?" How far would she go to stay an enigma?

"Yes, that's my name. Short for Maximara." After a few seconds, she looked up at him again. "May I ask you something? Nothing personal, I promise."

Miles laughed. "I don't mind if you ask anything personal." Of course, he knew why she didn't. If she asked something personal, he might reciprocate. For whatever reason, she didn't want him getting too close.

"Are you really that busy tonight, or have you lost interest?" She rushed on, "If you have, you can just tell me. I'm not a stalker type. I won't bother you."

His gaze moved to her mouth, and he thought of the incredible things she did with it. "See the big guy two tables over? Heavyweight fighter?"

She glanced around. "I can't really tell weight classes—oh." Turning back to him and leaning forward, she asked, "What about him?"

"I have a friend who works for the Body Armor

Agency. That's the bodyguard gig I'm thinking about taking. Well, my friend needs me to keep an eye on the big lug over there, so that's what I'm doing."

Accepting that, Maxi considered things, then asked, "For how long?"

"Until he leaves here."

"So you could be really late."

Gently, he asked, "Got somewhere you need to be?"

"Not really, no."

"So stay. Keep me company. Tell me where you got that name and what a personal shopper does. When it's time to go, you can follow me to my place."

Over the next half hour, between flirting, teasing and laughing, Miles managed to pry a little info from her. As a near stranger, she'd been hot.

Seeing her like this, less "on the make" and more re-laxed, only gave her more substance. When Tom got a call and stepped toward the front door, away from the din of conversation, to talk, Miles said, "I'll be right back," and followed him.

People entered and exited the bar, so Tom paid no attention when Miles moved to stand behind him, close enough to overhear.

"Right now?" Tom asked, looking out at the passing traffic, oblivious to everything else. "Yeah, I mean sure. I can make it." He nodded, repeating the name of a ritzy neighborhood as if to memorize it. "I'm famil-iar, yeah. I'll leave now, but that's across town, so give me a little time." He nodded again. "Thanks, Kern. See you soon." He disconnected and turned so fast, he damn near plowed into Miles.

"Tomahawk," Miles said, after he'd backed him off a little.

"Damn, man, didn't see you there." Distracted and in a hurry, Tom shoved the phone back in his pocket. "What's up?"

"Nothing. Just grabbing some air." Feeling like a sleuth and liking it, Miles asked, "You?"

"Meeting with a few sponsors. Big spenders." Smiling now instead of looking glum, Tom whacked him on the shoulder.

Miles stopped him from rushing off. "Sponsors for what? Got an upcoming fight?"

"If I can get Justice on board, yeah."

"I don't think that's happening."

"Hey, these guys can be persuasive. So don't count me out yet."

Miles watched him go inside to let his friends know he was leaving, then rush back out again. Once he'd driven down the road, Miles put in a call to Justice.

While the phone rang, he thought about life changes, and he thought about Maxi.

He'd made up his mind. Tonight would be a celebration, and he couldn't think of a better way to spend it than with a woman who burned him up, kept him guessing and didn't demand much in return.

CHAPTER SEVENTEEN

THE RESTAURANT WAS LOUD, the conversation at their table rowdy. Anytime Justice got his mom and granny out together, they had a great time. He didn't like the way Fallon had withdrawn. When his mother noticed, Justice subtly shook his head, warning her not to mention it. Marcus had thrown a lot at Fallon today, not only the possible danger but also the way they'd most likely resolve it. She deserved time to think about it, and hopefully she'd come to the right conclusions.

Let me protect you.

He couldn't take his eyes off her—something else his mother noticed. He saw Fallon smile as his granny described the way she'd taught him to dance. Many a night before dinner, they'd crank up the music and glide around the kitchen floor in their socks. Fallon obviously loved the story, but her smile didn't quite sparkle in her eyes as it usually did.

When his cell rang Justice barely heard it, but he felt it buzzing in his pocket.

He glanced at the screen, saw it was Miles and pushed back his chair.

Feeling like something was about to break, Justice

said to the table, "I have to take this," and stepped to the entry.

Miles got right to the point. "I was hanging at Rowdy's, keeping an eye on Tom as I promised. But a few minutes ago he got a call from someone named Kern and took off."

"Shit," Justice muttered, not wanting to believe Tom would be such a dick.

"He said it's about a sponsorship—for a fight against you."

Justice listened as Miles related the conversation. Like hell anyone would "convince" him. More like they meant to coerce him somehow, but that wouldn't happen either.

"You said he left?"

"Going to meet the guy."

Justice held the phone back to see the time. Nearing nine o'clock. Okay, not a crazy time for a meeting, but definitely not routine either. "Did he mention where?"

"Yeah, see that's the thing." Miles paused as if he dreaded sharing the rest. "Tom mentioned the same neighborhood where Fallon lives."

"That's too much coincidence for me."

"Maybe," Miles agreed. "But don't do anything stupid."

"Like?"

"Hit first and ask questions later. Be cool, okay? Just because he knows those dudes—"

"And is associating with them." *Maybe conspiring.*

"—doesn't mean he's guilty of anything. You've known Tom awhile. He deserves an opportunity to explain."

Justice indulged a deep, cleansing breath. It helped, but not enough. "Right." At the moment, the urge to destroy anyone who threatened Fallon burned hot. Unfortunately, he knew Miles had a point. "And pulverizing him won't get me the answers I need."

Moving past the idea of violence, Miles asked, "So what are you going to do?"

"I'm going to call Leese. Then I'm going to do my own conspiring."

SNICKERING, HE WATCHED from a safe distance away as Tom Nelson, aka Tomahawk, arrived at the destination. Like a sitting duck, Tom put his car in Park on the side of the road, ready and willing to wait.

As bait.

The big brute was far too gullible.

He had it all planned out, but several things had to align. Would Tom be patient enough? Given the prize, he'd wait as long as necessary.

Fortunately, only ten minutes passed before Justice Wallington's car came into view. Anticipation sizzling, he crouched beside the tree, the lighter in his hand.

Before anyone had arrived, he'd poured a generous amount of diesel across the road, followed by a trail over to where he hid. Once everything happened, it'd be easy for him to sink deeper into the lush landscaping. As always, he'd get away without a scrape—but the two fighters wouldn't be so lucky.

As a kid, he'd pulled this prank often. He'd found the panicked results of the startled drivers keenly satisfying.

With luck, the results this time would be even better.

As Justice's car drew nearer, he flicked the lighter, saw the flame dance, and at just the right moment, he put it to the trail.

In the darkness of the night, the red and yellow flame licked quickly across the road, flaring up just as Justice reached it. He watched the fighter hit his brakes hard, swerving sideways until the car slewed partially off the road and came to a shuddering halt.

Gleeful at that reaction, he hunkered down out of sight, listening for the woman's cries. Holding in his chuckles, he cocked an ear, waiting.

He heard only the hoot of an owl and the sound of the breeze playing with leaves overhead.

Nothing even remotely like female hysterics.

A second later the driver's door shoved open and the fighter emerged, one very pissed-off man.

In that brief moment while the overhead light glowed, he saw inside the car and knew the fighter was alone. *Where was Ms. Wade?* Her fear would have added nicely to this confrontation.

It didn't matter, he convinced himself. The results would be the same.

Predictably, Tom, who had parked only a short distance away, came jogging closer to help.

Fists would be flying in no time—he was sure of it.

As he faded back, he waited for the fun to begin.

JUSTICE STARED AT the slowly dying flame. *What the hell?*

Diesel, he thought, given the scent. He scoured the area, but the ritzy houses on this stretch of road sat acres apart from one another. Thick trees and high, manicured hedges lined the road to offer privacy.

Thinking he heard something in the woods beyond, Justice's eyes narrowed. He saw a shadow move and took a step in that direction.

"Justice?"

He jerked around at the shout and—surprise, surprise—found Tom jogging toward him.

Bewildered, looking at the flames, Tom asked, "What happened, man?"

Refusing to blow it by being too calm, or too enraged, Justice locked his hands down at his sides. "What are you doing out here, Tom?"

"Had a meeting, but the guy's late." He glanced at the car, still idling, with the ass-end over the shoulder of the road, almost in the gully. "You hurt?"

"No." Justice thanked God he didn't have Fallon with him. She, along with his mother and granny, were on their way home with Leese. Hitching his chin, Justice asked with lethal menace, "Who has a meeting here, on a dark road, at this time of night?"

Brows coming down, Tom stared at him. "Is this another accusation?"

"You're quick today, huh?"

Tom bristled. "I let you get away with that once, man. I won't take it kindly a second time."

"Take it any fucking way you want." Justice pointed at him. "Twice now shit has happened, and both times you're on the scene."

For a second, Tom looked like he might lunge for him.

Justice was counting on him wanting the sanctioned fight in the cage, not a street brawl.

At the last second, Tom visibly gathered himself and glanced around the area instead.

They stood to the side of Justice's car. The headlights cut across the road and into a line of thick shrubbery and pruned trees.

Rubbing the back of his head, Tom asked, "Did I see fire in the road?"

Aware of possibilities, Justice replied, "You did. A line of diesel, deliberately set."

Tom's gaze shot up. "Someone wanted you to wreck?"

"And here you are," Justice smirked.

Tom inhaled. "Yeah, okay, I admit, it looks bad." He glanced back at the car. "Fallon's not with you?"

"No."

"Small blessing, I guess."

He eyed Tom, surprised that he was staying so composed. That in itself made his cynicism grow. "What meeting?" Wondering if Tom would tell the truth, Justice asked, "Who's late?"

"Rich dude named Kern Arnold. He was at Stack's last fight…" Tom paused, then gave a rough laugh. "This won't exactly exonerate me, but Kern and his brother want to sponsor me—that is, if I can convince you to give me a rematch."

There'd be no rematch, but all he said was, "Sponsor you how?"

"Lots of bucks. Full ride." He stared at Justice. "They're big fans."

Did some lackey set the fire for Kern? Or was the

bastard sick enough to want to see the reaction himself? Was it possible that even now, he lurked there in the shadows, listening?

Damned coward.

Searching the area, Justice said, "I got the impression the brothers didn't know that much about MMA."

"Yeah, they're new to the sport. They like it. Stack's fight was their first live event, but they're really into the heavyweights now. They watched our last fight on the internet and they're hoping for a rematch."

Just as Marcus had said. But why spy on Fallon?

Almost as soon as he thought it, Tom gave him a credible answer. "I told them I didn't think you'd go for it, that you liked your new job and were hung up on Fallon." He quickly held up his hands. "Not that there's anything wrong with that. Just that it looks like you're going in a different direction now." He shrugged. "They said they could convince you."

Did they hope to get Fallon out of the picture, to force him to refocus? "I've told you at least a dozen times that it's not happening. I suggest you convince them, as well."

Tom scowled. "You're killing me, man. The girl is nice and all, but—"

"No buts." *Fallon was considerably more than nice.*

"The brothers said they could bring you around. God knows they have the money to do it. So at least hear them out."

Would they offer him money, Justice wondered, or did they plan another form of leverage? Maybe something involving Fallon?

He glanced up and down the road. "I think you got stood up."

Frustration deepened Tom's frown. "I'll call him and see what's up."

"Yeah, before you bother, we need to talk."

"That's what we've been doing, right? But you're still being a stubborn ass."

Justice walked over to the driver's door and got in.

"What are you doing?"

With a little effort, he got his car back onto the road. Tom stood there, hands on hips, watching until Justice backed up alongside him. With the push of a button, he lowered the passenger window and said, "Get in."

He could tell that Tom wanted to refuse, but then with a curse, he opened the door and slid into the seat.

"You're damned annoying, Justice, you know that?"

Calmly, Justice drove up the short distance to where Tom had parked, pulled in behind his Corvette and put the car in Park.

Half turning in his seat, he faced Tom. "I'm going to believe you're here for a meeting, but if I find out otherwise, I'll destroy you."

Rage growing, Tom barked, "To hell with it. We can settle this right now." He reached for the door handle— and the lock clicked into place. Incredulous, he glared at Justice. "Are you out of your fucking mind?"

Since he planned to tell all to Tom…maybe. But hell, he was willing to work with Marcus, and that had already put him over the edge of sanity. "Let me lay out some facts here for you, okay?"

"You've got about two seconds."

Justice decided to start with the most pressing issue. "Someone is deliberately placing you at the scene each time something happens."

The scowl lightened, and Tom scoffed. "What are you talking about?"

"You don't think it's a hell of a coincidence that Fallon would get elbowed down the steps when she's away from me, but close to you? Then someone calls the agency and labels *you* a threat. Now we're both on this road—a road where we normally wouldn't run into each other—and some asshole pulls a prank with diesel that could've gotten someone killed."

Tom glowered as he considered it then shook his head. "I told you, I'm here to meet Kern."

"But the bastard's not here, is he? It's just you and me. I don't mind telling you, with everything's that happened, if Fallon had been with me, there's a damn good chance I'd be even more pissed than I am. It wouldn't take much for one of us to lose our cool and end up—"

"Fighting," Tom agreed with thoughtful uneasiness. He rubbed his face. "So you think what? That someone wants us to battle it out? We're on a dark street with no one around."

Calmly, Justice pointed out the obvious. "If it's just us, who set that diesel on fire?"

Bewildered, Tom sat back in his seat. "That's a hell of a conspiracy you're spinning."

"Yeah."

"I have to admit, it does seem off."

"Big-time." Justice rested an arm over the steering wheel. "Without any bullshit, have you ever followed me?"

"What do you mean?"

Resting his wrist on the wheel, he gestured toward Tom's car. "In your Vette."

Knowing he was busted, Tom shifted. "Well, fuck, this is awkward."

Justice waited.

"It's not what you think."

"No? So what is it?"

"I was on that side of town to get my car serviced and I just happened to see you. Sure, I followed for a bit. I couldn't think of any reason for you to be over that way unless you were going to another gym to train, which would mean you weren't as out of the game as you claimed."

"Why would you give a shit?"

"Because I want a goddamned rematch!"

Justice studied him. "You didn't follow me to Fallon's?"

Slashing a hand through the air, Tom said, "No. Hell, I didn't know anything about her until I caught up with you at Rowdy's."

"No way you didn't see her with me in the car."

Coldly, Tom said, "For someone who doesn't want a fight, you sure like to sling out the insults."

"Well?" Again, Justice waited.

"I saw you had someone in the car, yeah, but not her specifically. I figured just a date, you know? I wasn't interested in following you anymore, but we kept going in the same direction until somehow I lost you. I ran a few other errands, then we both ended up at Rowdy's, so I guess we were headed in the same direction." He shrugged.

"What's the name of the place where you get your Vette serviced?"

Tom told him without hesitation, even naming the street. When Justice pulled it up on his cell, the route made sense. "Pure happenstance, huh?"

"Believe it or not. I don't care."

But Justice could tell that he did. Hell, no one wanted to be unjustly accused. "That's the only time you've ever followed me?"

"Swear to God, and I didn't exactly plan it that time."

Justice believed him. "Okay then. You want to know why I'm so skeptical?" By the time he finished explaining all his concerns with Fallon, the brothers and Marcus, Tom was outraged.

"What can I do?" he asked simply.

Justice told him.

MARCUS SAT IN uncomfortable silence inside the conference room of his offices. Across from him, Tom Nelson maintained a deadly stare. He was enormous, layered in muscle and presently in a bad mood. Or maybe he had no other mood—although, thinking back, Marcus remembered when Tom had met Kern and York at the MMA event. He'd been all smiles and "good old boy" charm then.

What the hell did these fighters eat? How many hours did they spend training?

Unlike Justice, Tom's mocking smile felt like a knife blade to his ribs. Justice, at least, had a little humor to him.

It had taken some fancy maneuvering to arrange the meeting. Justice wanted Tom and the brothers together, in front of Marcus, so that the puzzle pieces fit together in an unmistakable pattern. There could be no doubt, no suspicion of secret intent.

In the end, Marcus had called Kern to say he must meet with him that morning, only minutes after Tom had also requested a morning meeting. When Kern mentioned the conflict, Marcus offered to call Tom and arrange them to meet together in his office's largest conference room.

A small security camera was set up in the corner, and more importantly, Justice wasn't far away.

Hell of a situation to find himself in, Marcus mused. He currently relied on Justice, the man who had replaced him with Fallon, to keep him safe from harm.

Untenable, but what choice did he have? That same fighter would also keep Fallon safe, and that's what mattered most.

Getting up to pace, Marcus tried to ignore Tom's penetrating stare as it tracked him around the room. He was just about to demand that he cease and desist with the intimidation tactics when the door opened and his assistant announced the brothers.

Wearing wide smiles, Kern and York strode in. They'd dressed in casual clothes; khaki slacks on Kern, shorts on York, both wearing open-necked shirts and watches that cost as much as some people's cars.

Before Marcus could greet them, Tom growled, "Wasn't sure you'd show this time."

Why was Tom so damned hostile? If he didn't let up, he just might blow everything.

Marcus at least wanted to keep it together until the check cleared. The more ethical thing to do, he thought, would be to tear it up and toss it into the brothers' faces.

He wouldn't do it.

He'd earned the damned donation and knowing it'd be put to good use was enough of an incentive for him. Still, he had to keep the brothers trusting him another two or three days until they'd settled everything.

Taking the seat at the head of the long table, Kern smiled toward Tom. "Yes, I'm sorry about that. I got held up."

York sat at the opposite head of the table, stealing Marcus's seat. "Did you wait around very long, Tomahawk?"

"Got here five minutes ago."

Nonplussed at that reply, York shook his head. "Ah, no. I meant last night."

Shrugging, Tom sipped his coffee.

Determined, Kern leaned forward. "Last night—I tried to call but my cell service was acting up."

Again, Tom shrugged, and Marcus could see that it exacerbated both brothers. Were they hoping to discover what had happened last night? Or did they already know and only wanted Tom's accounting of it?

Marcus wasn't at all sure about Tom. He seemed sullen and unpredictable. Marcus's own ruse was enough to make his palms sweat, but at least he recalled what to say. "While we waited this morning, Tom and I have gotten better acquainted. He mentioned that he had unexpected company last night, so it wasn't a total waste."

"Oh?" Kern lifted his brows with fervent interest.

Finally, Tom deigned to play his part. "Justice Wallington had a mishap on the road, not more than a few yards from where you asked me to wait."

"Mishap?" Kern asked.

"Yeah. Some juvenile bitch playing a high-school prank. No big deal." Tom smiled.

"Do tell."

"You can imagine, he wasn't happy." As if they'd asked, Tom said, "No one was hurt."

Showing marked disinterest in that, Kern said, "Good thing," then asked eagerly, "So you and Justice. How'd that go?"

"Got a fight lined up."

Excitement caused a second of utter stillness before Kern and York celebrated with loud whoops. Kern left his seat to slap Tom on the shoulder, full of congratulations.

"So tell me," York probed, his tone cagey, "what turned the tide?"

Now that Marcus was onto them, the brothers were nauseatingly transparent.

"Guess there's more people like you two," Tom said, "fans who want to see me fight."

"And that mattered to Wallington?" York asked.

Tom snorted. "Why the hell would he care?"

He's toying with them, Marcus realized, appalled by the risk. Good God, were they all insane?

"Well," Kern suggested, somewhat unsure of himself in the face of Tom's attitude, "Justice was so dead set against fighting you—"

"He still is."

The brothers looked at each other, sharing their confusion, until Kern exploded. "You just said you had a fight!"

"I do, just not against Justice."

"But..." Kern pulled out the nearest chair and dropped into it. "The plan was a rematch."

"I had to give up on that," Tom said. "I'm set to fight Denver instead. He's another mountain, and damned good, so I'll get lots of exposure for the fight."

When Kern and York just stared at him, Tom continued pricking them with inane details. "It'll be the main event, probably in Vegas, but we're still waiting for the calendar to be finalized. My manager will let me know as soon as—"

Slamming his hand down on the table, Kern shouted, "What do you mean, you gave up?"

Marcus jumped in surprise.

Tom never even flinched. His flinty gaze met Kern's, and his slight smile slapped like an insult. "Not much choice. Some asshole is trying to make it look like I'd use Justice's lady to get my way."

York and his brother shared a fast, covert glance, so maybe Marcus was the only one to notice the clenching of Tom's jaw.

Kern cleared his throat. "You could—"

"No. If I press Justice now," Tom continued, "he'll never believe I didn't push the little lady down the stairs, or stomp on some fucking flowers or something."

"Uh...flowers?" York asked.

"Doesn't matter." Tom finished off his coffee. "Some

gutless punk is playing childish games, and because of that I have to change my plans."

"This fight was important to you," York insisted.

"Not as important as my rep. A real man would never use a woman to get what he wants, and I'll be damned if I'll let anyone think I would."

Flushing, Kern tried a different tact. "You explained to Justice that it wasn't you, and he believed you?"

"Hell, no. Justice wanted a piece of me, no doubt about that. Thing is, he refused an actual fight in the cage, and I told him I wouldn't risk an injury without an audience. He told me to stay away from him, and I agreed. End of story."

"We offered to sponsor you!" York accused.

"You still can."

Fuming, Kern snapped, "We wanted the damned rematch!"

"Get in line."

Everyone seemed to have forgotten him, Marcus thought, sinking back in his seat and staying still, content to be a silent observer. Tom's open disdain of the brothers, as if they were no more than troublesome brats, fascinated him. Kern's red-faced rage was a sight to behold. And York, his air conniving... Yes, fascinating— if it wasn't so dangerous.

Kern shoved back his chair so fast it hit the floor. "You don't understand. It doesn't have to be a professional fight. We don't care about that."

Tom curled his lip. "I care."

Edging his testy brother aside, York righted the fallen chair and turned to straddle it. He faced Tom with an implacable smile. "Here's the deal. Kern and I want to see you fight Justice, not some other goon. We've got a little wager on it, you see, and as Kern is the current loser in a string of bets, he's anxious to try to even the score."

"I'm betting on you," Kern offered for encouragement.

When Tom narrowed his eyes, unimpressed, York said, "You will fight Justice Wallington, wherever he wants—even in a goddamned alley for all I care—and we'll be your very generous sponsors for two years."

Tom lazily considered York. "So you're betting against me, huh?"

"There must always be a winner and a loser."

"This time," Kern said, "you and I will win, Tom. I'm sure of it."

Tom appeared unmoved by the pep talk.

"We'll supply you with comfortable living quarters wherever you train, cell phone, insurance, a food and entertainment allowance, and we'll provide any equipment or supplements that you might need."

Kern rushed to support his brother. "Two years, Tom. You won't get a more generous deal anywhere."

In a perfectly timed act, a knock sounded on the door, saving Tom from having to answer.

As if she owned the place, Fallon breezed in, then paused at the sight of the three extra men. "Oh, Marcus, I'm so sorry. Your assistant didn't mention that you had guests."

"No matter." Smiling, he stood. "I wanted to see you as soon as you arrived." God, she was pretty, always had been, but now that Justice had given her more confidence, she positively glowed. She'd changed her hairstyle a little, dressed in feminine clothes that showed off her body and smiled with sincere happiness.

Marcus wished it wasn't a farce, that her smile was for him, but in the years he'd known her, he'd never been as good for her as Justice had in such a short time.

Did the fighter really not mind those awful scars?

Seeing them had completely caught Marcus off guard. With time, he could have grown accustomed to them, but he'd never suspected, never considered... For the hundredth time, he cursed himself for reacting as bluntly as he had.

Fallon hadn't said it, but Marcus assumed she loved Justice. He saw it in the way she looked at the man, how different—how *carefree*—she was around him. Justice appeared to feel the same. There was a possessive look in the man's eyes that went beyond the duties of a bodyguard and a familiarity in the way Justice watched her. Intimate familiarity.

Fallon deserved happiness, so for her, Marcus would recite his lines and, hopefully, assist in securing her safety.

She hesitated at the door. "I can wait—"

"It's okay, this is both a business meeting and personal, but I wanted you to meet the Arnolds anyway." As he held out a hand to Fallon, he glanced at the brothers. They appeared confused by all the sudden changes. "Honey, these are the gentlemen who were so extremely generous toward the literacy fund-raiser."

Fallon smiled at the men. "Thank you so much, both

of you. I'm still stunned, and of course, so incredibly pleased."

York held out his hand. "York Arnold, ma'am."

"Fallon, please," she said, taking his hand in both of hers. "It's very nice to meet you personally, York."

"This is my brother, Kern."

Kern gently took her hand. "Obviously Marcus has excellent taste."

Surprising Marcus, Fallon leaned against his shoulder in an affectionate way. "Thank you."

"I saw you at the MMA venue," Kern said, as if he'd just remembered it. "Excuse me, but I thought you were with that fighter, Justice Wallington."

Giving a rueful grimace, Fallon nodded. "I found out that Justice isn't quite done with the sport. It's a commitment leaving little time for relationships."

"Surely no man would neglect you," York said.

"It doesn't really matter because Marcus won me back." In a teasing stage whisper, she confessed, "I made him work for it."

The brothers actually looked captivated.

"And I," Marcus said, "used your generous donation as a good excuse to get her to talk with me again."

"It worked," she said with a laugh.

Suddenly Tom shoved back his chair. "I need to get going."

Kern stepped toward him. "But—"

"I'll let you know this afternoon what I've decided." Tom paused. "Either way, thanks for the offer."

Nice way to leave them wondering. Marcus watched

Tom go, only half listening as Fallon picked up the conversation, keeping Kern and York from following.

After adequate time, Marcus reclaimed the room. "York, Kern, the reason I asked you to stop by is because we're creating a plaque to honor you for your lavish financial gesture. The plaque will hang in a prominent location in the new library. Now, thanks to you, at-risk children will have easy access to books."

York grinned. "I'm glad we could help."

"Let's celebrate over lunch," Kern said. "We can talk MMA, and maybe, Fallon, you can share a few tips on how to get Justice Wallington back in the cage for a rematch."

"I would love to help out," Fallon said with a laugh. "Unfortunately I already have another appointment for today." With Leese, who would ensure she got home safely while Justice kept an eye on the brothers.

Marcus's heart raced as he stood and walked her to the door. He looked down at her, wondering if she'd kiss him goodbye to seal the deal—but no, she patted his cheek, waved to the brothers and left.

Chagrined, despite the fact none of it was real, Marcus turned back to York and Kern. "Now, what was all that with Tom?"

CHAPTER EIGHTEEN

IN THE STOREROOM of Rowdy's bar, away from prying eyes, Justice pulled Fallon close and kissed her, first the tip of her nose, then her chin, her cheek, and finally he settled his mouth on hers. Her soft lips parted and he felt the touch of her damp tongue.

Groaning, Justice crushed her closer, taking her mouth in uncontrolled need, stroking deeply with his tongue, wanting to consume her.

"Excuse me." Avery, Rowdy's wife, laughed as she bumped her way past them, jarring Justice back to reality.

He lifted his head and saw Avery's long red ponytail swish as she reached high on a shelf behind them for a massive jar of pickles.

Justice easily stretched past her. "Let me." He fetched it down for her.

"Thank you." Hugging the jar to her body, Avery said, "Carry on!" A second later, they were alone again.

Fallon, trying to stifle a laugh, covered her heated cheeks. "Busted," she whispered.

Justice gathered her close and touched a finger to her now swollen mouth. God, he loved the taste of her, the way she fit against him. He pressed his forehead to hers and groaned again. His need was a live thing, always pushing at him.

Fallon smoothed a hand over his chest, then curled her fingers against his shoulder. "I missed you."

"Love hearing that." For only a few days they'd been playing this stupid but necessary game, yet it felt like an eternity. Damn it, he liked sleeping with her at night, waking with her in the morning. He'd grown used to her small body snug against his during the night, just as he'd grown used to regular sex, the hottest sex he'd ever had.

"Marcus has been nice," she said. "I thought I would be more uncomfortable with him, maybe even bitter, you know? But I'm not."

"Should I be jealous?" Stupid question; he already was.

She tucked her face against his throat. "Before you, I saw Marcus only as the man who'd rejected me."

"He's regretting that, I'm sure." *The putz.*

"Since meeting you, Marcus is just someone I know, someone I can think of as a friend." She tipped her face up to look at him with those big, soulful eyes. "His reaction to my scars was an eye-opener, but also real. I can't fault him for how he feels, but I'm glad I found out before we got any more involved."

"My reaction is real too, honey." He put his lips to her ear and whispered, "Seeing any part of you makes me hard."

She laughed. "That's the main reason I can now accept Marcus as an acquaintance, a friend and nothing more."

Marcus was no longer the man who hurt her. Justice

only hoped that made him more irrelevant. "You're saying I helped you get over the bad memory?"

"You obliterated the bad memory, and I love you
for it."

Justice's heart plummeted to his knees, then shot up
into his throat. *Love*. Jesus, he almost felt dizzy.

The urge to swing her up, twirl her in a circle and tell
her that he loved her, too, surged through him.

He held back only because she hadn't said it in a romantic way. She hadn't said, *Justice, I love you*.

Words he wanted to hear.

She'd only expressed her gratitude for the way he'd
gotten her past her insecurity. This was too important
to misunderstand; he wouldn't embarrass her by pounc-
ing on such a simple statement.

Her gaze stayed with his, her smile in place, and Justice knew he had to say something.

Straight from the heart, he decided. "You're the most
special person I've ever known, Fallon. I love everything about you." Watching the confusion flit over her
expression, he smiled to himself and kissed her again.

Soon she'd understand, but damn, the storeroom of
Rowdy's bar was hardly the place for declarations.

Hardly the place for him to be getting a boner either, yet after hearing that four-letter word, *love*, thrown
around, he knew he was almost there.

He broke off the kiss and cupped her face in his
hands. "Everything should be settled today." Then he'd
get her back where she belonged—with him.

"God, I hope so." Her smile teased. So did her fingers on his chest. "I miss your house, Justice."

A hint? She'd been staying with Leese and Catalina for the last few nights. No way did Justice want to risk her being home alone in her parents' mansion, and he sure as hell didn't want to tempt fate by pushing her at Marcus.

It amused Justice that his house could fit into the garage of her parents' mansion, but Fallon never looked at it that way. Even her dad had assured him how little she cared for the pampered life.

He had to taste her again. If Fallon was close, she drew him in, sharpening every physical need. "I miss having you there," he admitted against her lips. "A lot."

"That apartment I wanted to look at is gone."

Justice froze. *Good.* He didn't want her in an apartment.

Unsure why she'd mentioned it, he tried for a neutral tone. "Still determined to go that way, huh?"

"I'd like for each of us to have options."

He didn't want options; he wanted Fallon. This time, though, with him, her needs had to come first. He smoothed his thumb over her downy cheek, knowing he'd do damn near anything for her. "Soon as we get this settled, we'll talk about it more, okay?"

She nodded, her dark eyes staring up at him. "Are you sure you know what you're doing?"

"Hope so." Taking her hand, he led her over to a stack of boxes to sit. It sucked, having to sneak around to see her, but the alternative, not seeing her, would be far worse. "The bastard brothers now believe you're with Marcus, so hopefully you're not on their radar anymore." That had been his number-one goal. He'd hated thinking she might be a target used to twist him into lashing out.

"It's not me I'm worried about."

"Don't worry about me either. You know I can take care of myself."

"Yes, but those men—"

He shushed her, saying gently, "Tom talked with Kern and said he'd do his best to convince me to take the fight. They seemed to think that with you out of the picture, I'd have less reason to want to be a bodyguard, plus I'd have a lot of anger to unleash."

"It's all so idiotic."

"They accomplished one thing." Justice shared a grim smile. "I'm furious, but then, so is Tom. Only we're not directing it at each other."

Fallon leaned against him, her voice low. "Tom's still disappointed."

"Yeah, but he'll get over it." Tom had a nice future ahead of him; he didn't need a stupid rematch. "If things go off as planned, he'll be in the headlines a lot. That should guarantee him a good fight. The powers that be never miss an opportunity."

"I'm glad."

Justice rubbed the back of his neck. "The problem is that I don't want your name brought into it. Somehow I have to bust them without you being mentioned."

"I think it's a little late for that."

"No." He refused to believe that. "Your dad would have my head if, after everything he's done to save you from the press, I put you smack dab in the spotlight."

Slowly, Fallon stood to face him, her gaze direct and

her expression tight. "We've already agreed, numerous times, that my parents are overprotective."

"No argument from me." He understood them, but he also knew they hadn't done Fallon any favors by smothering her and, unintentionally, filling her with guilt whenever they worried.

"Since I met you, I've wanted you to know I'm independent."

"And you are, except when two psychos are plotting against you, willing to do whatever it takes to get their way."

She gave a sheepish grin. "Justice." Putting a small, warm palm to his jaw, she said, "I've wanted to keep you around, but not like this."

Keep him around? He wasn't going anywhere. "This," he emphasized, "isn't your doing. How do you think I feel? I'm supposed to protect you and instead you're being used because of me and a career I've already given up."

Frustration stiffened her shoulders. "I need you to be different, Justice. I need you to see that I'm capable of—"

He snatched her onto his lap and kissed away her gasp. "Now," he whispered, when she fell silent, "let me explain, okay?"

Gaze fastened on his mouth, she nodded.

Damn, but it was nice being wanted by Fallon Wade. "I'm not giving you special treatment, not like you think, anyway. If this was happening to my mom or my granny or any of my friends' wives, I'd be the exact same way." Did Fallon understand that for any woman he cared about—any woman he loved—he would do everything in his power to protect her?

"You would?"

"I'd be as bad as the brothers if I didn't."

After giving it some thought, she nodded. "All right. But you have to understand me, too. If busting those creeps lands my name in the press, I'm okay with that. I can handle it. It falls on me, Justice, not you."

He looped his hands around her waist. "You're pretty amazing. You know that, right?"

Laughing at his praise, she rolled her eyes.

"Hopefully it all goes off without a hitch." He glanced at his watch and knew Tom would be calling Kern right about now. This time, Kern and York would be the targets. "I've talked it over with Leese and my boss, Sahara. I've got Miles and even Brand on board to help." Thinking about Miles's willingness to jump in, he said, "Did I tell you Miles might be joining us at the agency? I don't understand why. He's at the top of his game."

"Maybe he just needs a change."

Justice shook his head. "The sport is in his blood. Something else is driving him, I just don't know what it is."

Fallon jumped when his cell rang. Justice knew she was nervous about everything and wouldn't be reassured until it was over. He spoke with Tom, got the confirmation and, stepping out of the storage room to snag a bustling waitress, asked for Miles.

Before his friend could join him, he cupped Fallon's face. "I need you again. Soon."

Nervously, she nodded. "Tonight?"

"One way or another." Seeing Marcus pretend to be with her had been hell. Still, Justice had to give the guy props for playing his role so convincingly. Any fool could see that Marcus still had strong feelings for her but he had set those aside to help.

Miles stuck his head into the cramped room. "Everything set?"

"Yeah. I'm meeting Tom there in a few minutes."

"Good. Best to get it over with." Miles glanced at Fallon while saying, "I'll let the others know and be right back."

"Thanks."

Hands clasped behind her, breath uneven, Fallon watched him. Justice could damn near feel her nervousness.

He couldn't take it. Without planning the words, with no conscious decision to share them, he heard himself say, "I'm in love with you."

Her eyes flared and her hands dropped to her sides. "What?"

She needed to hear it again? Yeah, he sort of did, too. "I'm in love with you. I don't mean to put you on the spot, and you're under no obligation—"

"Justice."

"I'd planned on talking to you about it—" *It.* What a stupid way to refer to something so overpowering, so all consuming. "After this was all settled. But, I dunno, I needed to share, I guess."

She put a trembling hand over her mouth.

Miles stepped back in. "Everyone's ready. I can

take Fallon out the back after you're gone. Cannon and Armie are going to follow, not that they don't trust Marcus, and not that I can't handle it, but you know how they are."

Still watching Fallon, Justice smiled. "Yeah, I do." He cupped her chin. "I'll let you know as soon as I wrap it up."

She flung herself at him, her arms tight around his neck, her breath choppy. "Please be careful."

"Hey," Miles said. "He'll be all right, honey. Honestly. It's covered."

Justice laughed, saying close to Fallon's ear, "I'm encouraged." He gave her a squeeze, kissed her temple and stepped away to sneak out the back door of the bar.

He'd had many fights, but this would be the biggest fight of his life because this time, there was a lot more on the line than recognition in a sport he loved. Regardless of the risk, he couldn't stop smiling. Soon as he rid himself of York and Kern, he could get back to Fallon.

That was a bigger payoff than he'd ever imagined.

LEESE DROVE THE CAR, Brand beside him in the front seat. Fallon was in back with Miles. The silence left her throat tight; these men, badasses all of them, were every bit as worried as she was. Slumping against the door and fighting off the fear, she watched the scenery speed past.

Brand twisted to look over the seat at her. His gaze, so sinfully dark, pinned her in place. "Tell me about the bodyguards you've had."

Drawn from her maudlin thoughts, Fallon started in surprise. "What do you want to know?"

"I take it Justice isn't the norm."

In a tart voice, she replied, "If you're asking if I've had sleepovers with other bodyguards, the answer is no."

Brand grinned, and he looked so sexy she had to sigh.

"You've had bodyguards since you were young, right?"

"Yes." She really didn't feel like chatting. She wanted to wallow in her concern. But how fair was that to the poor men assigned to keep her company? They were Justice's friends. She should treat them better. "My parents often thought it necessary to ensure my safety, at least at big functions. Usually the bodyguards were remote, not friendly like Justice. For different reasons, they were noticeable."

"Clichés?" Brand asked.

"Dark suits, precisely trimmed hair…even their body language screamed 'professional for hire.'" She gave it quick thought, then smiled despite herself. "Justice is the total opposite. He stands out, no way he couldn't. But it's not because anyone thinks he's been hired. It's just that he's so big and muscular, so cocky and—" Seeing Brand's grin, she cut herself off in midsentence. "I'm sure you understand, since you stand out, too."

"Thank you."

Oh, this one could be dangerous, she thought. Talk about cocky!

Miles turned in the seat to face her. "Was there ever

a time when your folks didn't have a bodyguard hovering over you?"

"Yes." And it had been tragic—because of her. "My sister and I convinced them we'd be fine at a lake property they'd purchased but hadn't yet remodeled. The cabin was secluded, so there weren't any other people nearby and no one knew we'd be there." Odd that she could talk about this now without a single shiver in her voice.

Because of Justice.

God, in so many ways he'd dragged her out of a troubled past and into a very bright future.

He said he loved her, and she didn't have a single doubt that it was true. She didn't need to prove anything to him.

And she no longer needed to prove anything to herself.

"My sister died at that cabin, and I was badly burned." No one interrupted as she told what had happened. Telling it the first time to Justice had been difficult. Now, it truly felt like a memory and nothing more.

Brand's gaze never left her. "I imagine that made your folks even more determined to protect you."

"Yes. That's why they hired Justice." She felt a small smile tug at her mouth. "My mother thought he might blend in better."

Miles snorted. "He blends in about as well as a longhorn bull in a herd of calves."

Fallon laughed. "Very true." She sighed, "I took one look at him and fell hard."

"Fell?" Leese asked, the first thing he'd said.

"In love. Or at least, in deep infatuation. It wasn't long before I knew I was lost, though. Justice is just so…exceptional."

"Yeah." Brand laughed. "Exactly how I'd describe him."

Maybe because she didn't have many friends, Fallon found herself confessing all. "I wanted to prove I didn't need a bodyguard, that I was as self-sufficient as any other woman. I had planned to get my own apartment and live off my own funds."

"But?" Miles asked.

"Justice told me that he loves me."

"Duh," Brand said. "We all saw the clues the first time he brought you around."

She remembered how each of them had treated her as Justice's girlfriend instead of his client. "Well, you guys are more perceptive than I am." *And I was afraid to hope.*

"So what are you going to do?" Leese asked.

Was he concerned for his friend, worried about her breaking Justice's heart? Not likely. "I'm not sure yet, but I love him, too. Right now, nothing else seems as important as that."

Her statement effectively lightened the mood and the rest of the drive was spent with the fighters asking her various questions about bodyguards, assuring her Justice could handle himself just fine, and telling her more about his past.

If so much weren't on the line, if she didn't have so many legitimate reasons to fret, she would have honestly enjoyed herself.

EVEN IN GYM SHOES, the cavernous room of the abandoned warehouse echoed his every footfall. Dust motes danced in the stale air and damp mold blackened the walls. Without being too obvious, Justice searched the perimeter of the room.

Broken equipment, piled off to the sides, offered lots of concealment. Only gray light filtered through the grime-covered windows.

The setting was perfect.

He strode to the middle of the cleared floor to join Tom.

Leaning against a section of dusty conveyor belt, anticipation bright in their eyes, York and Kern watched.

"You brought backup?" Justice asked Tom.

"Those two?" Tom laughed with derision. "They're just here to watch."

"Witnesses to your confessions, huh? I didn't think it'd be that easy."

"I'm not confessing shit." Tom squared off.

Impatient and very, very stupid, Kern shouted, "Enough chitchat, boys. Get on with it."

Justice stared at him with all the rage he felt. "Get on with what? You want to see us fight?" He curled his lip. "I wouldn't waste my time."

Tom bristled. "Then why the hell did you come?"

"To tell you to your face how pathetic you are." Justice pointed at him, his voice cold as ice. "And to warn you for the last time to stay away from Fallon."

Red faced, Tom shouted, "I told you, I never touched her!"

"You're a miserable liar."

Hands clenched in his hair, Tom strode away in mock frustration.

Smiling, Justice turned to go.

A hunk of metal sailed across the room and crashed into the wall with a clatter. "No," Kern shouted. "Hell, no, it's not stopping here! You two have to fight."

Justice flipped him off and kept going.

"Damn you, Tom, do something!"

That's it, Justice thought. *Take the bait.*

Tom asked, "What the hell do you expect me to do?"

"Throw a punch!"

More quietly, Tom said, "Then I'd be the coward he accuses me of being."

Justice paused to look at him.

"I didn't touch your lady," Tom swore.

"She's not his lady," York snapped. "She went back to Marcus."

"Doesn't matter." Justice folded his arms over his chest. "A real man never threatens a lady, any lady."

Throwing up his arms, Tom raged, "I agree with you!"

Wearing a mask of scorn, Justice moved closer. "Admit what you did. Admit you're a pussy that picks on women, and maybe then I'll annihilate you."

Through his teeth, looking far too sincere, Tom said, "I have never abused a woman in my life."

Maybe because Justice had once accused Tom of exactly that, Tom wore his insult with convincing umbrage.

"Then fuck it. No fight." He turned his back and strode away.

"Wait!" Kern threw something else, making a terrible racket.

A temper tantrum, Justice thought. The lack of control disgusted him.

"Tom didn't do it!"

At the sound of Kern's frantic voice, followed by the equally appalled rush of his brother's whispers, Justice paused.

"I did it."

Slowly, Justice turned. Pretending he didn't understand, he narrowed his eyes on Kern. "You did what?"

York gripped Kern's arm, trying to hold him back, but Kern had lost all sense. "I was coercing you."

"Coercing me?"

Unashamed, almost boasting, Kern explained, "I had her pushed down the stairs."

Icy anger filled Justice's veins, but he feigned only mild surprise. "And the flowers and the paint on the driveway?

"The call to the agency accusing me?" Tom asked.

"Yes, all of it."

York gaped at his brother. "Shut up, you idiot!"

"What does it matter? They can't do shit." Kern pulled out his wallet. "I'll pay for the flowers and the paint." He threw a thick wad of bills at them. The money separated midair, fluttering in individual bills to the dirty ground, ignored by both fighters. "I'll give you each an extra twenty grand, too."

Walking toward him, Justice said, "I don't think so, you gutless prick. How can you pay for terrorizing a woman?" Justice loomed over him, forcing him to back up a step. "How the hell do you pay for her bruises?"

SMUG AND UNCONCERNED, Kern said, "By not bruising anyone else?"

Yet another threat? "What are you talking about?"

"Fight Tom," he said. "Right here, right now."

Resisting the urge to punch the smile off Kern's face, Justice shook his head. "I don't think so."

"Oh, you'll do it," Kern growled, throwing caution to the wind. "Think about your mother, your grandmother."

Justice kept his expression set and said nothing.

"I've had you watched, of course. I know where they live." Kern fished out his phone and shook it at Justice. "One call from me, and my man will find new ways to convince you, I promise you that."

To keep him talking, Justice asked, "You really think you can get away with that? You want the fight so badly that you'd risk everything?"

"There's no risk to me," Kern boasted. "There never is."

Never is? So Kern had done this before?

"I want the fight and by God, you'll give it to me."

The silent "or else" hung in the air. Doing his own bit of gambling, Justice smiled. "If what you say is true, then you should know that I anticipated it." Yes, he had. He'd covered all his bases. "My family is safe, you psycho."

Kern laughed. "No one is ever safe."

Again, York tried to silence him, but Kern was be-yond reason, intent on bragging.

"You think tucking that little slut away with a friend

somehow protects her?" He leaned closer. "You'll do exactly what I say, and you'll do it now."

Fallon was with Leese, and no way would Leese let anything happen to her. Knowing it and convincing himself of it were two very different things, especially with the signs of insanity right in front of him. "Or what?"

Kern examined a nail. "Or I'll have my man burn Leese Phelp's house to the ground with everyone in it. Ah, I see that got your attention."

York said, "Jesus, Kern, you have to shut—"

Kern didn't listen. "I have men there, you know. It'll look like a gas leak. There's been no alteration to any insurance they have, the two pet dogs are still present, and they're all in the house. It'll be so tragic, no one will suspect a thing."

Panic tried to take hold, but Justice held it back. "You're full of shit."

"Boom," Kern said, fluttering his fingers into the air. "There will be nothing left but splintered debris. No one will ever suspect foul play."

Justice couldn't breathe. "That's not possible." *Don't let it be possible.*

"His house has natural gas, so of course it's possible. I've done it before," Kern bragged, "and no one suspected. Even if they did, so what? They couldn't confirm it, and they sure as hell could never peg it on me."

It hasn't happened yet. Justice clenched his fists, knowing he'd do whatever was necessary to keep Fallon from being hurt—even if it meant killing the man in front of him.

As Kern studied Justice's face, he whispered with satisfaction, "Yes, now you understand, don't you?"

"I understand."

"So throw a goddamned punch, already!"

Justice let out a breath. "Gladly." With one big step, he closed the distance between them.

Belatedly, Kern realized his error. He tried to lurch back and tripped into his brother.

Catching him by the wrist, Justice brutally squeezed until the cell phone dropped to the cement floor. He crushed it with his heel and, smiling at Kern, twisted his arm until a bone popped.

Kern screamed.

Justice silenced him with one solid hit to the jaw, breaking that, too.

York started to run and plowed headlong into Tom. "I don't think so," Tom said.

Police swarmed into the area.

York turned at the sight of a photographer recording everything, and his mouth flapped like a fish out of water.

Sahara stepped out, making a beeline for Justice. "I called Leese with the phone on speaker so he could hear. I didn't dare say anything to him for fear these miscreants would hear me." She touched his arm. "The line is dead now. An officer is already on his way there."

Justice inhaled shakily.

"Go," she whispered, "before you get detained here. Tom and I can handle this. But Justice, be careful."

Without another word, Justice ran out.

CHAPTER NINETEEN

FALLON STOOD ACROSS the street, her arms wrapped around herself, taking in the scene with disbelief. It wasn't that cold, but she couldn't stop shivering.

Brand looked down at her, then slipped his arm around her shoulders. "Reaction," he said in explanation. "It's a son of a bitch."

Brand was big and warm…but he wasn't Justice. "They wanted to blow us up." She still couldn't believe it. "All of us."

"Yeah." Brand pulled her in against his chest, now with both arms around her while he briskly stroked her back. "But they didn't succeed and we're fine. All of us," he repeated.

She didn't feel fine. Tears threatened, but she ruthlessly blinked them away. Her stomach knotted and her legs didn't want to support her.

"Come on," Brand said, leading her over to his car.

Fear squeezed her throat and she croaked, "I don't want to be alone."

"You're not." He didn't put her in the car, but guided her to sit on the front bumper. It was better. At least her knees weren't knocking anymore.

Leese and Miles had two men corralled on the curb

a few feet away. The men's faces were badly battered. So were Leese's and Miles's knuckles.

Brand had helped some with that, until he'd noticed her standing there, useless, scared...

"You're not a trained fighter," he said.

Fallon shook her head. No denying that. Until recently, until Justice, she'd barely been an adult. No, that wasn't true and she wouldn't insult herself. She'd been overly reserved, but she'd known all along what she wanted.

Justice had helped her to get it.

Where are you, Justice? "All I did was panic and get in the way."

"Not true. You were the first to hear the noise outside. Then we got that call from Sahara." He fell silent, his shoulders tensing, probably in memory.

For a second, they'd all been in indecision. The threats they'd heard... If they rushed outside, were there men waiting to cut them down? For a certainty, they couldn't stay in the house while being threatened with a gas explosion. After she'd heard the noise, Leese had made the decisions. He'd settled, uncomfortably, on going out first with Miles while Brand waited just inside the door with her.

Repeatedly, she had sniffed the air, but she hadn't smelled anything. That hadn't reassured her, though. How much of a gas leak was needed? How did a person go about causing a gas leak? The stove wasn't on—what else should she check?

Fortunately, Leese's wife, Catalina, along with their

two dogs, was visiting Yvette. Leese hadn't wanted her to be anywhere near possible trouble.

She and Brand heard the scuffle outside, the sounds of thuds and grunts and…pain.

Shortly afterward, Miles had called them out.

Did Brand resent having to babysit her while the others…engaged? Maybe. He'd gotten involved, only briefly, before returning to her side.

When Brand sat beside her on the bumper, Fallon leaned against him, seeking and offering comfort.

Sirens sounded in the distance, and shortly there were both police and firefighters on-site. Officers handcuffed the two battered thugs and dragged them away.

Miles, flexing his knuckles, came to stand before her. "You okay?"

"Yes."

Leese stepped up next, his hands still fisted. He looked to be in a killing mood but he said calmly, "Here comes Justice."

Heart leaping, she twisted around to see the car haphazardly parked. Before the engine had died, Justice jumped out.

Fallon said, "Excuse me," and then ran to him.

Behind her, she heard Miles laugh.

Laugh! How could any of them—

Justice caught her up in his arms and held her tight. One hand on the back of her head pressed her to his shoulder, the other low on her spine supported her since her feet were off the ground. He didn't say anything, just tucked his face to her neck and breathed heavily.

"I'm okay," Fallon whispered, teasing her fingers

over his short-cropped hair, inhaling his hot scent and relishing the strength in his embrace. "Justice? Let me look at you."

"No."

He sounded choked, and her heart swelled. She squeezed him tighter and said, "I don't want an apartment."

That loosened his hold enough for him to search her face. "You don't?"

Damn it, now she felt choked. Shaking her head, she swallowed the stupid tears and whispered brokenly, "I only want you."

His gaze warmed. "You have me, babe. I promise." He smoothed back her hair. "Tell me you love me."

"I love you so much."

His breathing evened out and he smiled. Then he laughed. Lifting her in his arms, he strode over to the others. "Hell of a night."

Brand cocked his head at Leese and Miles. "Those two had all the fun."

"It *was* fun," Miles said. "I mean, now that everything is okay. Hell of an adrenaline rush."

"So you're really going to do it?" Leese asked. "You're going to join Body Armor?"

"I think so." Before anyone could ask him why, he walked off to talk to an officer.

Fallon rested her head against Justice's shoulder. She didn't need him to hold her, but she liked it. She especially liked that Justice was such a big, buff guy who could do so with ease.

Before long, though, things got too chaotic for cuddling.

It was hours later when they congregated inside Leese's house. Catalina had come home and her two dogs were ecstatic with the company. Fallon sat on the floor in front of Justice, letting the dogs shower her with love.

Catalina was in the kitchen making coffee, whistling as if nothing out of the ordinary had happened. She saw Leese leave the room, go to his wife and hug her from behind.

They had such a wonderful life—a life she wanted, as well.

With Justice.

Behind her, the men talked quietly. Fallon was tired, but she enjoyed listening in on their conversation, learning more about how they thought, how they reacted to everything. Notes of serious reflection interspersed the joking insults and occasional murmurs of disbelief over what had happened.

When Tom and a beautiful woman showed up, Fallon could only stare in wonder.

Justice leaned down to say, "My boss, Sahara Silver. She owns the agency." Then he warned, "Prepare to be amazed."

And amazed she was.

Exhaustion and frustration weighed on Tom, but Sahara looked as if she'd stepped into a party—polished, fresh and energetic. Fallon knew she'd been at the warehouse during the entire confrontation, that she'd just spent hours talking to police and high-level contacts, ensuring that the brothers wouldn't be able to buy their way out of legal consequences, but looking at her, no one would know it.

Smiling, her stylish high heels dangling from the fingers of one hand—Sahara's only concession to the long, troubled night—she said, "I already talked with Senator Loy, and the prosecutor, of course. The Arnolds will not wiggle free this time. And, Tom, you were beautiful. So brave, so selfless. Please know that you'll be rewarded. I have friends at the SBC—that's the acronym, yes, for the Supreme Battle Challenge? Anyway, I've praised you and they're thrilled. You'll get great coverage from this. Who doesn't want to see a homegrown hero compete? I already feel sorry for your challenger."

As if he'd been listening to similar plans for a while, Tom's dazed but exhausted expression never changed.

Still talking nonstop, Sahara breezed in behind a dragging Tom—but drew to a halt when she spotted Brand. She drew a shaky breath and murmured, "Well, well. What have we here?"

"Hello, Sahara."

"Mr. Berry, what a pleasant surprise to see you again."

Fallon swiveled to see Brand, who only smiled lazily.

The rest of the men stared first at Sahara, then their friend and then each other.

When Fallon's gaze met Justice's, he only raised his brows, slowly smiled, and hauled her up to sit in his lap. "Tom will be okay," he whispered into her ear. "Sahara will see to it."

They drank coffee and ate some supposedly healthy treats that Leese had made. Catalina confided that Leese was an organized, neat-freak health nut, but in the very nicest ways. To Fallon, it sounded like bragging.

It was almost morning before Justice and Fallon headed home…to his house. They didn't speak much, but once inside, he led her straight to the bedroom.

"Tired?" he asked.

Seeing that look in his eyes, she nodded, but said, "Never too tired for that, though." Never too tired for him.

He gave her a crooked grin, and as he stripped, he said, "Tell me again."

"I love you."

"I'm never going to get tired of hearing it."

JUSTICE SAT WITH Fallon and her parents at his modest dining room table, using his inexpensive dishware and his stainless-steel utensils. Together, he and Fallon had prepared baked chicken, potatoes and carrots. Candles burned in the middle of the table.

He felt damned domestic—and liked it.

After finishing off seconds, Clayton Wade looked stiff and was mostly silent.

Rebecca, bless her heart, praised everything. His house, his yard, his food…

Suddenly Clayton laid his fork beside his plate and looked up. "You have good security here?"

An odd, out-of-the-blue question, but Justice didn't hesitate. "Yes, sir." He detailed the measures taken, doing what he could to reassure the man.

"I like what you did with my system. You're knowl-edgeable about it?"

Justice scratched his forehead, and realized that he was. Huh. So Leese was good with research, and he was good with security systems. "Yes, sir."

Clayton nodded, and drank more of his wine.

Fallon touched Justice's hand, then said, "I've been trying to look at apartments."

Rebecca's head snapped up.

Clayton froze. "Trying?"

"It seems every time we made plans, something came up."

Rebecca shared a knowing look with Justice, then smiled.

Justice kept silent.

"Apartments where?" Clayton asked.

"It doesn't matter now." Justice laced his fingers with hers. "She's going to move in with me."

Expression neutral, Clayton repeated, "Move in with…"

"Me." Justice held his gaze. Damn, this was awk-ward. It'd be a whole lot easier to say she'd be his wife. Her parents were old-fashioned, protective beyond be-lief, and Fallon was their only child. But what Fallon wanted mattered most to him. "I love her. I'll take good care of her."

Rebecca tipped her head to one side. "You're going to live together?"

"A first step, ma'am." Hopefully with a second step to follow, but Justice wanted to give Fallon the time she needed just to be, as she often put it, free. "You know Fallon has lived a reserved life."

"But no more," Fallon said.

"She deserves a long courtship." Justice grinned, knowing he'd marry her tomorrow, but… "She deserves romance. She deserves to be chased for a while."

Fallon fought a smile. "I do." Then she flushed. "I mean—"

Rebecca laughed.

Clayton shot his wife a quelling frown before turning his serious gaze on Justice. "Rebecca is correct. You have a very nice home. You may not know this, but Rebecca grew up in a house this size." His voice lowered, going thoughtful, then he covered his wife's hand with his own. "Her father was a welder and her mother a bus driver. My parents, second-generation hoteliers, were resistant to our marriage. None of it mattered to me, though, and none of it mattered to Rebecca."

With clear exasperation, Fallon said, "None of *what*, Dad? Those are both good jobs. Besides, it's not like Justice is a slug who refuses to hold a job. He's not into hotels, but he *is* a well-known, accomplished sports figure, and now he's a highly valued bodyguard at one of the most reputable, prestigious agencies. He's the most dedicated, motivated, sweet—"

With a one-arm hug and a quick laugh, Justice kept her from extolling him straight into sainthood. "I think your dad was giving his approval, honey."

"I was," Clayton assured him, "and I hope I didn't insult you."

"I'm not blind, sir. There's a huge difference in what I can offer her and what she has in store from you."

"Financially," Clayton said. "But then, Fallon has never been all that concerned with luxury."

"And there are other things," Rebecca added, "that are far more important."

Fallon beamed at them.

Giving them their due, Justice said, "You raised a wonderful daughter. She's beautiful inside and out."

Rebecca sighed. "He's also very romantic, Fallon. I like him a lot."

The next part, Justice knew, would be tricky. He hoped he didn't trip himself up. "Speaking of finances, I want you to know that I'm not a gold digger. If you and Rebecca were..." He used the same example Clayton had. "Well, a welder and a bus driver, it'd be all the same to me."

"Still," Clayton said, "you stand to inherit—"

"No, sir." Justice needed them to know that money didn't influence him. "I make my own way."

Clayton studied him. "Well, we can certainly discuss this further in the future."

Once we marry. That's what her dad was thinking, no doubt expecting. Justice said only, "The future is up to Fallon. But I'm here for the long haul."

Justice didn't mean to pressure her, but her parents' gazes shifted to pin her with their undivided attention.

She flushed before giving in to a laugh. "I'm here for the long haul, too, but I'm having so much fun right now, I don't want to spend time planning the future. I'd rather just enjoy the present for a while."

He could work with that, Justice decided. "Whatever you want, honey."

She fiddled with her napkin, glanced at him then lifted her chin. "Justice will no longer be my bodyguard. It's not necessary and of course he'll be taking other assignments. I was thinking of getting more involved in my own work."

"Travel?" Clayton asked.

"Yes, eventually. If that's okay?"

While her parents assured her they'd love it, Justice grinned, so damned proud of her.

"I think Justice and I need to have a normal life for a while. Without any threats, with him doing his own work and me doing mine."

Rebecca said, "I see. Yes."

Clayton slowly nodded. "You want some normalcy. A regular routine."

"I do." She rolled her eyes and laughed. "I'm forever saying that."

"Like you're answering a proposal." Justice gave her a crooked grin. "I like hearing it."

Fallon drew a deep breath, then twisted to face him. "What would you think about planning a wedding, oh, a year or so from now?"

A rush of emotion filled his chest until Justice could barely catch his breath. Fallon glowed with confidence, rightfully so, and he loved it. He loved her. Now and forever.

She'll marry me in a year.

He accepted that she didn't put it off out of indecision, but because they were already so content.

Together.

He ignored her parents and, smiling, leaned forward to brush his mouth over hers. "I think I have a year to show you that it's only going to get better."

Her palm settled against his jaw and she said sweetly, "With you, Justice, I never had a doubt."

To the sounds of her mother's happy excitement and her father's chuckles of amusement, Justice stood. "Guess it's time for dessert."

His life had taken a one-eighty from that of a bachelor fighter. And as he'd said, with Fallon, it was only going to get better.

* * * * *

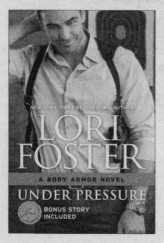

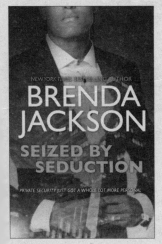

*To deflect some awkward questions, Ashley Ozark needs
a fake boyfriend for the weekend. That's why she kisses
Colton Cross, the cocky, arrogant bull rider she can't
stand. The problem is, Colton demands payment for his
services—in the most irreverent ways!*

Read on for a sneak preview of
WILD SEDUCTION
by New York Times *bestselling author Daire St. Denis!*

A sinful grin flashed across Colton Cross's face. "I'm of
a mind to collect."

"Collect what?"

"A couple more kisses."

After a glance over her shoulder to see if Jasmine was
watching—she was—and then a glance over his to see if
his friends were watching—they were—Ash went up on
tiptoes, placed her free hand on Colton's broad shoulder
and whispered in his ear, "No."

This did not deter him. He released her hand only so
he could slip his arm around her waist and pull her in
tight against him. "If you were my real girlfriend, we'd
be kissing right now," he said in a low voice, just for her.

She wedged a hand up between them, placing her
palm flat against his chest. Was it normal to have such
hard muscles hiding behind a button-up shirt? She didn't
think so. She pushed, and there was no give whatsoever.
"But I'm not your girlfriend. We're just pretending.
Remember?"

"Oh, I remember. But you want to put on a show." With a tilt of his chin, he indicated Jasmine. "So let's put on a show."

"How'd you know?"

Using his knuckles beneath her chin, he tilted her head up. "There's only one reason a woman wants a fake boyfriend."

"What's that?" There was way too much breathiness in her whisper for her liking.

"To make her friends jealous." He waited a half second, his eyes glued to hers. When she didn't move, didn't shove, didn't object in any way, he lowered his mouth to hers and kissed her.

This was not the kiss she'd expected. She'd expected something for show, pretending to make out with a passion he didn't feel.

That was not what this was. This was slow. Leisurely. Like he wanted to explore her lips, the inside and outside of them. Not to mention deep inside her mouth. His big hand cupped the back of her head, and he tilted her— gently—one way and then the other. When he finally pulled away, she was left, lips parted, panting.

"That ought to do it."

She blinked once, twice, three times before coming back to herself, suddenly clueing in to the fact that the whistles and catcalls were because of the show they'd put on.

Oh, shit.

What had she done?

Don't miss
WILD SEDUCTION by Daire St. Denis,
available April 2017 wherever
Harlequin® Blaze® books and ebooks are sold.

www.Harlequin.com

HARLEQUIN®

Red-Hot Reads

Save $1.00

on the purchase of
WILD SEDUCTION
by *New York Times* bestselling author
Daire St. Denis,
available March 21, 2017, or on any
other Harlequin® Blaze® book.

Available wherever books are sold.

Save $1.00

on the purchase of any Harlequin® Blaze® book.

Coupon valid until June 30, 2017.
Redeemable at participating outlets in the U.S. and Canada only.
Not redeemable at Barnes & Noble stores. Limit one coupon per customer.

52614763

Canadian Retailers: Harlequin Enterprises Limited will pay the face value of this coupon plus 10.25¢ if submitted by customer for this product only. Any other use constitutes fraud. Coupon is nonassignable. Void if taxed, prohibited or restricted by law. Consumer must pay any government taxes. Void if copied. Inmar Promotional Services ("IPS") customers submit coupons and proof of sales to Harlequin Enterprises Limited, P.O. Box 3000, Saint John, NB E2L 4L3, Canada. Non-IPS retailer—for reimbursement submit coupons and proof of sales directly to Harlequin Enterprises Limited, Retail Marketing Department, 225 Duncan Mill Rd., Don Mills, ON M3B 3K9, Canada.

U.S. Retailers: Harlequin Enterprises Limited will pay the face value of this coupon plus 8¢ if submitted by customer for this product only. Any other use constitutes fraud. Coupon is nonassignable. Void if taxed, prohibited or restricted by law. Consumer must pay any government taxes. Void if copied. For reimbursement submit coupons and proof of sales directly to Harlequin Enterprises, Ltd 482, NCH Marketing Services, P.O. Box 880001, El Paso, TX 88588-0001, U.S.A. Cash value 1/100 cents.

5 65373 00076 2   (8100)0 12274

® and ™ are trademarks owned and used by the trademark owner and/or its licensee.

© 2017 Harlequin Enterprises Limited

HBCOUP0417

Get 2 Free Books,

<u>Plus</u> 2 Free Gifts –

just for trying the Reader Service!

MERCEDES LACKEY

LUNA™